DAVID DICKINSON was born in Dublin. He graduated from Cambridge with a first-class honours degree in classics and joined the BBC. After a spell in radio he transferred to television and went on to become editor of *Newsnight* and *Panorama*. In 1995 he was series editor of *Monarchy*, a three-part examination of its current state and future prospects. David has two children and lives in London.

Praise for *Goodnight Sweet Prince*

'Dickinson textures his canvas with historical detail as thick as the oil paint on one of his favourite paintings by Turner.'

Kirkus Reviews

'Lady Lucy is a charmer and Dickinson's view of the royals [is] edgy and of course shaped by our times.'

Barbara Peters, *The Poisoned Pen*

By the same author

Death and the Jubilee

GOODNIGHT
SWEET PRINCE

DAVID DICKINSON

ROBINSON
London

Constable & Robinson Ltd
3 The Lanchesters
162 Fulham Palace Road
London W6 9ER
www.constablerobinson.com

First published in the UK by Constable,
an imprint of Constable & Robinson Ltd, 2002

This paperback edition published by Robinson,
an imprint of Constable & Robinson Ltd, 2003

A copy of the British Library Cataloguing in
Publication data is available from the British Library.

ISBN 1-84119-583-9

Printed and bound in the EU

10 9 8 7 6 5 4 3 2 1

For Patrick and Els

Part One

Blackmail

Autumn 1891

1

'Come, Powerscourt, come. I have a great secret to tell you.'

Lord Rosebery was waiting impatiently outside his front door as Powerscourt's luggage was taken into the house. Dalmeny, near Edinburgh, was one of Rosebery's many mansions.

'I've only just arrived. Why can't you tell me inside Dalmeny, rather than rushing me off like this?' Lord Francis Powerscourt sounded petulant.

'There are too many people in my house just now. I am taking you to Barnbougle, my little castle by the sea. Nobody will disturb us there.'

Rosebery led the way down the little path that led into the woods. A pair of magpies, predatory and delinquent, flew off ahead of them on some malevolent mission.

'I will tell you the most important part now, Francis,' said Rosebery, peering melodramatically around him as though spies or enemy agents might have been lurking in his woods. He drew his cloak tightly around him and whispered into Powerscourt's ear. 'Someone is blackmailing the Prince of Wales. The Princess of Wales fears for the life of her eldest son Prince Eddy.'

Rosebery stepped back with the special satisfaction of those who pass on secrets. Powerscourt was already mentally shifting through his previous cases. He had investigated murders in Simla and in Delhi, in London and in Wiltshire. Only once before had he encountered blackmail.

He had known Rosebery since Eton, and they had remained friends though they were so dissimilar. Rosebery was slightly below average height with the face of a cherub maturing slowly

3

into a statesman. He was very rich and much of his wealth was consumed in his annual, unfulfilled quest to win the Derby. Rosebery had been Foreign Secretary and was widely spoken of as a future Prime Minister. Powerscourt was a head taller than his friend, a head crowned with unruly black curls. Beneath them a pair of blue eyes inspected the world with detachment and irony, the lines of his smiles turning imperceptibly into wrinkles by the sides of his mouth and his eyes. He had served with distinction in India and Africa as Chief Intelligence Officer for various armies of the Crown. His skills in collecting and evaluating information had given him a second career as a solver of murders and mysteries at home and abroad.

'There it is!' said Rosebery, pointing proudly at a small castle right on the shore. 'Barnbougle. My ancestors were swept out to sea here, along with the bricks and mortar. I've had it restored.'

All around the little castle the waves were beating steadily, cascades of spray thrown against the walls. Far out in the Firth of Forth a coal packet was beating its way towards the North Sea, black smoke marking the afternoon sky.

Rosebery led the way through a large hall to his library on the first floor.

'Now then, Rosebery, tell me more about this blackmail.'

Rosebery sat by his fireplace, the lines of his bookshelves marching symmetrically towards the windows. 'There isn't a great deal more to say. The blackmail letters arrive at irregular intervals. They threaten to expose the Prince of Wales for his adulterous lifestyle.'

'Surely,' said Powerscourt, 'the mystery is that nobody has tried to blackmail the Prince of Wales before. His life is one long debauch. He keeps or has kept strings of mistresses rather like you keep your racehorses on Epsom Downs.'

'I sincerely hope that he has more success with his mistresses than I do with my racehorses,' said Rosebery ruefully. 'I should think that of the two, mistresses, if properly bred and trained, should be the cheaper option to maintain.'

'Do you know how the letters are written? Block capitals, disguised handwriting, that sort of thing?'

'Oddly enough, that is one of the few details the Prince of Wales' Private Secretary, Sir William Suter, chose to impart.

4

They are made up of letters cut out of newspapers, believed to be *The Times* and the *Illustrated London News*, and pasted on to a sheet of plain paper.'

'Are they delivered by hand?'

'No, they come by post, usually on Tuesdays. They are always posted in Central London on Mondays.'

Powerscourt turned to gaze out at the sea. Faint sounds of the angry waves carried up into the library. Rosebery was looking at his rare and valuable books.

'And the Princess of Wales, Rosebery? You said she was worried about the life of Prince Eddy.'

'She is, she is,' said Rosebery, picking out an ancient Bible from his shelves and blowing a small cloud of dust from the spine. 'Sir William did not say whether this was a mother's anxiety or if there was some other deeper reason for it.'

'Does Prince Eddy share his father's tastes? A life entirely devoted to pleasure with occasional breaks for opening new buildings and laying foundation stones?'

'I don't think the aphrodisiac of adultery has quite the same appeal for Prince Eddy as it does for the father. They say he likes men as well as women.'

'Dear God, Rosebery, what a collection.'

'They are all we have, Francis, God help us. They may live on the edge of scandal all the time, the Prince of Wales and his set, but they are the Royal Family and we must do what we can. But Francis, you will not be surprised to hear that they want you to investigate this blackmail. I told Suter I would send him a wire today, to say that you were on board, that you had accepted the commission.'

Powerscourt stared intently at his friend. 'It will be very difficult, Rosebery, almost impossible. No crime has been committed, apart from pasting up a few letters and sticking them in the post. There are never any witnesses with blackmail, as you know. There is nobody to question. Any correspondence that might have a bearing on the matter will be out of bounds. Payments from banks and bankers to blackmailers with or without scissors and paste and back copies of *The Times* are rather hard to trace. Messrs Finch's & Co., you know as well as I do, Rosebery, do not share their secrets with any passing lord.'

'I know, Francis, I know.' Rosebery had adopted the tone he used in the House of Lords with dim-witted and elderly peers. 'But you must do it. There have been far too many scandals involving the Prince of Wales and his family. One more could do untold damage to the stability of the constitution and the coherence of the Empire.'

'Those of us who have accepted the Queen's Commission in the past cannot refuse it now,' said Powerscourt sadly. 'I accept. But you will help me, won't you? You know these people far better than I do.'

'Of course I'll help you, Francis,' said Rosebery, rising to his feet and clasping Powerscourt's hand firmly in his own. 'I will help you in any way I can as long as your investigation lasts. But come, I must send that wire.'

Darkness was falling as the two men made their way back to Dalmeny, their boots crunching through the late autumn leaves.

'You and I have an appointment at the Prince of Wales' London residence at Marlborough House at nine o'clock in the morning on Tuesday. Five days from now.'

Lord Johnny Fitzgerald, Powerscourt's friend and companion in detection, was perched precariously on top of Slaughter, nearly one hundred feet above the ground. To his left were Conquest, Famine and Death, the Four Horsemen of the Apocalypse. To his right, more shadowy in the dusty shafts of light that fell into the bell tower, Matthew, Mark, Luke and John gave silent testimony to the gentler thoughts of the bell wrights who had cast these monsters two hundred years before.

Round his neck there hung a pair of the finest field glasses the Prussian Army could purchase. Up here, in the tower of his friend Powerscourt's Rokesley church, Lord Johnny could indulge his passion for bird-watching. There was a splendid view of Powerscourt's house Rokesley Hall just beneath him. To the south, beyond the hill, was the pleasant market town of Oundle with its fine eighteenth-century buildings and its architecturally less distinguished public school. To the east lay Fotheringhay with its square church tower, evoking memories of the incarceration of Mary Queen of Scots. To the west and the north lay the broad expanse of Rockingham Forest which ran for some ten miles before petering out at Kings Cliffe.

Above the forest great hunting birds would circle, rising impossibly slowly in great rhythmic sweeps up the air currents before hurtling down towards their invisible prey. In his lair, surrounded by the four evangelists and the four horsemen of the apocalypse, Fitzgerald would sit for hours at a time, watching the hunt, waiting for the kill.

Lord Francis Powerscourt was walking home from Oundle station. The boys from the school were playing a rugby match, the treble cheers of their supporters echoing shrilly back into the town. Powerscourt was thinking about Latin unseens, passages of Pliny, speeches from Livy, rhetoric from Cicero staring up at you from a page you had never seen before. You might recognize a couple of words the first time you read it through. The rest was a mystery to be unravelled. All his life Powerscourt had been fascinated by mysteries: puzzles as a small child, sitting by his mother's chair, a great fire burning in the hearth, the flow of Irish conversation passing literally over his head: codes and cryptograms during his time in the army in India, struggling in some stifling tent to decipher the messages of Her Majesty's enemies.

Each new investigation now seemed to him like another Latin unseen. You began with a few words, a few pieces of knowledge to be amplified and translated as the case went on. He remembered the satisfaction he found at school, as the meaning of the Latin slowly became apparent, revealed like invisible ink under the solvent of his brain.

Some noise from above reached Powerscourt, walking briskly down the hill. Fitzgerald must be here, watching his birds from the top of the tower.

'Johnny!' shouted Powerscourt. 'Johnny! Johnny!'

His cries had no effect on the bird-watcher up above. Powerscourt hurried across the drive to meet his friend in the churchyard.

Powerscourt and Fitzgerald had known each other growing up in Ireland. They had the special closeness of those who have fought side by side in battle. Fitzgerald was rash and impetuous and had been saved more than once by the cooler head and accurate shooting of his friend. They still served together on Powerscourt's detective missions. And on two occasions, as Powerscourt sometimes reminded himself, Lord Johnny had saved his sanity.

Over twenty years before Powerscourt and his three younger sisters had been devastated by the sudden death of their parents and three of their grandparents in the great influenza epidemic that decimated the Anglo-Irish aristocracy in and around Dublin. They were left in their huge mausoleum of a house, drenched in memories they could not escape. Two of Powerscourt's three sisters grew thin and pale and looked as though they would waste away. Powerscourt himself felt sick with the responsibility of unexpectedly becoming head of his family.

Uninvited and unannounced, Lord Johnny Fitzgerald and his mother came to stay. Quite what kind Lady Fitzgerald said to his sisters, Powerscourt never knew. But they began to get better. Johnny Fitzgerald took Powerscourt off for five days in which they walked right round the Wicklow Mountains, staying at country inns, rising early, exhausted by nightfall. And at the end of their march, Lord Johnny spoke harshly to his friend.

'Look here, Francis, forgive me if I give you some advice.' They were standing on top of the great marble staircase of Powerscourt House that looked out on to the fountain in the lake and the faint blue of the Wicklow Mountains beyond the gardens. 'You're all going to hell in a handcart if you stay in this house any longer. You must get away. All of you. You must begin again while you're all young enough to do it and before those lovely girls turn into old maids of mourning. I know a man who will give you a tremendous price for that house and for as much of the estate as you want to sell. A tremendous price.' Lord Johnny nodded his head vigorously in admiration of the tremendous price he had negotiated with a Dublin coal magnate before his visit. 'You should move to London. You'll get your sisters married off in no time at all over there.'

Reluctantly, then with increasing energy and vigour, Powerscourt followed his advice. They had all moved to London, the three sisters, possibly taking to heart the advice of Lady Fitzgerald, enthusiastic for new friends and a different society. The lovely girls were indeed all married now, producing nephews and one niece with a speed that sometimes alarmed their uncle as the intervals between birthdays grew shorter and shorter, the names of new babies harder and harder to remember. Soon he would have a cricket team composed entirely of Powerscourts if his sisters continued breeding like this.

'Johnny, I'm so glad to see you,' said Powerscourt. 'I think we have a new case. A real puzzle of a case. Come and have some tea and I'll tell you all about it.'

Fitzgerald had saved Powerscourt once in his twenties. He was to save him again at the end of his thirties.

At the age of thirty-six, in St George's Hanover Square, Lord Francis Powerscourt had married Caroline Stone, eldest daughter of Albert Stone, a wealthy landowner in Dorset. One year later their first child, Thomas, was born. Two years after that, mother and son were drowned when the SS *Amelia*, a passenger ship on the Dublin to Liverpool route, went down with all hands. One hundred and sixty-seven people died. For Powerscourt, it was as though death came for him once a decade. Parents, wife, child, all had gone. This time Fitzgerald carried him off to Italy for three months, hoping that Powerscourt's love of classical antiquity and the masterpieces of the Renaissance would cure him of the terrible grief.

On their return to England once again Lord Johnny suggested flight. 'You must get away, Francis, away to somewhere where you never knew Caroline, somewhere out of London. You don't need to be in London any more now. But if you stay you'll end up withered and shrunk like that old Queen Victoria and her forty years of mourning.'

So Powerscourt had moved again and now he was pouring tea in Rokesley Hall for his friend in the little sitting-room that looked out over the lawns to the churchyard and Lord Johnny's bells.

'I have been closeted with Lord Rosebery in his Dark Tower by the sea at Barnbougle. Somebody is trying to blackmail the Prince of Wales. The Princess is fearful for the life of their eldest son. They say, God help us all, that he likes men as well as women. I am bidden to a great conference with Private Secretary Suter in Pall Mall two days from now. That's it in a nutshell.'

Outside a couple of very small birds were performing a slow dance across the lawn.

'Bloody hell! Some shell. Some nut.' Lord Johnny Fitzgerald looked closely at his friend. 'That would be the very devil to crack. I'm not sure it can be done. Nobody's going to talk.'

'We can't give up at this stage, Johnny. We haven't started yet. I think I am going to make some inquiries about the Prince of Wales' finances.'

Fitzgerald helped himself to a couple of crumpets and a small mountain of butter. 'And I could make some inquiries into what the rich and discreet homosexuals of London get up to. Prince Eddy must be known in that world, if what they say is true.'

'Do you think we could get a man on the inside, Johnny? Blackmailers usually have inside knowledge from somewhere. The most likely place is from the servants at Marlborough House or Sandringham. I wonder if they'd let us put one of our own people in there, a senior footman or underbutler, somebody like that.'

'You could try it, Francis. I think I know a man who went to school with that Private Secretary Sir William Suter. He was a mean little sod then. I don't suppose he's changed.'

For two hours the two men talked until the fire had gone out and darkness had fallen over the Powerscourt estate beyond the windows. As they went off to dinner in Oundle's finest hotel, Lord Johnny had cheered up sufficiently to order a bottle of Chassagne-Montrachet with the fish.

'We're celebrating,' he told the wine waiter. 'I saw three kestrels and a hawk today.'

2

The blinds were tightly drawn. The door was locked and bolted. Two lamps cast fitful light over the long table. At one end was a large pile of newspapers and magazines. Lined up along the table, in four untidy rows, were the letters of the alphabet, cut loosely from their pages. The hands moved awkwardly with the paste as they composed a new message. Quite often the hands spilt paste on to the table or on to the floor. The hands had always been bad at art at school, always bottom of the class. This Sunday afternoon another message was almost complete, capital letters used in the middle of words, full stops in the wrong place, the letters themselves set at irregular angles on the page. The artist began to giggle, quietly at first, then almost hysterically as the message was completed. Tomorrow the message would go to London. There it would be posted in an obscure West End postbox. As the hands tidied up the letters and opened the blinds once more, the giggling stopped.

'I've always thought London is much more interesting at this time of the morning,' said Rosebery to Powerscourt as the two men set off to walk from Rosebery's house in Berkeley Square to their meeting with Private Secretary Suter at Marlborough House. A thin rain was falling, dusting the hats of the wealthy and the caps of the poor. At a quarter to nine the streets were jammed, not with the carriages of the rich, but with the deliveries that made their life possible: hams, geese, truffles, oysters, cases of claret and champagne. Carts laden with coal rubbed up

11

against the lighter vehicles of the window-cleaners; local bakers' boys were handing over great sheaves of loaves to undercooks on the pavements. Here and there an anxious butler or senior footman could be seen hovering around a furniture van with instructions to beware of the Queen Anne table in the hall and not to hit any of the banisters on the way up the great staircases.

The aristocrats of the early morning round were the liveried carriages of the great shops of London, the pale green of Fortnum and Mason, the dark green of Harrods, the dark blue of Berry Brothers and Rudd. At the bottom of Berkeley Street, just where it joined the fashionable artery of Piccadilly, three coalmen were locked in furious argument with a young Turk from Justerini and Brooks who refused to give way.

'I don't expect this will be an easy meeting,' said Lord Rosebery, picking his way delicately past a grocer's van that had drawn up on the pavement. 'Anyone dealing with the Royal Family has first to negotiate between the Scylla and Charybdis of the two Private Secretaries. Sir George Trevelyan, the keeper of Victoria's chamber, and Sir William Suter, the guardian for the Prince of Wales, have raised procrastination to an art form and obfuscation to depths undreamt of by Niccolo Machiavelli. They rarely say yes. They seldom say no. But between those two extremes they have made all negotiations into a perilous voyage, with many squalls for the unwary and little prospect of a safe arrival at the final destination. It is one thing to decide to send for you, my dear Powerscourt. It may be quite another to do something about any proposals you may have. I presume you have some crumbs of thought to bring to our humble table this morning?'

'I have indeed.' Powerscourt smiled, pausing only to look at the arsenal of weaponry on display in the windows of London's most exclusive and most expensive gun shop in St James's Street.

'I have spent much time reading in the London Library. I have spent even more time talking to my two sisters who move about on the fringes of the Marlborough House set.'

A junior footman showed them up to the Private Secretary's office on the second floor. It was a large well-proportioned room with high ceilings and tall windows that looked out over the gardens to St James's Park.

'May I introduce the Treasurer and Comptroller of His Royal Highness's Household, General Sir Bartle Shepstone?' Sir William had the impeccable manners of the well-tempered courtier.

The four men sat down round a table next to the window. To the right was a huge desk, cluttered with papers and correspondence, the raw material, Powerscourt presumed, of Suter's world. A full-length portrait of the Princess of Wales, standing by the lake at Sandringham, looked out at them from its command post above the fireplace.

'Let me say first of all how grateful we are for your presence here this morning,' Suter began, blessing each of them in turn with a wintry smile.

Sir William was tall, slightly stooped, with a high forehead and a well-tended moustache. His face, as Powerscourt observed it over the months ahead, was one of the most unusual he had ever seen. Years of dealing with the scandals of the Prince of Wales, scandals he knew about, scandals he could only suspect, had trained him to lock all expression out of his face. The grey eyes were always opaque. Neither smile nor grimace touched his lips. Sir William's face betrayed no emotions at all. Suter was a Sphinx.

'I presume, Lord Rosebery, that you have acquainted Lord Powerscourt with the information I imparted to you at our last meeting about the extortionate demands made of the Prince of Wales and the method of delivery?'

Rosebery nodded gravely. Extortionate demands, thought Powerscourt, that's not bad as a circumlocution for blackmail.

'We at our end of Pall Mall have naturally been giving thought to what might lie behind such unreasonable behaviour. We have been trying to identify the circumstances in which an extortionist could feel that a Prince of the Crown might prefer to offer some pecuniary obviation to prevent unfortunate outbreaks of publicity.'

'They ought to be controlled by law, these damned newspapers and magazines.' Sir Bartle Shepstone appeared to have turned red even thinking about them. 'Ought to be controlled by the laws of England.'

Powerscourt noticed that Shepstone was still wearing full military dress as if he was on parade. He looked as though he might have been an adjutant. Looking at his almost manic neatness, Powerscourt felt that this was a man who could have organized the transport of supplies through the Khyber Pass or a fleet of artillery down the more dangerous passages of the Nile.

Forty miles north of Pall Mall the station platform was invisible by the time the train pulled out of the station, billows of smoke drifting back to envelop the chaos it had left behind. The platform had disappeared beneath a miscellany of trunks, portmanteaux, valises, cabin trunks, shooting gear, hatboxes, shoeboxes, walking sticks and grips. Trying unsuccessfully to bring order to this sea of baggage were the accompanying staff who had decamped off the train, shouting at each other: two valets, two footmen, one groom, two loaders and an underbutler.

The station was Dunmow Halt not far from Bishop's Stortford. The arriving guest, with his large retinue of retainers, was the Prince of Wales. The hostess was Daisy Brooke, mistress of Easton Lodge in the County of Essex and adjacent lands that ranged over five counties. Daisy was also the current mistress of the Prince of Wales. When he was eighteen years old, the Prince of Wales had been stationed in Ireland with his regiment. Some of his fellow officers had introduced a Dublin actress called Nellie Clifden into his bed. His conversion in that camp at the Curragh was as sudden and as whole-hearted as that of Paul on the Damascus road. That long night the Prince of Wales found his mission in life. His calling was to have as many women as possible. Beautiful women, willing women, reluctant women, women in Ireland, women in England, women in France, women in Germany.

Daisy was the latest.

As the luggage chaos on the platform slowly struggled into order, Daisy and her Prince were riding merrily away, through the ornate red brick gates of Easton Lodge and into her estate. The late October sun blest the flat acres of Daisy's domain and Daisy's birds were singing the songs of autumn.

*

'Our conclusion was that there was one series of events which might have given rise to the feeling that money might be extracted in return for silence.' Suter coughed slightly, as if embarrassed at what he had to say. But he did not hesitate. 'I have taken the liberty of summarizing these events in the form of a memorandum. I felt it would be simpler to communicate in this fashion. I would ask you both to read it in turn and then return the paper to me. However distinguished our guests,' here came that wintry smile again, 'we do not feel it appropriate that any piece of paper should leave this room.'

There, thought Powerscourt. There was a glimpse of cold steel within the scabbard.

'But before you read that, I felt I should acquaint you with some of the blackmail documents themselves.'

Suter looked as if he had just stepped into a very disagreeable gutter. He took a small key from his waistcoat pocket and unlocked a drawer in his desk. He extracted a plain envelope and handed the contents round to his guests.

Powerscourt looked through them quickly. Then he looked through them again. He observed that the blackmailer had never mastered the art of cutting out letters or pasting them on to a page. The cutting was rough, there was always too much paste round the edges, as if the blackmailer was worried his messages would not stick. There was no proper punctuation as letters in upper and lower case, usually taken from different publications, sprawled their untidy way across the page.

The messages were usually brief. 'You were at Lady Manchester's with Lady Brooke. You are a disgrace. Unless you pay up, all of Britain will know of your deeds.' 'You were at a house party in Norfolk with Lady Brooke. The working people of this country will not stand for this behaviour. You will have to pay.' Powerscourt thought he could detect *The Times* and the *Morning Post* typefaces but there were another two he did not recognize.

'Does anything occur to you after your inspection?' Suter's voice called Powerscourt back to the meeting.

'Fellow seems to think he speaks for England. One of those damned radicals, I shouldn't wonder!' Sir Bartle Shepstone did not have a high opinion of radicals.

'I'm afraid,' said Powerscourt, handing back the venomous

15

bundle, 'that it is virtually impossible to deduce anything at all. The messy pasting, the untidy letters, could all be designed to throw us off the scent. I'm afraid,' he looked enigmatically at Sir Bartle, 'that they could as easily have come from a duke living in Piccadilly as a labourer in Peckham.' Privately, he thought the duke the more likely of the two.

Shepstone made a noise that might have been a grunt and might have been a cough. Suter hurried the business forward. 'The memorandum, gentlemen. Our memorandum.'

He handed a document to Rosebery. As he read it, Powerscourt became aware of the ticking of a clock in the corner. Buckler and Sons, the legend on its face said, Clockmakers, By Appointment to Her Majesty the Queen. Shepstone was peering at his shoes as if they too were on parade. Suter was looking out across St James's Park. Far off in the distance the chimes of Big Ben could be heard, tolling the half-hour.

'Most interesting. Most interesting. Thank you,' said Rosebery in his most pompous voice as he handed the document to his friend.

Powerscourt paused slightly before he began to read, his brows furrowed in intense concentration.

Frances Maynard, Lady Brooke, was twenty-nine years old. She claimed descent from Charles II and Nell Gwyn. She became an heiress at the age of three and had over £30,000 a year of her own. On her marriage to Lord Brooke, son and heir of Lord Warwick, she attained a magnificent position in society. Her marriage liberated her to pursue her own affairs while her compliant husband pursued his normal routine of hunting and shooting and very occasional forays to the House of Commons. Lady Brooke was certainly beautiful. She had in her eye the look of one who would not be deprived of her prey, be it man or fox.

'You know my station has just opened,' Daisy began, 'so we can now run special trains direct from London right to my front door.'

'Indeed I do,' said the Prince. 'It is a better station than the one I have at Sandringham. I suppose it must be more up to date.'

16

'Well,' said Lady Brooke, 'I'm going to have a party in the spring. And it's going to last a week. I'm going to have chess in the garden, with live actors from the London theatres dressed as pawns and castles and kings and queens. I'm going to have an orchestra that will play every night. I'm going to have the food brought over from Paris. I want you to help me with the invitations.'

The Prince of Wales' knowledge of society was encyclopedic, his society, Lady Brooke's society, for the Prince of Wales had never had any gainful employment in all of his forty-seven years. His hair was receding fast. A lifetime of seventeen-course dinners had taken its toll on his waistline. None of his circle and few of his subjects would have dared to call him fat, but the waistbands of his ceremonial uniforms needed regular attention from his team of valets.

His mother, Queen Victoria, was a jealous guardian of the powers and privileges of royalty, reluctant to share them even with her son. And politicians, however eager they might be to curry favour with the heir to the throne, had grown reluctant to let him know any secret or sensitive matter, as confidential Foreign Office documents were left lying about in theatre boxes or their contents circulated around the gossip channels of the capital.

The Prince of Wales had turned indolence into a profession and the pursuit of pleasure into a full-time occupation. Aristocratic birth and great wealth were the entry tickets. This was an exhausting life of entertainment and enjoyment, where thousands of birds were slaughtered in a single morning and where sleeping with other people's wives and husbands at country house parties was the expected order of the day or night.

Memorandum
From: Sir William Suter
To: Lord Rosebery, Lord Powerscourt.
At issue are the complicated relationships that have developed between Lord Beresford, his wife Lady Charles Beresford, Lady Brooke and HRH The Prince of Wales. The

events go back a number of years. These are the salient facts. Definite information about dates is sometimes difficult to ascertain.

1. Lord Charles Beresford forms a close friendship with Frances Maynard, Lady Brooke. This friendship lasts for a year or more and begins to become the subject of adverse comment in certain sections of Society.

2. Mindful of this, or of his position as an MP and junior member of the Government, Lord Beresford abandons the friendship and renews his marriage vows with Lady Charles.

3. Lady Brooke, meanwhile, resents the fact that Lord Beresford appears to have annulled their friendship and returned to his proper station. Her anger is further fuelled when she learns that Lady Charles is with child.

4. Lady Brooke writes a most intemperate letter to Lord Charles in which she pleads for him to return once more to her. This letter is full of compromising and embarrassing statements and should never have been despatched. Lady Brooke went so far as to suggest that Lord Beresford had no right to have issue with his own wife.

5. Peradventure, the letter is opened and read not by Lord Charles, as intended, but by Lady Charles. She is appalled by its contents and resolves to use the letter to undermine Lady Brooke's position in Society.

6. Lady Brooke throws herself on the mercy of the Prince of Wales. She appeals to him for help in recovering the letter before her position is seriously compromised. Lady Brooke forms a close friendship with HRH the Prince of Wales as she had before with Lord Beresford.

7. Lady Charles gives the letter to London's leading libel solicitor George Lewis for safe keeping. He writes a letter to Lady Brooke which incenses her further.

8. The Prince of Wales pays a call on Mr Lewis and requests that he show him the letter. Mr Lewis acquiesces but refuses to part with it or to destroy it without the agreement of his client. That agreement is not forthcoming.

9. Lord Beresford, wearied perchance of the intrigues of the women, returns to his earlier profession, the Navy. He takes command of a vessel in the Mediterranean.

10. The friendship between Lady Brooke and the Prince of Wales also becomes the object of censure in the less well-bred quarters of society. Acting as the champion of Lady Brooke, the Prince of Wales ceases to invite Lady Beresford to Marlborough House and lets it be known that he will not attend any social event where she may be present.

11. Lady Charles is deeply distressed at the social isolation in which she now finds herself. She writes to the Prime Minister, threatening to expose the friendship between the Prince of Wales and Lady Brooke to a wider public.

12. Lord Beresford returns briefly from the Mediterranean. He calls on the Prince of Wales at Marlborough House. He dares to call His Royal Highness a blackguard and at one point even threatens physical violence upon the person of the heir to the throne.

13. The Prince of Wales refuses to lift the obstacles to Lady Beresford appearing in Society. Her sister, Lady Paget, produces a scurrilous and defamatory pamphlet called 'The River', chronicling the friendship between the Prince of Wales and Lady Brooke. This pamphlet, unfortunately, circulates widely in Society.

14. Lord Beresford is currently threatening to return once more from his ship and summon the Press and Tele-graph Agencies to his house in Eaton Square and inform them of all he knows about the private life of the Prince of Wales.

'Daisy, my Daisy, I have not seen you now for nearly a week.'

'But now, my Prince, we have four or five days in front of us. The rest of the guests do not arrive until the day after tomorrow. Until then it is just the two of us.'

Of all the aspects of being a royal mistress, this was the one that Daisy loved the best. The farmers' families and the country people turned out to watch the mistress of Easton Lodge drive the heir to the throne through her grounds. For Daisy, this affair was about conquest. As a girl she had never known how pretty she was; only when she came out did she realize that she was one of the most beautiful women of her time, adored, worshipped, wanted by an army of male admirers. She wanted to be the most beautiful, she wanted to have the most handsome lovers, she wanted to make the most of her beauty while she could. Rather a last reckless ride to glory than the dull footsteps of the mundane and the everyday. To conquer the Prince of Wales, to display him rather like a new hunter, this was, she knew, as high as she would ever reach. And, deep down, she knew it would not last.

They were passing the parish church of Little Easton, where generations of her ancestors were buried. One of them had been Private Secretary to Lord Burleigh, Lord Chancellor and First Minister to Queen Elizabeth. Daisy felt she was carrying on a family tradition of royal service.

'I fear I bring bad news, Daisy.' Edward was continuing to wave his regal wave to the country people as they passed, his smile stitched firmly on to his face.

'Oh no,' said Daisy. 'I thought you could escape from the affairs of state for a few days when you come to my humble house.'

The affairs of state since they had last met consisted of one race meeting, two visits to the music hall and one men-only dinner at the Prince of Wales' very own pleasure ground, the Marlborough Club.

'It's Beresford. Lord Charles Beresford.'

Daisy winced as he spoke the name of her former lover.

'They say,' the Prince of Wales went on, 'that he has taken leave of his ship the *Undaunted* somewhere in the Mediterfjranean. They say he's about to return to London and cause trouble.'

The road past the church was lined with late windfalls of apples, pale green and watery red in the sunshine. They were ground into a cidery pulp by the hooves of the horses and the wheels of the carriage as they rattled past.

'What trouble can he cause a man in your position, my Prince?'

'You know perfectly well what he's threatening to do, Daisy. Make a public scandal. Publicity, he keeps saying, publicity, it's all he's got left to him. He says he's going to tell the world about my private life and about our love affair. Damn publicity! And damn Beresford!'

Part of Daisy didn't mind the world knowing about her love affair with the Prince of Wales. The greater the knowledge the greater the glory. But she knew that Society might not like it. Do what you want to do, but don't get caught.

As she looked across at the Prince she felt him growing ever more grumpy. Oh dear, Daisy thought, he's going to be difficult. We're going to have scenes before dinner and sulks after tea. This weekend is going to be a strain with the Prince moping about the house worried about his future. It might be worse than a strain, it might even be boring.

Powerscourt handed the memorandum back to the Private Secretary. He had memorized it word for word.

'Do you have any preliminary thoughts, Lord Powerscourt?' Powerscourt was to say later that Suter addressed him as if he, Suter, were a nervous patient before his dentist, fearful of some painful and bloody extractions.

'It is obviously a difficult and delicate matter,' Powerscourt replied, feeling himself falling against his will into the language and circumlocutions of the Private Secretary. 'There must be a number of people who might feel that they have the information which would enable them . . .' He paused before he dropped the word into the room. '. . . to blackmail His Royal Highness.'

'Blackmail' dropped like a stone. Sir Bartle Shepstone looked again at his shoes, as if the polish had suddenly worn off. Suter fidgeted with his moustache. Rosebery was impassive.

'But is it not the case that this information has been abroad for some time now? What I mean is this – why should the blackmailer wait until now before presenting his demands? And have those demands been met? Has the Prince, as it were, paid up?'

Shepstone looked as though he might explode at the impertinence. But Suter was made of sterner stuff.

'As yet there have been no such transactions. No suggestions have yet been made about possible transfers of money.'

'And would the Prince make such a transfer if the request were made?'

'I am not in a position to answer that at present.' Suter looked relieved that he could escape such a direct question.

'Are you sure,' Powerscourt went on, continuing to probe for answers, 'that there are no other matters apart from this which could give rise to blackmail? Forgive me if I raise such unpleasant thoughts. It goes with my occupation.'

Suter shrugged his shoulders. 'Who can say? Who can say?'

'No true-born Englishman would ever contemplate such behaviour. It would never occur to him.' Sir Bartle was growing red in the face again.

'Are you sure,' Powerscourt stuck to his last, 'that there is nothing in the current situation of Prince Eddy that might also give rise to blackmail?'

'Dammit, Suter, dammit.' The General was furious now, pounding the table as he spoke. 'Do we have to listen to these vile accusations?'

'I fear that you do. Nay, I am certain that you do.' The voice was very cold. Powerscourt had forgotten about Rosebery. 'If you wish to have these matters properly looked into,' Rosebery went on with all the political authority at his command, 'you will have to look at certain unpleasant facts. And that is one of them.'

Silence fell briefly over the meeting. Shepstone was restraining himself with difficulty. Suter glanced at the Princess of Wales above the fireplace. There was no reply.

'Lord Powerscourt, what would you have us do?'

'I can only make a few suggestions at this stage. Obviously I would like to look again at all the communications from the extortionist.' When in Rome, he reminded himself, talk as the Romans talk. 'I would like to speak with those present when the letters were received. I would like you to find an excuse for dismissing some respected member of your household, the senior footman perhaps, or somebody in such a position. I would then replace them with an equally competent servant in my sister's employ who has worked for me before in Army Intelligence. This would give us another source of information.

'I would like, with your permission, to speak to the Commissioner of the Metropolitan Police. Naturally I would not give him any details. But blackmailers often have a record, they have often struck before. I know the Commissioner from previous inquiries, and I have every confidence in his abilities and his discretion. If there has been a blackmailer at large among the rich of London, he will know of it.'

A frisson of acute distaste passed across Suter's face at the mention of the Metropolitan Police Force.

'I would also like to speak to the Superintendent of the Postal Services for this district to see what we could learn from watching the postboxes. And finally, I know that it is outside my position to say so, but I would advise that the Prince of Wales limits his appearances in society for a while. Sometimes the sight of the victim spurs the blackmailer on; equally the lack of sight may put him off.'

Sir William Suter had been making notes on a white pad in front of him. 'I regret,' he purred, 'that I am unable to give any direct answers to your requests at this stage.' Powerscourt felt that he did not regret it for an instant. 'I shall have to take advice from colleagues.' Powerscourt wondered how many times those words had been spoken in this room. He thought again of Rosebery's Scylla and Charybdis. 'Your proposals are interesting and ingenious,' Suter was well into his routine delaying mechanism now, 'but it would be impossible for me to say yea or nay at this meeting. Could I suggest that you leave it with me for a couple of days or so? Once I have an answer I shall, of course, give you a proper response. And thank you so much for the time and trouble you both have taken.'

Suter ushered them to the front door. Sir Bartle Shepstone remained seated inside, presumably, thought Powerscourt, to give vent to the true feelings of an outraged Englishman.

3

'Rosalind, I cannot tell you how angry I am.'

Lord Francis Powerscourt was cross. He was fuming in the study of his eldest sister Rosalind's house in St James's Square. Lady Rosalind Pembridge had removed her brother from the drawing-room in case his temper spoiled the evening for the rest of her guests.

'Francis, you are being unreasonable. You know you are.'

'I am not. I am not.'

His sister felt that Francis looked exactly as he had done when he was a little boy. The angry looks, the black curly hair thrown back over his forehead, the eyes flashing with defiance at some slight, real or imaginary.

'I specifically ask you to invite family members to dinner. Family members only. There are certain things I wish to ask them to do, relating to my current investigation. And what do I find? That you have chosen to ask somebody else along, without consulting me, and against my express wishes. Now I cannot talk about my investigation in front of strangers. Honestly, how could you be so stupid!'

Lady Rosalind regarded her brother's investigations as another of those irksome hobbies men have like hunting or fishing or shooting. She could not imagine how her brother could object to another person being invited to dinner. It would round off the numbers nicely, as she had said to her husband the night before.

'Do you not understand the English language?' Powerscourt was beyond gale force now, and on the verge of the typhoon.

'Family members only. O.N.L.Y. That's not too difficult for you, is it?

'Lady Hamilton is a very presentable young woman, Francis. You might like her. '

'Are you now so desperate that you have exhumed Nelson's mistress from the grave, Rosalind?'

'Not that Lady Hamilton, Francis. Don't be silly.'

Powerscourt was sometimes amused, sometimes angered, by the efforts of his sisters to marry him off. Eligible, healthy, single women were constantly paraded before him at his sisters' dinner tables. His younger sister Lady Mary specialized in society women just the wrong side of forty with social ambitions left to fulfil. The youngest, Lady Eleanor, married to her sea captain in the West Country, had an armada of naval widows on manoeuvres, still talking of ships and steam and prize money. Lady Rosalind went in for more eccentric offerings; in the past year she had brought forth a painter, then the Head of History at a leading girls' school – 'Think how much you like history, Francis dear,' – and then an American who might or might not have been the heiress to an enormous fortune.

Powerscourt looked them all over, he sampled their conversation, and he passed by resolutely on the other side. But now! After all he had said, his sisters just took no notice at all.

'Honestly, Francis, everybody is beginning to arrive. Are you going to calm down?'

'I think I shall go home now,' said Powerscourt gloomily.

'You can't possibly do that. The family is expecting you. So is Lady Lucy. She lost her husband with Gordon at Khartoum, you know.'

'I don't care if she is the Queen of Sheba or Cleopatra – she kept losing husbands too, didn't she? I want to go home.'

'Honestly, Francis, you sound just like your nephew Patrick. And he's only four years old.'

'All right, all right. But don't expect me to behave properly. You have left me in a most filthy temper.'

It wasn't until they were well past the fish that Powerscourt had the chance to talk to Lady Lucy on his left. Two glasses of Meursault had improved his temper greatly. Lady Lucy Hamilton was thirty-one years old. She was tall and very slim, with blonde hair, petite ears and a pretty little nose. Her eyes were a deep blue and quite disconcerting when they were wide open.

'Lady Lucy,' Powerscourt opened the batting and went straight on to the attack, 'how do you know my sister?'

'One meets your sisters all over town, Lord Francis,' said Lady Lucy with a humorous air. 'I met Lady Rosalind at Mrs Burke's the other day. I'm afraid I saw that look pass across her face and I knew I would meet you soon.'

'That look? Tell me more.' Powerscourt was drawn by the easy charm and the pretty looks of Lady Lucy into forgetting his previous anger.

'The look is something I know well now. It says, Here is another eligible person to introduce to my widowed brother or sister for matchmaking purposes. I see it in my own family all the time. Tell me, Lord Powerscourt, are your sisters always trying to marry you off to somebody or other?'

'Well, yes, as a matter of fact they are.' Rich helpings of roast duck were being handed round, a dark red cherry sauce dripping down the side. 'Lady Lucy, do you also suffer from a family trying to marry you off?'

'I do, indeed I do. But in my case they are mostly brothers. Men are so obvious in these matters, they've nearly given up on me now. Sisters, I should think, are more devious.'

'They certainly are,' said Powerscourt, 'and I have three of them. Like the three witches in Macbeth, endlessly stirring at their noxious brew, eye of this and hair of that. They stalk the streets of St James's at night, you know, potions bubbling in their hands.' Powerscourt drew his long fingers into the shape of a goblet and held it up to the candles.

'I can't believe they are as bad as all that, Lord Francis. I do have one very tiresome aunt, though.' Lady Lucy leaned forward to impress on her companion the gravity of her relations' behaviour. 'She doesn't invite what she considers to be suitable men one at a time, but in bundles of three or four at a single sitting. Repulsing one decent but undesirable male is not very difficult, but three or four can be very hard. But come, Lord Powerscourt. Let us be serious if only for a moment. One of your sisters told me that your wife and son were lost at sea some years ago?'

'Indeed they were. And your husband, Lady Lucy?'

'He went with General Gordon to the Sudan. He never came back. I cannot remember if they were meant to conquer the country or to give it back to the natives. It doesn't matter now. At least I have my little boy to remember him by.'

'Let us not trade sorrow for sorrow over the sorbet,' said Powerscourt as the duck was taken away .'How old is your little boy?'

'Robert is seven now.'

Lady Lucy was suddenly aware that she had broken one of the golden rules in this sort of conversation. 'Don't tell them you have a child,' her mother and her brothers had always urged her. Well, she didn't care if she had broken it. Lord Francis seemed a lot more pleasant than the usual run of sporting bores she met at her brothers' houses.

The middle of the room was dominated by a full-length portrait of Lady Rosalind, painted by Whistler just before her marriage to Lord Pembridge. Against a grey background, Powerscourt's sister looked radiant in black, her eyes sparkling merrily out of the picture.

At the far end of the table Powerscourt's other brother-in-law William Burke was holding forth about American railway stocks and South American bonds. At his end the conversation had turned to the prose of Cicero.

'That's what I started on when I began to teach myself Latin all over again. I thought I could help Robert, you see,' said Lady Lucy. 'I always found it quite easy to translate but rather boring after a while. All those orotund periods seem to strike the same sort of rhythm, don't you think?'

Powerscourt agreed wholeheartedly. Was she moving on to Sallust or Tacitus, he inquired, and he began a long exposition of how simply untranslatable Tacitus was, just untranslatable.

'Honestly, darling,' Lady Rosalind said to her husband late that night after all the guests had gone. 'Francis makes all that fuss about one extra person coming to dinner. Then they manage to have a distinctly flirtatious conversation about some dead Roman author called Tacitus. Getting on famously, they were. But I don't think he liked the duck. Was there anything wrong with the duck, Pembridge?'

'There was nothing wrong with the duck, my dear,' said her

husband loyally. 'But you can't have flirtations on the subject of dead Roman authors, Rosalind.'

'Oh yes you can. I only heard one of the bits he was quoting to Lady Lucy, but they sounded fairly rich to me. Their eyes were talking and I haven't seen our Francis' eyes like that for years.'

'Come to mention it,' said her husband, 'I think I heard them arranging to meet for luncheon at the National Gallery the day after tomorrow.'

'Really,' said Lady Rosalind. 'I wonder if Lady Lucy mightn't be the one after all.'

'There you go again,' groaned Lord Pembridge. 'They've only met for a couple of hours at a dinner party and you are marching them up the aisle already. Not so fast.'

'Don't be so sure,' said Lady Rosalind.

Lady Lucy went to sleep that night thinking about Powerscourt's deep voice and his hands with their long thin fingers. Powerscourt went to sleep thinking of the toss of Lady Lucy's head and her deep blue eyes.

The man collected his parcel from the blacksmith when it was dark. As well as his normal duties the blacksmith sharpened knives, a skill he had learnt in his previous career in the Army, sparks from knives old and blunt flying from his stone. The blacksmith didn't know why he had been asked to sharpen this one in secret, without anybody knowing about it. He didn't bother with things like that, he just liked getting on with his work.

The man unwrapped his parcel in a locked room. He took off layer after layer of paper. The blacksmith had used a lot of oil. The knife glistened in the firelight, distorted reflections of the room dancing on its silvery surface. Very gently he put his finger to the side of the blade. Even that brought a thin flow of blood. The man smiled and put the knife in a black sheath designed by its German makers. He tried putting it inside his boot. It fitted perfectly. The man smiled again.

*

Prince Eddy, Duke of Clarence and Avondale, eldest son of the Prince of Wales, was saying his farewells to his mother in the hall of Marlborough House. Twenty-eight years of maternal devotion had not dimmed the sadness Princess Alexandra felt at losing her eldest, even for an evening.

'Wrap up warm, darling. Have you got your gloves? And your scarf?'

Most young men would have felt deeply embarrassed at this display of affection more suitable to a child of eight or nine. But Eddy didn't care very much.

'Of course I have, Mother dear. Don't worry about me. I shall be back presently.' He kissed his mother affectionately on the cheek.

Eddy didn't care very much about anything. That was part of his problem. If only, he thought, as he hailed a cab passing in front of Marlborough House, if only they would leave me alone. All his life, he reflected, as the cab made its way towards Hammersmith, somebody had been after him to do things. When he was small they wanted him to learn things in books. Eddy hadn't seen much point in that. Then they'd sent him off to join the Navy and a different lot of somebodies had wanted him to learn another set of tricks. Climbing up ropes. Navigation with horrid maps and set squares and something mysterious called trigonometry. Knots. Eddy couldn't see much point in that. There was always somebody else to tie your knots for you and nobody in their right mind was ever going to ask him to navigate anywhere. Then there was the Army. Yet another lot of some-bodies tried to persuade him to march correctly, to grasp the rules of war, whatever they were, to learn how to command men and armies. Eddy couldn't see much point in that either though there were some fine fellows in the Army who became his friends.

And all the time people had kept on reminding him who he was and what he would inherit one day. And what his duty was. Eddy didn't want his grandmother to die. He didn't want his father to die. Least of all did he want his mother to die. Only after two of those deaths could his awful duty come upon him. That duty was still some way off. Anyway, he reflected, as he stepped out of his cab by Hammersmith Bridge, he had watched his father doing his duty all his life. He proposed to follow his example, but in his own way.

The wind was getting up as Eddy walked along the river bank towards Chiswick, flecking the dark waters with little spots of cream. A couple of barges, heavily laden, were trudging purposefully up the Thames. Eddy was wearing a plain grey suit and a dark coat, trying to look as much like his future subjects as he could. As he passed another tavern the sounds of raucous laughter floated out into the street. A flock of seagulls hovered expectantly around the water's edge.

He was nearing open country now. The Victorian villas had stopped their relentless advance along the river bank and the spire of St Nicholas' Church was behind him. There were no lights to be seen ahead, only the flickering of the moon across the water as the clouds scudded overhead. As he rounded a bend Prince Eddy could see a large house in the distance. That was his destination.

A mere eighteen months before, the nation had been shocked by the Cleveland Street scandal when a house at No. 19 was exposed as a homosexual brothel, run by a certain Charles Hammond. The scandal deepened when it was revealed that Lord Frederick Ravenscourt, an equerry to the Prince of Wales and to Prince Eddy, had been involved and had fled the country to escape disgrace or to avoid implicating his masters. The homosexual elite of London had reacted promptly. They abandoned Cleveland Street and began a six-month search for more suitable accommodation. They found Brandon House ideal for their purposes.

It sat in its own grounds a mile from Hammersmith Bridge in one direction, and the same distance from Barnes Railway Bridge to the west. To the north there was nothing between it and the grounds of Chiswick House where Eddy had played as a boy. South was the river, and the staff of Brandon House kept two boats permanently moored, oars tucked into the sides, in case a rapid escape was needed to the green fields of Barnes on the other side.

The Club, as it was known, had a very special set of rules. The entry fee was £500. The Club operated on the principle of mutual blackmail to survive. Membership was by personal recommendation only. And then the Club's management, half seriously referred to by the members as the Star Chamber, took and checked the names and addresses of two close family relatives of each member – wives, mothers, brothers, sisters. Any breach of the society's rules, which were remarkably strict, led to immediate disclosure, first to the family and then, if necessary, to the newspapers. Two well-known suicides of the previous decade were attributed by those in the know to the activities of the Star Chamber.

The house was built in the late eighteenth century. It had a kitchen in the basement, three grand reception rooms on the ground floor and a series of bedrooms on the two floors above. All the windows on the first two floors were heavily shuttered. The house rarely opened its doors before nine o'clock in the evening in summer and six o'clock in winter. Thin beams of light were shining through the shutters as Eddy entered the drive.

The staff of the Club were all former sergeant majors or petty officers from the Navy who encouraged proper discipline in the running of the Club's affairs. Its finances were looked after by a distinguished banker, its legal problems, on the rare occasions it attracted them, by a couple of MPs and a High Court judge. Once a month there was a masked ball. Once a year there was a fancy dress party when historical figures ranging from the Marquis de Sade to Cleopatra graced the White Drawing Room. And as he unbuttoned his gloves and greeted the duty porter the Duke of Clarence and Avondale was told: 'Good evening, sir. All the normal services are available this evening.'

4

'Just look at this thing, Johnny, look at it for God's sake.'

Powerscourt and his friend Lord Johnny Fitzgerald were in a small sitting-room on the top floor of his sister's house in St James's Square. It was known in the house as Uncle Francis' room. The presence of some scattered toys showed that his nephews were regular visitors.

'I mean, you've got to laugh really. They're so pompous, those Marlborough House people.' Powerscourt was holding a couple of letters up to the light. 'Twelve days ago Rosebery and I go to see Private Secretary Suter at Marlborough House. He says that he needs more time to consider some of the proposals I put to him, the ones we discussed at Rokesley, if you recall.'

Lord Johnny nodded, thinking more of the bottle of Chassagne-Montrachet with the fish than the minutiae of detection. He was working his way down a mere bottle of Chablis this evening.

'Of course, we said. So Suter says that he will let me know in a couple of days. After that I get the first little billet-doux, which I've got here somewhere,' Powerscourt looked around desperately as if it might be hiding behind one of his nephews' battered Roman legionnaires, 'and then I got this second one here today.' Powerscourt waved the missive up and down and began to read.

'"Marlborough House, Pall Mall et cetera, et cetera. My dear Powerscourt, Please accept my humble apologies for the apparent procrastination in response to your proposals. We have been in receipt of another of those blackmailing messages. It referred to the fact that HRH the Prince of Wales had been in Easton

Lodge with Lady Brooke. It commented, again, that the ordinary people of Britain would not countenance his behaviour and the monarchy would be brought down in scandal and disgrace.

' "Turning to the substance of your proposals, I regret to have to inform you that we require a further period of consultation and clarification before we can give you any more definite reply. It would be helpful if you could furnish us with a written memorandum outlining what we discussed in more detail. This would enable the consultation with colleagues to proceed at a more expeditious pace. I look forward to hearing from you. Your humble servant et cetera, et cetera."

'There,' said Powerscourt, 'you could win prizes for that lot. The Suter Prize, awarded annually to first year undergraduates for the most pompous piece of prose in England. And why should I write anything down? Do I not have my own little state secrets, my own red boxes, which are not to be passed around after dinner at Marlborough House or left on the billiard table at that Marlborough Club just a dice throw away across the street?'

Fitzgerald laughed, examining the label on his bottle of Chablis very closely. 'Never mind, Francis, never mind. Do you think that new blackmail message is important? Do you suppose the Beresfords have opened up a little newspaper cutting and pasting operation over there in Eaton Square, that they are the blackmailers?'

'They could be, of course they could be. But the messages could just as easily have come from the Archbishop of Canterbury or the Foreign Secretary for all I know. Anybody could have sent the things. They could even have come from inside Marlborough House itself.' Powerscourt was fiddling absentmindedly with a one-legged member of Napoleon's Imperial Guard, wounded in battle with a nephew.

'Why don't I tell you what I have discovered since our evening in Oundle? It's not very much, but it's better than nothing.'

'Very good, Johnny. Tell me all.'

'Now then,' said Fitzgerald, 'you remember we talked about Prince Eddy and whether or not he might be involved in the world of male brothels?'

Powerscourt's eye was drawn to one of his many paintings of the Battle of Waterloo. It showed a British regiment of the line forming square at Quatre Bras forty-eight hours before the great engagement itself. In the centre of the square stood the massive figure of a Regimental Sergeant Major guarding the flag of the Union and the colours of the regiment. Standing and firing was one half of the men in the square. Kneeling in the front row, bayonets poised to impale any French cavalry who dared approach, was the rest of the detachment, some of them little more than boys, shouting cheerful defiance at the enemy. On the fringes of the picture French cavalry whirled, lances raised, unable to break through. Around the participants there swirled the smoke from the rifles and the distant firings of the great guns.

Here, thought Powerscourt, was the glory of the British Army laying down their lives for King and country. And eighty years later, here we are discussing the male brothels of the eldest son of the Prince of Wales.

Lord Johnny was used to his friend's temporary absences, lost in thought at the non-striker's end.

'There was that place in Cleveland Street a few years ago, you remember. There's a few more that have sprung up in the same part of London, behind Fitzroy Square and round at the back of King's Cross station. But the rich people were terrified after Cleveland Street. They have no intention of getting caught ever again. They've upped sticks and bought a very fine house near the river beyond Hammersmith. Gentlemen arrive there at discreet intervals. There's a giant of a man on duty at the door who might well have been a Regimental Sergeant Major. Nobody seems to arrive until after dark. Now I wasn't there for long enough to find out if our Eddy is a customer or not. But I bet he is. And it wouldn't be too difficult to find out.'

'Did you try to go in?' asked Powerscourt.

'That I did not. It would have been rather difficult from where I was. Forty feet up a tree with cramp in my leg.' Lord Johnny laughed.

'I too have some intelligence to report.' Powerscourt's mood had suddenly turned sombre. 'The Prince of Wales has massive debts. At the last count he owes Messrs Finch's & Co., not two hundred yards from where we sit, the princely figure of £200,000.'

'So while I think I'm a bit of a hero for freezing up a Hammersmith tree, you've been going round breaking into banks. I didn't think you had it in you, Francis.'

'I don't,' Powerscourt grinned. 'But my second sister, Mary, is married to a man of business. Have you met William Burke, Johnny? He looks perfectly normal, eyes and ears in the usual place, devoted to his children, adores cricket, likes hunting with the South Essex. But he's one of those people who just understands money, where it comes from, where it's going, what's up and what's down. Our William is a director of some pretty big companies. One of them is Finch's Bank. God knows how he spirited the figures out of there but he says it's the biggest overdraft Finch's have ever seen.'

'£200,000 is an astronomical sum of money, Francis.' Vignobles, sun-drenched fields dripping with noble grapes swam before Lord Johnny's eyes. You could buy yourself entire villages in Bordeaux or Burgundy with that, St Estèphe or Margaux, le Montrachet or Pommard.

'William says that the richest man in England, who is a massive coal owner, or one of those shopping magnates like Maples or Lipton, has well over £100,000 a year in income, maybe even more. So the Prince owes twice as much as that. And William said the debt had not accumulated overnight. It had grown over a period of time, rather like a tree, getting bigger and bigger every year.'

'You don't suppose . . .' Fitzgerald and Powerscourt always discussed their cases in this way, throwing out the most fantastic ideas, some of which later turned out to be true. 'You don't suppose he's been paying this blackmailer for years and years, do you?'

'Well, he might have been,' said Powerscourt thoughtfully, 'or it may just be that he can't live within his income. I don't suppose Daisy Brooke is cheap to run. And there's something else. Rosebery told me that twelve or thirteen years ago Prince Eddy and his younger brother Prince George were sent round the world on a cruise, a cruise that lasted two whole years.'

'Was there any suggestion of scandal about that, Francis?'

'Rosebery couldn't remember. But he's going to find out for me. That means he'll probably ask the First Sea Lord himself . . . But I must reply to His Royal Private Secretaryship down the road.'

'Can you be as pompous as he is, Francis?' Lord Johnny had nearly finished his Chablis.

'Let me try, Johnny, just let me try. "Dear Sir William."' Powerscourt began writing at the little desk by the window, with the lamps being lit in St James's Square below. '"Thank you for your letter of 21st inst. I regret to have to inform you that it has never been my custom to set out possible avenues of inquiry on paper. Such documents have a habit of ending up in the wrong hands. I believe that such circumspection is also followed in your own establishment. I am, of course, only too happy to come and discuss matters with you or your colleagues at your convenience. I am anxious that the matters under discussion should proceed with all due despatch." Is that pompous enough, Johnny?'

'I don't think that man Suter would know pomposity if it came and stroked his beard. He's steeped in it, Francis. Positively marinated in pomposity.'

'Do you know,' Powerscourt was laughing now, 'I might just see if I can get a special dispensation to put my memorandum in for the Suter Prize this year.'

Trafalgar Square was jammed. The press of traffic was so great that every single vehicle, cart, carriage and coach had come to a full stop. A furniture remover's enormous van had toppled over by the edge of the fountain, its contents spilling out on to the road under the astonished gaze of a Landseer lion.

Waiting for Lady Lucy on the portico leading into the National Gallery, Powerscourt wondered if the whole of London would come to a complete halt one day. High on his column, ignoring the chaos below, his plinth festooned with pigeon droppings as the sails of his great ships had once been festooned with round shot holes, Horatio Nelson gazed imperturbably towards Big Ben and Parliament Square and the river that could carry him away.

Then she was beside him. Lady Lucy Hamilton, looking demure in grey but with a slightly raffish hat. Lady Lucy had wondered about the hat, even as she put it on. A little too fast? A trifle ostentatious for a morning rendezvous by the pictures in the National Gallery? It was pink. It was undoubtedly fashionable, and it certainly showed off her blue eyes. Never mind, if I dither about in front of this mirror any longer, thought Lady Lucy, I shall be late.

'Good morning to you, Lady Lucy.' Powerscourt wrenched himself happily away from the chaos in the square without. Looking at Lady Lucy, so charming with that smile of welcome, he felt suddenly that it might be replaced by a different chaos within. 'Shall we go inside? What would you like to look at this morning?'

'Do you have any favourites you would like to visit, Lord Francis?'

A party of art students rushed past them, sketch books in hand, pencils dropping out of their pockets.

'Well, I would quite like to look at a couple of Raphaels. Do you like Raphael, Lady Lucy?'

'Oh yes, I do.' She smiled broadly at him, wondering yet again about her hat. 'And I should like to look at some of the Turners.'

A curvaceous St Catherine, the curves of her dress suggesting the curves of her wheel, was followed by an austere Raphael Madonna, flanked by pillars and a couple of obscure saints.

'Do you think, Lord Francis, that there were conventions for what all these saints actually looked like? I mean, do you think there was some sort of artists' guidebook, only available to a select few of course, which said that St Jerome always looked sad and St Bartholomew happy? I know St Sebastian always appears with those beastly arrows and the four Evangelists usually have a book to write, but what about the rest?'

'It is a pretty thought, Lady Lucy. I have to confess that I don't know the answer.'

Behind them was a great rolling of wheels. A large trolley was conveying a full-length portrait of some seventeenth-century gentleman through the gallery. He was a sombre figure, painted in black with a Bible in his hand and a small dog at his feet.

Behind the trolley an anxious curator repeated instructions to the bearers to go more slowly, to mind the bumps in the floor.

'Where are they taking that Dutch gentleman? Are they throwing him out, do you suppose?' whispered Lady Lucy as the strange cortège passed within a few feet of them.

'Maybe the Last Trump has sounded for him,' said Powerscourt. 'His maker, or rather his restorer, is probably making the call not for the last judgement, but for his paint to be restored. I fancy he is going to the workshops for cleaning, that sort of thing.'

'It must be rather upsetting, if you're a picture,' said Lady Lucy, gazing at the retreating trolley as it rolled off towards the basement. 'One minute you're sitting happily on the wall, minding your own business, and then some horrid men come and take you away.'

'It's the same with people, don't you think?' replied Powerscourt. 'One minute you're sitting happily under the pictures on your wall at home, then Death comes with his trolley, and you're on your way. Down to the basement with you.'

'I don't like that at all,' said Lady Lucy, laughing. 'Let me take you to some Turners.' She steered Powerscourt away to a different part of the gallery. There were storms, shipwrecks, deaths at sea, blazing seconds of steam, sunsets, romantic ruins of ravaged Italian landscapes. Lady Lucy felt light-headed, dizzy, as she looked at them all.

'But look . . .' She planted Powerscourt on a bench looking out at *The Fighting Temeraire*. 'Is this not the finest of them all?'

At the far end of the room a party of students were rolling up their sketches and collecting their equipment. Two curators looked solemnly on, their faces bored or impassive. Outside the bells of St Martin in the Fields called the hour of twelve.

'They say,' said Powerscourt, stretching out his legs until they became a hazard for unwary passers-by, 'that this is one of the most reproduced paintings in England. There are nearly as many *Fighting Temeraires* hanging on the walls of Britain as there are portraits of Queen Victoria.'

'I know which one I would rather have,' said Lady Lucy disloyally, checking that her hat had not got completely out of hand. 'What do you think it means, Lord Francis?'

'What did Turner mean? Or what does it mean to the spectator? I've always thought that paintings, like people's faces, can have multiple meanings.' He stole a quick glance at Lady Lucy's face, mesmerized by the iridescent sunset, Turner's golds and coppers gleaming over the Thames. 'They say it has to do with the coming of the age of steam, don't they? This is the valediction to sail, condemned to be pulled by that ugly black tug on its final voyage to the breaker's yard. Farewell romance, hello smoke, farewell sail, hello mighty engines.'

'I don't think it means that at all.' Lady Lucy was quite vehement. 'I mean people may think it means that. But I think it's much more about Turner himself.' She leant back on the bench, combing her memory for the other Turners she had seen which would help her case.

'Turner, the Turner who painted this, this glory, was an old man when he did it. But when he was young, he made his name and his fame painting the ships and the battles of the great war against the French. This ship, the *Temeraire*,' she pointed dramatically at the ghostly vessel, 'took years and years to build in Rochester or somewhere like that.' Lady Lucy would have been the first to admit that her knowledge of naval construction yards was not that extensive. 'It sails the Mediterranean. It patrols in the Pacific. Its life is entirely peaceful, in spite of the guns on board and the fearful death toll of its broadsides. It only fights for one day, Lord Francis. Just one day. But that one day was at Trafalgar when the *Temeraire* was closely involved in the action right beside the *Victory* and our friend Nelson on his column outside, one day of everlasting glory. And Turner painted it at the time.

'After that, more patrols, more routine voyages, and then bit by bit, spar by spar, sail by sail, the great ship is taken to pieces. Then finally in 1834 or whenever it was, she is to be taken up or down the river by that horrid little tug to be broken up.

'But for Turner, for Turner, Lord Francis' – Powerscourt was bewitched by Lady Lucy's eloquence and her feeling for the painting – 'this was a symbol, a reminder of his own life, his past, his present, his future. Here was this ship of all ships, which he had painted as a young man so many years ago in her hour of glory. By the time the *Temeraire* made this last journey,

39

she would have been a hulk, she would have had no rigging, she would have had no masts. Turner has put them all back. That's why the painting is called *The Fighting Temeraire*. This ship, Turner's ship, his beloved *Temeraire*, has to make her last journey decked out as she was in her days of pomp and power, not like some beggar being dumped in the workhouse.'

Even the curators were listening intently now, staring spellbound at Lady Lucy.

'This is Turner's tribute to his vanished youth. The sunset is not just for the beautiful ship but for Turner himself. He knows that for him too the last journey will be coming soon. The crossing not of the Thames but of Jordan river cannot be very far away. This is Turner's last elegy to his youth, his past life, his own career, gliding unstoppably away from him. After the sunset comes the dark. Death. Oblivion. No more *Temeraire*, no more Turner. But we have this to remember them both.'

Lady Lucy stopped suddenly, as if worn out by so much emotion.

'I cannot tell you how impressed I am by your learning, Lady Lucy.' Powerscourt gazed at her with a new respect, with more feelings than he had brought with him into this gallery. Could she describe all the paintings with such eloquence?

Lady Lucy was grateful to him for listening. It makes such a change, she thought. So often when she wanted to talk about paintings or about books, men changed the subject to horses or cricket or fishing. But this was a man who could listen. She remembered her mother saying to her when she was just eighteen, 'Don't be taken in by their looks or how well the young men whirl you round the dance floors of London, my girl. Find yourself a man who appreciates your mind as well as your pretty looks.'

She turned to look at Powerscourt, who seemed to be inspecting the *Temeraire*'s rigging. Had she found such a man?

Christmas came and Powerscourt was still no further with the courtiers in Marlborough House. It was a long tennis match of letters from the baseline, neither player prepared to go to the net.

'What on earth are they doing?' Powerscourt had asked Rosebery in his library in Berkeley Square.

'The Prince of Wales can't make up his mind, I suspect,' said Rosebery, pouring them both a seasonal glass of white port. 'He wants to know who the blackmailer is. But he's terrified of what might come out of any investigations. Anyway, the Prime Minister has nearly settled the row with the Beresfords. Salisbury told me the Treaty of Berlin had probably been easier to negotiate.'

Rosebery had bought himself a racehorse for Christmas which he was convinced would win the Derby.

Prince Eddy became engaged to Princess May of Teck, to the delight and relief of both sets of parents.

Powerscourt bought Lord Johnny Fitzgerald a case of Chassagne-Montrachet.

His sisters clubbed together to buy Powerscourt a first edition of Gibbon's *The Decline and Fall of the Roman Empire*.

But Powerscourt's Christmas present to his nephews was the one closest to his heart.

Part Two

Sandringham

January 1892

5

The Voltigeurs were moving steadily down the slope, skirmishers who represented the advance guard of the French Army. Behind them, deployed behind and around La Belle Alliance, were the glory of Napoleon's Grande Armée, headgear glittering with the colours of different lands. There was a martial kaleidoscope, Lancers in red shapkas with a brass plate bearing the letter N and a white plume, Chasseurs in kolbachs with headgear of green and scarlet, Hussars with multi-coloured plumes, Dragoons with brass casques over tigerskin turbans, Cuirassiers in steel helmets with copper crests, Carabiniers in dazzling white and the Grenadiers of the Old Guard in massive, plain bearskins.

Across the valley the British, a motley army in motley uniform, waited for their fate.

'Fire!' said a small voice. 'Fire!'

'Bang! Bang! Bang! Bang!' shouted two other small voices.

'If I take a big puff on my cigar,' said Lord Francis Powerscourt, who normally loathed cigars but felt that sacrifices had to be made in the interests of history, 'we can have smoke all over the battlefield.'

This had been his Christmas present to three of his nephews, a huge board portraying the battlefield of Waterloo in minute detail, and toy soldiers representing all the different varieties of troops on duty that June day.

William, Powerscourt's eldest nephew, was eight years old and in command of two younger soldiers, Patrick and Alexander. Patrick was the drummer boy, equipped with a replica of the equipment used to drive the French infantry to success and glory across the battlefields of Europe. Alexander was the bugler, trained to give the different orders to the men of Wellington's command.

'After the artillery bombardment,' Powerscourt puffed bravely on at his cigar, enveloping the battlefield with smoke, 'the next thing is the attack on the farm at Hougoumont. Four regiments of veterans,' he pointed to a small cluster of models, 'began to advance towards the farm. Beat the drum.'

As William moved his troops forward through the smoke Patrick beat out the *pas de charge*: boom boom, boom boom, boom a boom, boom a boom, boom boom.

'Splendid,' said Powerscourt. 'Now, Alexander,' he brought in the youngest, 'you are standing beside the Duke of Wellington, here, on his horse Copenhagen. Your job is to sound the bugle call that sends out his orders. Look! He has seen the French advancing towards the chateau. Reinforcements are needed. Now! Blow!'

It could not be said that Alexander was master of the full repertoire of bugle calls from the reveille to the retreat. But he did make a great deal of noise.

'*Alors,*' cried Powerscourt, 'some of the French did manage to get inside the building. And I'll show you what happened then. Pretend that this door is the main entrance to Hougoumont. You three go outside, with your drums and bugles, and push as hard as you can to try to get in. You're going to be French just for once, and I'm going to be Colonel Macdonnell who closed the gate.'

The three boys pushed as hard as they could. 'Make more noise! Shout in French!' Powerscourt was getting carried away. Cries of '*Allez! Allez! Vive la France! Vive l'Empereur!*' – Powerscourt himself had taught them that one – sounded out across the upper levels of the house and floated down to the drawing-room two floors below. With a mighty heave Powerscourt at last closed the door. Three small boys fell backwards on the floor in a tumbling melange of arms and legs.

'Powerscourt! Powerscourt!' shouted Rosebery. He burst into the room, taking in the battlefield at a glance. 'I think you'll find that you have put the British cavalry a bit too far to the left,' he said absent-mindedly, surveying the order of battle. 'But come, Powerscourt, come, we must go at once! Reasons on the way!'

Rosebery led a swift charge down three flights of stairs, pausing only to give apologies to Powerscourt's sister at the bottom. 'A thousand pardons for this invasion, Lady Rosalind! We shall return to fight another day!'

With that Rosebery bounded down the flight of steps, pulling a bemused Powerscourt behind him into the night, and hurried his friend into a waiting brougham.

'Liverpool Street! As quick as you can. I have a train waiting!'

'A train?' said Powerscourt feebly, wondering if this was all another dream.

'Yes, yes, yes. If you want to get anywhere in a hurry in this country you have to order yourself a special train. I've done it before.'

Even at this moment of crisis Powerscourt found time to reflect on his friend. Most people in a hurry would consult timetables, seek out alternative routes, fret over possible delays on the line. Rosebery simply hired a train, and the best that money could buy, thought Powerscourt, as the engine pulled them slowly out of the station, real smoke billowing out over London's suburbs.

'Where are we going? What is the rush?'

'Rush? Rush? Wild horses couldn't get us there fast enough. We are going, my dear Powerscourt, to Sandringham. Something terrible has happened. Some disaster we don't yet know about.'

He thrust a cable into his friend's hand.: 'Come immediately. Most urgent. Bring Powerscourt. Brook no delay. Suter.'

'Death closes all,' Powerscourt muttered to himself, 'but something ere the end, some work of noble note, may yet be done, not unbecoming men that strove with Gods ... sorry, I have been reading Tennyson again last thing at night.'

'What makes you think of death, Francis?'

'Think of it, my friend,' Powerscourt went on, who had thought of little else since they fled the battlefield of Waterloo. 'If there was some natural act, like a fire or the roof falling in, they would send for the fire brigade or the builders. If it were the death of an aged uncle or aunt, the family would not be summoning you in the middle of a January night. They would not be sending for me. They would be sending for the tribes of relations and a couple of parsons. Bishops, more likely. Maybe Archbishops.'

'Are you possessed of second sight as well as a photographic memory, Francis?' Rosebery was peering closely at his friend as if another telegram was about to appear, etched across his forehead.

'Certainly not,' Powerscourt laughed. 'But it seems to me the most likely explanation is that there has been some dirty work afoot in Norfolk. Death not by natural causes is usually called murder. But we must wait for some hard intelligence before our speculations run away with us.'

The two men sat silently, lost in their thoughts. Rosebery was wondering about the political implications of a royal death. Powerscourt looked troubled.

'I am sure that it is impossible to underestimate the effect a strange death could have on the Royal Family,' he said, watching Rosebery's cigar smoke drift down the carriage. 'I have been thinking about this a lot lately,' he went on, looking out at the occasional ringlets of light that gleamed faintly against the East Anglian sky. 'Somewhere at the back of all the royal minds there must be a fear, maybe not a fear, an anxiety, a tremor in their dreams. On the surface, of course, all is serene, the palaces, the pomp, the pageantry. But underneath?'

'Think of it,' he continued, in what for him was a most animated fashion, 'like a painting by Claude. There's a huge mythological landscape, elegant classical buildings, assorted Greeks and Romans like Dido and Cleopatra up to no good. You know the sort of thing.'

Powerscourt drew a large frame in the condensation of the window between them. 'All the normal Claude tricks are here, the fantastic buildings, the intense sunlight, the faint sense of being in another world. I expect you've got a Claude or two, Rosebery, lying about the place?'

'I've got three, actually,' admitted Rosebery, 'maybe four. I can't remember. But what's going on in this one here?' He pointed to the Old Master taking dim shape on the railway carriage window.

'Here,' said Powerscourt, drawing an ill-defined blob at the bottom of the frame, 'is the fantastic palace, the grand pillars, the colonnades, the battlements, flags waving in the sunshine. And here, on an elaborate and bejewelled royal throne, we find the little Queen, resplendent not in a bonnet as so often, but in a proper crown. Around her are disported the usual crew, the courtiers, the secretaries, the equerries, the waiting servants – a mass of uniforms and all the decorations in the kingdom. I think Claude would have fun with that.

'But here, behind them, in the park,' Powerscourt's finger added a series of semicircular blobs to the window of the Great Eastern, 'we have a series of statues. Some of them lurk invisible at the end of a terrace until you turn the corner, some of them are in semicircles, standing rigidly to attention waiting for time's last roll call. Right at the back we find some of Royalty's distant predecessors, Henry VII, Richard II, two small princes in the Tower, a reminder to their successors in the big house down here at the bottom of the picture, that their ancestors waded through rivers of blood to sit upon a throne. And threw a previous monarch out to get there.

'At the back of the semicircle, here, Charles I on execution day. Kings of England can lose their heads, even on a balcony above Whitehall. Then, slightly closer to the house we find Robespierre, the man who struck Terror not just into the hearts of the French, but into the hearts of every crowned head in Europe. In his left hand he holds a model guillotine and at his feet, a tumbril, with the powdered heads of the aristocrats already overflowing. Do you not like the tumbril, Rosebery?'

'No tricoteuses, Powerscourt?' said Rosebery with a smile. 'No room for Madame Defarge and the knitting needles of death?'

'No room on the plinth,' said Powerscourt, turning back to the window. 'The picture is nearing completion. At one edge of the semicircle, nearest the house, we place the Queen's relation and colleague in Royalty, His Most Serene Majesty Alexander II, Czar of all the Russias, blown to pieces by a terrorist bomb twelve years ago and with a face so disfigured that his relatives fainted when they went to kiss him a last goodbye in his coffin.

'On the other side we have Lord Frederick Cavendish, Her

Majesty's appointed representative, Viceroy of Ireland, stabbed to death by Fenian assassins in Dublin's Phoenix Park in 1882, just ten years ago.

'And last of all, right here,' Powerscourt added another artistic blob, 'we have a bearded agitator, pamphlet in hand, fist raised in defiance, cap on head, speaking of troubles yet to come. At the far left-hand corner of the picture' – Powerscourt's hand almost reached the emergency cord – 'a small black cloud threatens the blue serenity of Claude's landscape, a thunderstorm perhaps, a stroke of lightning.'

6

They found the Duke of Clarence and Avondale shortly before seven o'clock in the morning. The front of his night-shirt was saturated with blood.

Blood red.

There was so much blood that Shepstone, veteran of many a battlefield, described the room later as smelling like a cross between a butcher's shop and an abattoir.

Eddy's bedroom was on the first floor of Sandringham House, looking out over the gravelled sweep of the main entrance. It was not completely flat, but sloped gently downwards to the window. Below the sash was a small lake, whose surface glistened eerily in the candlelight.

Blood scarlet.

Tributaries flowed from the end of the single bed across the floor towards the lake, matting the carpet and, where the floor was bare, seeping through the floorboards.

Blood river.

On the dressing-table was a copy of the Bible and Eddy's diary, open on the day of his death. Hanging on the back of the door was his full dress scarlet uniform, last worn on his birthday just a few days before. Both of his wrists had been viciously slashed. From them both trickled a small but regular flow, running down into the mattress.

Blood crimson.

The main arteries in the legs had been severed too, adding to the blood river traffic towards the lake by the window. And his head was barely attached to his body. The murderer had slit his throat from ear to ear, leaving it lolling dangerously off the pillow. At the age of twenty-eight, Albert Victor Christian Edward, Duke of Clarence and Avondale, second in line of succession to Victoria's throne, had breathed his last. Clarence was a corpse.

Blue blood.

Blood royal.

The Prince of Wales was in torment. On him, and on him alone, rested the responsibility of what to do about the murder of his son. What would happen if this death and the manner in which it occurred were made public?

There was only word that came into his mind, and it came in letters as high as the rooftops of Sandringham itself.

Scandal.

Scandal as the newspapers began to speculate about the murder of a Royal Prince asleep in his own house, in his own bed, surrounded by members of his own family. Scandal about his own private life that had threatened to erupt before Christmas with revelations about his affair with Daisy Brooke.

Scandal about his dead son.

Waves of anger at the death of Prince Eddy were sweeping through the Prince of Wales. For ten or fifteen minutes he would feel overwhelmed, drowned in anger. Then it would subside, only to reappear at a time of its own choosing.

The Prince of Wales was always restless. He marched out of his study and down to the billiard room on the far side of the house where he knew he would not be disturbed. Somebody had left the balls on the table. It was an easy shot. The Prince of Wales picked up a cue. He bent over the table, his stomach pressing against the side. He missed.

He tried another cannon on his billiard balls. Surely, he thought to himself, the red and the white will not dare to disobey their master's will. They did. He missed again.

Scandal lay around his family like the covering of some very expensive diamond from one of those great jewellery houses in the fashionable Faubourgs of Paris. Heaven and his bankers knew, the Prince of Wales had bought enough favours with their products over the years. The gems came in boxes, wrapped in layer upon layer of the most exquisite tissue paper. As you peeled off each rustling layer, you felt sure that here, at last, was the treasure, only to be cheated of your prey.

Eddy lay at the bottom of the box. Or the bottom of the coffin. Edward remembered his conversation with Alexandra about Eddy's future, some months before, with another wave of scandal threatening to break.

'Send him away! Send him away, for Christ's sake! Europe, the colonies, I don't care. Anywhere, as long as he's out of this country for at least two years!'

And Alix, pleading softly, 'Oh no you don't. Not this time. You did that years ago, and it nearly broke my heart. This time Eddy is staying here.'

Against his better judgement, he had given way. Eddy had stayed here. Now look where it had got them. Of all the scandals, the ones surrounding Prince Eddy were the most serious.

Prince Edward knew a lot of it, he thought he knew most of it, but even he did not know if there were other layers, waiting to be unpeeled in the unforgiving light of publicity and a nation's fury. Layer upon layer of the tissue papers of scandal.

The billiard balls lay in their pools of light, the dark green baize a pitch waiting for another match. Death stopped play.

The Prince of Wales made up his mind. He summoned Sir William Suter and Sir Bartle Shepstone to a meeting in the drawing-room at the back of the house.

Another wave of anger was upon him, flooding through him like a typhoon of fury.

'Private Secretary,' he said. 'Treasurer and Comptroller of my Household. I do not need to tell you gentlemen the reasons why I feel this matter should be concealed. Not the death, of course, but the murder. The scandal would be intolerable. I feel that no word of it should leak out to the outside world. But I do not know if it can be done.'

Private Secretary Suter had attended some very strange meetings on some very strange subjects with his master. He was not particularly surprised at this one. He looked at the Prince as if this was some normal question of routine, a visit of inspection to the fire brigade in Birmingham, the laying of another foundation stone in Shoreditch.

'Get Rosebery here as fast as you can. And that investigator friend of his, Powerswood or Powersfield or whatever he's called.'

'Lord Rosebery and Lord Francis Powerscourt are on their way, Your Royal Highness.'

'And when they come, gentlemen . . .' The Prince of Wales stood up. He looked old suddenly, his hair in disarray, his eyes hurting with the force of his anger. 'I think we want two things.' Shepstone, ever the faithful courtier in a crisis, began taking notes in a small blue book. 'We want to know if the thing can be concealed, covered up. And then, we want – Powerscourt? Is that what you said his name was, Suter? – we want him to find who killed my son.

'When he does, Shepstone, you will know what to do. We may not be able to summon the laws and the courts of England to our aid, but there are older laws than those. Vengeance is mine, saith the Lord. I will repay. Even unto the third and fourth generation of them that mock me. All of those involved in this murder must pay for their knowledge. With their blood. Not my son's.'

The Prince of Wales strode from the room. In the corner, beside the bookcase, the grandfather clock struck five. Less than twenty-four hours had passed since the discovery of the body.

Sir William Suter stared vacantly at the grandfather clock.

Sir Bartle Shepstone stared at the fire. Then he wrote some more in his little blue book. He filled three pages with his recollections of the words of his master. He thought he preferred the New Testament God of love and forgiveness to the Old Testament trumpet call of Vengeance is Mine. But he knew where his duty lay.

'Rosebery! Powerscourt! Thank God you have come.' Sir William Suter and Sir Bartle Shepstone were unanimous in their welcomes. Powerscourt noted with interest that neither was wearing mourning clothes.

'Tell us the facts, man. Tell us the facts.' Rosebery was leaning on the mantelpiece in the drawing-room at the back of Sandringham House looking out over a plain of white snow and an icy lake.

'Well, I will try,' said Suter, grimacing with distaste at the prospect of reliving the past twenty-four hours. 'The body of the Duke of Clarence was discovered at shortly before seven o'clock this morning. Lord Henry Lancaster, one of the equerries or gentlemen in waiting to the Duke, went in to inquire after his health – he had been suffering from a heavy cold – and to see if he wanted breakfast brought up to him. Thank God it was Lancaster, and not one of the parlourmaids gone in to clean the room.'

'How was the body lying?' Powerscourt asked the question quietly.

Suter looked at him carefully. Perhaps this was the world Powerscourt moved in, a world where murderers stalk the corridors by night and corpses are found in the morning. A world where the smell of blood lingers on in the nostrils long after you have left the room. 'He was lying on his back. His throat had been cut. So had his wrists and the great blood vessels in his legs. The blood was lying all over the floor.'

'My God!' exclaimed Rosebery. 'And this is England, not the Rome of Nero or the Borgias. How terrible.'

'Quite so. Quite so.' Suter acknowledged the outburst as one might tolerate a tantrum from a small child. But his face was as impassive as ever, a mask that concealed the workings of his mind. 'Lancaster thought quickly. He summoned one of the other equerries, Harry Radclyffe, and put him on permanent guard outside the door, with instructions to say that the Duke was asleep and was on no account to be disturbed. I informed the Prince of Wales who told his wife and the rest of the family.

'Dr Broadbent examined the cadaver and gave it as his opinion that the murder had taken place between eleven o'clock the previous evening when Lancaster bade him goodnight and saw him off to sleep and five o'clock in the morning. Broadbent has, naturally enough, been sworn to secrecy. The Prince wanted to have you gentlemen here before we decide how to proceed.

'Less than a dozen people know what has transpired here. The Prince is firmly of the opinion that the murder must be covered up, that we invent some story to conceal the truth. That, rather than the particular circumstances of a person's death,' he said, staring balefully at Powerscourt, 'is our immediate concern.'

'Good God, man, this is England! This is Victoria's grandson! This was Victoria's grandson.' Rosebery corrected himself. 'How can you think of covering it up? Think of Parliament! Think of the laws of England! Think of the ancient constitution!'

'I am not aware,' said Suter coldly, 'that any of your colleagues or predecessors have actually bothered to write it down. The ancient constitution, I mean. That gives us some flexibility.'

'Come, Rosebery.' Sir Bartle Shepstone had spent most of the discussion gazing sadly out of the window, as if time might suddenly decide to run backwards. 'You have always been an adviser to the Royal Family on the constitution. Is there anything that says we couldn't conceal it, cover it up, if such be the parents' wishes?'

Rosebery looked long at a portrait of the Princess of Wales by the bookshelves. There seemed to be three or four Alexandras in the room, radiant as a bride, happy as a mother surrounded by three of her children, regal as the Princess of Wales in formal attire and a dazzling tiara.

'There is nothing in the constitution,' he said finally in the manner of one who has been taken to a lunatic asylum and has to address the inmates, 'that says you could not cover it up. There are the laws of the country, conspiracy to pervert the course of justice to name but one. I would find it easier to answer the question if I knew the reason for it, if I could sense what prompts this perversion of justice.'

'Nobody is trying to pervert the course of justice, Rosebery. That is why Powerscourt is here. We want him to find the murderer.'

Powerscourt said nothing. Inside, he felt sick. If the murder was covered up, he could ask no questions, he could make no inquiries, he could not conduct his business. It would be like playing cricket not just blind but with only one hand.

'The reasons, I think, are simple.' Suter was counting them off on his fingertips as the last light ebbed away from the white world outside. 'It is a choice between two evils. Of course, if it is covered up, that is a terrible thing. But think of the alternative. We have the police tramping all over Sandringham and Marlborough House. Think of it, Rosebery. Inspector Smith who has spent his life investigating the criminal gangs of the East End of London comes to interrogate the Prince of Wales. Superintendent Peters polishes his best black boots and proceeds to talk to the Queen Empress at Windsor Castle. They do not know the world in which we live.' As Suter thought of these outrages the colour drained slowly from his face.

'Then there are the opposition politicians, radicals and suchlike. Every jumped-up backbencher will be on his feet in the House of Commons trying to ask the question nobody has asked before. The one designed to cause maximum embarrassment to the Royal Family. The newspapers will go mad. Initially of course we'll have the black mastheads and the loyal and pious editorials. Grave loss to the nation and the Empire. You could write those now, Rosebery, I expect. But give them a week and they will be all over the Royal Family like vultures. Vultures over a corpse. They will start to rake up every single of scrap of gossip that has circulated in the drawing-rooms of London for the past three years. That could prove embarrassing and difficult for all concerned. Think of the foreign newspapers and what they will make of it. Think of the rejoicing in Paris and Berlin as a murder and a series of scandals in Britain's Royal House are all over their front pages. Mourning dress won't be worn for very long.'

And then Rosebery could see it all.

The need for secrecy, the need for silence.

Fear was the key. Fear of some unspoken scandal that had not yet been brought out into the light of day. Fear that if the stones were lifted, something so terrible would crawl out that it could endanger the whole position of the Royal Family. Fear so strong that it left the risky and hazardous course of covering up the murder as the better of two options.

Powerscourt tried to find the thread that linked his earlier investigation, the investigation that never was, with these terrible events at Sandringham. Somebody blackmailing the Prince of Wales, fears for the life of Prince Eddy. They must have thought it had all gone away, he reflected, looking at Suter and

Shepstone and remembering the final letter from Marlborough House, written on the last day of the old year, that seemed to close the account. What had it said? 'I am happy to be able to report,' Suter had written in his best Private Secretary prose, 'that the circumstances that led us to consider the possibility of availing ourselves of your expertise have changed for the better.' This cold January evening, thought Powerscourt, they have certainly changed for the worse.

'Gentlemen. Gentlemen.' Suter was calling the meeting to order. 'We are due to meet the Prince of Wales in one hour's time. Rosebery, I would be grateful if you could marshal your arguments against what I have suggested. The Prince wishes to avail himself of the best possible advice before he reaches his final decision. I must go to him now. Sir Bartle here will answer some of your more specific questions.'

Suter walked slowly from the room. As he closed the door faint sounds of women weeping could be heard from the floors above.

'Was there any sign of a murder weapon? Was the window open or closed?' Powerscourt felt suddenly like an intruder as he began his inquiries.

'No murder weapon was found,' Sir Bartle Shepstone replied. 'I do not know about the window – but obviously members of the family have been tramping in and out of the room all day. You can see it tomorrow, and Lancaster will talk to you, of course.

'I have ordered reinforcements of a sort,' Shepstone went on. 'A detachment of two dozen Guardsmen, commanded by a Major Dawnay, including a doctor and a trained undertaker, should be with us soon. They are part of a special section of the Household Division and are sworn to secrecy in the event of unusual missions like this.'

'I never knew of such a special detachment,' said Rosebery, with the air of a man who found it difficult to believe that such things could exist without his knowledge or approval.

'Oh, they are very very secret, my dear Rosebery. When you are Prime Minister you will know all about them, and the special units of the Metropolitan Police Force. But they will be able to help us with the body.'

Powerscourt suddenly remembered that Shepstone had won the Victoria Cross for outstanding bravery in the Indian Mutiny. He made a mental note to tell his nephews that he had talked with an old man with a white beard who had a VC; the Indian Mutiny, he suspected, would seem as remote to those little boys as the Spanish Armada.

'How many people are in the house just now?' Powerscourt returned to Sandringham.

'Well, the family are here. And the Tecks, of course – Princess May was engaged to be married to Prince Eddy, as you know. About half a dozen young men, friends or equerries of Prince Eddy.'

'And how many servants are there about the place?'

Sir Bartle shook his head rather sadly. 'Do you know, I have no idea about that. Some of them live in, of course, and some of them come from the neighbouring villages. Seventy? Eighty? I've never thought about it.'

'Any reports of strangers in the vicinity?' Powerscourt felt he wasn't making much progress so far. He didn't suppose it would get any better.

'Odd that you should mention that, Lord Powerscourt.' Shepstone was looking very tired suddenly. 'There have been reports of a party of Russians and some Irishmen in the neighbourhood. The Prince of Wales is convinced one of them must be responsible.'

'Let me ask the key question for our next round of discussions.' For much of the conversation Rosebery had been marshalling his arguments for the Prince of Wales, lost in thought on the settee. 'How many people know what has happened? How many people know the truth?'

'I should think it cannot be more than a dozen, maybe fifteen at most. But all of them are either members of the family, or members of distinguished families who can be relied upon to do their duty.'

Powerscourt raised his eyebrows at the assumed link between birth and virtue. If all those of good birth and position had done their duty according to the honour of their class and the dictates of their Commandments, he reflected bitterly, we probably would not have a bloodied corpse on our hands, stiffening into rigor mortis in an upstairs bedroom.

The Prince of Wales seemed quite small that evening. He looked as though some powerful machine had emptied most of the air from his body. His eyes were red from weeping, his face pale and drawn. And though he was wearing one of his darker uniforms, he looked as though he no longer cared for the medals and decorations that hung loosely from his tunic, as if they too were in mourning.

'My friends,' he began, 'thank you for coming to see us in this time of trouble. Thank you, Rosebery, thank you, Powerscourt. We shall never forget your assistance.

'Rosebery, I do not think I shall make a final decision until the morning. But I want you to try to persuade me that we should tell the truth. My own inclination, as I believe Suter told you, is to conceal it.'

If you have led the life of Prince Edward for the past thirty years, the love affairs, the gambling, the discreet trips *en garçon* to the pleasure palaces of Europe, thought Powerscourt, concealment must have become a way of life. There are only so many evenings you could pretend to be playing billiards at the Marlborough Club.

Rosebery began with expressions of concern and sympathy for the family at the time of this terrible tragedy. He spoke of his long acquaintance with Alexandra and Edward, his frequent trips to Sandringham and Marlborough House, the weekends at his own houses, Mentmore or Dalmeny. He referred to his long intimacy with Queen Victoria and his friendship with the members of her Household. 'I have often said, Your Royal Highness,' he bowed slightly to the Prince of Wales, 'that I have only met two people in my entire life who frightened me. One was that old bully Bismarck. The other is rather a smaller figure, your mother, the Queen.'

The Prince of Wales smiled a wan smile, Shepstone managed the ghost of a laugh. Powerscourt had never heard Rosebery speak in the House of Lords. He had heard him once on a platform with Gladstone in London where his elegant eloquence made the Grand Old Man sound long-winded and lugubrious. He had never heard him as forceful as he was this evening.

'Of course I understand the reservations you might have about bringing this sorry affair into the cold light of day. Of course I can see that concealment has its attractions, and that the opiate of secrecy is a powerful and addictive potion. Of course I can sense your fears of what might lie on the other side of those locked doors, of what dark phantoms might emerge to trouble yourself and your family.

'But, Your Royal Highness,' Rosebery was speaking very quietly, looking now at the Prince of Wales, now at the silent figure of Suter by the fireside, 'I think there are other higher considerations, other flags to which we should pay allegiance. I would ask you to think about truth. Truth first of all in relation to my own profession of politics. Of course it can be a filthy business, despoiled by bribery and corruption, debased by fraudulent appeals to the electorate and the sordid traffic of faction. But some six hundred members of the House of Commons and a thousand members of my own chamber the Lords swear a solemn oath of loyalty to the Queen. It is a matter of high seriousness when you do it. Think of their feelings and their reactions when they learn that their own Prince of Wales has concealed things from them, that he has lied about such an important matter as the death of one who is second in line to the throne. There is no uglier sight in politics than the House of Commons when it knows it has been deceived. They will count up the sums of money voted each year to maintain the standard of living of the Royal Family, and their instinct will be to take revenge in whatever fashion they can find.

'Think of the truth and the Church of England. It is not the force it once was, weakened by Darwin and by defections to Rome, but it remains the national Church of this country. People died at the stake to bring it into existence. Its bishops are appointed in the name of the Queen, who is Head of that Church, as you will be one day. Can you stand there at your Coronation, surrounded by the Princes of the Church as well of the State, and say that you will keep God's holy laws and uphold his Commandments?'

There was no noise in the room save for the soft cadences of Rosebery's voice. Outside snow was falling steadily, wrapping those inside with further layers of white.

'Think too about something more intangible but more valuable even than truth. Think of the relationship between the Royal Family and the ordinary citizens of this country. For some of them, who have attended our great public schools or served in the military, loyalty and patriotism are centred on the person or persons of the Queen and her family. You can be loyal to a flag or to a regimental colour or to your house at Eton, but the supreme loyalty which inspires people to die for this country is channelled through the Queen and the Princes of the Blood. The middle classes absorb this as they are brought up; go into the homes of the ordinary people of this country, working hard to better their lot and that of their families who will come after them, and you will see that loyalty burning bright by fireside and hearth. On the walls there are portraits of the Queen or pictures from the distant parts of her Empire. These people are the ones who turn out to wave the penny rattles when a Royal passes by, or will queue for hours to line the Jubilee parades. They trust you – will you betray that trust? Break that trust and you break the link that unites the people with their sovereign. Break it – and get found out – and all the King's horses and all the King's men will not put that trust together again.

'If you do not take the side of truth in this matter, think of the other trusts and the other duties you are betraying. Think of the duty of honesty, the requirement to tell the truth, however unpalatable it may be. The fabric of the country, its moral centre, its legal system, is held together by the assumption that people will tell the truth. If you do not, why should your subjects? In the name of honesty, in the name of your responsibilities to the Parliament and Church of this land, your land, our land, I appeal to you to do what you must know to be the right thing to do. Tell the truth. Face the consequences. Honour your obligations to your country.'

Even as he finished, Rosebery knew that it wouldn't work. He had the sense as he spoke that he was swimming against the tide.

'My dear Rosebery,' said the Prince of Wales. 'I am so grateful to you. I always suspected that your eloquence would make you Prime Minister one day. Now I am sure of it. But on this occasion, just for once, I am going to follow a maxim of my father's.'

Powerscourt groaned inwardly at the thought of some heavy German apothegm from Prince Albert.

'He always said you should sleep on things before taking a decision. That is what I propose to do. But could I ask you gentlemen, particularly you, Lord Powerscourt, to give thought to how the matter could be concealed, were that the decision. And could I ask you to put your thoughts down on paper for me – rest assured that it won't fall into the wrong hands.'

'No more than one side of a sheet of paper,' Suter advised as the Prince went off to his own quarters. 'Otherwise there may be a scene. Shall we say nine o'clock in the morning, gentlemen? Thank you so much for your assistance.'

With that Suter and Shepstone glided off into the night, leaving Rosebery and Powerscourt in possession of the drawing-room.

'Nine o'clock,' said Rosebery ruefully. 'I shouldn't think he's been up at nine in the morning since he was nine years old. What do you think the old hypocrite is going to decide, Francis?'

'I have absolutely no doubt,' said Powerscourt, 'that he is going to want to cover it up. What do you say to Death by Influenza?'

7

Few people slept well at Sandringham that night. Outside further falls of snow drifted down, covering the great slate roofs and the gravel driveway and lying in weird patterns on the tall trees.

The Rosebery Powerscourt Memorandum, written in Rosebery's best copperplate, was waiting in the little drawing-room of Sandringham House for the nine o'clock meeting.

Subject: The Days Ahead.
1. If the murder is to be covered up, there has to be another cause of death. Death by Influenza is the best solution. Prince Eddy was already suffering from a cold. There have been a number of tragic deaths from this disease in recent weeks. Another would not be surprising.
2. For Death by Influenza to work as a cover story, the Prince must, as it were, be kept alive for a couple more days. This afternoon or tomorrow a notice should be pinned to the Norwich Gates here and outside Marlborough House reporting that there is grave cause for concern and that additional medical staff have been sent for from London. This will appear in the newspapers the following day.
3. Tomorrow two further bulletins should be posted. Each one should be more sombre than the last. They will appear in the papers on Tuesday.
4. On the appropriate day, a last bulletin should be posted in the usual places, reporting that the Prince has passed

away. If that happens early in the morning, say eleven o'clock, it will give the papers ample time to prepare special editions.

5. Sir George Trevelyan, Private Secretary to HM The Queen, is an expert at dealing with all the newspapers. He is particularly close to the editor of *The Times*. He should be let into the secret of the illness and entrusted with the task of liaison with the Press.

6. Returning to today, it is essential that the military gentlemen have access to the body and that the room be cleaned up. A Service of Prayer for the sick Prince should be held in the church this afternoon. Attendance should be recommended if not compulsory for all the domestic staff. While that is in progress, the body could be seen to. A brief inspection could be made of the roof to see if there has been any unexpected traffic up there.

7. Only two other people should be told the true nature of Prince Eddy's death. One is the Prime Minister, whose authority may need to be invoked to expedite future inquiries. The other is the Commissioner of the Metropolitan Police, who has files on all known Irish subversives, and may be able to assist with possible foreign suspects.

The Prince of Wales read slowly, pausing occasionally to polish his glasses. Suter and Shepstone were busy making notes on the pads in front of them.

'I think this is an excellent plan,' said the Prince of Wales, rising from his seat to gaze out of the tall windows at the white wilderness beyond. 'Now I must make up my mind. I did not feel I could do so until I saw what the alternative plan might be. Suter, Shepstone, do you think it could work?'

The faithful courtiers gave it as their opinion that if everything was properly managed, and if there were no unforeseen circumstances like a leak of the truth along the way, then indeed it could be successfully implemented.

'Never say yes and never say no,' Powerscourt said to himself, remembering Rosebery's words from the past. 'Your backs are well covered, gentlemen. Nobody will be able to blame either of you if things go wrong. No doubt you've written your reservations down on those little bits of paper, just to be on the safe side. If the plan fails, all the blame is going to attach to Rosebery and me.'

All his life Rosebery had been fascinated by the way people made their decisions. He had watched politicians take great decisions in haste or on a whim, or because they couldn't think of anything else to do, or because they felt they had to be seen to do something, in one case because the minister was going to be late for the opera. As he watched the Prince of Wales, standing by his Norfolk window, he knew that this was the most bizarre decision he would watch in his life.

'All right. All right,' said the Prince of Wales. 'I want my son's murder to be concealed. That is my final decision. Will you gentlemen see to the details?'

Sir William Suter was the first to break the silence that dropped on the room after the Prince of Wales' departure.

'Gentlemen,' he announced with the satisfied air of one who is back in control of the meeting, 'we are most grateful to you both. Let me try to divide up the tasks that yet remain if this plan is to succeed. We have a few days left in which to maintain the necessary deception. After that we must bolt the lie into the history books.'

That, thought Powerscourt, realising that he might have underestimated Suter, was rather good. Cheating history. Deceiving the future.

'Lord Rosebery, could the Royal Family impose on your kindness and your generosity one more time? Your suggestion about Trevelyan is excellent. Could we ask you to make all speed to London and communicate with him in person? I dare not trust these tidings to a letter, nor yet to the telegraph machine. It is vital that he knows what we know as soon as possible. The Prince of Wales' train is at Wolferton station now, waiting for whatever passengers it may have to bear. If you were to set out at once we could have Trevelyan on board by early afternoon.'

'Hold on a moment.' Rosebery spoke very softly. His head

was in his hands and he sounded as though he was speaking from somewhere very far away. 'Hold on a moment, gentlemen, I beg you.'

Suter, Shepstone, and Powerscourt stared intently at Rosebery, his delicate features contorted by some inner strain. He looked up.

'Of course I should go and talk to Trevelyan in London or Osborne or wherever he is to be found at present. But consider, pray. We are about to embark on one of the great deceptions in the history of the monarchy in this nation. I do not doubt the sincerity of those who wished it thus, or the power of the reasons for that choice. But we must have a plan. If we are to cheat history, as you, Sir William, implied earlier, we must make sure that the cards, as it were, are properly sharpened, the form book doctored, the dice weighted in our favour.

'We have one enormous advantage. Nobody would ever suspect that such a deception was being practised. History is always written by the conquerors. They get their version in first. The vanquished may rot in some prison cell or die upon the battlefield. They never tell their story, and if they do, it is usually too late.

'But, gentlemen, we must prepare our ground. First we must fix the date of death. Then I suggest we work backwards from that date to this Sunday morning, deciding in advance what information we give out. It is as if we were writing a play backwards. We know the last act, the death of the Prince, just as Shakespeare must have known that *Hamlet* had to end with the death of his Prince. Hamlet was Danish too – appropriate for this household. But we have to write Acts One to Five of this drama, if the thing is to work.'

'Are you suggesting, Rosebery,' Suter sounded like a man going into uncharted waters, 'that we should write everything down as if it were a play?'

'I am not sure yet. I think we need to think about it calmly. Can anyone think of the single most important fact that we do not possess? But a fact vital to our success?'

'Oddly enough, I can. I thought about it this morning, Rosebery.' Powerscourt was staring at the snow-covered lake outside.

'And what do you think it is, Francis?'

'Quite simply, it is this.' Powerscourt glanced around the room, Suter looking disturbed by the fire, Sir Bartle looking vacant as if hoping the murder and the cover-up would melt away, Rosebery pacing up and down the room like a cat. 'We know it is possible that Prince Eddy could die from influenza. People are dying from it all the time. But we can't just tell the world he's died from it, just like that. There has to be a history, announcements of the illness in the papers and so on. But we don't know how long it might take. It could take two days. It could take ten, or twenty. Until we know how long that is, we cannot fix the date for the end of Rosebery's Act Five. And, don't you see, until we know the date of the end of Act Five, we don't know what to put in the four acts in between. Until we know that, we are, quite simply, in the dark.'

'Are there any doctors in this house?' Rosebery was obviously anxious to push things forward. 'Doctors who know, I mean?'

'Dr Broadbent is still here. Dr Manby cannot be very far away. I could summon him now.' Suter looked reassured at the prospect of action in the world of Private Secretaries rather than playwrights.

'I suggest you summon them both at once. Perhaps we could reassemble here in one hour's time.'

Rosebery left the room, beckoning Powerscourt to accompany him. They went out of the front of the house in the unforgiving cold, snow dribbling occasionally on to their thick coats. Soldiers were everywhere, patrolling discreetly out of sight, making circuits of the lakes and shrubberies. Where did Shepstone's Major Dawnay get them all from, Powerscourt wondered? He started with fourteen. Now he must have at least fifty. If it went on like this, Dawnay would have a whole regiment by the end of the week.

The two doctors were a study in contrasts. Manby, tall, slim, looked to be in his early thirties. He had the air of the countryman about him, in his healthy cheeks and his casual tweeds. Broadbent was a creature of the town or the city, portly, his hair receding, his suit the most respectable black, his bag large and formidable.

A circular table and six dining-room chairs had been appropriated from another room and sat by the corner, waiting for meetings.

'Dr Manby, Dr Broadbent.' Suter was at his most unctuous. 'Thank you for interrupting your business to give us of your wisdom. You both know the circumstances in which we are placed, and the solution that has been advocated to our difficulties. We just need a little practical advice. Rosebery?'

Courtier to the last, thought Powerscourt. Pass the parcel, pass the body, pass the corpse. Let Rosebery ask what might be called the fatal question, and no blame could attach to Suter in the future.

'Gentlemen,' said Rosebery in his best House of Lords voice. 'Our question is a simple one. How long does it take for somebody to die of influenza? We are talking of a young male, some twenty-eight years old, to all intents and purposes in good health.'

'That is not as easy a question as it sounds.' Broadbent looked down at his bag, as if medical secrets or influenza victims were contained inside. 'It depends on so many other factors.'

We could be here all day at this rate, thought Powerscourt, as the man in the black suit tried to wriggle out of committing himself.

'One sees so many different varieties of symptoms, you understand. Age is only one factor, maybe not even the most important one. There have been cases where the illness has dragged on for three or four weeks and the patient has recovered, others where the disease has worked itself through much more rapidly.'

Powerscourt glanced at Rosebery to see his reaction to the delays. Would the former Foreign Secretary lose his temper?

A flicker of irritation shot across Rosebery's face. 'I think we are talking at cross purposes here. Both you gentlemen know what we are talking about. There are reasons I cannot divulge why the manner of Eddy's death has to be concealed. All I can say is that those reasons are to do with state security.'

Rosebery had just thought of state security. He paused to let its full impact sink in. It was, Powerscourt reflected, the perfect justification for the cover-up. It covered everything, like the snow outside.

'We intend to tell the world,' Rosebery continued, 'that Prince Eddy died from influenza, not from murder. We need to announce his illness. We need to invent medical bulletins for every day before his second death, if you follow me. We would like that process to be short, so that the normal routines of mourning can be properly observed. At present the situation is intolerable for members of the family. But we do not want it be so short that it looks implausible or improbable. Dr Manby, you are the local man here. What do you feel would be a reasonable period of time? For the thing to be plausible, I mean.'

'Of course, I share my colleague's reservations,' Manby began.

Good God, thought Powerscourt. Another one. More bloody qualifications. They'll start talking about the Hippocratic Oath soon. But he was wrong.

'The key factor, I think, is whether it is influenza alone or if there is some accompanying illness which might speed up the process. Pneumonia comes often with influenza – two of my patients have recently died, not from the influenza, but from its terrible twin disease. If the pneumonia came quickly, you would expect the patient to go through a period of fluctuating conditions, apparently recovering one day, very high temperatures and a relapse the next. In those circumstances, the patient might die after four or five days, though that might be too abrupt. Anything between six and nine days would fit the prevailing trends of such a condition in Norfolk at the present time.'

'Would that analysis meet with your approval, Dr Broadbent?' Rosebery was anxious to carry the meeting with him, before further medical complications set in.

'Of course, I do not know the particular circumstances in these rural areas.'

Here we go again, thought Powerscourt, casting a surreptitious glance at his watch.

'But in general, that is a very fair description of the progress, the possible progress of the disease.'

'Thank you, Dr Broadbent.' Rosebery interrupted him neatly at the end of the sentence. Powerscourt felt Broadbent had been good for another three or four minutes of intervening conditions and unfortunate side effects.

'Let me try to sum up our position with a concrete example.' Rosebery smiled a thin smile at the medical gentlemen. 'Let us say the Prince contracted the beginnings of influenza at the end of last week. We already know that he was suffering from a cold. On Friday, two days ago, he is taken seriously ill. Pneumonia symptoms appear quickly. The patient comes and goes in the manner described by Dr Manby over the weekend and through the first three days of next week. By Thursday, he could be dead.'

'I am afraid that that is all too plausible,' Dr Manby said. 'Wouldn't you agree, Broadbent?'

Surprisingly, Broadbent did. Even more surprising was what Rosebery did next.

'Suter, do you have some pens and paper in here?'

Sir William produced some from the drawers on the table.

'Gentlemen, I am going to give you some rather gruesome homework. And I am afraid it must be done now. It's the express wish of the Prince of Wales.'

Rosebery's making that up, thought Powerscourt. He's making it up to make sure they don't wriggle out of what he wants them to do.

Rosebery wrote rapidly on five separate sheets of paper. Sunday. Monday. Tuesday. Wednesday. Thursday.

'I would ask you to remember that what you write for the Prince's condition on Sunday will be the first news to appear in the papers. One bulletin should suffice. It will appear in the Monday editions, Monday's bulletins appearing on Tuesday and so on. For each day from Monday to Thursday, gentlemen, we require two medical bulletins. They will be signed in your names. They will be pinned up on the railings of Sandringham House and at Marlborough House.

'They can be brief, the bulletins, but they must be plausible. Just a couple of sentences at a time will do. Bring in the pneumonia as you feel appropriate. I think you might write a third bulletin for broadcast late on Wednesday. And I think you should also write one holding version which could be used if we find that we need another one in a hurry. No change in the patient's condition, that sort of thing.'

'Do you know when you want him to die, Lord Rosebery?' Manby was looking practical, pen poised over his Sunday hymn sheet.

'I do indeed, Dr Manby. I was just coming to that. Prince Eddy, Duke of Clarence and Avondale, is to die at 9 a.m. on Thursday morning, in time for the papers to prepare special editions for the Friday.

'Now, I suggest that we leave you to this distasteful task. These other gentlemen and I are going to prepare the background material that will be distributed to the newspapers at the same time as the bulletins.'

Rosebery was now in complete control of the situation. 'Successful generals,' he said to the two doctors as he prepared to lead the rest of his small army from the room, 'leave nothing to chance. Everything is planned. Everything is prepared. If we want our version to be believed, we are asking people to believe in one huge lie. They are much more likely to do so if we can support the big lie with a host of smaller ones.

'We are going,' he looked at Suter and Shepstone, 'to invent the host of smaller lies to buttress the bulletins, when he first felt ill, when the first doctor was called, any trips he might have made outdoors, shooting or that sort of thing, which could have brought on or aggravated his condition.'

'Lord Rosebery.' Broadbent sounded plaintive. 'Haven't you forgotten something?'

'I'm sure I have, my dear Broadbent. Please enlighten me. At times like this we need all the help we can get.'

'This is Sunday,' said Dr Broadbent. 'Do you mean to say that you intend to get the first bulletin into the papers tomorrow?'

'Indeed I do. That is why you gentlemen must make haste. The Prince of Wales' special train is waiting to take me at full speed to London. There I shall meet the Queen's Private Secretary. Together we have an appointment with the editor of *The Times* early this evening. 'That is when, for our purposes, the history of this affair will begin to be written. The Official History, I mean. For that other history, the secret history, the history of secrets, could I paraphrase from the Danish play, the rest must be silence.'

8

Suter had posted notices of the Service of Prayer for the Sick all round the house and grounds by 10.30 in the morning. It was to start at three o'clock.

The staff filed into the little church two by two. Butler, footmen, housekeepers, parlourmaids, nursery maids, grooms, gardeners, blacksmiths, carpenters, coachmen, all arrived to insult their separate gods by praying that one already dead might live.

Powerscourt thought that the prospects of a Resurrection in East Anglia were rather remote. He had planned to spend the time talking to Lancaster, but received a message from Shepstone that his presence was specially requested by the Princess of Wales.

'My soul he doth restore again,' the congregation sang, slowly at first, and then with more conviction as the tune took hold.

> 'And me to walk doth make
> Within the paths of righteousness,
> E'en for his own name's sake.'

The singing was quite loud now, floating out from the little church across the white landscape and the frozen lakes.

> 'Yea, though I walk in death's dark vale,
> Yet will I fear none ill:
> For thou art with me, and thy rod
> And staff me comfort still.'

On the upper floor of Sandringham House Shepstone's special forces moved with extraordinary speed. Prince Eddy's bed and all the bedclothes were rushed out of his room and buried in the woods. The carpet was removed, the floor scrubbed, and a new bed with clean sheets installed. Mats that were almost indistinguishable from the previous carpet were laid upon the floor. His bloody clothes were taken away and a new series of pictures of his family, borrowed from his mother's quarters, placed on the dressing-table. His old dress uniform which had been splattered with blood was replaced with a cleaner, freshly pressed model.

'O most merciful God, open thine eye of mercy upon this thy servant, Prince Eddy, who most earnestly desireth pardon and forgiveness. Renew in him, most loving Father, whatsoever hath been decayed by the fraud and malice of the devil, or by his own carnal will and frailness . . .'

Canon Hervey hurried over the words carnal will and frailness. He had been chosen as Rector of Sandringham for the quality of his voice, which appealed to Princess Alexandra, and the brevity of his sermons which appealed to her husband. His beautiful speaking voice filled the little church as the thin afternoon sun lit the stained glass windows of the Last Judgement.

The embalmers took Prince Eddy's body away to the top floor, to special attic rooms that were kept locked and whose key was in the sole possession of the Princess of Wales. These had been night nurseries years before, but were later turned into store rooms for her children's toys.

So here among a small armada of toy boats for sailing on the lake, among dolls and teddy bears that were gifts from the crowned heads of Europe, and toy soldiers from the armies of Prussia and France, the corpse was cleaned and the embalmer's art set to work to disguise the ravages of his murder. 'Somebody may want to see the body,' Sir Bartle had warned them, 'so you'd better make it bloody good.'

'Oh Lord, look down from heaven, behold, visit and relieve this thy servant Prince Eddy.' The congregation were very still, almost all of them on their knees, praying for a Prince who would be their master one day, if he lived. 'Look upon him with

74

the eyes of thy mercy, defend him from the danger of the enemy, and keep him in perpetual peace and safety, through Jesus Christ our Lord. Amen.'

It's too late, it's too too late, Powerscourt thought. The danger of the enemy had already struck with terrible force. Eddy might have found perpetual peace, but safety had eluded him.

Was the murderer in the church, Powerscourt wondered suddenly? He gazed desperately at the backs of the congregation, at the members of the Household and the equerries kneeling with their straight backs in the royal pew. These hands clasped together so decorously in prayer, had one pair of them also wielded a knife with the skill of a butcher? Had one of these worshippers a collection of bloodied clothes, hidden away at the back of a cupboard, or thrown into a pit in the woods?

Sir George Trevelyan, Private Secretary to Queen Victoria, was waiting in Rosebery's drawing-room in Berkeley Square. The fire had been lit, the carpet swept, the chairs and ornaments dusted. Rosebery's houses ran like clockwork, whether he was in them or not.

'Sir George, thank you for taking the trouble of coming all the way up from Osborne. I trust you had a pleasant journey?'

'Indeed, I did, Lord Rosebery. There are times, as I am sure you know as well as I do, when it can be a relief to get away, especially when there are a lot of relations in the house.'

Trevelyan had been in his position for over twenty years. Contemporaries said that he knew how to manage the Queen better than any man since Disraeli – and Disraeli had used outrageous ladlefuls of flattery. Trevelyan didn't. His management techniques were more oblique: patient campaigns by letter, subtle delaying tactics until the Queen's wrath had subsided, reminders of how matters had been managed in the past. On at least one occasion, to Rosebery's certain knowledge, Trevelyan had invented fictitious chapters of English constitutional history to get his way and persuade the Queen onto the proper course. This usually involved sending for Gladstone to form the next Government.

'The relations,' Rosebery sighed. 'Ah, yes. I can imagine how you must feel about those relations. But, come, Sir George, I have a terrible tale to relate. When is the man from *The Times* coming?'

'Barrington should be here in about half an hour. I thought we might need some time together beforehand. He is bringing one of his people with him. Barrington says his own shorthand is completely unintelligible. He can't even read it himself.'

Briefly Rosebery related the terrible events at Sandringham. He left nothing out, the deep wounds, the blood sprayed around the room, the prostration of Alexandra and the cold fury of her husband.

'The point is, Trevelyan, the point is this. They want to conceal the nature of the death. They propose to announce on Thursday, this coming Thursday, four days from now, that he died of influenza. My purpose is to warn *The Times*, to soften them up, if you like, to prepare them for the blow.'

'Good God!' said Trevelyan. 'Dear God in heaven. The poor family.' He closed his eyes for a moment and said a silent prayer. 'Do you think they are right, Rosebery, to conceal the murder from the world?'

'The time is past when one could speak of right or wrong. They have taken their decision. It is a perilous course. But they were prompted, as you can well imagine, by the fear of scandal and the newspapers prying into all their lives.'

'What should we tell the Queen?' Trevelyan's first loyalty was always to his royal mistress, happily surrounded by other members of her family and the waters of the English Channel on the Isle of Wight.

'What should we tell the Queen, indeed.' Rosebery looked troubled. He paused to stare into the fire. 'I can only relate the views of the Prince of Wales. He explained his position very clearly to me as I was leaving Sandringham.'

Prince Edward, wrapped in a dark green cape, had marched Rosebery up and down the little platform at Wolferton station, talking passionately of his fears, the lampposts, adorned with a premature crown for the Prince of Wales, shining bravely against the winter air, the engine already fired up, sending impatient clouds of smoke into the night.

'The Prince of Wales is frightened of his mother. I think he is more frightened of her than of anybody else on earth. He doesn't want to tell her. He fears her wrath. He fears for her health. Worst of all, he fears that she might not be able to keep such a secret to herself, that the scandal of Eddy's murder would somehow find its way into public gossip.'

'My God, Rosebery, you could well be right there. The Queen would be bound to tell somebody, probably her favourite daughter in Berlin. In half an hour the thing could be all around the Wihelmstrasse and the Unter den Linden. I don't think Prime Minister Salisbury would thank for us that.'

Footsteps could be heard, echoing across one of Rosebery's marble halls. There was a knock on the door.

'My lord. Sir George. The gentlemen from *The Times* are here. Mr Barrington. His chief reporter, Mr Johnston.'

'Barrington, how good to see you again! Thank you for coming.' It was certainly true, thought Rosebery, that Trevelyan was on excellent terms with the man from Printing House Square.

'Please sit down, gentlemen, please.' Rosebery placed his visitors side by side on a great leather sofa.

'I fear,' Trevelyan began, 'that we have some serious news concerning the Duke of Clarence and Avondale.'

'I hope you will have no objections, gentlemen,' the editor of *The Times* was at his most charming, 'if my colleague here makes a shorthand record of our conversation? It helps us to get our facts straight.'

'Of course, of course.' Trevelyan volleyed back some courtier's charm of his own. 'The Duke has contracted a most severe bout of the influenza. Most severe.'

'Oh dear, oh dear,' said Barrington, assuming already his air of mourning, planning perhaps the black-edged columns around his leader page which would greet a royal death. 'So many of our great men are suffering from it at present.' He shook his head sadly. 'The influenza is raging all across the Continent of Europe. The Bishop of Southwark is in crisis with it. They say that Cardinal Manning is at death's door.'

So far so good, thought Rosebery. The ground here is fertile. 'May I just fill in with a few more details, Mr Barrington? I have come this very evening from Sandringham.'

'Please do, Lord Rosebery, please do. We are most grateful to you.'

'The doctors believe that the illness took serious hold on Friday evening. The most serious development is that the influenza is accompanied by pneumonia. Dr Broadbent, who attended on the recent illness of Prince George, is in attendance. Dr Manby, the local man, a most capable physician, is also on call. I believe that Dr Laking may be summoned over the next twenty-four hours, if he is not already there.'

Doctors' names, Rosebery had always felt, would give the lie some serious substance. One man might not be telling the truth, but a trinity of doctors?

'Let me tell you what the proposals are for the dissemination of further information. From tomorrow, regular bulletins about his progress will be posted on the Norwich Gates at Sandringham and at Marlborough House.'

'Who else is in residence at Sandringham House at the moment?' Barrington leaned forward. Rosebery kept thinking of him as a bloodhound hot on the scent of death. His colleague took shorthand at a prodigious speed, his pen coming to rest a few seconds after the speaker had finished.

'Duke and Duchess of Fife, Duke and Duchess of Teck and their children, Prince and Princess of Wales obviously, Prince George, Princess Maud, Princess Victoria, a number of friends and equerries who had come to celebrate the Prince's birthday on Friday.' Rosebery took great care, on Powerscourt's instructions, not to give the names of any of the equerries. The shorthand pen hurtled across the page, the scratching of the nib filling in the silences as Rosebery spoke.

'We feel,' Rosebery nodded gravely at Sir George Trevelyan, 'that the first announcement in the newspapers should confine itself to a bald announcement of the illness, accompanied, if you feel appropriate, by a list of those in residence at Sandringham.'

'Of course, of course.' Barrington nodded gravely in his turn. If the newspapers were as tame and as docile as this all the time, Rosebery felt, we would not be in such difficulties.

'However, there is some background information about the possible origins of the disease which could, perhaps, be included on the following day, should the illness persist, of course.'

'*The Times* would be most grateful to you, Lord Rosebery, Sir George.' Trevelyan thought that Barrington sounded like the Ambassador from a major power proposing the terms of a treaty at the Foreign Office.

'On Monday of last week the Duke felt unwell as he attended the funeral of Prince Victor of Hohenhoe. On Tuesday he remained at Sandringham. On Wednesday he went shooting – and that, as I am sure you will remember, even in the warmth of London, was a very cold day. On Thursday he felt unwell again and on Friday he felt ill again on his birthday.'

Suddenly Rosebery felt completely blank. He had forgotten something. Like an actor, he had lost his lines. But there was no prompter, only Trevelyan, and he hadn't yet read the whole script. Had Eddy attended his birthday dinner party or not? Had he stayed in his room, according to the legend he and Suter and Shepstone had concocted earlier that day? Or had he attended and had to leave early? He simply could not remember.

He pressed on regardless. 'And that, gentlemen, is about as much as we can tell you at present.'

Silence fell on the room, the shorthand nib quiet at last. Barrington looked at his watch.

'Lord Rosebery, Sir George, please forgive me. Time waits for no man, not even *The Times*.'

Trevelyan wondered how often he had used that quip in the past twenty years. 'I must return to my offices. We must include this story in the first editions. We should be on our way. We are most grateful to you. I shall despatch a reporter to Sandringham at once.'

Times present turned into *Times* past as the two men were ushered from the room.

'I think that went as well as might have been expected, Lord Rosebery. We need to co-ordinate further plans.'

'Indeed, indeed.' Rosebery was staring at his empty sofa.

'Do you think Barrington brings that other chap with him everywhere he goes? A silent amanuensis? I don't believe he spoke a single word all the time he was here.'

'Perhaps he is the Official Scribe,' said Trevelyan, 'like those characters with tablets who used to follow Eastern potentates around their palaces, writing down every word.'

Rosebery laughed suddenly, the tension draining away. 'Do you suppose he tastes Barrington's food as well?'

Snow had turned into slush in the ancient streets of King's Lynn, seven miles south west of Sandringham. Powerscourt splashed his way through the entrance hall of the King's Head hotel and found Lord Johnny Fitzgerald drinking beer and William McKenzie drinking tea in a private sitting-room on the first floor. His reinforcements had arrived.

'Powerscourt! At last!' Fitzgerald eased his tall frame out of the best chair and shook his friend warmly by the hand.

'It's turning into a gathering of the clans here tonight.' McKenzie was a small, silent man in his early thirties. He was what they had called in India a tracker. Trained in his native Scotland in the complicated arts of stalking stags, he had transferred his skills to tracking humans. In India, as in his homeland, they spoke of him with awe.

'I am so glad you are both here.' Powerscourt sank into a chair by the fire and looked at his companions. 'Let me tell you what this business is about.'

Powerscourt left nothing out, the great slit across the throat, the other arteries slashed, the pools of blood on the floor. He told them of the plan to conceal the death from the public and the authorities. He filled them in on the activities of Major Dawnay and his band of mysterious experts with their arcane skills, military and civilian.

'Do they expect us to find out who did it? I suppose they do.' Fitzgerald took a long draught from an enormous tankard of ale. 'How in God's name are we supposed to do that, Francis? Blood in puddles all over the floor. It's like a butcher's shop on slaughter day.'

'All we can do,' Powerscourt surveyed his small forces, 'is to begin from the beginning. That's what we have always done in India or in London. In Wiltshire, you will remember, we had even less to go on than we do here. I think . . .' He paused to gaze with horror at an extremely sentimental picture of the Scottish Highlands hanging on the wall. 'I think we have to start by trying to eliminate the outsiders.

'Johnny.' Fitzgerald had just completed his tankard and was eyeing it curiously, as if amazed that it could be empty so soon. 'There have been reports of Russians in the vicinity. Reports have reached the Sandringham servants that there are Russians at Dersingham, at Hunstanton, at Fakenham even. There are also reports of Irishmen in the neighbourhood.'

'Where the hell is Fakenham?' Fitzgerald was notorious for his total ignorance of geography, even of countries he had lived in for years.

'It's north and east of Sandringham. This map on the wall should help you. The Prince of Wales is convinced that one or more of these Russians, if they exist, killed his son. Myself, I rather doubt it but I intend to keep the Russian ball in play for as long as possible. I don't think I want them to know just yet where my suspicions lie.

'And you, William McKenzie, I need your skills as never before. I need to know if you can tell if anybody has been trying to break into or out of Sandringham. There are great walls all around the estate and the gates are locked at night. It will be very very difficult with all this snow about.'

'Difficult, difficult, but not impossible, I dare say.'

Suddenly Powerscourt felt very tired. Tomorrow, he knew, would be another trying day at the big house. But as he looked as his two companions, already peering at the map and discussing tomorrow, he knew he was no longer alone.

It was so like Francis, his eldest sister Rosalind reflected bitterly, to disappear like that. One moment he was playing happily with her children upstairs, that ridiculous board thing with all those toy soldiers and the Battle of Waterloo, the next moment he was gone.

And then there was Lady Lucy, entertained at dinner here in her house in St James's Square, taken to look at the boring pictures in the National Gallery, friendship possibly ripening into something more substantial. Now she had been abandoned, like one of those Greek people, dumped on some hot island while the hero sailed away and forgot to change his sails.

Lady Rosalind Pembridge had invited Lady Lucy Hamilton

to tea. She was very fond of Lady Lucy. Maybe she could get some information about how the friendship was progressing. Maybe she could set Lady Lucy's mind at rest about the ridiculous habits of her brother. But she had even more important matters on her mind as she poured the tea and proffered some egg sandwiches.

'I'm thinking of changing the curtains in here, Lady Lucy. Pembridge says I can spend a couple of hundred pounds or so. Patterned or plain, do you think?'

'They've got some beautiful fabrics in Liberty's just now,' said Lady Lucy, aware that curtains can be a difficult and troublesome question.

'I've got a man from Liberty's coming round tomorrow morning,' said Lady Rosalind. 'He's going to bring a whole book of things with him. He tried to interest me in some Japanese designs. He said they were the coming thing. Have you seen these Japanese designs, Lady Lucy?'

'I have seen some of them. And they are very pretty. Very peaceful, I think. What does Lord Pembridge think about it all?'

'Pembridge!' Lady Rosalind laughed a sardonic laugh. 'Pembridge wouldn't notice if his curtains were made in Tokyo or Timbuctoo. He really wouldn't.' She shook her head sadly at the lack of interest of the other half of the human race in things of beauty. Her mind jumped sideways, to her brother. 'Have you heard from Francis at all, Lady Lucy?'

'I had a note from him. In fact I have had a couple of notes from him.' Lady Lucy smiled a private smile to herself. 'He's somewhere in Norfolk. He didn't tell me where. He said it had to do with his work and was very difficult.'

'That's so like him.' Lady Rosalind poured some more tea. The lamps were being lit in the great square outside. 'When we first lived in London years ago, before we were married,' she looked as if it was hard to remember the time before she was married, 'Francis used to take us to balls and things, the three of us girls. I suppose he was doing his duty. But even then you'd look round sometimes for a spare man, to fill in a gap on your card, or to take you in to supper, and Francis would have disappeared! Vanished into thin air! He always came back before

82

the end of course to take us home. But it was so irritating. Eleanor, my youngest sister, once hit him over the head with her bag on the way home.'

'Is he a good dancer? Francis, I mean. When he's actually there.' Lady Lucy had a sudden vision of herself and Francis floating round one of the great ballrooms of London, not talking, their eyes waltzing into the future.

'Well, he is, since you mention it. He's very good. But you're never quite sure if his mind is with you. The feet are fine, the brain may have wandered off somewhere else.'

Lady Lucy smiled. She could see it all.

'You might think,' Lady Rosalind went on, warming to the character assassination of her brother, 'it would have stopped once we were all married and he didn't have to go to these balls and things. The disappearing Francis, that is. But no. It went on. It still does. Have you met his great friend Lord Rosebery?'

Lady Lucy said she had met him at her brother's house years ago.

'When Rosebery was Foreign Secretary, a couple of years back, he invited Francis to some very important dinner at the Foreign Office. Ambassadors, one or two other Foreign Secretaries, those kind of people. I think there was some big conference on in London. All goes well until the pudding. Francis sits in his seat, makes polite conversation, doesn't spill anything on the floor. Then one of the waiters brings him a note with the crème brûlée. Rosebery said it was a particularly fine crème brûlée, much better than you get in Paris. Francis reads this note. And then he just disappears. He vanishes through the kitchens. The German Ambassador, Count Von somebody or other, finds himself talking to an empty chair. The wife of the French Foreign Secretary from the Quai d'Orsay is addressing her remarks to a crumpled napkin. There is a gap in the glittering party, as if a tooth has just fallen out. Francis has disappeared into the night. Even Rosebery was quite cross about that.'

Lady Lucy laughed. She felt Francis must have had a very good reason for disappearing. But she wasn't sure she should say so.

There was a tentative knock at the door.

'Who can that be at this hour?' Lady Rosalind looked peeved. 'Pembridge never comes back this early.'

The knocking continued.

'Come in!' called Lady Rosalind.

A nervous small boy poked a tousled head round the door. William Pembridge, eight years old, had been chosen by his brothers to lead this deputation to the terrifying world of the downstairs drawing-room.

'William, what are you doing here?' The voice was kind, but firm.

'It's the battle, Mama. We don't know what happens next.'

'Battle? What battle, William? Are you three fighting up there again?'

'No, Mama, we're not fighting.' William looked weary, exhausted perhaps by his mission to the lower floors. 'We don't know what happens next. At Waterloo. On that big board game. The one Uncle Francis gave us, the one with the soldiers.'

'Here we go again. Here we go again. Francis, Francis.' Lady Rosalind sighed in exasperation, as if brothers were even more troublesome than sons. 'Francis, Lady Lucy, very kindly bought the boys this big board thing for Christmas. It's a huge model of the site of Waterloo with soldiers and toy farms and all sorts of things. The four of them used to play with it happily for hours up there. Four little boys together. Then Francis disappears in the middle of the early stages of the battle and rushes off with Lord Rosebery into the night. Now the boys are upset. What seems to be the trouble, William?'

'We don't know what happens now. After the farm at Hoggymut. Do you know, Mama?'

'Don't be ridiculous, William. Of course I don't. I don't think your father knows either. You'll just have to wait until Uncle Francis comes back.'

William looked very sad. He would have to report failure to his brothers. They were so looking forward to the next part of the battle. 'But Uncle Francis may not come back for a bit. You said he'd disappeared.'

'You know what your uncle is like as well as I do, William.'

'Maybe I can help.'

William looked doubtfully at the slim elegant figure of Lady Lucy. Girls didn't know about battles and important things like that.

'You see, I know quite a lot about Waterloo. My grandfather fought there. He was with the cavalry. He used to tell us about it when we were little. And when we were bigger, come to that.'

'The finest day of my life, the proudest moment of my whole career,' the old General used to say in his last years, looking into the fire with his nearly blind eyes. 'What a day! What a charge!'

'Lady Lucy has far better things to do than go upstairs with you and play toy soldiers, William. Back you go upstairs. Off you go now.'

'Please, Mama. Couldn't Lady Lucy come up for a minute? It would make a big difference.'

'Of course I'll come up. I'd be delighted to help out, if I can.' Lady Lucy assured Lady Rosalind that it was no trouble at all. As William opened the door of the drawing-room his two brothers nearly fell in. They had been listening at the keyhole.

'I'm Patrick,' said the middle brother. 'I'm the drummer boy who leads the French Army when they charge.'

'And I'm Alexander,' said the smallest one. 'I've got the bugle. I blow when the Duke of Wellington says so.'

They looked up at Lady Lucy with hope in their eyes.

'Now then,' said Lady Lucy, surveying the battlefield on the top floor. 'The attack on the farm at Hougoumont has failed, I see.'

She explained about the British cavalry charge down the slope, the horses galloping ever faster, galloping to disaster as the French decimated them in the valley below. She wondered if any of these model horsemen had been based on her grandfather. She explained about the advance of Napoleon's Imperial Guard up the slope, led by Marshal Ney, spurred on by the relentless beat of the drummer boys. She explained how the British waited for the enemy, lying behind the slope, waiting for a corps that had never been defeated in twenty years of warfare.

Down below in her drawing-room Lady Rosalind had an image of Francis and Lucy living in a large house. The top floor was a whole series of huge boards. Battles, soldiers, guns, drums were laid out across the attics.

Malplaquet, she thought. Blenheim. Oudenaard. She stopped. She couldn't remember any more battles.

9

The Times, Monday, 11th January 1892
The Influenza
Illness of the Duke of Clarence and Avondale

We regret to announce that the Duke of Clarence and
Avondale, who is with the Prince and Princess of Wales at
Sandringham, is suffering from a severe attack of influenza,
accompanied by pneumonia. A telegram last evening from
Sandringham states that his Royal Highness' strength is
well maintained. Dr Laking has been at Sandringham since
Saturday. All the Duke's engagements have, of course, for
the present, been cancelled.

'You must have seen lots of dead bodies, Lord Powerscourt?'
Lord Henry Lancaster was the man who had found the body of
Prince Eddy. He was the younger son of the Duke of Dorset,
twenty-five years old, tall and very slim, his fair hair blowing in
the stiff North Sea wind. Powerscourt had taken him right away
from Sandringham House to walk in the dunes and the sand
beyond Hunstanton, a few miles up the coast.

'I mean, I've seen a few,' he went on, as if not wanting to
seem a complete innocent in such matters, 'but you must have
seen lots and lots.'

Powerscourt looked at him with a sudden rush of sympathy.
He had thought of this interview as an interrogation in his mind;
he had rehearsed in his analytical way the various avenues he

would explore, the points where the evasions would most likely come, the lies he might be told. Now he saw that it was not the mind of the historian that was called for, but the empathy of a father. Well, his period of fatherhood had been brief, but he had served a long and often painful apprenticeship as an elder brother.

'Well, I saw quite a few in India in some of those Afghan wars and things, you know. It's always all right in the heat of battle when the blood is pumping through your veins. If it's going well, you think you're immortal, that you can't be killed that day. It's only afterwards that men grow sad when they think of their fallen comrades. Like Byron in *Childe Harold* where he talked of

"the unreturning brave, – alas!
Ere evening to be trodden like the grass
Which now beneath them, but above shall grow
In its next verdure, when this fiery mass
Of living valour, rolling on the foe
And burning with high hope, shall moulder cold and low."

'I had to recite that in front of the whole school when I was twelve years old,' said Lancaster. 'I can still remember it word for word.'

'Of course,' said Powerscourt. 'You would remember something like that.'

They had crossed the dunes and were walking along the shore, an angry sea stretching its dark grey lines towards a faint horizon. Now, thought Powerscourt, now was the time to begin his questions.

'What was it like when you found him?' he said, throwing an idle stone far out into the waves. The stone was ice cold on his hand.

'It was terrible, terrible.' The young man shuddered as if trying to recover something he wanted to forget. 'There was the smell.' He trembled slightly. 'It was thick, very thick so that it was almost hard to breathe and strong like some terrible perfume of the dead.' He paused. Powerscourt said nothing. He waited.

'Then there was the blood. They tell you it's red. This wasn't just red. It was black in places and where it was still dripping from his wrists it was this unbelievably bright red, as if it had been polished. There was a huge puddle of it over by the window.'

'The army doctors will be able to tell us quite soon when he died. They were examining the body last night when everybody had gone to bed. You see, I don't know why, I think he may have been killed first and then those other cuts made which caused all the blood.'

Even as he spoke Powerscourt regretted what he said. It was not for him in these circumstances to show off his clever theories. The special forces may have searched the roof and the grounds, they may have been conducting inquiries near and far about mysterious strangers in the area, the Prince of Wales may have been convinced that the murderer was some foreign fiend, some Russian or Irish fanatic in the pay of Her Majesty's enemies. Powerscourt was virtually certain that the murderer had slept between clean sheets in a clean bed as a guest in Sandringham House before venturing up the stairs to slaughter Prince Eddy. And here he was, confiding his innermost thoughts to a man who must be one of the main suspects in the affair. How stupid! He cursed himself for his folly.

'But tell me,' Powerscourt hurried on, trying to conceal the import of what he had just said, 'was he lying on his back when you saw him?'

'He was. And, you know, I've been trying to get this out of my mind ever since, but he had a sort of silly grin on his face even with his throat cut like that. You've seen the body, I presume?'

'Yes, I have,' said Powerscourt, 'and I'm afraid that is rather a good description of it. Was the window open when you saw it?'

'Yes, it was, but the breeze wasn't enough to get rid of the smell.'

'What else did you notice?'

'Well, I'm afraid I'm not trained in these matters . . .' His voice trailed away. The roaring of the wind and the crashing of the waves meant that the two men were almost shouting at each other. Their words were being carried away over their shoulders to be lost over the dark expanse of the North Sea.

'I mean anything apart from the dead man, was there anything unusual about the furniture or the clothes or anything?' Powerscourt was leaning close to Lancaster as he spoke.

'I don't think so.' The young man sounded doubtful. The wind got up suddenly and a small wall of howling sand battered their eyes and faces. It would, felt Powerscourt, be the perfect cover for somebody with something to hide. Was this the moment for the lie?

'You didn't tidy anything away, or clear something up off the floor?'

'How did you know, how did you know?' Lancaster spoke very softly, and as he looked at Powerscourt, there was a terrible supplication in his eyes. Powerscourt was to wonder for weeks afterwards what it meant. For the moment, he remained silent. 'There was a picture on the floor. It had been smashed into little tiny pieces. It must have taken a great deal of force to do it. It looked as if the murderer had swivelled the heel of his boot on the glass and the picture over and over again. It was as if there was as much hatred going into that as had gone into the murder itself.'

'And could you tell whose picture it was?' Powerscourt spoke slowly now.

'Oh yes, you see that's what must have made the murderer so cross, the fact that the image wouldn't be reduced to a pulp. It was Prince Eddy's fiancée, Princess May of Teck.'

'And what did you do with the pieces?'

'I – I tried to pick them all up,' said Lancaster, his slim frame swaying in the wind. 'I put them in my pocket and when everybody was busy, I took them into Sandringham Woods and threw them on to a pile of rubbish. Look here, you do believe me, don't you?'

Powerscourt had no idea who to believe any more. But after his earlier mistake, he knew what he had to do. 'Of course I believe you, Lord Lancaster.' He put his arm round the young man. 'Of course I do.'

As they drove back to Sandringham House Powerscourt asked about the other equerries and the pattern of their duties.

'Ever since he became ill on his birthday there were six of us on duty round the clock, four hours at a time. On the day he died, I remember saying goodnight to him and then I was on duty from three to seven. There were nurses on duty on the same pattern but they had a different sitting-room to us.'

'So when you came on duty at three, what were you told?'

'The nurse told me Prince Eddy was sleeping and was not to be disturbed. It was only in the morning that I looked in to see if he wanted any breakfast or any cold drinks. That influenza makes people very thirsty.'

'And who were the other equerries?'

'Well, there was Harry Radclyffe, Charles Peveril, William Brockham, Lord Edward Gresham, Frederick Mortimer.'

'And who was on duty just before you?'

'That was Harry Radclyffe. The nurse said he'd gone off to bed when she told me Eddy was asleep.'

'I see,' said Powerscourt. 'I think I may need to ask you some more questions later on, if you don't mind.'

'Not at all.' Lancaster sounded relieved that the interrogation was over.

As they drove round the bend and in through the Norwich Gates, another of Shepstone's bulletins had already appeared on the railings.

Sandringham, Monday evening.
   The illness of the Duke of Clarence and Avondale continues to pursue a somewhat severe course, but His Royal Highness' condition and strength are full.
      Bartle Shepstone, Comptroller of the Household

A small crowd had gathered outside, including one or two men who were dressed for London, not for Norfolk. They had sharp inquisitive faces and were already asking questions of the local people.

Newspapermen, thought Powerscourt. They're here already.

'I am so sorry, Lord Powerscourt, that we should meet in such melancholy circumstances.' Major Edwin Dawnay, officer commanding the bizarre collection of soldiery summoned by Sir Bartle Shepstone, was walking away from the front door of Sandringham House. 'I have heard so much about your work in India.'

'You are too kind, Major Dawnay, too kind. And the circumstances are indeed melancholy, if not macabre.'

Powerscourt shuddered slightly as he thought of the murderer alone in Prince Eddy's room with the bleeding corpse, searching for the photograph of Princess May, stamping on it in a fit of frenzy as he tried to reduce it to rubble, the blood already flowing freely from the dead man's veins, the glass on the picture shattering into smaller and smaller pieces as the onslaught went on. The dead man had not been safe in there. Even the photographs of the living had to be slaughtered too. 'Your men have been very busy this afternoon, I understand.'

'Yes they have, and a pretty good fist they have made of things so far,' Dawnay replied. 'But come, Lord Powerscourt, there must be a reason why you have brought me away from the house.'

'There is,' said Powerscourt, pausing at the top of the great gravel drive. The light was fading fast now. The snow felt crunchy underfoot. Powerscourt drew the Major behind a hedge. A small creature of the Sandringham undergrowth shot out beneath their feet and disappeared into the white wastes beyond. 'I would like to draw your attention to the roof, Major Dawnay.'

'The roof?' Dawnay wondered inwardly if the man was losing his wits. It was a perfectly normal roof, the Royal Standard of the Prince of Wales faintly visible from the flagpole.

'Count five windows to the left of the main entrance. Go up one. That is the room in which the unfortunate Prince was murdered.'

Dawnay counted the windows, still uncertain of the sanity of his companion. 'You mean the window with the stone surround, rather than the normal red brick? With a little ornamental crest on top of it?'

An early owl hooted far off in the distance. The bells of Dersingham church tolled the hour of five.

'Just so,' said Powerscourt. 'Now it is my belief that the window was not fastened shut on the night of the murder. You may well ask why it was left like that in temperatures like these, but sufferers from influenza or whatever it was have been known to do strange things. I wonder if the murderer could have climbed over the roof, dropped down the side of the house, opened the window, murdered Prince Eddy, and escaped the way he came.'

'God bless my soul!' said Major Dawnay.

'Let us walk round to the other side of the house and see where he might have started from. Do you have any good climbers in your party, Major?'

We can clean up a dead body. We can set a bloodstained room to rights, thought Dawnay. Now this Irish peer wants to know if we are also trained as mountaineers or cat burglars.

The two men were looking at the back of the house, where the light was slightly better. 'I would draw your attention,' Powerscourt pointed with one of those long fingers that had so fascinated Lady Lucy Hamilton, 'to the second floor, just to the right of the flagpole. There are at least six windows along there. That is the general area that our mountaineer might have set out from.'

'You mean the equerries' quarters?' Major Dawnay was aghast.

'Major Dawnay, you and I are trained in the arts of discretion, of remaining silent and not telling what we know. It is, unfortunately, at the heart and core of our professional lives. It was because I knew that I could trust you absolutely that we are here.' Powerscourt was whispering now as a couple of dim figures could be seen walking towards the main entrance. 'Do you have any climbers?'

This is not a man who is going to give up easily, thought Dawnay. If he ever gives up at all. He could sense a steely determination in his companion, concealed in company by the rattle of repartee or a languid charm.

'As a matter of fact, we do. I think we have two. But I presume that for your purposes you only want one?'

'Correct. Now, I think that it might be rather difficult to attempt the traverse from one of those rooms themselves.'

Dawnay didn't like to think of what might happen to any intruder, creeping through one of the equerries' rooms in the small hours of the morning, only to vanish out of the window into the night and the roofs above. He doubted if they would get out alive.

'But if we look further along this side of the house. Four or five windows along there is a small door, leading to the lawn. Do you have it? I think our climbing friend might start his expedition from there, don't you? There seem to be lots of handholds and things. I don't know if he would bring ropes and climbing gear like that?'

'Ropes?' Dawnay was thinking hard, his eyes measuring distances and elevations in the gloom. 'It's hardly the main face of the Matterhorn. But I should think ropes might be necessary, yes. But look here, Powerscourt, I am assuming that the person who may have climbed over the roof a couple of nights ago had time to do a certain amount of reconnaissance by day. He'd have wandered round the place, perhaps looking at the roof from a distance with a small telescope or something similar?'

'I am sure that is the case,' said Powerscourt. 'Would you rather the scaling of Sandringham took place tomorrow night and not tonight? To give your man time to check out the task beforehand?'

'I am sure that would be more realistic. We wouldn't want to have to explain why one of my men died climbing the walls of Sandringham, would we, Lord Powerscourt?' Dawnay was rubbing his hands together now to keep warm, the noise of his palms lost in the night air. 'Shall we say two o'clock in the morning? And I presume that you do not wish me to mention this to a single living soul?'

'Two o'clock would be excellent. And I fear that silence would be even better. And the silence must include everybody.'

'Even Shepstone?'

'Even Shepstone'. Powerscourt's voice sounded very cold. Where does he go in his mind, Dawnay wondered as they trudged back to the main entrance, what ghastly journeys does his imagination take him on? For he could see now that the key to the whole investigation lay in Powerscourt's head as he formed and reformed pieces of a blood-red jigsaw puzzle in his brain.

*

The Times, Tuesday, 12th January 1892
The Influenza
The Illness of the Duke of Clarence and Avondale

The announcement of the serious illness of the Duke of Clarence and Avondale caused universal regret yesterday, and this was shown by the large number of inquiries made at Sandringham House. In addition to personal inquiries, messages were received to such an extent as to tax to the utmost the powers of the private telegraph at Sandringham. With regard to the origin of the Duke's illness, it is stated that after returning in Monday of last week from the funeral of Prince Victor of Hohenhoe, he did not feel well, but he went out shooting on Wednesday, and it is feared that he then aggravated his disposition. On Thursday he remained at Sandringham House all day, but the symptoms were not to be distinguished from an ordinary cold. He was worse on Friday and indeed felt so unwell that he did not leave his room and was not present at the birthday dinner given in his honour. On Saturday it was deemed necessary to call in the advice of Dr Laking, who, with Dr Broadbent, had been in attendance during the serious illness of Prince George of Wales. Throughout the whole of Saturday and Sunday the Duke suffered considerably from a severe attack of influenza, accompanied by pneumonia, but the doctors were able to report that his strength was 'well maintained'.

'Foreigners, bloody foreigners!' Lord Johnny Fitzgerald was lying once more on the sofa in the sitting-room at King's Lynn. Powerscourt noted that he had two large tankards of beer waiting patiently by his right hand. William McKenzie had a pot of tea and a plate of biscuits.

'We're all bloody foreigners round here,' Fitzgerald went on, in pained tones. 'I'm a bloody foreigner. You're a bloody foreigner, Francis. William's a bloody foreigner. In this part of the world you're a foreigner if you come from Peterborough, for God's sake. They look at you all the time. They stare at you as though you had two heads. If you buy something in a shop the rest of the natives all fall silent in case you're an enemy agent.'

'It must have its advantages, surely,' Powerscourt laughed. 'If we are all marked men, then other strangers must have been spotted here before us.'

'Indeed they have.' Lord Johnny took a refreshingly large gulp of beer and wiped the foam from his chin. 'Which brings me to my report.' He lay back on the sofa and gazed at the ceiling. A large spider had escaped the attentions of the parlour-maids and was preparing an elaborate mesh for its victims. 'Russians first. Those servants at Sandringham were right. There has been a party of Russians in the neighbourhood. But I'm sorry to have to report that they are extremely respectable Russians.' Fitzgerald sounded as though he had difficulty in grasping the possibility of Russians being respectable.

'There are six of them,' he went on. It's the same as the equerries, thought Powerscourt suddenly. Six of the best. Six good men and true. Half a dozen. Half a jury.

'They come from St Petersburg,' Fitzgerald went on, 'from some Institute of Science and Technology at the university there. They're led by a certain Professor Ivan Romitsev. His two assistants are called Dimitry Vatutin and Nikolai Dekanozov. Didn't I do well remembering that lot?' He looked around for applause and wonderment.

'The other three gentlemen – please don't ask me to remember their bloody names but I do have them written down somewhere – are technicians. All of this little band are concerned with advanced forms of printing. They are trying to modernize the facilities in some great industrial complex at a place called Vyborg in St Petersburg. They came by sea. They went to a big new plant at Peterborough to look at the new machines they have there, which were, I believe, imported from America. They are on their way to see more printing machines in Colchester and in London.'

'How come they were spotted in Sandringham, Johnny?'

'I'm coming to that. Will you let me finish my report now?' In protest at the interruption, Lord Johnny took another giant's mouthful of his beer.

'They are all loyal subjects of the Czar, this lot. They planned their journey so they could have a look at Sandringham on their travels. Isn't the Czar's wife, Mrs Czar or whatever they call her, isn't she related to Alexandra up at the big house? Once they heard there was a royal palace, as they thought, in the neighbourhood, they had to go and see it. I think these Russians expected some enormous structure like those huge palaces and things they have in St Petersburg. Summer Palaces. Winter Palaces. Do they have Spring and Autumn Palaces too? Maybe Sandringham was the British Winter Palace. If you're a Russian, that is.

'I have to tell you, Francis,' Johnny laughed as he remembered his Russians, 'they were very disappointed when they saw Sandringham. That isn't a palace, they said as their carriage brought them up to the main gates to have a look. It's far too small. It's more like a big dacha, a sort of summer house in the country. I don't suppose you'd better include that in your report to the Private Secretary and the Comptroller General of the Household, Francis. Not a palace at all. Far too small.'

'Could you imagine, Johnny, in your wildest dreams that any of these gentlemen from the Institute of Science and Technology could be a secret agent, a revolutionary? Looking at printing machines by day, devouring anarchists' manuals by night?'

'No. Absolutely not. I got very drunk with these Russians the other evening. That is to say, they got very drunk, I got a little bit drunk. And I think they are as innocent as our own printers over there in Peterborough.

'There are also some Irish in the neighbourhood.' Lord Johnny continued his report. 'And I don't mean you and I, Francis. There are five Irish in a party of workmen extending the telegraph lines north and west of Sandringham.'

Telegraph lines, thought Powerscourt. In his lifetime he had seen the steady advance of these wooden posts across the length and breadth of Britain, like some enormous army being dressed across the parade ground of a nation, linked not by arm to shoulder, but by roll upon roll of wire. 'Be not afraid,' he thought with Prospero, 'the isle is full of noises'. Messages of joy and despair were whispered along the uncomprehending cables. Births, marriages, deaths. He wondered if his brother-in-law the canny Mr William Burke had investments in telegraph pole companies or wire manufactories. Almost certainly he had. There were other inventions, stranger still. Voices, human voices, being carried down the lines. New vehicles that relied not on horses but on engines for power. Some brave new world – he went back to Miranda in *The Tempest* – is being born at the end of our century. No more the Age of Reason. No more the Age of Enlightenment. Welcome to the Age of the Machines.

'Francis, hello-oh, hello-oh. Are you there?' Lord Johnny had known Powerscourt for so long he had grown accustomed to these temporary leaves of absence. Compassionate leave, he always thought. The poor bugger's brain has run away with him again.

'Of course, of course.' Powerscourt wondered if he shouldn't join William McKenzie in a pot of tea. 'The Irish, you were saying.'

'I have talked to them too, of course. And I've got their names. They all play for the same cricket team in Skibereen. Can cricketers be revolutionaries, do you think?'

'Charles Stewart Parnell,' said Powerscourt, 'God rest his soul, was the captain of the County Wicklow cricket team. But I don't suppose he'd be classed as a revolutionary, do you think?'

'Not quite, not quite.' Fitzgerald started on his second tankard of beer. 'Anyway, I don't think any of these characters is our man. They work so bloody hard on those poles, drive them into the ground, make them straight, up you go to fix the wire on top, next one, please, hurry up there, – those foremen are slave drivers, I tell you – that they wouldn't have the energy left to wander round the countryside in the middle of the night with a butcher's knife in their pocket.'

'That's a clean bill of health for the Russians and the Irish, then.' Powerscourt didn't sound surprised. 'You have done well, Johnny, you must have been working very hard. I am very grateful to you, as always.'

'I have to tell you that I shall always be a welcome guest at the Institute of Science and Technology in St Petersburg.' Johnny Fitzgerald was laughing now. 'And at the humble home of the good Professor what's his name. They promised to take me on a tour of the Russian vodka factories when I come to call. Anyone care to join me?'

McKenzie shuddered at the thought.

'William.' Powerscourt turned to his Calvinist tea drinker. 'Have you been able to find anything out in the dreadful snow?'

'Yes and no, Lord Francis. Yes, in this sense. I have been all around the grounds of Sandringham House. The snow makes it very difficult to come to firm conclusions. I do not think anybody has been trying to get in or out, by unorthodox means, if you see what I mean. They could have always used the front door. That's a bit of a yes. The no is that I cannot be sure, sir. I would like to have a day or two more to work on it. I have an appointment with some poachers later this evening. They may have more intelligence.'

'I would like you to join me tomorrow morning at the big house, William. I will meet you at the main entrance by the Norwich Gates at, shall we say, ten o'clock? I have asked one of the military gentlemen to see if it is possible to climb over the roof at Sandringham and gain entrance to the death chamber on the other side. This man is an experienced mountaineer, they tell me, but I would welcome a second opinion.'

'Ropes, naval ropes,' said McKenzie, 'they used to have things that could catch on to anything, other ships, fortifications, battlements, that sort of stuff. And they keep inventing more equipment on the Continent for those daft people who go climbing in the Alps.'

10

The Times, Wednesday, 13th January 1892
The Illness of the Duke of Clarence and Avondale

Expressions of sympathy with the Prince and Princess of Wales and hopes for the speedy recovery of their son continued to pour in to Sandringham yesterday from all parts of the country in the shape of letters and telegrams, while at the gates and lodges of Sandringham Park the number of personal calls from people residing in the neighbourhood was also very great indeed. The first bulletin, posted at the gates of Sandringham House, was as follows.

. Sandringham, Norfolk, Jan 12. 10.30 a.m.

With regard to the illness of the Duke of Clarence and Avondale, the inflammation of the lungs is pursuing its course, and the strength is well maintained, but no improvement can yet be reported in His Royal Highness' condition.
W. H. Broadbent MD
F. H. Laking MD

Powerscourt always remembered questioning the five other equerries as an exercise in futility. He met with a brick wall of good manners, perfectly plastered with the soft easy charm of the upper classes. One by one, walking in the grounds, or in the drawing-room of Suter's meetings, he talked to them as they came off their roll call of sentry duty on the upper floor.

His questions were always the same. So were the answers.

Had they seen anything unusual on the night of the murder?

No, they had not. Harry Radclyffe, Charles Peveril, William Brockham, Lord Edward Gresham and the Hon. Frederick Mortimer were unanimous.

Had they had noticed anything unusual in the room where Eddy died if they had seen it?

'Only a great deal of blood,' the Old Etonian chorus replied.

Had they heard any strange noises in the night, either inside or outside the house?

No, they had not. Except for Lord Edward Gresham who thought he had heard a horse riding away from the house towards the woods sometime in the night. No, he was afraid he could not be more specific about the time.

Could they think of any reason why somebody might want to take Prince Eddy's life?

No, they could not. It was an outrage. It was a scandal. When the murderer was caught they would all be quite happy to wring his neck.

Did they know of anything in Prince Eddy's life which might have made him enemies?

'Absolutely not,' the equerry chorus replied. Eddy had been a jolly fine fellow. Not too quick on the uptake at times, but there was nothing wrong with that. Never too good at grasping the rules of the military, but nothing wrong with that either.

Had any of them ever heard Eddy talk of somebody who wished him harm, who wanted to injure him in some way?

No, they had not.

'If you remember anything, anything at all, that you think might help unmask his killer, will you please get in touch with me at once. At once, wherever you may be.'

All solemnly assured Powerscourt that of course they would do that. Absolutely. No question of it. Jolly important to find out the truth.

And as he reviewed his interviews Powerscourt thought he had gained one tiny scrap of information, the horse in the night. That was all. For the rest he had been wasting his time. Whether they had all agreed on a common line beforehand he did not know. But they had certainly come across with one. And of one thing Powerscourt was virtually certain. One of them was lying. Maybe, he thought in his darker moments, maybe all of them were lying.

Powerscourt stopped counting when he reached fifty-two. He ran his eyes over the rest of the crowd assembled outside the Norwich Gates at five to ten on a cold January morning. Seventy, maybe eighty souls, he said to himself, have gathered here, the snow still falling lightly, dusting the elaborate filigree of the metalwork on top of the gates. For what? A glimpse of some royal personage on the far side of the great wrought-iron structure? A sight of Sir Bartle Shepstone, or one of his auxiliaries, pinning the latest bulletin about the health of Prince Eddy to the railings? Or were they really ghouls, hoping to be the first to see the announcement of a royal death?

'Good morning, Lord Francis.'

William McKenzie had appeared suddenly by his side. He had not, as far as Powerscourt could tell, come through the gates themselves.

'Good morning William. Where on earth did you come from?'

'Oh, I have my own ways in and out of here by now, Lord Francis. I always feel it's best to remain inconspicuous.'

'Indeed, indeed. Come, we must make our meeting with Major Dawnay and his climbing friend. I think he is called Bateman.'

'Lord Fitzgerald asked me to bring you these.' William McKenzie fished in one of his many and voluminous pockets, and produced Lord Johnny's Prussian glasses. 'He says you could read the maker's name on the slates on the roof with them.'

Three soldiers on horseback trotted slowly past them as they made their way up the drive, the horses' breath hanging long and slow in the cold Norfolk air.

'Lord Powerscourt! You, sir, must be William McKenzie. Good morning to you both!' Major Dawnay had the cheerfulness and good temper of a man who has just escaped from the overheated interior of Sandringham House. 'And this is Corporal Bateman, gentlemen. He tells me he passed a most interesting night!'

Dawnay led the way round the path, scarcely visible in the snow, to a position some two hundred yards from the back of Sandringham House. Powerscourt raised his glasses and passed them over to Dawnay.

'I should not think these came from this country,' said Dawnay appreciatively, as if British manufactures were of inferior stock. 'These are German, I fancy.'

'Sir, sirs,' Corporal Bateman seemed unsure as to whether he should address his superior officers in the singular or plural, 'my brief was to see if it was possible to climb from one side of the house to the other in the snow. The particular windows to which I was referred' – he's beginning to sound like a policeman making his report, thought Powerscourt – 'were those six just to the right of the flagpole, if you would like to cast your glasses there. Access to those windows being denied, I was then asked to see if I could effect the passage from a standing start, as it were, on the ground by those flowerbeds to the right.'

How Bateman could tell there were flowerbeds there at all, Powerscourt never knew. The snow wrapped up every living thing.

'Well, gentlemen, I have to tell you that I had some special equipment sent up here when I heard of this mission. But it is all equipment that can be readily purchased at reputable stores in London and the big cities, special ropes with these little grappling hooks at the end.' He took a coiled piece of rope from his pocket.

'It's like a cross between a grappling hook and a rope ladder, is it not?' McKenzie had come to the aid of his fellow mountaineer.

'It is exactly that, Mr McKenzie. Exactly. You throw it up, it catches on a roof or a chimney, and up the rope ladder you go. I have to tell you, gentlemen,' Bateman suddenly looked around him in case the wrong ears might be listening, 'that it is a simple matter to cross from one side of the house to the other. I made my ascent upwards from the flowerbeds you have noted. In various places on the roof – you can't see them with this snow', Dawnay was fiddling with the range controls on the Prussian glasses – 'there are little ladders. Quite new, they are. I imagine they were installed after the recent fire to enable people to escape.

'Some five minutes after my departure' – the man is sounding like a train timetable now, thought Powerscourt – 'I was outside the window of the late Prince Eddy. I could have walked in and murdered him, gentlemen. If he had been there, that is.'

Corporal Bateman paused. This was becoming one of the longest speeches of his life. And to two superior officers, one of them a lord.

'It only took me another five minutes to return to the flower-beds where I started. Half an hour after that, there was not a trace of my activities on either side the roof. I looked most carefully, then and in the morning. The snow covered everything like a blanket.'

'Well done, Corporal! Well done, indeed.' Major Edwin Dawnay was proud of his man.

'Tell me,' said Powerscourt, 'did you find anything while you were up there? Anything unusual?'

'Funny you should mention that, Your Lordship. I don't know how long it had been there, or if it means anything to you gentlemen. But I found this.' He paused to rummage in his pockets, which were, Powerscourt noted with interest, even more capacious than those of William McKenzie. He drew out a small piece of rope ladder with one of the grappling hooks at the top missing. It was only two inches long, but its purpose was very clear.

Bateman and McKenzie disappeared into a private conversation of their own about makes of rope ladder, strength of line, chances of fracture.

'Do you think the murderer left this up there, Powerscourt?' Dawnay sounded alarmed, as if the murderer had suddenly taken shape and was liable to emerge at any moment from Sandringham Woods or peer down at them from the rooftops above.

'It's perfectly possible,' said Powerscourt. 'Then again, the fire brigade might have used those things when they were putting in the ladders.'

My God, he plays it very close to his chest, thought Dawnay. Pound to a penny Powerscourt or one of his friends will be round to the local fire brigade within the next twenty-four hours asking about bits of rope ladder left on the roof.

But Powerscourt hadn't finished yet. Not by any means. He was coming to what was, for him, the most important question of all.

'Tell me, Dawnay,' he said nonchalantly, as though it were a mere trifle, 'did anybody in the house hear anything? Anything at all?'

'Of our friend Bateman's activities, do you mean? That's the curious thing, Powerscourt. Nobody heard a thing. Not even the dogs barked during the night.'

'Nobody heard a thing?' Powerscourt looked very thoughtful indeed. 'How very interesting.'

Powerscourt was sleeping heavily. There was the light touch of a hand on his shoulder. He turned. There was an urgent whisper in his ear.

'Lord Francis. Lord Francis.'

Powerscourt wondered if some strange new dream had come to haunt him, the hand on his shoulder shaking, shaking, shaking.

'Lord Francis. Please wake up. Please wake up. Please.'

With a groan, Powerscourt suddenly shot up in his bed. 'William, what on earth are you doing here? What time is it, for God's sake?'

'I will tell you all outside,' whispered William McKenzie. 'You must get dressed at once and come with me. Don't put your boots on till we get away from the house.'

With his boots in his left hand, Powerscourt tiptoed out of his room, down a corridor he had never seen and down stairs he had never climbed. How had William McKenzie, his trusty tracker, found him in the dark? What was going on now? Where was he taking him?

They passed out of a small door at the side of the house. Powerscourt put his boots on and followed McKenzie out into the night. Their feet crunched heavily on the snow. The sound was magnified as they passed between a clump of trees. Surely somebody in the house must have heard them, thought Powerscourt, looking back in alarm. They sounded like the Blues and Royals changing the guard.

'William, please tell me what's going on.' Even a whisper sounded like a sergeant major on the parade ground.

'There's another body, my lord. I found it an hour ago when I was having a wee patrol round the grounds. I met one of Major Dawnay's men doing the same thing. The Major is there now. It's about a mile from here.'

Admirably succinct, thought Powerscourt. Another body. God in heaven. When would it stop?

The cold seemed to start at the ears. Then it made an orderly progression downwards, tip of nose, lips, hands, fingers, toes. Those were the first bits that fell off the Athenians in the great plague in Thucydides, Powerscourt suddenly remembered, wishing he could keep his memories in better order. A different sort of plague seemed to have struck the coast of Norfolk. Two bodies in four days were enough for a tennis match in hell or heaven.

They were deep in the forest now. McKenzie moved so silently that at times Powerscourt thought he had lost him. Perhaps, he thought, this is the darkest hour before the dawn. And there really is a dawn chorus, he realised, as a ragged burst of birdsong broke through above the trees.

'Nearly there.' McKenzie was still whispering even though Sandringham House was over a mile behind.

In a small clearing ahead, Major Dawnay had a torch of sorts that cast fantastic shadows on the trees.

'Powerscourt, my dear Lord Powerscourt. Thank God you have come.'

He turned his guttering candle to his left. The body of a man was lying on the ground. He was wearing the full dress uniform of the Coldstream Guards. He looked as though he had fallen over unexpectedly. The ground was covered with blood, and with bits of light grey and brown matter that Powerscourt presumed must have been his brains. The porridge-like material had also fallen all over his shoulder and made terrible stains on his epaulettes. Lord Henry Lancaster, the equerry who had found the body of Prince Eddy, had joined his master in death.

'I think he shot himself through the head. Or somebody else

shot him through the head. The doctor will be here presently. Do you think it is murder or suicide, Powerscourt?'

'God knows. God knows.' Suddenly Powerscourt wished he were at home in Rokesley, inspecting the sales catalogues of the great auction houses, or walking through his grounds. 'We mustn't move anything until the doctor comes. May I?' He borrowed the makeshift torch from Major Dawnay and walked slowly around the body.

'There's no sign of anybody else coming this way, my lord.' McKenzie, as ever, seemed able to read his thoughts. 'I checked it all out before anyone else got here. There's only one set of footprints in the snow. No traces of a horse. Unless somebody was swinging through the trees like some African ape, Lord Lancaster was the only person to come here.'

It wasn't surprising that he was the only person to come here. They were one or two hundred yards off the main road between Wolferton and Sandringham, a road designed to show off the size of his estate and the splendour of his grounds to the Prince of Wales' visitors. Some estate, some sights to be shown to the new arrivals now, thought Powerscourt. One corpse, restored to some sort of life, was waiting in an upstairs attic. Another was lying awkwardly on the ground, the brains staining the dark Sandringham earth.

There was another set of rustling, like animals moving through the trees. Two more faces peered up into the light of the torch.

'Dr Spencer.' Dawnay greeted his man. His guide, presumably McKenzie's colleague on night patrol, was carrying a makeshift stretcher.

'When bodies come, they come not single one, but in battalions.' Dr Spencer prided himself on his knowledge of the classics. 'Let me have this torch just now.'

The doctor peered intently at the dead man's head. He looked particularly closely at the right temple. He glanced distastefully at the ground. He handed a standard Colt pistol to Major Dawnay. 'I can't give you a proper opinion about anything much at present. No doubt you gentlemen will be wanting something to occupy your thoughts at a time like this. I think – but I will not be held to it until later – that the man killed himself. The gun to the right temple is quite a popular form of suicide these days.'

Dr Spencer paused and looked around. Faint, very faint, from over the sea at Snettisham came the first intimations of dawn. 'We must move the body. Now.' The doctor spoke with all the authority of the medical profession, used to handling the living and the dead.

'Great God, Powerscourt,' Dawnay sounded more alarmed than Powerscourt had ever heard him, 'where are we going to take the body? This morning, this morning of all mornings. In a few hours' time, the Royal Family, the whole lot of them, are going to file into Eddy's bedroom to say their last farewells. At nine o'clock Shepstone is going to post the notice on the Norwich Gates, saying that Prince Eddy is dead from the influenza. We can't . . .' His voice trailed away as he thought of the horror of it all. 'We can't have another body lying in the hallway or hidden in the drawing-room while Death by Influenza is played out upstairs.'

'Take him to Shepstone's house. It's not that far from here. We can keep him away from the main house for the time being.' Powerscourt felt that the arrival of another corpse would bring on hysteria, or worse, in Sandringham House. You were welcome there when you were alive, he said mentally to Lancaster, now being loaded on to his temporary bier, you're not wanted when you are dead. You're too embarrassing. We'd rather not think about you today.

There was a whispered dialogue between Powerscourt and Dawnay. McKenzie and his colleague had raised the temporary stretcher. As they marched slowly through the wood Powerscourt could hear the Dead March from *Saul* booming in his head. As the pall bearers passed over fallen branches their boots sounded like pistol shots in the dark.

'Do you think he was murdered, Lord Francis?' said Dawnay, walking through a dark glade.

'There are a number of possibilities.' Powerscourt was always amazed to find his analytical powers still operating, however bizarre the circumstances. 'Possibility Number One,' he groped for a frozen finger in the gloom, 'is that the murderer of Prince

Eddy decided to kill Lancaster too. For reasons unknown. Perhaps relating to the conversations the equerries must have had among each other after the death. Perhaps relating to the conversations they had with me. But I doubt it. William McKenzie was the best tracker of man or animal the British Army ever possessed. He tells me only one set of footsteps went to Lancaster's last resting place. I believe him absolutely. So it may be suicide.

'Possibility Number Two,' he continued, noting with alarm that the stretcher ahead had nearly lost its load, 'is that Lancaster was the murderer. He was, you will recall, the man on guard for most of the night Prince Eddy was killed. He had the time. He had ample opportunity. Overcome with remorse, he takes his own life. Our job is over. We know the murderer. We can all go home.'

'Do you really believe that, Lord Francis?' Dawnay sounded highly dubious about Possibility Number Two.

'Possibility Number Three is that he killed himself because he knew too much. Maybe he knew who the murderer was. Maybe he couldn't bear to tell us. Maybe he couldn't bear to betray a friend.'

The light was getting brighter now. Shepstone's house suddenly loomed out of the faint morning mist.

'How do you think we should get in? Ring the front door? Good morning, we've brought a corpse for breakfast. Have you got any porridge?' Powerscourt felt flippancy spreading over him, like a disease.

'I fancy we may have to rely on the talents of your friend McKenzie,' said Dawnay, smiling despite himself at the thought of porridge. 'If he can bring you out of the main house with only the vaguest idea of how to get in or out, a Shepstone burglary should be easy enough.'

An hour and a half later, Sir Bartle Shepstone came downstairs in his best Paisley dressing-gown, a Christmas present from his sister some years before, to meet the most unusual collection of guests. One was obviously dead and was lying on the kitchen table, the blood on his face and jacket drying into strange patterns. Working round the body was Dr Spencer, talking to himself occasionally and writing frequent notes in a small black pocketbook. Powerscourt and Dawnay were drinking tea from his best china cups. There was a smell of burning toast in the air.

'Sir Bartle,' Powerscourt began after one moment of shock and silence, perhaps in tribute to the dead man, 'may I apologise for our early arrival. Major Dawnay, you know. This is Dr Spencer whom I presume you also know. This was Lord Lancaster.' He pointed to the kitchen table. 'We found him in the forest a few hours ago. Dr Spencer is carrying out the normal medical inquiries at a time like this. We think he may have committed suicide.'

Sir Bartle Shepstone gathered his dressing-gown around him and surveyed the field of battle.

'Quite so, Lord Powerscourt, quite so. Good morning, gentlemen. I presume you have brought Lord Lancaster here because you felt the main house was out of bounds.'

'On this of all days, we did,' Powerscourt replied, wondering precisely how Shepstone had won his Victoria Cross. 'Major Dawnay and I felt the house with all its sorrow was not the place for another cadaver.'

'Quite so. Quite so,' said Sir Bartle. 'I think I shall get dressed now. Any chance of a cup of tea?'

11

Suter called them to attention in Sandringham House two hours later, Sir Bartle Shepstone looking completely unperturbed by the strange invasion of his house earlier that day, Dawnay looking elegant in a discreet tweed suit. Rosebery had reappeared from London in a dark blue pinstripe. A footman brought an envelope for Powerscourt, who stuffed it absent-mindedly into his pocket.

Powerscourt was peering idly out of the great windows where rain, sometimes sleet, was washing away the snow of previous days. Occasional parcels of snow and ice from the roof were tumbling on to the Sandringham lawns. Some of the evidence might be washed away on the roof. The rest would melt on the grass.

'I think we should begin with a short moment of silence for Lord Lancaster,' said Suter at his most sanctimonious. 'If he had not come to this house, from friendship and from duty, maybe death would not have called him away.'

Suter bowed his head. Shepstone crossed himself slowly and mouthed what looked to Powerscourt like the Lord's Prayer. Dawnay looked resolutely at the carpet, eyes open, lips not moving. Maybe he's lost his faith, thought Powerscourt, fresh interest developing in the efficient Major. Rosebery looked impassive. Powerscourt himself scurried through the Nunc Dimittis.

'I turn now to the arrangements for this morning.' Suter returned to Private Secretary mode. 'At 8.30 I propose to bring the members of the family into Prince Eddy's room. This will be

111

for what could be described as the last vigil. Those present will be described in their positions in tomorrow morning's newspapers. All those involved have given their consent.'

'I'm afraid that was my idea.' Dawnay, the unbeliever, spoke apologetically. 'For the lie to stick, I felt we had to conform as closely as possible to the events that would have occurred if the lie were true, if you see what I mean.'

Sir Bartle came to his rescue, his white beard looking more than ever like that of some Old Testament prophet.

'I am sure you are right, Dawnay.' The prophet shall speak to the unbeliever, thought Powerscourt. 'If Prince Eddy were really dying, all the members of the family would gather round his bed for his last hours. For the final vigil. I am not sure myself that I should wish to be surrounded by all the members of my family as I passed away, but there it is. That is undoubtedly what this family would do.'

Private Secretary, Comptroller of the Household and the ubiquitous Major Dawnay departed to the chamber of death on the upper floor.

'Charades, my dear Francis.' Rosebery sounded weary. 'They're going to play charades upstairs over that poor boy's last moments. This family are very good at them. They're just going to have another round.' Rosebery had taken up his favourite position, leaning on the mantelpiece, his legs crossed in front of the fire. 'Charades are their life after all. Their whole existence is one long protracted game of charades. They spend their time dressing up, quite literally in the case of the Prince of Wales with his scores and scores of uniforms. Dressing up defines who you are. When you have on that uniform, be it Colonel of the Guards or the weeping widow in black, everybody knows what you are. Everybody knows who you are. So do you. As long as you enter the part with vigour, as they will, no doubt, this morning, all will be well. Royalty's on parade, it's time for charades – play up and play the game.

'But come, Francis,' Rosebery tore himself away from Royal Charades, 'what does our postman friend bring you this morning? Is the death toll about to rise yet again?'

Powerscourt suddenly remembered the letter in his pocket. It was simply addressed. Lord Francis Powerscourt, Sandringham

House. Powerscourt opened the envelope carefully. The letter was written on Sandringham House notepaper.

Dear Lord Powerscourt,
By the time you read this, I shall be dead. I am sorry for all the trouble I am causing to my family and friends and to yourself.

I am sure you will come to understand that I had no choice. I could do no other.

Semper Fidelis.

Lancaster

Powerscourt read the letter twice and handed it to Rosebery. He could see in his mind the tall young man, hair blowing in the wind, walking alongside him on that blustery beach at Hunstanton two days before. He heard the cries of the gulls. He saw again the look of supplication in Lancaster's eyes as he told him about the smashed picture on the floor. He imagined a solemn younger version of Lancaster – twelve years old, had he said? – reciting a section of Byron's *Childe Harold* to his school. Lancaster himself had joined the ranks of those who would not come back:

'the unreturning brave, – alas!
Ere evening to be trodden like the grass.'

'How tragic, how tragic,' said Rosebery, handing the letter back to his friend.

Upstairs, Sir Bartle Shepstone smoothed out his paper and began to read, in a firm steady voice.

'"*The Times*, 15th January 1892. We have received from General Sir Bartle Shepstone, Comptroller and Treasurer of the Household, the following description of the Duke's last hours and death:

'"'Sandringham, Norfolk, Thursday, 14th January 1892. After the issue of the evening report of the 13th relating to His Royal Highness the Duke of Clarence and Avondale there was a

113

decided improvement in his condition, which continued up to 2 a.m. on the 14th, and a reassuring message was sent to the Queen at midnight. At 2 a.m.," ' Shepstone paused in his reading to let the time sink in, ' "serious collapse came on which threatened to be immediately fatal; and the members of the Royal Family were summoned to his bedside." '

'Semper Fidelis, Powerscourt, Semper Fidelis,' repeated Rosebery. 'Is that the motto of his family or of his regiment?'

'It could be either,' said Powerscourt, 'but I don't think he means it in quite that sense.' He glanced again at the letter as if it might have more to say. 'I suspect it means what it says. Forever Faithful, Always True, Always Loyal. But it could mean loyalty or faith to almost anybody, don't you see? Did he mean faithful to Prince Eddy because he knew why he was killed and could not say? Did he know that dark secret in Eddy's past which led to his bloody demise? Quite possibly he did. Then again, did it mean that he knew the dark secret and dared not speak of it through loyalty? Was he being faithful to the good name of the Royal Family? Was he being faithful to the nation, loyal to his country?

'Or, look at it another way, Rosebery, did he know who the murderer was? Or what motive the murderer had for killing Eddy? Was he shielding his friend, the murderer? Semper Fidelis, Forever Faithful, always loyal to his friend?'

' "The Reverend F. A. J. Hervey, domestic chaplain to the Prince of Wales, was therefore sent for, and read the prayers for the dying in the presence of the assembled family. His Royal Highness gradually sank, and expired peacefully about 9.10 a.m." '

Outside the small window there were noises of manoeuvre on the gravel. A group of horsemen were practising with an empty gun carriage, the last bier for the dead man on his final journey from Sandringham, through the Norwich Gates, down to the royal station at Wolferton, on to Datchet station and the Chapel of St George at Windsor. At nine o'clock the royal party in Prince Eddy's bedroom began their last separate prayers for the dead.

'At present,' Powerscourt looked both defiant and very determined to Rosebery, like one who has taken up a great challenge and will not let it go, 'I do not know what Semper Fidelis meant when Lancaster wrote it. The minds of those about to commit suicide are seldom at their clearest. But I knew him slightly, I know his family slightly. Before this sorry affair is over, I am going to find out the answer. To his death and to his memory, I too shall be Semper Fidelis.'

In the nation's capital the first news of the death of the heir presumptive reached the Mansion House.

'Our beloved son passed away this morning. Albert Edward'

The Great Bell of St Paul's tolled its sad message across the city. As the Royal Family began to shuffle from the bedroom, other messages followed down the telegraph lines to London.

'Sandringham, 9.08 a.m. A change for the worse has taken place, and fear not much hope. Shepstone.'

'Sandringham, 9.35 a.m. His Royal Highness passed away at about 9.10 this morning. Shepstone.'

Part Three

The Journey to Venice

12

Lord Francis Powerscourt was staring intently at the Basin of St Mark, crowded with the shipping of Venice. One whole wall of the great drawing-room of his house at Rokesley Hall was covered with reproductions of Venetian canvases, limpid panoramas of the Serenissima by Canaletto, the solemn oligarchy of fifteenth-century Venice, painted by Gentile Bellini, clad in their most resplendent robes, parading round St Mark's Square in honour of a new Doge.

Here Powerscourt found comfort. Here he could relax. Eight days in Sandringham had left him drained, as if he had been living in a hothouse. A Hothouse of Death where the inmates came to worship, feeding off the rituals and the details of doom. He had walked for one whole day since his return to Northamptonshire, through the great Rockingham forest and across his fields to Fotheringhay. Now at last he could talk to Lord Johnny Fitzgerald in peace.

Lord Johnny had replaced the beer of King's Lynn with two bottles of Nuits St Georges. Fine burgundy, he assured Powerscourt, is a powerful stimulant to thought.

'Johnny . . .' Powerscourt tore himself away from his Venetian daydream, wondering if the nobles processing around Piazza San Marco were as difficult to deal with as the British Royal Family. 'It's time to take stock.'

'I've been thinking about this murder too, Francis. I don't feel we have very much to go on. Did those old miseries ever let you talk to members of the family about what happened on the night he was killed?'

'There are many old miseries up there, Johnny. The particular old misery you are referring to on this occasion is Sir William Suter, Housemaster of Sandringham.'

Powerscourt remembered bitterly his entreaties to the Private Secretary. If he was meant to investigate, then surely he must be allowed to ask a few questions. Did they want him to attempt to solve this terrible crime or not? Did they have any idea of how difficult his task was when he had no information to go on?

It was a waste of time. Sir William assured him that nobody had heard anything at all unusual, that he need not bother himself with inquiries that would lead him nowhere and cause needless offence to members of a family under severe strain.

'Do you think they had anything to hide? Could they have been protecting one of their own? Was that why they wouldn't talk?' Lord Johnny had finished his business with the corkscrew and was eyeing a rich ruby glass of Nuits St Georges.

'They may have. They may well have. But I don't think we should start there. Now then, Johnny, let's go right back to the beginning. Who might want to kill Prince Eddy, Duke of Clarence and Avondale?'

'All right, all right, let's think about motives.' Fitzgerald took a sip of wine to aid his mental processes. 'Suppose you're the Government. I don't mean . any particular minister, just the Government in general. There's Victoria, entombed in black in Windsor or Osborne or Balmoral or wherever it is in perpetual mourning for Albert and John Brown. She's not going to last much longer. Then they get Edward on the throne. King Tum Tum himself.'

Powerscourt wondered if the burgundy had the power to turn its consumers into republicans, the tricolour exported not by force of arms but by dusty bottles and Premier Crus.

'Edward VII, he'll be, won't he?' Lord Johnny went on. 'I think they could probably cope with him all right. The Government, I mean. They'll just invent lots of ceremonial stuff so he can dress up all the time. But look what they get then on the throne of England. They get that listless homosexual half-wit. Or they would have got him. You're not going to be very happy as Prime Minister or Foreign Secretary going in to bat for Britain with that clown at the top of the order. So why not get rid of

120

him now? How's that?' Johnny Fitzgerald looked pleased with himself, as if he had just clean bowled an opening batsman facing his first ball.

'Perhaps they did, Johnny. That's not bad at all. One of those equerries, in the pay of one of those secret departments Shepstone told me about, sets off to Sandringham to save the nation. I think it's entirely possible. Only one thing makes me wonder about it.'

'What's that, Francis, you're not going to tell me that Governments suffer from fits of morality?'

'Certainly not,' Powerscourt laughed. 'But I just wonder about time scales. Different people have different time scales, I think. If you're the Royals, Rosebery tells me, you have a very long time scale indeed, even longer than aristocrats. You think of the survival of your house, the crown on each succeeding head, twenty, fifty years into the future.

'But if you're the Government, you have a very short time scale. You don't think much beyond the next election. Eddy wasn't going to be a real problem until he came to the throne, and that would have been some time away, way beyond the next time the country goes to the polls. That's why I don't think it very likely the Government did it. But it's not impossible.'

'Government as twenty to one outsiders in the Prince Eddy Memorial Stakes, then.' Lord Johnny drew his fingers into a pinnacle and eyed them carefully. 'Family Time now,' he said cheerfully. 'Happy Families. Royal Families. Family Life. Family Death. Which of his relations might want to get rid of him? Let's begin with Victoria.'

Lord Johnny moved the pinnacle of his fingertips to a crown above his head. 'You're the Queen. You're the Empress, first emperor in Britain since the Romans. You're Victoria, waterfalls, whole swathes of Australia, railway stations named after you. You want your family to remain on the throne for ever. You have grave doubts about our earlier friend Edward King Tum Tum on the throne, your throne. But think of the doubts you must have about his eldest son.

'Think of them, Francis. All her life Victoria has been plagued by the memory of her wicked uncles, Uncle Clarence – note the name, my friend – with his ten illegitimate children, that awful old rake Uncle Cumberland. Then there was Uncle King, Uncle George IV with his mistresses and his debauchery in that Brighton Pavilion and everywhere else. And here is her grandson, Grandson Clarence, who seems to combine the vices of all of them with a few extra ones of his own.

'So what do you do? You harden your heart, you put out the word, very quietly, that the family would be better off without him, and you climb happily into deep mourning when you hear of his passing.'

'You should have been a barrister, Johnny. Case for the Prosecution against Her Majesty completed. How about the case against the father?'

Lord Johnny poured the last of the first bottle into his glass and held it up to the light. 'The Prince of Wales? I think that's easier still. Remember the blackmail that started all this business off? Let's suppose the blackmailer isn't putting the squeeze on because of something the Prince of Wales has done, but for something his son has done. The best way to get rid of the blackmailer is to get rid of Eddy – then there's nothing left for him to be blackmailed about. Didn't you tell me that the father wanted him out of the country for two years on some cultural and political tour of Europe, a sort of nineteenth-century Rake's Progress? When he couldn't get his way that way, then he just got rid of him. Now then, your turn. What do you say to the mother, Francis?'

'I will not hear a word said against Princess Alexandra,' said Powerscourt primly.' 'I regard her as above suspicion.'

'Are you falling a little bit in love with the Sea King's daughter from over the sea, Francis?'

'I think everybody falls a little bit in love with her, Johnny. She's just that sort of person.'

'I see.' Lord Johnny looked very grave. 'And shall I have to inform Lady Lucy of this sad development? I am sure it would break her heart, Francis. And she speaks so highly of you all over London town.'

Powerscourt made as if to throw a cushion at his friend. 'Leave Lady Lucy out of it. That is a private matter.' He blushed a deep red.

'What can you say of the brother, Johnny, – I give the sisters exemption from suspicion, along with their mother.'

'The brother, the brother . . .' Fitzgerald looked very thoughtful, as if he thought a bet on the brother might be a sound investment. 'He's a very solid sort of chap, isn't he. Reliable, a bit dull, our George, not very much there in the brains department. I seem to remember you telling me he doesn't like change. At his age, for God's sake. What is he, twenty-five? But you would have to say one thing for that sort of character. He's absolutely perfectly fitted for the throne. Stupid, boring, not likely to cause anybody any trouble, he's an ideal king, the perfect monarch. So, either the conspirators, whoever they might be, know that they have the perfect substitute for the appalling Clarence. Or the substitute himself is the plot, and nips next door to slit his brother's throat. That's easy.'

'I'm sure you could make out a case for almost anybody in Norfolk wielding the knife, Johnny, in this sort of form. Let me try this out on you.'

Powerscourt walked to the window and drew back the curtains. The night was full of stars. Powerscourt suddenly remembered he hadn't seen a single star all the time he was at Sandringham, only clouds and the ever-falling snow.

He looked at the tombstones in his graveyard, watching through another night. He had remembered most of the names and the inscriptions by now, after ten years in the house: Albert George Mason, Mary Mason, his wife, William their son, departed this life aged five years, Charlotte their daughter, gone to her Father in heaven after seven. And mine eyes shall see God. Gone but not forgotten. Suffer the little children to come unto me. For Thine is the Kingdom.

A young fox was perched on top of one of the gravestones, as alert as a guardsman on duty. In the distance, on one of his tenant's barns, an owl hooted into the night.

'I think – no, I am sure,' Powerscourt spoke initially to the gravestones, to those who had departed long before Prince Eddy, 'that the key to the whole mystery lies with the equerries. We know that there were no outsiders, according to William McKenzie. We know, thanks to you, Johnny, that there were no

123

Russians, no murderous Russians I mean. I have to check with the Commissioner of the Metropolitan Police about the Irishmen and the telegraph poles, but I suspect their messages were peaceful. I do not believe any of the servants did it. Not many of them sleep in the house, and those that do are a very long way indeed from Eddy's bedroom.

'But this is the devil of it all, Johnny. Any one of your plausible theories sits happily with the equerries. The Government could have asked one of them to do it, as you suggested. They could have been agents of Queen Victoria, or the Prince of Wales, or even the brother Prince George. Or they could have been the loyal servants of the Crown, anxious to rid it of a future problem, as we said. Or they could have been mixed up with the blackmailing business, in one way or another.

'Good God,' suddenly Powerscourt turned back from the window and his contemplation of the fox. 'You don't suppose that Eddy was the blackmailer, do you, Johnny? Blackmailing his father in the first place, then turning to one of these equerries as well for yet more money? A second helping, or maybe even a third?'

'Eddy the blackmailer? God in heaven, that would make things complicated, wouldn't it? It would certainly explain why nobody wanted to speak to you. They were all too frightened to confess that they have been fingered too. Perhaps he was blackmailing the whole bloody family.'

Powerscourt felt lost. Just when he thought he had advanced his inquiry a little way, it slipped back and fell away. Then he recovered.

'Johnny – have you left any wine in that second bottle? Ah, thank you – even if Eddy is the blackmailer, I think the way forward is clear. And I think it divides into two halves. The first is concerned with the equerries: Lord Henry Lancaster, dead or alive. Harry Radclyffe. Charles Peveril. William Brockham. Lord Edward Gresham. The Honourable Frederick Mortimer.'

'Ten to one on all of them in the Prince Eddy Memorial Stakes.' Fitzgerald the bookmaker was busy with his odds. 'Fifteen to one Queen Victoria. Twenty to one Prince of Wales. Twenty-five to one Prince George. Thirty to one the Government. Fifty to one The Field. Roll up! Roll up!'

'We must investigate the equerries' lives from the cradle to the present day.' Powerscourt declined to take a wager yet. 'We need to find out about every action, every friend, every love affair with man or woman. I feel that my sisters and your relations will prove invaluable allies here. You see, it could be that there were very personal reasons behind Eddy's death. Look at the way he was killed, the picture of his fiancée smashed into small pieces all over the floor. The murderer might have had his own very private motives for the killing. Revenge maybe. Or it could be that the murderer wanted people to think that. The fiancée's picture could be a distraction, a red herring.'

'And the second thing, Francis?' Lord Johnny reckoned that there was at least one glass left in the bottom of the second bottle.

'The second has to do with scandal. Eddy's scandal. He brought some terrible scandal with him to that house last weekend. There may be one or two or even three scandals. I suspect they go back ten or twelve years. That is what the Prince of Wales knows and dare not speak about. That is what Princess Alexandra knows about or fears. And Suter knows that they know something that he doesn't. He is left to guess at what it might be. There are lies and secrets falling over each other to obscure the truth. You see, there was one very strange thing about the way they reacted to Prince Eddy's death. It only struck me yesterday when I was walking back from Fotheringhay in the dusk.'

'What was that, for God's sake?' said Fitzgerald, fascinated by the prospect of new information.

'Just this.' Powerscourt had resumed his place by the window looking over his graveyard. The fox was still on parade. 'Everybody was very sad. Everybody was very upset. But I don't think anybody was surprised. It was as if they had been expecting it.'

That night Powerscourt had another dream. He was in a large children's playroom on the top floor of Sandringham House. There was only one child in the room. It was Prince Eddy. He was sitting on the floor. He was surrounded by copies of *The Times* and the *Illustrated London News*. Prince Eddy was cutting out letters one by one with scissors and a large knife and pasting them on to a page. He smiled happily as he worked.

Letters of blackmail. Blackmail letters. Only when he looked very carefully could Powerscourt see that the knife was dripping with blood.

... I think at this stage that both the normal and the unusual will be of interest. Everyday gossip below stairs as well as the rumours of life above that circulate in all great houses, any suspicion of a secret, any whiff of scandal. In short, my dear James, in this, as in all the inquiries we have undertaken together, please keep your eyes and ears open at all times. I know you will, and I look forward to reading your reports or to hearing them in person if you feel that would be more appropriate.

The old Indian rules apply. Please destroy all correspondence.

Powerscourt

The letter's author was writing at a great hurry in the upstairs drawing-room of his sister's house in St James's Square.

Sudden changes had been occurring in the domestic staff at Sandringham and St James's. Wilfrid Theakston, senior footman for many years at Marlborough House and Sandringham, had been taken ill unexpectedly and was granted indefinite leave of absence. The Prince of Wales' household were fortunate to find a speedy replacement in one James Phillips, senior footman to Lady Pembridge, who happened to be sister-in -law to Lord Francis Powerscourt. Phillips was Powerscourt's man; they had served together in India and in all but one of his investigations since.

Even this change had met with the normal reluctance from Suter and Shepstone. 'Dammit, man, this is like taking a spy into our own house!' Shepstone had protested.

For once Powerscourt had lost patience.

'You would appear to have had a murderer in your house for some days. For all we know he may still be there. I can't see that a pair of eyes and ears below stairs is a matter of much consequence in these circumstances.'

Suter turned red. Shepstone muttered something into his beard. But they had agreed.

Powerscourt had been writing a lot of letters. He wrote to Lord Rosebery asking for names and addresses out of the Government machine. He wrote to the Commissioner of the Metropolitan Police, requesting an interview on a matter of the utmost delicacy. He wrote to the Russian Ambassador. He wrote to the London end of the Irish Office in Dublin, asking for an interview with the senior man engaged in countering terrorism and subversion in that unhappy island. He wrote to Sir William Suter, asking when the equerries at Sandringham at the time of the murder had started their tours of duty. And he wrote to Lady Lucy, accepting an invitation to tea in her little house in Chelsea.

Rosebery was looking very cheerful, seated in the small library at the back of the first floor of the Athenaeum in Pall Mall. The room had no discernible wallpaper, only books. Two dark brown globes sat on either side of the fireplace. A Chinese chess set lay on a table by the window, the game unfinished, White in the ascendant. Powerscourt saw that the Black forces had been reduced to a solitary rook, a couple of pawns and a beleaguered king – all the rest were prisoners, neatly locked up according to importance behind the White lines.

'I've just been spending a great deal of money, Powerscourt,' said Rosebery happily.

Powerscourt wondered how large a sum would constitute a great deal of money in Rosebery's book.

'About £15,000, since I can see you thinking about it!' Rosebery laughed. 'It is a rare library of ancient volumes, many from the Renaissance, that came unexpectedly on to the market in Rome. But come. To more serious business. I have a lot of information for you. First,' Rosebery delved into a folder in front of him, 'here are six of these letters. They're like a blank cheque – you fill in the name and address as you think fit – requesting the recipient to provide all the help and assistance in their power to Lord Francis Powerscourt in the conduct of his current investigation, which is of the highest national importance. They're signed by the Prime Minister in person. I thought that might be going it a bit strong myself, until Salisbury reminded me that somebody had just murdered the heir presumptive to the throne.'

Powerscourt placed the letters solemnly in his pocketbook.

'The man you want to see about the *Britannia*, that naval training ship Prince Eddy and Prince George attended all those years ago, is the Admiralty archivist. He's called Simkins, I think, and he lives in some obscure place in the Admiralty just down the road. He knows you're coming. The man you want to see about the Irish up their telegraph poles is called Knox. He'll be in London tomorrow and will see you in the afternoon – I just thought I would give your own request a bit of a nudge there.'

Rosebery smiled the patronising smile of the man on the inside, helping out a new arrival in the Whitehall jungle.

'Now, if that is all there is for now, my dear Powerscourt, I had better hasten to my bankers. They will not be best pleased if they discover unexpectedly that I have just written a cheque for £15,000.'

13

The waiting area at the Admiralty was the largest Powerscourt had ever seen, enough to hold an entire ship's company. The pictures on the walls, reaching ever higher towards the plastered ceiling, were all of great warships under sail. Not a single vessel was powered by steam, after a mere thirty years still too modern for the First Sea Lord and his lieutenants.

Perhaps, thought Powerscourt, its size was to accommodate all those who waited here in the Navy's great days a hundred years before during the Napoleonic Wars; gun manufacturers anxious to show off their latest cannon, chartmakers with fresh maps of unknown lands, mad inventors with startling new versions of compasses and sextants, orolobes and longitudinal clocks. Here desperate captains with no commands, living on half pay, their uniforms patched by loyal wives and mistresses, loitered in hope of preferment. Here Howe and St Vincent, Collingwood and Nelson had come for their sealed instructions. Here they had planned the twenty-year-long blockade of Napoleon's France. Here they had planned Nelson's funeral, his body brought to the heart of London on its last journey up the River Thames.

'Lord Powerscourt, sir? This way, if you please.'

A solemn porter broke Powerscourt's reverie and led him through the labyrinth to his destination. Powerscourt doubted if he could have found his way out unaided. They climbed staircases with yet more paintings of the age of sail. They went past entire departments labelled Navigation, Gunnery, Engines. At last, at the end of a dark corridor lit by a single skylight, they found the door called Archive.

'Come in, come in. Who are you?'

Everything about the naval archivist was thin. His frame was thin and looked very old, his nose was thin, his long bony fingers were thin. His voice was a thin whine. Even his room was long and thin, like a naval galley; it stretched back for nearly a hundred feet in the gloomy light, files rising towards the roof like midshipmen climbing the top-gallants.

'Mr Simkins, how kind of you to see me. My name is Powerscourt. I believe you are expecting me.'

'Are you writing a book? Most of the people who come here are writing books.' Simkins peered at Powerscourt over his thin spectacles.

'No, I am not writing a book.'

'Biography then. You must be one of these biographers.'

'I'm afraid I am neither of those. I believe you have had a letter about my visit.'

'An article for one of the naval societies perhaps? The history of a particular ship? I don't recall an HMS *Powerscourt* ever gracing the waves, but I could be wrong.'

Powerscourt suspected that Simkins was deaf. The dust had gathered in layers round the edges of his great desk, almost invisible between papers and files from long ago.

'Can't believe they've sent somebody to see me who isn't a historian. First time in thirty years apart from some rum manufacturer from the West Indies who got sent up here by mistake. Letter, did you say? Letter from where? Letter from whom?'

'It's a letter from the Prime Minister's office.'

'Who is the Prime Minister now? I seem to have forgotten.'

Powerscourt wondered if Simkins ever left this office. Maybe he sleeps here as well, he thought, guarding the secrets of the naval past with his bony frame and his peaceful spectacles.

'It's Lord Salisbury, Mr Simkins. Lord Salisbury.'

'I heard you the first time. There's no need to shout.' Like many deaf people Simkins had sudden, unexpected bursts of perfect hearing, like the calm in the eye of the storm. 'Salisbury, you say. Not a naval man, I think. Is he one of those Hatfield Salisburys? Cecils, all that sort of thing?'

It seemed to be easier for the archivist to place the Prime Minister in the sixteenth century rather than the nineteenth.

'The same,' said Powerscourt.

'Here we are. Why didn't you say what you were about at the beginning? Now then. I see what you are after.' Simkins peered over his spectacles once again. 'You are a historian after all. You want to know the names of the officers commanding HMS *Britannia*, naval training ship, in 1878, 1879, and the captain and officers of the vessel *Bacchante* which took the two young Princes round the world. Damned strange name for a ship, the *Bacchante*, don't you think, Lord Powerscourt? Weren't the original Bacchantes lusty maidens with very few clothes on who danced about in the Greek islands getting drunk and worse?'

'I believe they were. Maybe it referred to the elegant way the ship danced across the water,' said Powerscourt feebly.

'I knew it. I knew it.' Simkins had risen from his chair and looked round the room.

'Other people lose their spectacles all the time. I keep losing my steps. My steps to get up there to the top row of my files. Now where can they have got to?'

'There is a pair of steps leaning behind that revolving bookcase,' Powerscourt suggested hesitantly, unsure how many pairs of steps might be in play.

'No good. Too short. Couldn't reach.'

Powerscourt wondered if his mission was about to fail for want of a tall pair of steps. He looked about more keenly. 'I think that might be a pair over there in the corner.'

'Which corner?' Simkins turned round quickly. 'Ah, this corner. Now we are in business, Lord Powerscourt.'

Simkins placed the rickety steps against a wall and began to climb. 'My filing system has become more confusing as the years pass. More confusing to me, I mean. I began filing everything under the name of the ship many years ago. By the time I got to F for *Fearless* I realised that wasn't going to work. Tried filing it all alphabetically after that. No good, that only got as far as D for Denmark. Then I tried filing under the name of the First Sea Lord, but that didn't seem to work either. Are you any good at filing, Lord Powerscourt?'

'Hopeless Mr Simkins, absolutely hopeless.'

'Here we are.' Simkins tottered uncertainly down his steps. 'We're fortunate that both *Bacchante* and *Britannia* begin with B.

If they'd begun with T or V you might have had to come back next month. Now then.' Simkins filleted the first file expertly. '*Britannia*. 1876–1879. Captain Williams. He didn't last very long – most of them stay there for years and years... My goodness me. My goodness me.'

Simkins looked up at Powerscourt with new respect. 'You might be on to something here. For your book, I mean. Every single officer on board left at the same time as Captain Williams. Every single last one of them.'

'What does that suggest to your expert eye, Mr Simkins?'

'Clear-out. I've never seen anything like it. There wasn't a war on in 1879, was there?'

Powerscourt remembered that W for War had never featured in the Simkins filing system. He wondered if entire conflicts could go unnoticed up here. What would happen to a war in Zululand? Or Zanzibar?

'I don't believe there was.'

'Don't like the look of it. Don't like the look of it at all. Could have been a court martial. Could have been a scandal. But the whole thing was kept very quiet. One day they were all there. Next day they were all gone. That'll be a good chapter for your book.'

Simkins handed Powerscourt a single sheet of paper. 'There's the names of all the officers and the last addresses we have for them. It should be up to date. And here are the names of the officers on the *Bacchante*. Hello, hello. You do seem to pick them, Lord Powerscourt. This file has four stars on it.'

'Four stars? What on earth does that mean?'

'I'm trying to remember. I invented this star system over thirty years ago.' The archivist looked hopelessly around his long thin room, as though he might have written the key to the stars in the surrounding dust. 'Got it. Knew I wouldn't forget. Memory goes on the blink every now and then, rather like these new steam engines on the ships if you ask me, then it comes back. Where was I?'

'Four stars?' Powerscourt prompted gently.

'Four stars? Four stars? Of course. That means two things. It means refer to the Prime Minister's office before release. And that further files are held in other Government Departments.'

Powerscourt's heart sank as he contemplated a guided tour of the archivists of Whitehall, each one possibly more eccentric than the one before.

'That means you can't have those names. The ones from the *Bacchante*.'

'But my letter comes from the Prime Minister's office in the first place.'

'What letter? Did you say you had a letter? Who did you say the Prime Minister was? I've forgotten it again.'

'My letter comes from the office of Lord Salisbury, the Prime Minister.'

'The Hatfield person?'

'Correct.'

'Why didn't you say so? Of course you must have these names. Forgive me the things I have forgotten.'

'Not at all, Mr Simkins. I am most grateful to you.'

As he left, Powerscourt was sent away with best wishes for the success of his book. Further messages followed him down the narrow passageway. The archivist's parting remark pursued him down the stairs: 'Make sure you get yourself a good filing system for your book. Never quite managed it myself.'

The strange fact only struck Powerscourt when he was underground. He reckoned his train was only a couple of hundred yards from Sloane Square when it shuddered to a halt. He took out the list of officers from HMS *Britannia* and gazed with dismay at Simkins' handwriting. It was extremely small, written with a very thin nib.

Captain John Williams, Station Road, Amble, Northumberland. Amble. Amble. Where the hell was Amble? Then it came to him. A castle. A castle by the sea, a Percy castle, a Hotspur castle and the River Coquet twisting its way to the sea and a small fishing village called Amble. Bloody miles from anywhere.

Lieutenant James Forrest, Sea View, Greystones, Co. Dublin. Other side of the Irish Sea.

Lieutenant Jack Dunston, Borth Road, Aberystwyth. Other side of the Welsh Mountains.

Lieutenant Albert Squires, The Scores, St Andrews. Other side of the Scottish border. Christ, it's going to be like a tour of the extremities of Britain, Powerscourt thought bitterly, if I have to go and see all this lot. And they're all by the sea, he noticed, for yachts and boats and memories of the Navy.

And then it struck him. Surely, if they had been working in Dartmouth, Devon, they would have lived near Dartmouth. That's what most people would have done. You would have thought that one, or maybe two of them, would have stayed down there. After all, most naval people lived in a long sweep from Hampshire to Cornwall to be near the great ports and naval establishments on the south coast. But they'd all gone. Every single one of them. It was as if they had fled. Or been told to flee. In disgrace? In shame? In exile? They'd fled to places as far away from Dartmouth as they could possibly get.

The train resumed its fitful journey into Sloane Square. Powerscourt clutched his small parcel and set off for Markham Square, home, at No. 25, to Lady Lucy Hamilton.

'Lady Lucy, I'm so sorry I'm late. The trains, the trains . . .' He held out his hands in supplication and excuse.

Lady Lucy smiled, a secret sort of smile for Powerscourt. 'You'd better have some tea,' she said, pointing to a great tray laden with sandwiches on the table in her upstairs drawing-room. Powerscourt thought he had never seen so many sandwiches for two people. There were brown ones, white ones, sandwiches with crusts, sandwiches without, ones with little sprigs of greenery on the top. Did she think he was a giant or something, with a giant's appetite? Were they to embark on some sandwich eating competition, all proceeds to the poor and needy?

'I thought,' she said defensively, 'that Robert should join us. He was going to bring a friend but his friend isn't allowed out at the moment.'

'Is he ill – the friend, I mean?'

'Not exactly, no. Something to do with broken windows, I think.'

'Ah,' said Powerscourt solemnly, 'so he's temporarily confined to barracks. Good behaviour ensures parole at a later stage.'

'Exactly so.' Lady Lucy smiled her smile again. 'But even at seven years old they can eat an incredible number of sandwiches. Robert will just have to manage as best as he can on his own.'

A small face peeped nervously round the door. The face had a small nose, blue eyes like his mother and a shock of fair hair. The hair looked as though Robert had been attempting, without success, to get it into some sort of order before grown-up tea.

'Robert, darling, come and meet Lord Francis Powerscourt. Robert, Lord Francis, Lord Francis, Robert.'

Lady Lucy's two males shook hands solemnly like Wellington and Blucher meeting at the end of Waterloo.

'Sandwich, Robert? Sandwich, Lord Francis? Let me pour some tea.'

It was true, Powerscourt thought, about the sandwiches. The great piles began to dissolve rapidly.

'I've brought you a sort of present, Robert,' said Powerscourt between mouthfuls. 'I don't know if it'll be all right.' Lady Lucy suddenly remembered that Powerscourt was well supplied with a cricket team of nephews of his own. She felt sure that he would have a reasonable idea of what a Robert might like. Some men were completely hopeless. A friend of her father's had presented him recently with the complete works of Ovid. Ovid!

'It's a sort of boat thing,' said Powerscourt, struggling with the wrapping. He had bought it in the shop of temptation, as he referred to the place where he had spent so much money on the Voltigeurs and the Imperial Guard for his nephews.

It was a small yacht, with two sails, perfect rigging so you could adjust everything, a tiny rudder, polished wooden decks.

'Wow! Wow!' said its new owner, taking delivery of the vessel into his own hands. 'Thank you very much. Thank you so much.'

His mother breathed a small sigh of relief. Forgotten thank yous, she knew, were sometimes hard to forgive.

'Does it sort of go? Does it move?' Robert was turning it over in his hands with great care.

'It does. The man in the shop promised me it sails very well. Maybe you could try it out in the bath?'

'But there isn't any wind in the bath. Not in my bath anyway.' Robert looked solemnly at Powerscourt as if he might be the secret owner of force five sou'westerlies blowing through his bathroom.

'Maybe you could try bellows,' said Powerscourt, looking at a very ornate pair in Lady Lucy's grate.

'Wouldn't that make a lot of mess? The soot might get all over the sails,' said Robert doubtfully. 'And I'm not sure Mama would like that. Would you, Mama?' Robert looked as if he thought bellows in the bath might produce the same result as his friend's broken windows. Not allowed out, confined to barracks.

'The Round Pond in Kensington Gardens. That's where the man in the shop said it would do very well.' Powerscourt was trying to extricate himself from bellows and soot.

Lady Lucy had a vision, of the three of them going every Sunday afternoon to the Round Pond, Robert racing away through the trees, herself and Powerscourt – were they arm in arm, she wondered? – the boat sailing proudly across the waters.

'My only worry about that,' said her consort, unaware of this weekly pilgrimage, 'is that the boat might get lost. It might get stuck, I mean.'

'What do you mean, stuck?' said Robert anxiously.

'Well, I mean, it might sail out as far as the middle, and not come back again. Somebody would have to wade out and get it.'

'Lord Francis, Lord Francis, are you hopelessly impractical or what?' said Lady Lucy, fresh from her walk with her males.

'Well, I am as it happens. Hopelessly impractical I mean. Am I wrong about the boat?'

'Don't you see, if there is enough wind to take it to the middle, the wind will keep it going to the other side. Isn't that right, Robert?'

'Because it's round, you mean.' Robert was thinking hard. 'You just have to walk round to the other side. It wouldn't get lost at all. Or I don't think it would.'

'Anyway, Lord Francis, you must come and see us one weekend and we can make an expedition to the Round Pond. I quite like Kensington Gardens anyway.'

Powerscourt smiled. 'That would be delightful. But, Robert, before your ship makes its maiden voyage you will have to give it a name. What are you going to call it?'

'I don't know yet. I'll have to think about it. Can I take the ship up to my room now, Mama? I need to work out where to put it.'

'Of course, Robert, off you go.'

'What a charming son, you have, Lady Lucy.' Powerscourt had finished his tea and was looking with awe at the depleted sandwiches.

Lady Lucy blushed a fetching shade of pink. 'Thank you, Lord Francis, thank you so much. But come, some more tea?'

'Lady Lucy, please forgive me. I arrive late. I must leave early. It has nothing, I assure you, to do with the company. I could happily sit here for the rest of the evening. But I have another appointment I cannot break.'

'Not more tea?' Lady Lucy had a sudden vision of another, different, Lady Lucy pouring out cups of Earl Grey and affection for Lord Francis Powerscourt.

Powerscourt laughed. 'No, not more tea. I have to see the Commissioner of the Metropolitan Police.'

'Lord Francis, you're not in trouble, are you?'

'My dear Lady Lucy, of course I'm not in trouble. It's just something I am working on at the moment.'

'Will you tell me about your work, one day? If you can, that is.'

'Of course I will. But, if I don't go now, I shall be late and then they probably will arrest me.'

Powerscourt climbed into his coat and paused by the front door to say goodbye. Lady Lucy stood beside him.

'Thank you so much for tea, Lady Lucy. I shall write to you about our next meeting.'

'I hope it will be soon, Lord Francis.' She leaned forward and brushed a speck of dust from his collar. Well, she thought there had been a speck of dust there.

'Goodbye.' Powerscourt stepped reluctantly into the night.

'Goodbye.' Lady Lucy watched him go. What was that he had said? 'I could happily sit here for the rest of the evening.' She smiled and closed the door.

As he climbed into his cab Powerscourt thought that Lady Lucy would be a good name for the boat. Lovely lines. Graceful. Elegant.

He leant forward to give the driver his destination. 'Could you take me to Scotland Yard? Thank you so much.'

'My dear Lord Powerscourt, how very nice to see you again!'

The Commissioner of the Metropolitan Police was tall and thin, with the upright bearing of the former Guardsman. He must be nearing retirement age by now, thought Powerscourt, he's been in this impossible job for years and years.

'Sir John, it is a pleasure to meet you again.'

'How long since our last encounter?' Sir John was counting the years off on his fingers. 'Five, or is it six?'

'I fear it is seven now. None of us is getting any younger.'

In 1885 Powerscourt had been working on a particularly unpleasant case and had to call on the assistance of the Metropolitan Police Force. Powerscourt had treated them with great courtesy, with tact and, he hoped, with charm. They in their turn had done everything in their power to help him. And at the end of the case, over a very fine dinner in his club, the Commissioner had promised Powerscourt that if ever he needed help in the future, all he had to do was to ask.

'I need some assistance, Sir John. I have come to throw myself on the mercy of your force once again.'

'What can we do to help?' The Commissioner opened his hands wide on the table in front of him. Powerscourt saw that on the walls of his office there were four huge maps of London, divided into North, South, East and West. On each map were small red circles, presumably denoting the scenes of recent crimes. East London is looking particularly red this evening, he thought, parts of it almost obliterated by the circles.

'Two questions, if I may. The first relates to blackmail. And you will not be surprised to learn,' Powerscourt rose from his chair and stood by the great map of West London, 'that we are talking about what is known as Society, living here,' he pointed to London's most fashionable and expensive quarter, 'in this area of Mayfair and Belgravia. Not many of your red blobs here, I see.'

'Crime is not for the few who are rich, most of the time. They don't need to bother. It is London's more numerous poor who have to resort to it, either to find enough money to live on, or they are fuelled by drink. So many of our cases in this red area over here,' he pointed a sad finger at the reprobate East End, 'are related to drink.'

Powerscourt remembered that Sir John was the treasurer of the local church in his little village in Surrey where most of the inhabitants did not know of his occupation and thought he worked in a bank. He also remembered, though he could not recall where this information came from, that Sir John painted rather gruesome watercolours of the Thames in his spare time.

'Blackmail in Belgravia, as the headline writers might put it,' Powerscourt went on with a smile. 'What I want to know is this, Sir John. Do you have any records in recent years of a black-mailer, either an insider or an outsider, operating in what is called Society? And if there is such a man, is there any sugges-tion that he may be at work now?'

Sir John was worried about Powerscourt's eyes. There was some strain, some worry there behind and beyond the particular requests he was making. He remembered those eyes from before, always courageous, always curious, always delighting in the hunt for the truth.

'My second query is more delicate yet. It concerns London's homosexual fraternity, the rich ones again. I understand that they have recently purchased a house by the river between Hammersmith and Chiswick where they may go about their business in peace. Is there any evidence of blackmail being carried out there, or any other criminal activities?'

'We know about that house, we've known about it for some time.' Sir John looked carefully at his map of West London as if the mark of Cain might have suddenly appeared over Chiswick. 'We find it easier to leave those people alone as my officers find any investigation so very distasteful.'

Sir John stared intently at London's West End on his map. 'How soon would you like this information, Lord Powerscourt? I do not have to tell you that we shall begin work as soon as we can.'

'I have to go on a long journey the day after tomorrow.'

Powerscourt looked for railway stations on the maps. 'I may be away for some time. Could I call on you again in about ten days' time?'

'Of course you can. That will be a pleasure.'

After packing Powerscourt into yet another cab, the Commissioner watched him go, his coat pulled tightly round him in the fog. I'll say he's going on a journey, he said to himself, as Powerscourt's cab disappeared round the corner, a journey of discovery. God help him on his way, the Commissioner thought, returning to contemplation of his city, laid out in four maps across his wall, criminal red spattered all across the East End.

14

There were primroses everywhere, plaster primroses, stucco primroses. Were those marble primroses? Powerscourt had never really noticed them before. A field of artificial primroses surrounded the London home of Archibald Philip Primrose, fifth Earl of Rosebery. Now he thought about it he remembered seeing Rosebery once in evening dress, a pair of cuff links adorned with golden primroses glittering among the candles.

'Lord Powerscourt. Good morning to you. I regret to have to inform you that my master is not at home. He should return presently, if Your Lordship would care to wait.'

William Leith, Rosebery's butler, was a short square man with a gloomy expression like an undertaker off duty. Powerscourt remembered Rosebery once getting rid of a butler who was taller than himself. 'Couldn't stand the fellow looking down at me all the time,' he had complained, 'made me feel like a fag at Eton.'

'It was not Lord Rosebery that I wished to speak to on this occasion,' said Powerscourt, stepping into the hall.

'Indeed, my lord.' Leith deftly removed Powerscourt's coat and hat.

'I need some advice from you, Leith.'

'Indeed, my lord.' Leith deposited the coat in a vestibule off the hall.

'I have to go on a long train journey, or journeys. I am not sure yet how many journeys.'

'Indeed, my lord.' A flicker of interest, indeed pleasure, crossed Leith's face. Rosebery, in his more frivolous moments, referred to Leith as the Traveller's Friend. He had a prodigious memory for the train timetables of Britain, an encyclopedic knowledge of the routes across the Continent of Europe. Rosebery believed he had recently purchased volumes of railway information about America and Africa. 'If you want to get to Vienna without going through Germany, or if you need to reach Brindisi or Berlin in a hurry, Leith is your man. What he doesn't know, he looks up. What he can't look up, he finds out by devious means. He may have his own secret agents in Thomas Cook and the Compagnie of Wagon-Lits. I believe his library of railway timetables may one day be more valuable than my own humble collections.'

'Perhaps Your Lordship would like to step this way. My lord.' Leith ushered Powerscourt into his office half-way down the stairs into the basement.

I'm in the Holy of Holies, thought Powerscourt. Now I get to see the Ark of the Covenant itself. I wonder if Rosebery has ever been in here. Two walls were covered with books of timetables. The other two had railway maps of Britain and Europe, many places marked with Leith's microscopic writing.

'St Andrews in Scotland. Amble in Northumberland. Aberystwyth in Wales. Greystones, County Dublin, in Ireland. Those are the places I need to get to. I may only need to go to one of them if I find what I am looking for on the first journey. Or I may have to go to them all.'

'Indeed, my lord. Your Lordship has been given a list of difficult destinations.' Leith pulled a couple of volumes from his shelves. 'Greystones, my lord. I fear it may be in County Wicklow rather than in County Dublin. No matter.'

Scarcely pausing to consult his library, Leith fixed his eyes on the ceiling, his face a smile of pleasure. The lights in front of him in his driver's cab were green, the green flag waved in his mind and he was off.

'Evening train to Liverpool, my lord. Euston. I would suggest Your Lordship takes the 3.30 as it is less crowded than its successors. Night boat to Dublin or Kingstown, preferably Kingstown. Arrives 7.30 in the morning. Local service every half an hour, stops at Greystones. I feel Your Lordship should be able to catch the 7.45.

'Amble is easier, my lord. Express to Edinburgh, stopping at Morpeth. My Lordship and I travel that line regularly. The ten o'clock from King's Cross is the fastest. Cab to Amble, not very far. Or irregular local service to Warkworth. Very infrequent, my lord.

'Aberystwyth, 9.15 from Euston, change at Birmingham and change again at Ludlow. Very slow journey from there, my lord. Very slow. Stopping train.' Leith looked down sadly as though stopping trains were a cross he had to bear. 'Or you could take the 9.20 express to Cardiff. Paddington, I fear. Change at Cardiff on to the 4.15 North Wales connection. Very slow again. Mountains, my lord.

'St Andrews, same train from Euston as for Amble, my lord. Continue to Edinburgh Waverley and change there. The eight o'clock from King's Cross would enable you to catch the seven o'clock non-stop service to St Andrews.

'Or, my lord,' Leith, like his trains, was drawing to a halt, 'you could circumvent all those problems of changes and connection by taking a special.'

'A special, Leith?'

'Indeed, my lord. A special train. My Lordship takes them frequently. You simply hire one train and it takes you everywhere you want to go.' Leith's face took on a rapturous expression as if he wished his last journey to be taken in a special, non-stop express to St Peter's railway station.

'I don't feel a special would be appropriate on this occasion.' Powerscourt could sense Leith's disappointment, the funeral director's look swiftly obliterating the glory of the special. 'But I shall certainly bear it in mind for future occasions.'

'Indeed, my lord. I have written down all the relevant details, times and so on, for Your Lordship. Is there anything else I can tell Your Lordship about these trains?' Leith contrived to look impassive and hopeful at the same time.

'Only this, Leith. Let us assume that one journey may suffice. Which of those places is the easiest to get to?'

'The easiest to get to, my lord? There can be little doubt of that. Their engines are newer than most, my lord. Their carriages are better upholstered than most.' Leith shuddered at the memory of some badly upholstered seats, his master's fury echoing down the train. 'They are usually punctual. Amble, my lord, is by far the easiest place to reach, if that fits in with Your Lordship's plans.'

'Indeed it does. I am most grateful to you, most grateful.'

Powerscourt wondered if the Russian Ambassador would serve him tea in a samovar. He did not. He served the finest Indian tea in the finest Meissen china.

Count Vasily Timofeyevich Volsky, Ambassador from the Court of the Romanovs, Nicholas II, Emperor and Autocrat of all the Russias, to the Court of St James was charm personified. 'He's extremely rich,' had been Rosebery's verdict. 'Extremely rich. Thousands and thousands of acres. Far more than I've got. Palaces full of paintings all over the place. Far more than I've got. Terrible wife. Probably can't wait to get back to St Petersburg. God knows why they all want to go back to Mother Russia, but they do.'

'Lord Powerscourt, I can be very brief in answer to the questions you raised in your letter. Is there any record of Russian anarchists or revolutionaries operating outside our country? The answer, I fear, is no. They confine their criminal activities to our own poor homeland. I do not believe they have ever operated abroad. Exile, of course, many of them are in exile in Paris or Geneva or even here in London, but they are always well behaved when abroad. They save their wickedness for home.'

He looked sadly at Powerscourt as though grieving for the sins of his compatriots.

'And these gentlemen whose names you gave me. You said you were certain they were law-abiding citizens, but felt you had to check. I admire your thoroughness, Lord Powerscourt. These are all good citizens. The Professor I have met myself. He likes to read Pushkin in his garden. What could be more peaceful than that?

'I do not know what you are seeking. I do know the answers are not be found in Russia. May I wish you good luck in your mission, Lord Powerscourt? '

*

One last call, thought Powerscourt. Then the London end of this part of the investigation will be over. After that comes the bit I am not looking forward to, the voyage round the remains of HMS *Britannia*, that strange cruise of the *Bacchante* all those years ago.

Dominic Knox, of the Ireland Office, welcomed him into an enormous room overlooking Horseguards Parade. Out in St James's Park the afternoon parade of nannies with perambulators was in full swing, the overfed ducks crowding round the hands that fed them. Knox was a small wiry man, casually dressed, with a neat goatee beard.

'Now then,' he seated them both in two comfortable chairs looking out over the trees towards Buckingham Palace, 'let me try to help you in your business. Do you know much about the security operation in Ireland, Lord Powerscourt?'

'I am glad to say that I do not.' Powerscourt wondered if he was in for a lecture for the rest of the afternoon. At least there were no dusty files hiding on the top of rickety steps.

'Well, let me enlighten you. It is huge, the security operation, that is. Everybody remembers the assassination of Lord Frederick Cavendish and Secretary Burke ten years ago in the Phoenix Park. But the ferment started long before that. There were nineteen separate attempts on the life of Forster when he was Chief Secretary of Ireland before Cavendish. Nineteen, Lord Powerscourt.

'Secret societies flourish over there like mushrooms in the dark. Fenians, Irish Republican Brotherhood, Invincibles, Captain Moonlight, once you think you have got to the bottom of one of them, another one pops up somewhere else. They're like weeds, particularly obstinate weeds. You know how you can do battle with an obdurate bramble; you trace the damned thing back to its roots, you follow the roots along the earth, eventually you pull it up and think you have won. One week later the bramble is back again. That's what Irish secret societies are like.

'Dublin Castle now has one of the largest networks of informants in the world. Every one of these secret societies is infiltrated by the police or the Government. Some of their meetings probably have more informants in the audience than real people attending the meeting. Informants are tripping over each other to pay their subscriptions. Soon we'll need informers to tell us about the other informers. I'm sure that a lot of them are doubles, working for the Irish secret organizations and reporting back on us. Maybe there are trebles, quadruples, it could go on for ever.'

'Jesus Christ only had twelve, and one of them was a double,' said Powerscourt flippantly.

'If he'd come down to Ireland about four or five of his disciples would have been working for the other side. Thirty pieces of silver is pretty cheap these days when you think of the amount of money handed over to these Irish Iscariots.'

Knox looked down at a file in his hand. Out on Horseguards a troop of cavalry was rehearsing, the crisp upper class orders carrying across the park to the nannies and the babies on their peaceful progress through the afternoon until it was time for tea.

'I come to your particular requests, Lord Powerscourt. We have run your names from the telegraph pole operation through our files in Dublin Castle. None of them appears. That does not mean that they may not be men of violence – any sensible assassin would take good care to keep out of our books, after all. But I think it very unlikely.

'Sometimes they venture across the Irish Sea to place bombs in London. But on the whole, the Irish are obsessed with their own little island, their own place in it, the relative rights of any of the foreigners who have settled in it for the last 800 years. They look backward, not forward. They look inward, not outward.

'In short, Lord Powerscourt, I think it unlikely that any of these telegraph people are dangerous. But I could be wrong. The English usually are, where Ireland is concerned.'

A small collection of admirers had gathered round Lady Pembridge's new curtains in St James's Square.

'Aren't they just divine? I think the colours go so well with this room, Rosalind!' Mary, Mrs William Burke, middle sister of Lord Francis Powerscourt, was paying tribute to her elder sister, proud proprietress of the new materials hanging in splendour across the great windows of her drawing-room. 'And the finish!

They're so beautifully made!' Linings were fingered, pelmets assessed.

'Do you know,' said her sister, 'I tried to interest Pembridge in the colours and the design. I might as well have asked the lions in Trafalgar Square. Completely hopeless. No idea about design at all.'

'I think they're all like that,' said her sister. 'Husbands, I mean. It's probably just as well,' she went on, thinking of the expense on the new sofas in her own house the previous year.

This was a gathering of the clans, a special Annual General Meeting of the Powerscourt family, summoned for a conclave by the eldest brother.

'They may get pretty inquisitive. In fact they are bound to do so, I'm afraid,' Lord Powerscourt had said to Lady Lucy as he prepared her for the initiation rites into a family evening in St James's Square.

'And what will they be inquisitive about, Lord Francis?' Lady Lucy was inspecting her dress for the fifth time as they prepared to leave her house in Markham Square.

'Why, inquisitive about you, Lady Lucy. Remember, my youngest sister, Lady Eleanor, has never met you. She will be consumed with curiosity, far worse than the Cheshire Cat.'

'I think I shall be able to manage, thank you,' Lady Lucy smiled. 'At least it won't be as bad as four brothers shouting at you over Christmas dinner about why you haven't found a husband yet. One of them even told me I was over the hill. Fancy such a thing. But seriously, Lord Francis, I am flattered and pleased that you have seen fit to invite me to dinner this evening. Does this mean that you now consider me to be one of the family?'

Powerscourt was growing accustomed to her teasing. 'My dear Lady Lucy,' he laughed, 'I am delighted to welcome you into the bosom of my family. But beware of the perils that lurk within.'

There she was now, looking perfectly at home as she talked to William Burke by the fireside, her blue eyes sparkling in the flames. At the other end of the room, the conversation had moved on from curtains. Powerscourt knew it would.

'So where did you say Francis met her, Rosalind?' Eleanor, like her brother, was beginning her investigations, pursuing them steadily, amassing evidence.

'Why, they met here, I think. Lady Lucy came to dinner one evening and I believe it all started then. Pembridge claims he heard them fixing up an assignation at the National Gallery.'

'Is she artistic, then? That would be good for Francis. But is she practical? Some of these artistic women make a point of neglecting their houses and their husbands.' A vision of some sordid dwelling in Hampstead or Soho, filled with unfinished canvases and opened jars of paint, passed through Eleanor's mind.

'Oh, I think she's practical enough,' said Rosalind, looking across at the slim figure by the fire. 'She's got a little boy from her first marriage. The husband was killed with Gordon at Khartoum, you know.'

'Really, really.' Lady Eleanor, being married to a naval captain, currently on manoeuvres in the Mediterranean, was impressed. Clouds of glory were attached to this particular widow. 'But tell me this, Rosalind.' Eleanor also glanced over at Lady Lucy, a look intercepted with amusement and resignation by her brother. 'Are they, you know, are they serious about each other?'

'I think they might be very serious,' said Rosalind thoughtfully, 'there's something about the way they look at each other now. As if there isn't anybody else in the room.'

Further discussion was interrupted by the dinner bell. Powerscourt observed that Lady Lucy had been placed at the opposite end of the table from him, flanked by Eleanor on the right of Lord Pembridge and Mary on his left. He himself was surrounded by Rosalind and the good William Burke, conversational rescue missions in the direction of Lady Lucy difficult, if not impossible, to undertake.

Portraits of Pembridge ancestors lined the walls, bouncing off the huge mirror over the fireplace: a Restoration Pembridge, dressed in flamboyant red, his hat at a rakish angle, looking every inch the successful cavalier, a late eighteenth-century Pembridge with flesh-coloured hose and a black jacket and a puffy, dissipated face. Powerscourt remembered Burke telling him that this particular Pembridge had lost a great fortune gambling with Charles James Fox. There was a slightly later Earl, now the master of all the acres he surveyed, gun in hand, dog at his heels, probably repairing with hard work and good husbandry the damage done to the family fortunes by his predecessor. Family gossip, so much more vicious than any other, swirled round the table. Powerscourt had always been amazed at the way in which family members were prepared to say the most terrible things about each other, things that they would never countenance coming from an outsider.

'There he was. I mean, there he was.' William Burke was telling the story of a cousin, recently fallen on wicked times. 'At breakfast he was married. Had been for twenty years, in fact. He had the normal breakfast, two kippers, strong coffee, a mountain of toast. He was always very particular about the marmalade, wasn't he, my dear?' He smiled at his wife, in search of confirmation of his cousin's strange habits at the breakfast table. 'It had to be that thick stuff with lots of bits of rind or whatever they call it piled very high on the toast so you could hardly see the bread.

'Anyway, that was breakfast. By lunchtime he was gone. He never came back. He simply disappeared. Word came a few days later that he had been seen crossing the Channel with a young lady. Then he was reported in the South of France with the same young lady in Cannes or Antibes, one of those places. No questions asked in the hotels, no sign of him ever returning. He just fled at fifty and abandoned the whole lot of them.'

'I suppose they'll save on the marmalade bills.' Powerscourt was unable to resist the aside.

'Francis, you are awful! There is this poor woman, William's cousin's wife, deserted at her age. And all you can think of is the marmalade,' said his eldest sister, never happier than when telling her brother off.

'But was it Cooper's Oxford marmalade? Or that stuff in the funny jars, Tiptree I think it's called. It comes from somewhere in Essex.'

'Do shut up, Francis!' All three sisters joined forces to berate him. Witches, thought Powerscourt bitterly, remembering the days when they had ganged up on him as a boy and stolen his

149

catapults. As he looked for assistance to Lady Lucy he thought he saw a sudden conspiratorial smile flash down the table to him. A private smile from Lady Lucy was worth the whole cauldron of his sisters' wrath.

The last servants had cleared the last plates and the last glasses from the table. The doors were closed.

Pembridge, looking every inch the paterfamilias, coughed meaningfully and tapped his fingers loudly on the table.

'Ladies and gentlemen,' he began, smiling at them one by one round the table, an extra strong smile for the pretty Lady Lucy. Francis has asked us here this evening because he wants to enlist our help. Francis, the floor is yours.'

All evening Powerscourt had wondered about the tone he should adopt in addressing this particular gathering. After his marmalade gaffe he knew he couldn't be flippant. No jokes, he said to himself. For God's sake, no jokes. He knew that his two brothers-in-law were likely to take him much more seriously than his sisters, however dearly they loved him. The witches, he remembered, had always thought of his investigations as yet another male hobby, not to be taken seriously.

'I need your help,' he began, deciding that a policy of abasement might be the best tactic. Throw yourself on their mercy. 'I am engaged at present on a most difficult and important investigation. Two days ago I saw the Commissioner of the Metropolitan Police. He has promised me all the assistance at his command. I have in my pocket,' he paused to draw out one of his letters from No. 10 Downing Street, 'a number of letters from the Prime Minister. The recipient is left blank for me to fill in as I choose. The letter instructs that every possible assistance is to be given to Lord Francis Powerscourt who is engaged on a mission of the utmost national importance.'

He paused, looking round the table. They had fallen silent and rather serious, Pembridge looking like some hearty squire from the Pembridge past, William Burke the man of affairs, serious about his duty to Queen and country, Rosalind impassive, Mary and Eleanor curious, Lady Lucy suddenly looking rather frightened on Powerscourt's behalf. Maybe this is all going to be very dangerous, she thought suddenly.

'Francis, can you tell us anything of what this matter is about? Anything at all?' Asked Lady Rosalind.

'I am afraid that I cannot. It would not help matters and it might make life more difficult for everybody involved. Especially me.' He gave a self-deprecating shrug.

'But you can't expect us all to help if we don't know what it's about.' Lady Eleanor neatly fulfilled her brother's prophecy about her curiosity.

'What is it that you would have us do, Francis?' asked Lady Mary, practical wife of a practical man.

'I would prefer it if you wouldn't all talk at once for a start,' said Powerscourt, exacting a minor revenge for the marmalade war.

The men laughed, a male combination against women and wives.

'What I want is very simple. I want information about a number of people. I want information about their families, information about their finances, information about their fortunes, if they have any, or have recently lost them all. Informal information, the kind that comes easily in conversation, and, if I dare to use the word in this company, gossip. I have suddenly become a great fan of gossip. The kind of things, I am told, that ladies have been known to talk about when they are together. Not that there is anything wrong with gossip.' He thought briefly of the witches conspiring again, spells cast, potions prepared, strange smells rising from the heath.

'I have here,' he said, anticipating what he knew was the next question, certainly from his sisters, 'a list of the people involved. I should say that there is no suspicion at all that any of them has done anything wrong.' He passed glibly over the lie, not daring to tell the family that one of his names might have murdered the heir presumptive to the throne. 'No suspicion at all.'

Lord Henry Lancaster, Harry Radclyffe, Charles Peveril, William Brockham, Lord Edward Gresham, the Honourable Frederick Mortimer. Powerscourt recited the names easily. He used to recite them to himself in moments of boredom, shaving, or waiting for the underground railway trains to appear.

'But, Francis –' began Rosalind.

'What exactly is it –' said Mary Burke.

'Do you seriously expect us –' asked Eleanor, her face bright with interest and curiosity.

'There you go again. You're all talking at once. Just for a change.' Powerscourt smiled at his three witches, as if their spells were kindly. 'One at a time, please.'

'Francis,' said his eldest sister Rosalind, taking on the rights of birth, 'do you actually expect us to go about interrogating people about these young men? As if we were policemen or something?'

'I do not,' said Powerscourt. 'I merely thought that at what you feel to be the appropriate moment you could try to steer the conversation in their direction. You haven't heard anything about them for a while. Is it true that such and such a one is engaged to be married? Or that so and so has lost the family fortune? I am told,' he smiled a rueful smile as he continued, 'that ladies in society do actually have conversations of this sort from time to time.'

'Did you know that one of those young men is dead, Powerscourt?' Pembridge interrupted, looking very grave. 'Lancaster. He was killed in a shooting accident in Norfolk, somewhere near Melton Constable, I believe. Terrible business.'

So that was what Dawnay had done with him, thought Powerscourt. He remembered the Major's promise that he, Dawnay, would look after the business of the body in the woods, the brains scattered around the Sandringham trees. Forever Faithful. Semper Fidelis.

'Yes, I did.' Powerscourt too looked sombre. A hush had fallen in the dining-room, faint reflections of Pembridge's shirt and Lady Lucy's hands visible in the polished table. 'But I am afraid that he too must be included in these conversations. His death, dare I say it, might provide a useful point of introduction.'

'What do you want us to do with this information? Just tell you the next time we see you?'

'No, I don't want you to do that. I want you to write it down.' This brought howls of pain and anguish from the three sisters.

'Francis, you can't be serious.'

'We're not going back to school.'

'This isn't some essay prize is it, Francis?'

William Burke came to his rescue. 'If I may say so, that is a most sensible suggestion. People in my line of work are always forgetting exactly what people said to them. The only way to be sure is to write it all down. One of the companies I am attached to has declared it to be company policy now. Writing things down, I mean.'

'And what should we do when we have written it all down in our little notebooks?' Lady Eleanor was retreating defiantly.

'You could give it to me in person. Or you could post it to me here.'

Powerscourt thought the battle was won, the witches retreating, the cauldron off the boil.

'Tell me, Francis,' William Burke spoke again. 'Tell me about this financial information you want. Do you think there might be anything untoward about the situation of these young men?'

'I would be most interested to know' – Powerscourt looked round the table once again, daring to drop in the one word which he knew would command universal attention – 'if any of them were being blackmailed. Or, for that matter, if they might have been blackmailing anybody else.'

15

Morpeth railway station arrived precisely on time, fulfilling the promises of Lord Rosebery's train-obsessed butler. The sun was setting as Powerscourt set off towards the Queen's Hotel in Bridge Street, grey clouds chasing each other across a darkening sky. The following morning, at ten o'clock, he was due to call on Captain John Williams of Station Road, Amble, one-time commander of the naval training ship HMS *Britannia*. Powerscourt had written his letter most carefully, timing his visit for the early morning when full defences might not yet be in position.

An enormous building, easily the largest in the little market town, was set back from the houses and the streets. The windows were small, narrow and barred all the way up to the top floor. A small mean entrance promised little welcome to the new arrivals. Northumberland County Lunatic Asylum, said the discreet sign on the driveway.

Powerscourt wondered how many were locked up inside. It must be hundreds, he thought to himself, hundreds and hundreds of lunatics, gathered together in this inhospitable northern town. The ones who couldn't talk. The ones who wouldn't talk. The ones who couldn't stop. Silent people, lost to this world, possibly lost to the next, are wandering round this ghastly building.

Powerscourt suddenly remembered the haunting poems of John Clare, locked up in an asylum in his own county town of Northampton all those years ago. The defiant verses:

'I am: yet what I am none cares or knows,
My friends forsake me like a memory lost:

154

I am the self consumer of my woes . . .
And yet I am . . .'

Were there hundreds of John Clares in there, scribbling furious
protests about their own sanity, ever doubted by the hostile
nurses and the overworked doctors, Julius Caesars, King Charles
Is, Jesus Christs on patrol in the darkened corridors? Once you
were in there, thought Powerscourt, hastening on his way to the
saner quarters of the Queen's Hotel, you might never get out. It
was a sort of earthly limbo for the not yet dead, a prison for
those whose most serious crimes had been committed inside
their heads.

Captain Williams' house stood in a little terrace of fishermen's
cottages, looking out over the river and the sea. A mile or so
away inland the Percy castle at Alnwick stood proudly on its
hill, surveying from its ruined battlements both land and sea.

Captain Williams himself opened the door.

'I suppose you must be Lord Powerscourt,' he said doubtfully,
as if hoping that some other visitor might have knocked on his
door. 'I suppose you'd better come in.'

'Thank you so much,' said Powerscourt cheerfully, looking
quickly round the little sitting-room. 'How very good of you to
spare the time to talk to me.'

Captain Williams' sitting-room had seen better days. The
wallpaper was beginning to peel off the walls. There were gaps
on the walls, cleaner wallpaper visible, as if pictures had been
removed, or sold, or pawned, though Powerscourt doubted if
this little hamlet would boast a pawn shop. The fire in the grate
sputtered hopelessly, trying in vain to light a room where the
gloom seemed to have sunk into the furniture itself.

Captain Williams wasn't in much better shape himself. He
must have been very tall when he was younger, Powerscourt
thought, looking at the hunched figure in the chair. His hair had
gone. His teeth were going, black and yellow against the sad
pink oval of his lips. His spirit seemed to have gone too, his
clothes hanging listlessly off him, as if he didn't look at what he
put on when he rose in the mornings. The eyes were red and

Captain Williams tried to hide them, staring down at the fading patterns of his carpet rather than looking directly at his visitor. Drink, thought Powerscourt. The man must drink like a fish to have eyes like that. Appropriate in a place like this, fish everywhere. Good God, he can't have been drinking already, it's only ten o'clock in the morning. Even Johnny Fitzgerald, always drinking but seldom drunk, didn't start at this hour of the day.

'Did you come by train, Lord Powerscourt?'

'I did, I came up yesterday and stayed the night at Morpeth.'

'They say the trains get faster all the time nowadays.' Captain Williams sounded as if he were playing for time, small talk postponing whatever interrogation might follow.

'I've brought you this.' Powerscourt took out one of his letters from Downing Street, now enclosed in a plain white envelope belonging to the Queen's Hotel, Morpeth, and addressed in a clear hand.

'You said you had a letter.' Williams fumbled for his spectacles, perusing the document with a look of growing terror on his face. 'Your business must be pretty important then, Lord Powerscourt.' Captain Williams wondered if he could spirit himself away somewhere for a bracing dose of brandy.

Powerscourt looked at him sharply, the hands trembling as he handed back the letter. Thank heavens I came in the morning, he said to himself. God only knows what he's like in the afternoons.

'My wife has gone out for the day.' Captain Williams looked desolate, as if his wife could have driven off what might follow.

'What I want to know is quite simple, Captain Williams.' Powerscourt tried to sound as gentle as he could. 'What exactly happened at the end of your time in charge of HMS *Britannia* all those years ago? When you had the two young Princes in your charge.'

'I knew you would come.' Captain Williams wrapped his jacket ever closer round his thin frame. 'Ever since, I have always known that somebody like you would come. Asking questions. Raking up the past. Dredging up things that happened long ago. Why can't it be left in peace? Why can't I be left alone? It wasn't my fault, I tell you, it wasn't my fault.'

Powerscourt felt sorry for him for a moment, a lost old man, waiting thirteen years for the knock on the door, the letter through the post. He, Powerscourt, was the exterminating angel, come to destroy what was left of an old man's peace of mind. He thought of Prince Eddy and the rictus of death on his face, blood lying in pools across the floor, he thought of Lord Henry Lancaster lying dead in the forest. Semper Fidelis, he said to himself. Semper Fidelis.

'Why don't we go for a walk?' said Powerscourt suddenly, trying to temper perseverance with mercy. 'You might find it easier outside. You can tell the waves. You can tell the seagulls. You can tell the sand-dunes. I shall just be listening in.'

'A walk?' Captain Williams looked at him as if he were mad. Walks, however good they might be for clearing the mind of drink, didn't appear to feature in the old man's morning routine.

'A walk by the sea.' Powerscourt pressed his case. 'At least it's not pouring with rain.'

Two figures set out from the little cottage, the old man hunched against the bitter wind, a threadbare coat small protection against the elements, Powerscourt wrapped in his warmest cape, buttoned right up to his throat. They crossed the river and began to trudge through the sand.

One hundred yards out to sea, sometimes two hundred, great breakers began to form, crests of foam flying proudly behind them as they crashed in towards the beach. The spray was like fine rain, drifting in towards the sand-dunes and the distant castle. A lone seagull tried an unequal contest with the wind, now stationary, now blown backwards with the force of the blast. The noise thundered along the solitary beach, waves driven forward on their final journey as far as the eye could see.

'Begin wherever you like,' Powerscourt shouted, trying not to sound too hostile.

'That's very kind of you. Very kind of you indeed.' The voice was thin and bitter. Powerscourt strained to hear it through the gale, and huddled ever closer to his companion.

There was a pause, their feet scrunching though the sand. Powerscourt waited. Far out to sea, two ships were pitching violently in the swell. More seagulls tested their wingpower against the wind. Powerscourt waited.

'I suppose it all began when those young officers took Prince Eddy off to Portsmouth.'

Captain Williams' words flew past Powerscourt. He strained to catch them, like a slip fielder diving after a thick outside edge.

'They were meant to bring him back that night. That had all been agreed. I remember it so clearly.' Captain Williams turned to Powerscourt, red eyes weeping with the weather.

'But they didn't. They disobeyed orders.'

A pause followed as the Captain's mind was forced back thirteen years to the events preceding his disgrace.

'They took him to some seamen's brothel. They said they wanted to make a man of him. They said it was time for a boy who would be a king one day to become a man. And after a couple of hours, they went back and took him to another one.'

'Another brothel?' Powerscourt tried to shout the words gently.

'I'm afraid so. There may even have been a third one before the night was out. And then he was brought home. I threw the book at him for disobeying orders, not coming home when he was told. Do you know what he did, Prince Eddy? He just smiled at me, that rather silly smile of his.'

A smile he took with him to the grave, thought Powerscourt, remembering Lancaster's description of the corpse.

'What we didn't know, of course, was what went on with the older boys in the dormitories last thing at night.'

Oh my God, thought Powerscourt. Oh my God. He remembered Lady Eleanor's husband's accounts of some of the activities that went on in places like the *Britannia*. The sea was now depositing great sausages of foam on the shore in front of them. As the wind drove them along the beach, they gradually evaporated, the foam blown away across the dunes.

'There was a group of five of them,' Williams went on, hurrying now, as if he was thinking of a large drink when his ordeal was over.

Five of them, thought Powerscourt bitterly. Just like those bloody equerries.

'Illicit sexual relations, that's what the admiral who conducted the inquiry called it. Five of them having illicit sexual relations with each other. They all got ill. Very ill.'

'Ill with what?' Powerscourt was whispering now.

'Syphilis, that's what they said it was. Syphilis. I'd never heard of it until then.'

Ulcers, Powerscourt remembered, it started with ulcers. Then fevers, headaches, spots, lesions, pustules. The New World's revenge on the Old, carried back across the Atlantic by Columbus's sailors and their successors to be spread round the cities of Europe. The French pox, very difficult to cure. Sea journeys, he said to himself, didn't they think that long sea journeys might be the answer? Get yourself a ship, call it the *Bacchante* for want of a better name, pack on board the offending Prince and his brother, send them all round the world. Sea journeys. No chance of infecting anybody else, he said to himself, that bloody boat will have been patrolled night and day, the crew and passengers vetted right down to their buttonholes. God in heaven.

'The Prince's father was very good to the other boys, the ones who were ill. They said he paid for their treatment too, that he looked after them very well.'

It wasn't really blackmail at all, thought Powerscourt. It might be self-defence. Was it twenty thousand a year above his income that the Prince of Wales had been spending for years and years? He was sure that William Burke, ever reliable with the arithmetic, had told him that early on in his inquiry. It wasn't really blackmail, just regular payments, treatments, maybe abroad, expensive doctors, young men with their futures ruined but still financially afloat, courtesy of Marlborough House and Messrs Finch's & Co., Bankers. Years and years of payments, probably still going on. No wonder they didn't want to talk to him. No wonder they hadn't been surprised when Eddy was murdered in his bed.

'Come, we had better get back now. I'm sorry that was so difficult for you. I'm very grateful to you. Do you have the names of the other boys?'

'I do, oh yes, I do. Oh yes. Sometimes I take out that list and I wish they had never been born.'

The Captain's first act on returning home was to disappear into a scullery behind the kitchen. Powerscourt could hear liquid being poured into a glass. There was a pause, followed by what might have been a gulp, then the sound of more liquid being poured. Williams came through the door, looking rather better.

'I got so cold, Lord Powerscourt. Medicinal whisky helps restore the circulation. Can I get you a glass?'

'Just a very small one,' said Powerscourt. He wondered how much you would get if you asked for a large one.

'The addresses, if you could be so kind.' Powerscourt cradled the glass in his hands, amazed at the improvement in Williams' demeanour.

Another piece of paper disappeared into his pocketbook. He left Amble in the same carriage that had brought him there.

Captain Williams stood at his door and watched him go. For the rest of his life he would remember his visitor on this day, the walk on the beach, the seagulls flying backwards, his visitor straining to catch his words as the wind blew them away. Another ghastly memory to add to his collection.

Powerscourt read the addresses on his way back to the hotel. At least this lot aren't scattered all around the four nations of Great Britain, he thought to himself. But when he thought of his next round of conversations, once more exhuming the past, once more distressing the old, he almost wished they were.

I shall actually be quite glad, he said to himself as his carriage rattled along the windswept lanes, to see that lunatic asylum once again.

A note from Rosebery, asking him to call at his earliest convenience, was waiting for Powerscourt on his return to his sister's house in St James's Square. There was a note from Lord George Scott, former captain of the *Bacchante*, saying that he would be honoured to meet with Lord Powerscourt at the Army and Navy Club the following morning. There was a report from James Phillips, his footman spy in Marlborough House, saying that there was no gossip about Prince Eddy's death in the servants' hall and that the Prince of Wales had gone to stay with Lady Brooke at Easton Lodge. And a note from Lady Lucy, a delicate whiff of her perfume still lingering about the notepaper, asking him to lunch at her house in Markham Square the following Sunday.

We are going to have a christening party for Robert's boat. I think it should take place after lunch at the Round Pond in Kensington Gardens. I shall, of course, provide the necessary champagne.

Robert has decided to call the boat *Britannia*. Don't you think that is very patriotic for one so young?

Yours ever,

Lucy.

Powerscourt's heart sank. Not even the single word Lucy at the bottom of the page could cheer him up. Not Lady Lucy, not Lady Lucy Hamilton, not Lady Hamilton. Just Lucy. Please don't call it *Britannia*, he thought, dear God, please not *Britannia*. He would never be able to look at the little craft without thinking of illicit sexual practices and a naval inquest which despatched its victims to the four corners of the kingdom, a broken man whispering his terrible confidences into the teeth of the wind as the great breakers rolled in from the sea.

'Francis.' His sister appeared, apparently rushing from one appointment to another. 'We have all been so busy working on your behalf.'

'The curtains are looking particularly fine this afternoon, Rosalind. It's as if they were chosen specially for this late afternoon light.'

'No gratitude,' said his sister, 'no gratitude. Flippancy is my only reward.' She dashed off to her next appointment, thinking that it was nice of brother Francis to mention her new curtains, even if he didn't afford them the respect they deserved.

William Leith, Rosebery's inscrutable butler, opened the door. 'My lord. His Lordship is in the library. Your coat, my lord.'

Coat, hat and gloves departed to the Rosebery vestibule.

Leith coughed. 'Might I make so bold, my lord, as to inquire if Your Lordship has yet availed himself of the travel arrangements we discussed?' A flicker of a smile crossed his impassive face.

'Leith, my good man.' Powerscourt wondered suddenly if he could try his luck again. It's like having your very own travel agent, he thought to himself. 'I have indeed. Your arrangements worked like clockwork. Now, I wonder if I could take advantage

161

of your good offices and your expertise once more.' He handed over another list of places, scribbled out on the train home from the North. 'I am sorry that the writing is a trifle uncertain. I wrote it on your train coming back from Morpeth.'

'Did Your Lordship catch the 8.15 or the nine o'clock? My Lordship speaks highly of the speed of the 8.15.'

'The 8.15 it was, Leith. And the train was very fast.'

Leith glanced down at the list of places. 'My lord. These places. I shall prepare a memorandum for you to take away.' My God, thought Powerscourt, a memorandum, the man even sounds like Rosebery in one of his pompous moods.

'Could I suggest once again, if I might,' here came the deprecating cough, the note of pleading, almost of supplication, 'that if Your Lordship wishes to make the rounds of these localities, a special might prove the most expeditious method for attaining your objectives?'

Specials once again. The man is obsessed with specials. What on earth is so special about specials? Powerscourt resolved to ask Rosebery.

'Please include the details in your memorandum. That would be most kind.'

'Thank you, my lord. If Your Lordship would like to step this way. Lord Powerscourt, my lord.'

Leith glided away back to his lair half-way down the stairs, to enjoy moments of communion with the domestic timetables of Britain, Surrey, Gloucestershire and Hampshire in particular.

'Rosebery, how good to see you.'

'Powerscourt, how kind of you to call. Come and sit down.'

'I have a confession to make to you, Rosebery. I have been using the expertise of your butler for information about train times.'

Rosebery laughed. 'You have certainly come to the right place. I keep increasing his wages in case he defects to Thomas Cook or the Travel Department at Harrods.'

'But why the obsession with specials? Every time I ask, he recommends a special.'

'Ah, specials,' said Rosebery thoughtfully. 'I have a certain weakness for specials myself. For Leith, I think,' Rosebery looked into his fire, 'specials simply represent the highest form of travel.

They're almost metaphysical. Your own train, your own driver, your own route, no other passengers cluttering up the place with luggage and children and the other impedimenta of mass movement. If Leith ever went to Plato's Cave and was asked about a Form or an Ideal, he wouldn't talk about Love or Truth or Beauty. He'd talk about a special train, chugging slowly out from the darkness of the cavern to join the Great North Eastern line at Peterborough.

'But come, enough of trains.' Rosebery abandoned his inspection of some ancient volume on the table. 'Trevelyan told me the other day that there had been a frightful row between the Queen and Disraeli about that boat you were interested in, the *Bacchante*. He said the Queen seemed to wish to vet every single person on board her. Do you have any news, Francis?'

All the way back on the train Powerscourt had wondered about who he should tell about Captain Williams' confessions about the *Britannia*. Rosebery, of course. Johnny Fitzgerald, of course.

About Durham, he began thinking about telling Lady Lucy. By York he had decided against it. Then he asked himself if he would have told Lady Lucy if he was married to her. Just supposing he was married to her, that is, a purely hypothetical question. I don't have to marry her just in order to be able to tell her, he said to himself. Do I? By Peterborough he had decided that he would tell her if it became really necessary. But what did really necessary actually mean? By King's Cross he was back where he started. He just couldn't decide.

But he could tell Rosebery. He did.

Rosebery walked up and down the whole length of his library. Pictures, books, curios were simply blotted from his mind as he took in the import of the revelations on the Northumberland shore.

'My God, Francis. What a mess. Where does this leave everything? What do you make of it?'

'It seems to me that a number of things come from it. First, we do not yet know what happened to the five boys. But if they have been ill intermittently – some of them may have died by now, for heaven's sake – that would be an ample motive for them or for other members of their families or friends to murder Prince Eddy.

163

'Second . . .' Powerscourt held up a hand to quell a Rosebery intervention. 'Second, this may be the secret of the blackmail charges and the Prince of Wales. They've been going on for a long time, you told me right at the beginning. Of course they have. These are the payments for doctors, cures, compensation, call it what you will, payments above everything else for silence. If you're the Prince of Wales you don't want a single word or even a syllable of this stuff leaking out. You've got to feel sorry for him in a way. There he is, leading a perfectly ordinary life of adultery and debauchery. Up pops his son and does something far far worse. Of course it's blackmail in one sense. We do not know how the payments were arranged. We do not know who took the initiative. I reckon the Prince of Wales would have paid anything for silence. Don't you?'

'He would, he would. So you think that someone connected with these five families could be the murderer. Or the blackmailer. Or both.'

'I do. Or I think I do. It's possible. A long arm of revenge reaches out from Dartmouth thirteen years ago and cuts Prince Eddy's throat.'

'Would it explain the violence of the murder itself?'

Rosebery had turned pale. Powerscourt didn't feel too good himself, discussing these fantastic propositions in one of London's finest private libraries in Berkeley Square, train timetables being prepared for him down below.

'It might. I have always thought that it could be a revenge attack, a life for a life, a death for a death. 'But we do not yet have enough information. I am seeing Lord George Scott, captain of this *Bacchante*, tomorrow. Maybe he will have more information. And I have the addresses of the five boys from the *Britannia*.'

'God help you, Francis. May God bless this *Britannia* and all who sailed in her. But I very much doubt if he did.'

Lord Johnny Fitzgerald materialized out of the night air of London and presented himself in Powerscourt's little sitting-room in St James's Square. The apparition was clutching a bottle with even more devotion than usual.

'Powerscourt, just look at this one here.' Fitzgerald

unwrapped his packet with the reverence Rosebery brought to volumes of Renaissance verse. 'Armagnac, Francis. Look at it. And this bottle is sixty years old. Will you be taking a glass of this nectar here?'

'I will not. Not for the moment, thank you.' Powerscourt shuddered at his memories of the last man with a bottle, the trembling hands, the bloodshot eyes, the look of ruin.

'Have you signed the pledge now, Francis? Shall I book you in for a Temperance meeting at the Methodist Central Hall?'

'I have seen your future, Johnny. And it is not a pleasant one.' Powerscourt tried to remain as grave and as severe as he could. 'I can now tell you what you will look like in about thirty years' time, if you do not mend your ways. There is still time. It is never too late. Rejoice more for the one who is saved than for the ninety and nine who did not stray.

'Let me tell you precisely what will happen to you, you poor addict. Believe me, I saw the signs, the portents of your future, only the other day.' Powerscourt looked intently at Lord Johnny's face. 'Your hair will fall out.' Fitzgerald checked briefly on his extravagant set of brown curls. 'Your eyes will sink into your face. They will be red and bloodshot from over-indulgence in the golden liquids provided by the wine merchants of London. Your teeth will turn yellow and black. Your hands will shake. Your spirits will be broken by too many of the other kind. You will lose all faith in yourself and in your own future. Despair will hang over you like a great cloud, blocking out God's own sunlight.'

'For God's sake, Francis. I'm definitely having a glass of this stuff now. It's a fine preacher you would have been, if only you could have kept a straight face.'

'I think I may partake of a very small measure of that Armagnac, Johnny. Medicinal purposes only, you understand. That's what the man said.'

Powerscourt told the story of Northumberland for the second time that day. There's only Lady Lucy left to tell, now, he thought to himself. If I do tell her.

Lord Johnny Fitzgerald was stunned into silence. There was no need to tell him what the implications were. He would have worked them out as fast as Powerscourt himself.

The two men sat staring at the bottle of Armagnac. J. Nismes-Delclou, said the label. Specially bottled for Berry Bros and Rudd, St James's Street, London. High-pitched voices strayed upstairs, announcing the return home of the working women of the house.

'Let me really cheer you up, Francis. I have come to make another report. And I fear I may have yet more suspects to put into the pot.' He took a large gulp of his Armagnac, shivering slightly as it passed down his throat. 'They make it a different way from the brandy, you know. That's why it's so fiery.

'Anyway, Francis, I thought I would resume my investigations into that club in Chiswick, the secret one with the homosexual rich of London, gathered by the waters of the Thames. I spent three days up a tree once again. Bloody cold it was too. I expect my hair would have started to fall out if I'd stayed up there much longer. I have to confess that I did have a bottle of Armagnac in my pocket. But it was only a small one, Your Reverence. Just a little one.' Fitzgerald's hands cupped themselves round a very small container indeed.

Powerscourt didn't think they made Armagnac in half or quarter bottles, but he thought he would let it pass.

'On the third day – why do things always happen on the third day, Francis? – I saw a man I knew. I waited till he came out and I followed him home, not two hundred yards from where we are sitting now. He's married, this character. I went to his bloody wedding. He must be able to look in two directions at once, God help him. The next day, I bumped into him just before lunch. I'd been loitering outside his offices all morning, pretending to be waiting for somebody. Lunch followed. Not Armagnac this time, Your Reverence. I have to confess to the Temperance Movement that it was Claret. Pomerol, Château Le Bon Pasteur, would you believe. Two whole bottles of the stuff it took. The Lord's my Shepherd, I'll not want, he leadeth me the quiet waters by. Waters by the Thames. Sorry, I'm getting carried away like you, Francis.

'I said, may the Good Lord forgive me, that I was interested in men. Or boys. But only if it was safe, no danger, no threat of arrest from the peelers. Half-way down the second bottle, he opened up. He told me about the place by the river, about the entry fees and the precautions and all the other things we knew before. But, Francis, this is the thing. This is the thing.'

Powerscourt leant down and poured a generous measure into Lord Johnny's glass. It seemed very quiet, up there at the top of the house.

'There is a crisis in the affairs of the club in Chiswick. Members keep getting ill. One or two of them have died in recent years. The symptoms are all the same. Spots, fever, lesions, pustules.'

Syphilis again, thought Powerscourt bitterly. Most people could go through their whole lives without hearing mention of the word. Now he had encountered it twice in the space of a week. 'Do they know where it is coming from, Johnny. This disease, I mean.'

'No, they don't. But they are worried, very worried. Petrified, in fact. They are thinking of closing the whole operation down. Don't you see, Francis, don't you see? I'm sure you do.' Powerscourt stared intently at his friend, a dark shadow of fear passing over his face, 'We could have another boatload of suspects. Somebody may be infecting these homosexual characters down there. We know a member who has syphilis, he may never have been cured, the heir presumptive to the throne. God knows how many more people he may have infected down there. God knows how many more lives have been ruined, husbands and brothers who may have to face telling their wives and families how they got ill, devoted fathers trying to summon the courage to break it to their own children that they may be dead in a few years, sores and rotting bits all over their bodies.

'Let's just suppose one of these unfortunates thinks he may have caught the disease from one of the members, our Duke of Clarence. Precious Prince Eddy. What would you want to do to him? I tell you what I'd do. I'd cut his bloody throat. I'd cut every single artery in his body and hope the blood spilt all over the floor. It wouldn't matter if you are caught and hung. Think of it. You may as well die from the hangman's noose as from the horrors of tertiary syphilis.'

Powerscourt felt very tired. Here was another collection of suspects, even less likely to tell the truth than the ones before.

'Johnny, Johnny. I thought there were about ten possible

suspects, or ten suspect families before tonight. I say families because brothers, even fathers might want to take revenge for ruined lives. How many more of them do you think there might be down by the riverside?'

'I don't know. I could only guess. Maybe six. Maybe a dozen. Maybe fifteen at the outside. Not more.'

'Every time I think we have moved a step forwards, we go backwards. I felt quite cheerful the other day, looking up at the Northumberland County Lunatic Asylum. Maybe I should go in and join them.'

'Never give up. That's what you've always said, Francis. Never give up. Even at the bottom of that bloody great mountain in India.'

Powerscourt smiled at the memory. That was it. Never give up. He watched without complaint as Lord Johnny Fitzgerald poured out two glasses of Armagnac. Bloody great big ones, as Lord Johnny himself would have said.

16

I wonder how much he knows? I wonder how much they told him? I wonder how much he'll tell me. Lord Francis Powerscourt was walking to the Army and Navy Club, thinking about his forthcoming interview with Lord George Scott, one time captain of the *Bacchante*.

A bright January sun had come out, casting great shadows from the bare trees of St James's Square. Powerscourt paused at the junction with Pall Mall, lost in thought. A slim figure, wrapped up to the chin in splendid furs, was dancing through the traffic to talk to him. If they chose Scott because he could keep his mouth shut, Powerscourt reflected, then maybe he'll go on doing it. I'll get nothing out of him at all.

The slim figure came to a halt beside him and looked up at him brightly.

'Lord Francis! Lord Francis! Hello. Hello. Anybody at home?'

It was Lady Lucy.

'Lady Lucy, why, how delightful to see you. How very delightful indeed.' Powerscourt looked her up and down as if he had not seen her for years. 'What are you doing here at this time of the morning? It's only a quarter to nine. I thought young ladies of fashion never went out before eleven o'clock at the earliest.'

'I am not one of those young ladies of fashion, Lord Francis. Later this morning I do have an appointment with a young lady of fashion. She is said to have been romantically involved with one of your equerry persons. I rise to go about your business, Lord Francis. And anyway,' she smiled at him, their eyes already

169

carrying on a private conversation of their own in the midst of London's early traffic, 'I have to buy one or two things in Fortnum and Mason, just up the road.'

'You look like Anna Karenina in that coat, Lady Lucy. Why do I think you look like Anna Karenina? I have never met the woman.'

'You're thinking of that illustration on the first edition that came out in English, the one they put on the cover. That showed a young woman wrapped up to the throat in furs.' Lady Lucy did not mention that the young lady, or the model on whom she had been based, was outrageously beautiful. 'But if I am Anna Karenina, who are you, Lord Francis?' Here came that teasing look again. 'I think you must be Vronsky. Are we going to an illicit assignation? I have to say that I don't particularly want to throw myself under a train. Not at the moment anyway.'

'I'm not sure I would care to be Vronsky. Not today. I am going to be late for my appointment.'

Lady Lucy could not bear to let him go. Surely Anna had held on to her Vronsky through thick and thin?

'Lord Francis, I have some news for you. About those matters we spoke of at dinner before you went away. How was away? Was it satisfactory?'

'Since you ask, away was terrible. But I did get to see a nice lunatic asylum. I'm thinking of retiring there. Would you care to join me?'

Lady Lucy's eyes danced. 'I would think of joining you wherever you were, Lord Francis. But only as long as I knew you were sane in wanting to be with me.' Had she gone too far, she wondered. Should she have said that? It was only what she felt.

The object of her affections was looking at his watch. 'Would you by any chance be free in a couple of hours' time, Lady Lucy? We could have coffee and biscuits in Fortnum and Mason. But I don't suppose you'll be in there all that time.'

'You'd be amazed at how long I could spend in there. I shall see you then. But there's one thing, Lord Francis. I'm so terribly sorry.'

'Why are you sorry?'

'The information I have found out for you. About your equerries.'

'Yes, what is it?' Powerscourt was growing anxious. Not more bad tidings at this time of day. He had had enough to last him a month.

'I'm afraid I haven't written it down. Not yet anyway. But I will. Write it down, I mean.'

With that, she was gone, gliding through the throng to the shops of Piccadilly, the high collar still visible against the crowd. Maybe I should turn into Vronsky after all, thought Powerscourt, watching her disappearing figure. It might be quite nice. He corrected himself. It might be very nice indeed. After all, Lady Lucy's husband was dead, wasn't he?

Polish. There was polish everywhere, polish on the boots coming down the steps as he walked up the steps, polish on the sword handles, glittering in the winter sun, polish on the scabbards, clanking beneath them, polish on the belts round the waists of the military, some small and tight, some tight but expansive. Polish, even on the hair, was the order of the day at the Army and Navy Club.

Polish, and noise, thought Powerscourt as he presented his credentials at the desk. Army boots, Navy boots, maybe even the odd civilian boot like his own, echoed across the marble floor and up the great ornate staircase to the rooms above. The noise was deafening. He had to shout.

'Lord George Scott. I believe he is expecting me.'

A uniformed porter, boots so polished that you could see reflections of the club's ceilings as he walked, led Powerscourt to a small room at the back of the library.

Lord Scott was a tall slim seafarer with a clipped beard and a neat clipped moustache. He had a clipped way of speaking too. Maybe it was all those naval signals he had to send, telegraphic messages despatched from distant parts.

'How d'ye do. How d'ye do. Please sit down. Ordered coffee. Lots of it. We won't be disturbed.'

Powerscourt presented his credentials, another of his letters from Lord Salisbury. I may have to go and get some more of these soon, if they keep going at this rate, he said to himself.

'Met this Salisbury fellow, have you?'

'Only once,' Powerscourt replied.

'Don't know much about him. Good man, do you think?'

'My friend Lord Rosebery thinks very highly of him. But he says Salisbury's as devious as they come.'

'Have to be. Have to be. In that position, I mean.' Lord George Scott poured two cups of coffee and decanted three spoonfuls of sugar into his own. 'Need sugar. Don't know why. Bloody doctors told me. Now then. The *Bacchante*. You're here to talk to me about all that. Been combing my memory. Looked up a few records. Checked the odd time and place. Why don't I run that lot up the yardarm first and then you ask questions.'

Powerscourt said that that sounded an excellent plan.

'Damn strange business, whole thing. 1879, that's when it started. Met the Prince of Wales a few times by then. Shooting party in Yorkshire, one or two rubbers of whist. Always had to lose to the Prince of Wales at whist. Don't suppose you knew that.

'Had no intention of ever taking two bloody Princes on some bloody jaunt round the world. Not given any choice. Hauled up before those First Sea Lords and given no option. Old fools said it would be good for my career.

'Normal thing, Powerscourt, when you run a ship, you get to choose your officers. Not this time. Not the men either. Officers picked by one lot of admirals. Crew picked by another lot of admirals. Officers all old, rather decrepit. No dashing young flames there. Crew old, ugly, past their peak. Think they must have emptied one or two workhouses to provide me with that lot.' Lord George Scott shook his head sadly at the memory of his decrepit crew.

'Whole lot of nonsense before leaving about whether boat would sink or not. Had to take the old hulk out into North Atlantic and into the middle of a big storm. See if she would survive or not. Nobody seemed to have thought of what happened if she did sink. End of *Bacchante*, end of Captain Scott, end of crew. Naval disaster. British can't sail any more. British

172

ships can't float any more. Bloody papers making mincemeat of Royal Navy.'

Powerscourt could see that whatever his reservations about the First Lords of the Admiralty, Lord Scott's loyalty to the Navy was as strong as ever.

'Great row about accommodation. Somebody somewhere obsessed with it. That other boat they thought of using, *Newcastle*, had sort of sealed compartments, isolated accommodation. That was the appeal of it. Keep one lot of people away from the other.

'Where should Prince Eddy sleep? Where indeed. Many a time I would have pushed him overboard myself. Had to put him in my cabin. Build a sort of extra bit of space. Not allowed to mingle with rest of crew at all, only with his brother and the officers. Very strict instructions on that from my Lords of the Admiralty. Sealed packets, all that kind of stuff.'

Lord Scott poured himself another cup of coffee, a further three spoonfuls of sugar disappearing inside.

'Where was I? Accommodation. Prince Eddy spent most of his time in my cabin. Two whole bloody years of it. All kinds of lies put about. Prince learning naval trade, ropes, navigation, gunnery. All complete rubbish. Some kind of parson person with them. Name of Dalton. Sanctimonious old bore, like most bloody parsons. More like a guard for his precious Eddy. Never let him out of his sight.

'When you've grasped all that, you've got the main points. Didn't matter where we went really. Could have sailed round and round the Isle of Wight for two years. Wouldn't have made any bloody difference. Always had feeling that object of the exercise was to keep Eddy as far away from England as possible.

'One other thing. Nearly forgot.' Lord Scott took another mouthful of his sickly brew. 'Didn't just have a bloody parson person on board. Doctor person as well. Not naval. Ordinary bloody doctor. Seasick all the time. Had to be dosed round the world with his own medicine. He spent a lot of time with Prince Eddy. Special patient. Special examinations now and then. Everybody else had to leave the cabin. Don't care for doctors. Don't care for parsons. Didn't care much for my Lords of the Admiralty after all that either.

'That's it. Your turn now.'

He paused. Powerscourt didn't know where to begin.

'An admirable narrative, Lord Scott. I am much obliged to you. If I could just bowl you a couple of questions, I would be even more grateful.'

'Fire ahead. Fire ahead.' Scott had the air of one who would not be frightened by any broadside, however weighty and numerous the cannon balls.

'Those sealed orders you mentioned, the ones from the Admiralty. Did they make any mention of illicit sexual relations?'

'Good God, Powerscourt! How d'you know that? Mindreader, are you?' He looked up at Powerscourt with fresh respect and poured out yet more coffee. The great clattering of boots on marble had died down now, silence ruling over library and entrance hall. 'Pages of sealed orders about that. Pages of it. Crew to be lectured on evils of illicit sexual relations at regular intervals. Me, parson, doctor, all reading riot act. Ferocious floggings for transgressors. Waste of time. Crew could have hardly managed licit sexual relations, whatever they are. Dried-out collection, no juice in their limbs. Know what I mean? Never seen anything like it in all my years afloat.'

'Did you have any idea when you set out how long the voyage was going to be? Or did it get extended as it went on?'

'Never worked that out at all. Never clear.' Scott had abandoned the coffee and moved into the attack on the Army and Navy Club biscuits. Crumbs were spoiling the symmetry of his beard. 'Thought we could have come home after six months myself. God knew why we were sailing round the world in the first place. More orders kept coming. Keep sailing. Like some ancient curse. Never get home. Endless voyage. Voyage that never stops. Voyage to the back of beyond. And back again. Ancient mariners.'

'One last question, if I may. You said earlier that you suspected that the real purpose was to keep Prince Eddy out of England. What made you say that?'

'Thought that for years. Never told anybody. Not until now. Not until you. Before the voyage, terrible business on board *Britannia*. All hushed up. Officers cashiered, crew dispersed, ship's cat itself sworn to silence. Scandal of some sort. Dreadful scandal. Never knew what it was. Nobody did. Dangerous to ask questions. But if Prince Eddy was involved, maybe a need to get him out of the way. Families send naughty younger sons to the colonies. Keep them out of sight, out of harm's way. Same thing here. Eddy sent to the colonies. Literally. I bloody well took him there.'

Another of William Leith's trains was taking Powerscourt out of London to another appointment with James Robinson, The Limes, Church Road, Dorchester on Thames, father of one of five boys involved with Prince Eddy on the *Britannia*. Glimpses of the Thames through the windows offered the promise of a more peaceful world. Two schoolboys at the end of his compartment in black jackets, white shirts and black ties were complaining about Caesar and Cicero.

'We've only got half an hour left to finish these two passages off, or we're for it,' said the taller one.

Latin dictionaries lay open on their laps.

'I think I can manage this first bit,' said the little one, 'look up *aedificavit*, can you? That comes at the end of the sentence. Must be the bloody verb.'

Powerscourt was trying to make sense of the recent revelations. Scandal on the *Britannia*, that was certain. But then? Did they send Eddy away because he was ill? Was the *Bacchante* really a sort of hospital ship, specially equipped with doctors and parsons? Could they only come home when he was cured? Or when they thought he was cured? Was he cured?

Or did they send him away so they had time to hush everything up? Did it take the Prince of Wales two whole years to conceal the scandal? Two years in which the mere sight of Eddy could have blown the whole thing apart? No wonder they wanted to conceal the details of Eddy's death, he said to himself. No wonder they wanted to hide the murder. They've been hiding things for years. It must be second nature to them by now, almost a way of life.

'Thank heavens that's over,' said the tall black jacket as the two boys gathered themselves to leave the train. 'But why did

Cicero have to write such long sentences? Wouldn't those ordinary Romans have forgotten the beginning by the time he got to the end?'

'Think of Gladstone,' said the little black jacket. 'I'm not sure he can remember the start of a sentence by the time he gets to the end. If he ever does. Same thing really.'

And why, thought Powerscourt, watching the thatched cottages on the river go by once more, why should somebody wait thirteen years to kill him? Why not try to do it before? Presumably the Prince of Wales despatched money to keep everybody quiet, heaps and heaps of money probably. So why didn't they all keep their mouths shut, like they were meant to? Perhaps they had.

The Limes was a compact suburban villa. It had seen better days. The windows were in need of attention. Paint was peeling in large black flakes from the front door. Captain Williams' wallpaper came back to Powerscourt as he waited, wallpaper peeling off the walls, the bare patches where pictures had once stood.

He knocked firmly on the door.

A small fierce man of about sixty opened it. Dogs could be heard yelping in the background. Old copies of *The Times* and the *Illustrated London News* were piled up on a little table in the hall.

'Are you Mr Robinson? Good morning to you. My name is Powerscourt.'

'Get out!' said the small fierce man. 'Get out!'

'I wrote to tell you I was coming. I have in my pocket a letter from the Prime Minister for you.' Long experience had taught Powerscourt to place his left foot firmly against the jamb of the door.

'Get out. I don't care if you have a letter from the Prime Minister or the Archbishop of Canterbury or the Pope in Rome. Just get out!'

'Our conversation would be entirely confidential. Nobody would know anything about it. I give you my word.'

The little man had turned quite red now. Powerscourt thought he could see tears forming in the corners of his eyes.

'Do you understand English? I said Get out! Before I put the dogs on you.'

'Please don't put the dogs on me. I'm very fond of dogs,' said Powerscourt, hoping against hope that he could charm his way into the house.

'For the last time, Get out! Don't come back! Don't ever come back!' The little man was actually crying now, tears rolling down his cheeks.

Powerscourt beat the retreat. 'My apologies for upsetting you Mr Robinson. I'm going now. And don't worry. I won't come back.'

The barking of the dogs pursued him down the little drive. From somewhere inside he could hear a man weeping, and a softer woman's voice trying to comfort him. Mrs Robinson was soothing the little man, fierce no longer, as though he were a small child. She sounded as though she had done it before.

Two hundred yards away the churchyard nestled under its yew trees. Birds, river birds replaced the noise of the barking dogs and the agony of Mr Robinson. Fresh graves, thought Powerscourt, that's what I am looking for. Well, fairly fresh, not more than a year or two old. Lines of ancient memorials swept away towards the church path, names virtually eroded by time and weather. Here and there a defiant cross or angel marked a richer passing.

On the southern side, on the far side of the church, he found the more recent graves.

Mary William Blunt, beloved wife of Thomas Blunt, of Dorchester, passed away 15 January 1890.

Andrew James Macintosh, churchwarden of this parish, beloved husband of Elizabeth, father of Tabitha, Daniel, Albert. 18 July 1891. May he rest in Peace.

Maud Muriel Smythe, beloved wife of John Smythe, of Dorchester. 25 August 1891. Gone, but not Forgotten.

Peter James Cooper, beloved husband of Louise, father of the twins, 12 September 1891. May he see God.

Simon John Robinson, passed away 25 September 1891, beloved son of John and Mary Robinson, The Limes, Dorchester. Lord forgive them, for they know not what they do.

Powerscourt sank to his knees and prayed. He prayed for the Robinsons, all three of them, he prayed for the growing community of the dead who seemed to surround him, he asked

God's forgiveness for his morning call on the Robinson household. He prayed for his family. He prayed for Johnny Fitzgerald. He prayed for Lady Lucy.

Lord forgive them, he thought as he rose from his knees, a respectful gardener waiting to do his work, for they know not what they do. Who, for the family Robinson, was them? The Prince of Wales and his household? The boys on the *Britannia*? Was it even, he thought fancifully, the tumours that marked the latter stages of the disease, eating away at the victim's bones and his brain, unwitting and unfeeling instruments of God's purpose?

The vicar, the church noticeboard proclaimed, was The Very Rev. Matthew Adams, BA Oxon, M.Litt, London, of The Vicarage, Dorchester.

Mrs Adams opened the door. No dogs this time, Powerscourt thought, as she showed him into a cold sitting-room.

'My husband has just popped out,' she said brightly. 'But he'll be back presently. Would you like to wait in here? He won't be long.'

Biblical scenes adorned the room, great vistas of the lake of Galilee and the Mount of Olives. Powerscourt wondered if the vicar painted in his spare time, holidays always spent with canvas and brush. 'I'll just be a few moments more, dear, I've got to finish these angels.'

'Good morning to you,' said the Rev. Adams cheerfully as he strode into the room, a handsome man of about forty years, eyes wary beneath the smile.

I presume he knows I'm not bereaved or anything like that, thought Powerscourt. Probably his wife gives him a clue when unexpected visitors arrive, the weeping, the demented, the lost souls of Dorchester.

'Please forgive this unannounced intrusion, most impolite of me. My name is Powerscourt. I have had some rather unsatisfactory business here in Dorchester, and I would welcome your local knowledge.'

Powerscourt handed over his card. He explained that he was engaged on an investigation which, by its nature, had to remain secret. He showed the Rev. Adams a copy of his letter from the Prime Minister.

'Is there anything wrong? With the Government, I mean?' The Rev. Adams looked as though he would be reluctant to add the troubles of Westminster and Whitehall to the heavy burdens of Dorchester upon Thames.

'Anything wrong with the Government? No, I don't think so, no more than usual. My concerns are with a recent parishioner of yours, recently interred in your churchyard. Simon John Robinson.'

'Young Robinson.' The eyes grew warier still. The vicar edged himself further back in his chair. 'What can I tell you about him?'

'Do you know what he died of?'

'Oddly enough I don't. One usually hears, you know, what people die of. I don't think he actually died here. I think the body was brought from somewhere else.'

'Were the family well off?'

'I'm not their bank manager, Lord Powerscourt, but then I don't suppose they tell even you anything at all. Sometimes I feel it would be helpful in our parish work if the banks could let us know who was in financial trouble and we could provide help of a different kind. But they don't of course. Where was I? Ah, yes, the Robinsons. I think they were quite well off, they always seemed to live well. The son, Simon, was away a lot. He had been in the Navy for a while, you know.'

'Was he still in the Navy at the time of his death, do you know?'

'No, he wasn't, but they said he was in receipt of a generous naval pension which supported him in all his trips abroad.'

'Any indication,' Powerscourt raised his hands towards the vicar, 'that the rest of the family are not so well off now? Presumably the naval pension had to stop with his death.'

'There was some talk of them selling up shortly after he died. But then that stopped. Normal financial service seems to have been resumed now.' The vicar smiled a weak routine smile. Maybe they teach smiles in the theological colleges, thought Powerscourt, the polite smile, the sympathetic smile, the concerned smile, smiles for all seasons.

'Any brothers and sisters?'

'I think they were all boys. No daughters. Poor Mrs Robinson.

I'm sure she would have liked a daughter. She always says how lucky we are. We've got two of each.'

The smile of the happy family man this time. 'Two of the brothers are abroad. Canada, or is it Australia? The other one works up in London and comes down from time to time.'

'Do you know what he does in London?' asked Powerscourt, feeling it was time to leave.

'I do, as a matter of fact. He works in a grand shop near Piccadilly, but they've got branches all over London. They specialise in guns, shooting stuff, hunting knives, that sort of thing.'

Hunting knives. Powerscourt could feel the colour drain from his face. Sharp hunting knives. Sharp enough to slit your throat. Sharp enough to sever your arteries.

'Are you unwell, Lord Powerscourt? You look as though you had seen a ghost.'

'I'm fine, I'm fine. I have these little turns every now and then.' He smiled back one of the vicar's weaker smiles.

Ghosts. Ghosts of boys on the *Britannia*. Lord forgive them for they know not what they do. Ghosts that lay under trees in Sandringham Woods, messages left for the living. Forever Faithful. Semper Fidelis. Ghosts dancing in the rigging of the *Bacchante*, sailing on a journey to nowhere. The living ghost on the beach at Amble with the red eyes and the sunken spirit. It wasn't my fault I tell you. It wasn't my fault.

'Would you like a cup of tea? Something to eat?'

'No, I'm fine. The walk to the station will do me good, I promise you.'

The vicar walked him down to the town and escorted him right on to the platform itself. He's making sure I've gone, thought Powerscourt. Dorchester doesn't want to see me any more. Or they'll put the dogs on me. Or sons from gunshops in Piccadilly, armed with hunting knives.

17

Maybe, Powerscourt said to himself, it's because women, or more specifically, his sisters, weren't educated properly. Back in St James's Square Powerscourt was surrounded by his sisters' notebooks, reporting their conversations across London about his six equerries. Random thoughts spilled across the pages, random sentences with no order and no logic. Surely, thought Powerscourt, those governesses must have taught them something up there in the schoolroom. Or maybe not. Maybe they had just gossiped all day long, looking out over the soft hills of Wicklow, dreaming of balls and horses as yet unridden.

Powerscourt's mind kept wandering back to one phrase, just three words, spoken by the Rev. Adams as he sat in his chair underneath the Mount of Olives in The Vicarage, Dorchester on Thames.

Generous naval pension. That's what he said. Powerscourt was so taken by the phrase that he had written it down in his notebook and looked at it on the train back to London. He looked at it a lot. He didn't think you got generous naval pensions. If you got naval pensions at all.

William Burke had laughed. 'My dear Francis,' the financier had said, 'the Royal Navy and the First Lords of the Admiralty are not known for the generosity of their pensions. Quite the contrary. If they can get away with it, they don't give you a single farthing. And the idea that they would start paying out to somebody – how old did you say our chap was, late twenties, was it – it's absurd. I wouldn't go as far as to say it was impossible,' the banker's caution came to the fore, 'but it's very very unlikely. Very unlikely indeed.'

Suppose the payments coming from the Prince of Wales were disguised, disguised as generous naval pensions. It was a cover story, a convenient fiction to disguise the fact that the money came from Sir William Suter and Sir Bartle Shepstone, Private Secretary and Comptroller to the Household of the Prince of Wales. They wrote the cheques. The recipients welcomed another instalment of their generous naval pension. The blackmail circle was complete.

His mind wandered again, to the note he had sent to the Commissioner of the Metropolitan Police asking him to check on the movements of a man called Robinson, first name unknown, employed in the gunshop off Piccadilly. His parents lived in Dorchester on Thames. Could the Commissioner establish where this Robinson had been on the weekend of the 8th and 9th January. Had he, by any chance, been in Norfolk? This request was most urgent. Lord Powerscourt was most grateful for the assistance.

The notebooks of his sisters, lying unread on his table in St James's Square, called him back to work.

It really is a remarkable collection of documents, he thought, nearing the end of his sisters' writings. Future historians will find it fascinating. Who was poor, who was rich, which families rowed and which did not, which families were selling their paintings to Americans to keep themselves afloat, which younger sons drove their parents to despair. The marriages, fixed not in the hearts of tomorrow's husbands and wives, but in the scheming brains of their mothers: where they bought their furniture, where they bought their curtains, where they bought their kitchens, where they met their lovers.

Charles Peveril's mother was widely believed to have had an affair with William Brockham's father, an affair that went on for years. This, according to Powerscourt's sister Mary, must be the key to the whole affair. Quite how, she did not reveal, as further bits of gossip chased each other across the page. Harry Radclyffe's father drank too much. Frederick Mortimer's father kept selling parcels of land, thousands and thousands of acres at a time.

But of blackmail, of secret payments, dark shadows falling across a family's fortunes, there was not a word. William Burke confirmed the absence of blackmail when Powerscourt met him downstairs.

'Francis, I promise you, I have written it all down. But I have left the document in my office. Let me give you the main points now.'

He drew Powerscourt aside to stand by the windows. The lamps in the square showed not a soul walking the streets of St James's. The great square was empty, except for its resident colony of crows.

'Money,' said Burke, familiarity and reverence in his voice. 'As far as money goes, they're about average for their kind. It all depends on who got out of land in time. Four of them are still heavily invested, or mortgaged, in land. They're getting worse off all the time. Two of them got out of land, like you, Francis, and put their money elsewhere. They're getting richer most of the time. But of blackmail, in the active or the passive sense, I can find no trace at all.'

Before he went to sleep Powerscourt looked again at some more of his correspondence, at two letters in particular. They came from the parents of two of the five boys who had been with Eddy in the *Britannia* affair. Both were very happy to see him. They would be delighted. But they both recommended that he should speak first to a Mr William Simmons, of The Laurels, Shapston, Dorset. 'He is much better acquainted with these matters, better qualified to speak, than I am.' The wording was identical in the two letters, as if they had agreed it beforehand, decided together what they were going to say. Or had the Simmons of Shapston, Dorset, agreed the wording with the other two?

Tomorrow he would find out.

The spire of Salisbury Cathedral disappeared slowly into its valley as Powerscourt's cab took him up into the rolling hills of Dorset.

He had expected Shapston to be a pretty little village with a pond, a cricket pitch and rows of neat houses with well-tended gardens. It wasn't. There was a very fine Jacobean mansion above the little hamlet, and a disparate straggle of miscellaneous houses. There were a great many cows. The cows seemed to think they owned the place.

The Laurels was a two-storey building with a thatched roof and a very ancient front door.

'Welcome to our humble abode, Lord Powerscourt! Welcome!' gushed Mrs Simmons, as she took his coat in the large hall. Mrs Simmons was a well-built woman in her mid-fifties with a look of command in her eye. A couple of feet behind her, William Simmons waited to shake his hand. Powerscourt wondered if the gap summed up the relations between them, Mrs Simmons always in the lead.

'This is the dining-room in here.' She seemed to be giving Powerscourt a tour of their humble abode. He shuddered at the sight of the dining-table and chairs, but the curtains looked satisfactory. 'We only use this suite in the winter if William has to entertain clients from the bank, isn't that right, dear? And this is the entrance to the cottage, our little extension here, the East Wing we like to call it.' She laughed a bright laugh. 'Alfred, our son, the one you are interested in, Lord Powerscourt, these are Alfred's quarters.

'Now then,' she went on gaily, 'this is the drawing-room. I expect you'd like to sit down, Lord Powerscourt, after your long journey. And I expect you'd like some coffee. William always likes a cup of coffee at this time of day.'

It was a handsome room with a blazing fire and a door opening out on the garden. A couple of robins picked their way delicately across the lawn, their red breasts very bright in the sombre winter landscape of withered grass and bare fruit trees.

'I think we'll wait until the coffee comes before we begin our conversations, Lord Powerscourt. Muriel always likes to be in the thick of the action. I sometimes wonder if she won't come down to the bank in Blandford one day and try to take over.' Simmons smiled a rueful smile. He looked a lot shrewder than his wife's comments suggested. He was nearly six feet tall, expanding round the waist, with a very thin moustache and a splendid watch chain adorning his waistcoat.

'Here we are! I expect you thought I'd lost the coffee!' sang Mrs Simmons, reappearing with a tray.

Powerscourt took out his letter from Prime Minister Salisbury and handed it round for inspection. Simmons read it respectfully and passed it over to his wife.

'Oh, I say! I say,' said Mrs Simmons, 'isn't this splendid! Downing Street comes to Shapston! How appropriate that the letter comes from Lord Salisbury too. Just a few short miles away. What will they say about this in the bank, William?'

'It must never reach the bank, my dear. Never. Or anywhere else for that matter. The whole business has been kept a secret for all these years. It must remain so.'

Powerscourt thought he could see what Mr Simmons might be like in his bank, firm words to those who strayed. Perhaps he wasn't in his wife's pocket after all. Perhaps he just played along with her because that was the easiest thing to do.

'Mr Simmons. Mrs Simmons. I knew you would accept the need for secrecy. And I know that you will observe that need in the future. Perhaps I could give you an indication of what I am interested in.'

Powerscourt looked round the room. That was a mistake. The walls, he saw, were covered with old maps, maps of Dorset, maps of Blandford, maps of Salisbury. Some of them looked as though they could have cost a great deal of money.

'Forgive me for interrupting!' pealed Mrs Simmons. 'I couldn't help noticing that you were admiring our collection of maps, Lord Powerscourt! It's one of William's hobbies. He'd go anywhere to find an interesting old map, wouldn't you, dear!'

'Everything in its place, Muriel. There's a time and place for everything, as I always say. Lord Powerscourt, you were saying.'

'I have talked to some of the officers who were involved in the unhappy business of the *Britannia*.'

'That was too dreadful, too dreadful, Lord Powerscourt!' Mrs Simmons could not be contained. 'Forgive me for interrupting again. I'll always remember where I was when we heard. William was mowing the lawn in our other house, much smaller than this one, I fear. And I was making him a steak and kidney pie for his lunch. It was Cook's day off. It's William's favourite, steak and kidney pie. And then we heard the news! I dropped William's kidneys all over the floor! Oh, I am so sorry.' Her husband was glaring at her with a look of fury on his face. 'I won't interrupt again. I promise. I'm so sorry, Lord Powerscourt.'

Powerscourt smiled at her, one of the smiles he had learnt from the Rev. Adams in Dorchester. 'As I was saying, I have talked with some of the officers on *Britannia*. I have talked with some of the officers on the *Bacchante*, the vessel that took the two Princes round the world. But I would really like to know how the families of the other boys reacted to these sad and unfortunate events. I don't think we need bother with any of the medical details Mr Simmons.'

Powerscourt turned to Simmons on his left. He had the fire in front of him. Mrs Simmons, on the right, was poised for speech, like a bird of prey.

'I have given this matter a lot of thought since your letter, Lord Powerscourt,' Simmons was addressing the shareholders of his bank, 'and I will try to keep it brief. Shortly after that *Britannia* business was over, the parents of the five boys met in London. We were trying to decide how to proceed, what to do for the best, how to look after our children in the future. The parents decided to ask me to be the spokesman for our little group. I have been so ever since.'

'They wanted a man of business, Lord Powerscourt! They wanted somebody used to dealing with the affairs of the world. Isn't that right, William?'

Simmons carried on as if there had been no interruption. 'I wrote, in confidence, of course, to the Prince of Wales' Private Secretary, William Suter. I pointed out to him that, thanks to the actions of his master's son, all of our sons faced a very uncertain future, one where there would be a great deal of expense. There would be medical bills, trips to Europe, maybe to America in search of new treatments. I didn't ask for any money at that stage. I waited to see what the reply might be.'

'And there was the worry! The worry and the uncertainty of it all! Five of us mothers needing some form of recompense for all the pain we were going through! Enough to break any mother's heart!'

Simmons sailed on. 'I received an immediate reply, requesting a meeting in London. Mr Suter – he wasn't Sir William Suter then, was he, Lord Powerscourt – said that the Prince of Wales had been thinking about this very carefully for some time.'

I'll bet he had, thought Powerscourt. I'll bet he didn't intend to hand over a penny if he could avoid it. He waited until the loaded pistol was held to his head.

'Suter more or less told me that we could name our price. So we did. But there was one condition. And I am sure you could guess that in one, Lord Powerscourt.'

'Silence,' said Powerscourt.

'Total and absolute silence. We all had to sign a document drawn up by his lawyers. Even Muriel signed it, didn't you?'

'There was nothing to say that we couldn't talk about it in the privacy of our own homes, William dear. And we did very well out of it in a way. A few years after that we were able to move in here, weren't we?'

Powerscourt remembered a conversation about blackmail with a very intelligent Superintendent of the Metropolitan Police several years before. They had been on their own in the back room of a quiet pub by the river.

'It's like this, my lord,' said the Superintendent, drinking his pint slowly and deliberately. 'The first thing the blackmailer has to do is to get his claws into his victim.' He squeezed the back of his left hand very firmly with the fingers of his right. Briefly, the blood drained away. The skin went white. 'Then they start asking for more. Year one, it may be just a preliminary finger, my lord. By year two the blackmailer feels he can ask for a bit more. Then a lot more. After a while the blackmailer starts to feel that his victim owes him the money, that he, the blackmailer, deserves it. Very strange that.'

'Could I ask you about the arrangements, Mr Simmons? How the money was paid and so on.'

'Oh, it was all very honest and above board, Lord Powerscourt.'

'William wouldn't have had it any other way, would you, my dear? What would the bank have said if there had been anything strange about it all?'

What indeed, said Powerscourt to himself.

'It came every month. The story we all agreed on was that

they could be referred to as naval pensions for the boys. If anybody asked. But nobody ever did. The money came like clockwork. From a branch of Finch's in London.'

'And did you find that the whole business became more expensive as time went on? What with the doctors and the treatments and all that sort of thing?' Powerscourt was trying to sound as innocent as he could. He needn't have worried.

'Of course it did, Lord Powerscourt!' Mrs Simmons was indignant. 'Every year it became more expensive! We've been to Switzerland, to London, to America to see the doctors there. We had to buy new clothes and new hats for all these trips. And if we stayed on for a little holiday afterwards, then no one was going to object, were they? Think what we were all going through! Think of the shame if it ever came out! I could never have raised my head in the village again! We'd have had to move! I think silence is beyond price, don't you agree, William dear?'

'Have the arrangements always worked smoothly? No unfortunate mishaps along the way?' His Superintendent came back to Powerscourt. Something he'd said was teasing away at the back of his mind.

'If any of the arrangements about paying the money ever go wrong, then it's panic all round, my lord. Frightful panic. Very hard to put the genie back in the bottle again.'

'They've always worked very well,' said Simmons. His wife had temporarily vanished from the room. 'They've only gone wrong once and that was fairly recently. But we managed to sort that out.'

'And the boys themselves, young men, I should say. I know that one of them died last year. Are all the rest all right?'

'As well as can be expected, that's what the doctors say. Sometimes they go for years with no trouble, then it flares up again.'

'And your own Alfred? Does he live here with you?'

'Lord Powerscourt! Do have some of my special cake! My modest effort always wins the prizes here in the village. I once had a third place with it at the Dorset County Show!'

Mrs Simmons had returned, triumphant, with an enormous fruit cake, and a small, leather-bound book.

'There! A generous slice for you, Lord Powerscourt! William always says there is no point in having mean portions of my cake!'

'Our son is quite well. He's our only child,' Simmons carried on, 'he lives most of the time here with us.'

'William was able to secure him a small position in the bank, Lord Powerscourt! So kind of William! And, unlike most boys of his age, Alfred really loves living with his mother! Isn't that right, dear?'

'Is he here at the moment?'

'No, he's not.' Simmons was rendered almost speechless by a mouthful of his wife's fruit cake. 'He's been away since the start of this year. He's gone to a friend of his in Norfolk, somewhere near Fakenham. Alfred goes there often. He's always been excellent with a rifle. I think they do a lot of shooting.'

Powerscourt took refuge in his cake. One *Britannia* brother was good with the hunting knives perhaps. Another one was good with a rifle. They could be a deadly pair up there in Norfolk, not far from Sandringham. He began composing another note to the Commissioner of the Metropolitan Police.

As he left The Laurels, he was trapped again by Mrs Simmons.

'Lord Powerscourt! We can't let you leave until you've signed our little visitors' book! All our guests do! And if you could sign it Lord Francis Powerscourt, that would be too nice for words! Otherwise they mightn't believe you were really a lord! Dearie me! That would never do!'

For the first time in his life, he signed himself Lord Francis Powerscourt. Simmons shook him warmly by the hand as he left, saying that if he needed further help, then he must come again. Mrs Simmons assured him that he would always be more than welcome in her humble home. There was another cake recipe she could perfect before his next visit.

18

'Just you sit yourself in the back of the boat, Francis.'

'I think they call it the stern, Johnny.'

Powerscourt and Fitzgerald were setting off from Hammersmith up the Thames to view the secret house of London's homosexual rich. Powerscourt wanted to see the building for himself. It was late in the evening, a cold wind blowing across the river. Fitzgerald had procured an ancient rowing boat from somewhere.

'The thing is, Francis, I'm getting very superstitious about that house. Twice now I've seen single magpies on my way back from there. No matter how long I waited I never saw another one. And I'm fed up with being stuck up that bloody tree. So we'll creep up on them the way they're least expecting. Christ, Francis, sit still, for God's sake. We'll all be in the water at this rate.'

The rowing boat seemed to have a will of its own, swaying, lurching, dipping at unpredictable moments.

'Which way are we going, Johnny?'

Powerscourt wondered if he could swim back to the bank, as the vessel zigzagged its way towards a fatal rendezvous with the bastions of Hammersmith Bridge.

'Shut up, Francis! I've just got to get the bloody thing into the middle of the river. The current's not so bad there.'

At last the boat settled into a rhythm, Fitzgerald's powerful arms moving them upstream. Hampton Court, thought Powerscourt, we could reach Hampton Court if we kept going, or Oxford. Though not at this rate, not this year. Even in the middle the current was still strong, progress very slow, the splash of the oars unnaturally loud in the middle of the Thames.

To Powerscourt's right lay the waterfront of Hammersmith lined with taverns and fine houses, occasional sounds drifting out across the water. To his left, beyond Hammersmith Bridge, the trees of Barnes kept silent vigil over their progress. Strange pieces of river jetsam floated by on their passage towards the open sea: pieces of wood in fantastic shapes, bits of material that might have once have been clothes, bottles without messages. A rowing eight, dressed entirely in black, shot past them going the other way, a ghostly light at the front of their boat, the current sweeping them downstream towards Putney.

'Nearly there, Francis.' Fitzgerald took a brief break from the oars and drank deeply from his hip flask. 'Look! You can just see the lights through the trees.'

The river had taken them round a bend. Hammersmith Bridge was no longer visible behind. Ahead the cold black waters of the Thames reached out towards the waterfront of Barnes, a mile or so away on the opposite bank. A couple of rooks stood sentinel on the top of the trees around the house.

There were lights on all across the top two floors. Powerscourt thought business must be brisk. Maybe it was one of those special evenings, a dinner dance or a masked ball. There was a stone balustrade running right round the top of the building, shafts of moonlight blinking intermittently through the clouds. Sentinels, he thought, watchmen on duty, searching a dark London for the unexpected visitor, the sudden rush of officers in uniform towards the front door.

'It's a grand place if you want to be alone, isn't it?' Fitzgerald was panting slightly from his efforts, holding the little boat steady in its place. They could see a small jetty to their right, a couple of boats moored, ready for a quick escape across the water. 'I had another chat with my friend, Francis.'

'The one with the Pomerol?'

'The one with the Pomerol,' Fitzgerald agreed. 'He said two things that are relevant to our purpose, I think. The first . . .'

A muffled sound came to them from very close by. It echoed slightly across the water and disappeared into the trees.

Fitzgerald rowed on, past the house, round another bend in the River.

They waited. Neither spoke. They waited for two minutes, perhaps three. The River Thames was silent save for the timeless murmurings of the water. Then Fitzgerald turned the boat around. The current took them back towards London. Only slight adjustments were needed to hold their course.

'What the hell was that?' said Powerscourt as the house disappeared from view.

'I think it was the front door opening and closing. Another member, another client. He must have been bloody quiet going up their driveway. We didn't hear any footsteps, did we?'

'No, we didn't. That place gives me the creeps. You were saying, Johnny?'

What must we look like, thought Powerscourt? Two men, huddled in a tiny boat, going up and down the river in the middle of the night. Excise men, perhaps, going to inspect some forbidden cargo, or grave robbers, avoiding the main roads.

'Two of them have died in the past two years. I think that's what I was about to say. My friend shuddered when he told me about it. I expect he wondered if that was how he was going to go. Mad or blind or paralysed, or all three, his bones eaten away.

'But I talked to him about blackmail, about whether any of our friends back there might have been blackmailing each other. He said he thought it was virtually impossible.'

Fitzgerald was whispering. Powerscourt had to lean forward to catch his words, the little boat bobbing precariously once more.

'You remember the constitution of their club, Francis, each member having to give the names and addresses of two referees who didn't know about their perverse habits. That threat is always there. Step out of line and you'll be exposed. My friend said they were all so frightened of being blackmailed by their own club that they couldn't possibly think about blackmailing anybody else.'

These were calmer waters, thought Powerscourt, a little bit choppy, perhaps, tiny waves beating helplessly against the shore, sailing craft bobbing about, minute bow waves inching across the pond.

The Round Pond in Kensington Gardens was host to Powerscourt and Lady Lucy and two small boys on a peaceful Sunday afternoon.

Lunch had been taken quickly in Markham Square. Lady Lucy had christened Robert's boat *Britannia* by pouring a glass of champagne across the front.

'I thought it might break. The boat, I mean. If I broke the bottle across the bows in the approved manner.' Lady Lucy sounded as if she had been launching ships all her life. Perhaps she had, thought Powerscourt, a thousand of them, maybe, sailing across the blue waters of the Aegean to a tryst with death at windy Troy.

Robert's friend, Thomas St Clair Erskine, recently released from jail or temporary domestic confinement, informed them solemnly that his ship was called the *Victowy*, his rs rolling like the original *Victowy* on patrol out in the Atlantic.

'Can we go now? Can we go and sail them?'

Even Lady Lucy's cook's best apple pie, laced with slivers of orange and fortified with nutmeg, could not hold them. The boys ran, not too fast in case they dropped their boats, the grown-ups following more sedately behind.

Anxiety, great anxiety, surrounded the maiden voyage of the *Britannia*. Robert, his face drawn with nerves and concentration, kept making final adjustments to the sails. There were learned seven-year-old conversations about the direction of the prevailing wind. At last she was off, wobbling at first, then making steadier progress on an arc of a journey that left her marooned on the shore once more, not far from the launch position.

'I do hope it's going to be all right. The boat I mean. Think what would happen if it didn't work.' Lady Lucy turned to Powerscourt, a male consort who ought to know about such things.

'We didn't learn much about sails and things in the Army,' said Powerscourt defensively.

'Oh dear. Oh dear.' Lady Lucy hurried towards the shore. Robert's boat had performed two more irregular journeys before returning to port and refusing to move at all. There seemed to have been a mutiny on board. Robert was close to tears. His friend was urging him to let the sails out so that *Britannia* could take advantage of the breeze, blowing strongly across Kensington Gardens.

'Then it might fall over and sink. I don't want it to sink. Why won't it go, Mama? Everybody else's boat is going fine.'

Lady Lucy's look of helpless despair brought rescue from an unexpected quarter. An old gentleman, dressed in a dark blue coat, buttons brightly polished, muffler round his neck, had approached the sad party.

'Could I offer you assistance? I have some experience in these matters.' The old gentleman addressed his request to Lady Lucy. The two boys looked up at him warily. 'I do know about sailing ships, I promise you. I sailed in one of them for years.'

The two boys stared at him, wonder in their eyes. Here was a man in a sailing ship. Perhaps he had climbed all the way to the top of the masts when he was young. It was nearly as good as meeting W.G. Grace himself.

'How very kind of you,' said Lady Lucy. 'If you're sure it's no trouble.'

'No trouble at all. We can't have these boats not sailing properly, can we?'

'It's Wobert's boat, sir.' Thomas had obviously decided that the old gentleman must have been a naval captain, if not an admiral. 'It just wolls awound in the water, sir. The wigging must be wong.'

There followed a long inspection of the errant *Britannia*. The old gentleman bent down slowly to the water's edge. Powerscourt wondered if he had back trouble, or stiff joints. Lady Lucy thought she had seen a miracle. Knots were undone. Rigging was adjusted. The tiny rudder was repositioned on the advice of the ancient mariner.

'If you put it like that, the ship is bound to go round and round,' he said kindly. 'Now, Robert, just make sure all those knots are tied properly. They are? Good. Put her back in the water. Give her a little push. Big ships have tugs to tow them out to sea when they are launched. Nothing wrong with giving it a push. Same thing really.'

This time around the *Britannia* performed creditably, sailing steadily across the pond and ending up beached on the far side beside a very large dog. The two boys hurried to the rescue. 'I told you it was the wigging,' shouted Thomas triumphantly. 'The wigging must be wight now.'

And so it went on all afternoon. The light was fading when the sailing ships were finally withdrawn from service, their keels inspected for damage underneath, the sails shaken clear of water. The old gentleman took his farewells. He leant down as he said goodbye to the two boys.

'I was once the captain of a sailing ship, you know, a real one. HMS *Achilles* she was called. Back in the 1860s that must have been. Very fast she was too. As you would expect with a name like that. I come here most Sunday afternoons. My wife can't get out any more. Her navigation systems have all gone. Maybe I shall see you here again. Good afternoon to you both.'

'Wasn't he a nice old gentleman,' said Lady Lucy, her hand poised over a Spode teapot back in Markham Square.

'I think it made his day,' said Powerscourt. 'I wonder if he'll be there again the next time the boys go sailing.'

'Lord Francis,' Lady Lucy's slender arm reached out to pour the milk into his tea. 'You don't take sugar, do you?'

'How clever of you to remember,' Powerscourt replied gallantly, thinking that Lady Lucy was looking a little apprehensive.

'You remember I said I had something to tell you about those equerries of yours. The day we met at the bottom of St James's Square.'

Lady Lucy as Anna Karenina, thought Powerscourt, himself a reluctant Vronsky, the high fur collar and its owner tripping off towards Piccadilly. 'Of course.'

'Well, I still haven't written it down. I mean I have written it down, but it didn't seem to make sense. It's such a strange story, almost like a fairy tale from long ago. I was always very fond of fairy tales when I was a child, Lord Francis. Were you?'

'I used to get very frightened,' said Powerscourt, thinking that Lady Lucy's childhood must be twelve to fifteen years more recent than his own.

'A long long time ago, twenty-five or twenty-eight years ago . . .' Lady Lucy spoke quietly, her eyes and her mind far away. Powerscourt thought she must tell Robert bedtime stories like this, the little boy's head tucked up against the pillows, his mother's soft voice coming from some still place deep inside her. '. . . a little boy was born into one of England's oldest families. His mother was quite old, in her late thirties or early forties. This was her last child. All the rest were daughters. And she loved him so much. She watched him growing up on the great estate. She cried in secret when he went away to school. All through the long terms she waited for him to come home. Home to his mother.

'When he was quite small his father ran away. He went off to Paris or Biarritz or one of those places where wicked husbands go and he never came home again, not even to see his little boy. The sisters got married and went away. There was only the mother and the little boy left in the great house with the park and the lake in front of the windows. The little boy used to go boating on the lake, rowing his mother round and round until it was time for tea.

'The little boy grew up. He was a very pretty little boy, they say, and very handsome when he turned into a young man, almost like a prince with his very own castle. All the girls fell in love with him. And his mother didn't like that. She didn't like that at all.'

It was growing dark outside. Lady Lucy got up and drew her curtains, pausing to toss a couple of logs on the fire. Her granddaughter clock ticked hypnotically behind her chair.

'Not very far away, ten or fifteen miles away, there was a great city. As the little boy grew up, the city grew up too. But while he was growing in feet and inches the city was growing by the thousand, tens and tens of thousands of people, all crowding in, looking for work and happiness.

'More tea, Lord Francis? I could make some more if this lot has gone cold.'

'No, thank you.' Powerscourt didn't want to break the spell.

'Most of the people in this city were poor. Terribly poor, poor souls.' Lady Lucy shivered slightly although the room was warm from the fire. 'But some of them were very rich. They made things. They ran great businesses. They owned shops. The man in our story, Lord Francis, owned a great many shops, grocers' shops, in the great city and the other cities round about. He became the richest of them all. And he had a daughter, an only daughter. They say she was beautiful, so beautiful that the young men were almost frightened of her beauty.

'The young man brought lots of girls back to his house in the country. There were dinners before the great dances and balls of the county, hunt balls, charity balls, that sort of thing. His mother looked at all these young women, coming to take her beautiful son away, and she sort of hated them. She couldn't bear it. But he never grew attached to any of them. Perhaps he was being kind to his mother. We don't know. Perhaps, like the prince in the story, he was waiting for someone else to come along.

'They did, of course. Perhaps they always do. One day, the prince met the grocer's daughter. I don't know where it was. But they fell in love just like in the fairy stories. The young man had resisted all the great beauties of county society all his life. Now he fell over in a great rush, as if he was in a waterfall, hurtling towards the bottom. Can you have waterfalls of love, Lord Francis?'

'I'm sure you can, Lady Lucy. I'm certain of it.'

'Where was I?' Lady Lucy was temporarily knocked over by her torrents of emotion. 'Inside a month they were desperately in love. They wanted to get married. But there was a complication, Lord Francis. There usually is. The girl was a Roman Catholic. Her parents were very devout. They didn't want her to marry a Protestant, even if he came from one of the oldest families in England. They said they would forbid the match.'

Lady Lucy took a sip of her cold tea. Powerscourt watched her tell her story, his mind racing ahead. He wondered where it would end. He didn't like to think about the end.

'But there was a complication on the other side too. The boy's mother didn't want her precious son marrying a grocer's daughter, however rich her family were. And she certainly didn't want him marrying a Roman Catholic. She said she would forbid the match too. She said she would bring the boy's father home from wherever he had gone, whatever he had done in the meantime, to stop this marriage.

'So they were all stuck. The young man, the beautiful girl,

two sets of parents. Maybe it would have been better if the parents had never been so obstinate. What were the young lovers to do? What could they do?'

Lady Lucy paused once more, looking at the flames dancing in the fireplace as if the answer might be hidden in the blaze. 'I don't think young lovers are ever very sensible, do you, Lord Francis? The young man had to choose between his love and his mother, between his past and his future, perhaps, between old age and the glory of youth.

'The young man started taking instruction in the Catholic faith. They say he followed his lessons far more intently than he ever did at Eton. When he was accepted, or whatever happens to them, they were married. The boy's mother refused to attend. Not to a grocer's daughter, she said. Not to a Roman Catholic. Not in some pagan chapel, decked out with bleeding hearts and the false idolatry of Rome.

'Well, some of them were happy now, especially the young lovers. The girl's father bought them a lovely little house between the city and the old house where the young man was born. The girl became pregnant, there was tremendous happiness all round. But it didn't last, Lord Francis. It didn't last.'

Lady Lucy looked thoughtful. Her eyes were far away, lost in the fairy story.

Powerscourt waited for the end, for some horror yet to come. The faces of the equerries he had questioned at Sandringham flashed through his mind. Five of them, one of them must be the young man in the story.

'Then she lost the baby. She had some sort of terrible accident. The young man was away on military duty at the time. I think I forgot to tell you that he joined his father's regiment. It was a terrible accident. The baby died. The young mother died. The young man rushed home to find his life in ruins, the love of his life lying at the bottom of a great set of stone steps, the baby dead inside her.

'There was a row about the funeral, about where the body was buried. The boy's mother wanted the girl and her grandchild buried in the family vault in the family chapel in the family seat, even though she had refused to attend the wedding. The girl's parents refused. They said it was their grandchild too. I don't know where they were buried in the end.

'But the point of the story, Lord Francis, is this.' Lady Lucy leaned forward and fixed her blue eyes on Powerscourt's face. She looked at him intently. 'The young man told very few people about his wedding. I suspect he thought of the pain it would cause his mother, all those county women inquiring about the church service and making pointed remarks about the price of groceries. I don't think he told any of the other officers in his regiment. I don't think he told any of his other friends.

'But Prince Eddy knew. Prince Eddy knew the girl. When the husband was away, they say that Prince Eddy was never away from the house. They say that he was forcing his attentions on her. Maybe he thought married women were fair game, just like his father. Well, I don't think this girl was. Fair game, I mean.

'On the day she died, they say that Prince Eddy was at the house, that he was seen running away after a scream, a horrible scream that went on and on and on. They say that he didn't go back, Prince Eddy. He just kept on running, running away.

'I don't think I know any more. It's a terrible story.'

Powerscourt rose from his seat and walked over to the fire, as if to break the spell. 'Who told you the story Lucy? Where does it come from?'

'Two people, Francis. I had to invent some terrible pack of lies to get the story out of the second one. One of them was a cousin of the dead wife. The other was the uncle of the boy. You see, he's my uncle too, in a roundabout sort of way. He's my late husband's father's brother, uncle-in-law, if you see what I mean. I think he heard it from the boy's mother.'

The truth was lying about on your own doorstep, thought Powerscourt. While he had been charging round England in a variety of trains, Lady Lucy merely talked to her relations round the corner.

'And what is the name of the young man?'

Lady Lucy paused. She suspected that everything would be different after she told him. Then her courage came back.

'The young man is called Lord Edward Gresham.'

Powerscourt had wondered about that for some time. Had

there been something not quite right about his demeanour at Sandringham? Nothing tangible, maybe the kind of thing that would come over you if you had murdered the heir presumptive to the throne and smashed the picture of his fiancée into small pieces on the floor.

'Lord Edward Gresham. Lord Edward Gresham, equerry to His Royal Highness the Duke of Clarence and Avondale. The late Duke of Clarence and Avondale, Prince Eddy.' Powerscourt was already thinking about more journeys. 'And his mother is Lady Gresham, Lady Blanche Gresham, of Thorpe Hall in War-wickshire. And the great city must be Birmingham. Am I right?'

'You are, Lord Francis. You are. 'The young man in the fairy story, the young man with the dead wife at the bottom of the stone steps, is Lord Edward Gresham.'

19

It really was the most improbable ceiling. High above were putti in angelic plaster frozen into the corners, plaster maidens draped in scanty wraps, plaster maidens carrying trumpets or spears or sheaves of corn. Wrapping them all together in a filigreed embrace, the elaborate plasterwork itself danced round the four walls and the over-elaborate corners. In the centre, in an oval shape, was an allegorical painting in pinks and vivid reds. Apollo in his chariot, on a hunting mission, was surrounded by yet more female forms with plaster thighs and plaster breasts.

'Most people stop here, my lord,' said Lyons, the butler of Thorpe Hall in the county of Warwickshire. 'To look up. The ceiling was built in 1750, my lord, by a man called Gibbs, James Gibbs, my lord.'

While Powerscourt gazed up at the baroque ceiling and the delicate outlines of the chariot above, Lyons deposited his hat and coat in some distant corner of the great entrance hall. Powerscourt wondered what the decoration was like in there. Hatstands made of plaster perhaps, contorted putti disguised as coat hooks preparing to bear the weight of the visitors' cloaks.

'This way, my lord.' The hall was very long, a number of ornate doors closed on either side.

'Lord Powerscourt, my lady.'

He was shown into a great salon with large windows at either end, paintings lining the walls. Lady Blanche Gresham advanced from her chair at the far end of the room to greet him. There was ample time to take in her stiff elegance, pride and dignity in each aristocratic step on her slow walk across the carpet.

'Lord Powerscourt. I am delighted to make your acquaintance. Please sit down.'

An imperious nod indicated that he was to retrace his steps with her to the seat by the window, the journey long, the stiff frozen lawn outside beckoning them on.

'Lord Rosebery wrote to me about you. Do you know Rosebery well?' The question was almost a command.

'He is one of my greatest friends, Lady Gresham. I have known him for many years. And I have a letter for you from the Prime Minister as well. I did not like to entrust it to the postal services.'

Lady Blanche was tall and slim. Powerscourt thought she must have been in her early sixties, probably born in the reign of William IV. She was wearing a long black skirt and a silk shirt of deep red. Round her neck was a string of pearls which she fingered from time to time as if checking they were still there.

'Rosebery I knew as a young man. This Salisbury I don't know at all.' The Prime Minister was dismissed as though he came from poor stock or had made his money in trade. 'Rosebery was quite charming. He came here to a house party many years ago. I think Disraeli was here that weekend.'

Powerscourt wondered how Disraeli had gained admittance if Salisbury was *persona non grata*. Charm and flattery, he supposed, the usual Disraeli tricks.

'He was most amusing, Rosebery I mean. He kept us all quite entertained for the days he was here. Such elegant manners.' Her voice was high. It cracked from time to time, like glass in a mirror. 'But you haven't come here to reminisce about Thorpe Hall in the days of its glory, Lord Powerscourt. How can I be of assistance to you in your business?'

There was something very special about the way she said Thorpe Hall, as if it were sacred, something to be kept safe from strangers.

'I wanted to ask you a few questions about your son, Lady Gresham.'

'My son? My son?' Lady Blanche Gresham sat ever straighter in her chair, her back stiff, her eyes haughty.

'The first thing you have to remember about my son, Lord Powerscourt, is that he is a Gresham. A Gresham.'

That emphasis again. Earlier Greshams, Greshams in uniform, Greshams in repose, seemed to nod their approval, staring down from their family seats on the walls of the long long room.

'Greshams have played their part in the history of England for over six hundred years, Lord Powerscourt. They may have come over with William the Conqueror. We cannot be sure. One of my ancestors was burnt at the stake in the reign of that dreadful Queen Mary, burnt to death for his beliefs. They say that the other Protestants who perished with him cried out as the flames took hold. They repented. They said they were sorry, they hadn't meant it. The Gresham spoke not a word, Lord Powerscourt. Greshams don't cry.

'I have looked at the records of the time, our family records somewhere in the attics of this house where we sit. The priests were corrupt, Lord Powerscourt. The abbots were greedy. They took from the rich. They took from the poor. The friars were more interested in the sins of the flesh than the redemption of souls. Those indulgences! Sold to indulge the whims of a Pope in Rome who wanted to glorify his city with the buildings of this world, not with the blessings of the next.'

Powerscourt could see that an alliance with a Catholic family might present a few problems here in Thorpe Hall.

'My family,' she went on, 'have been active in the business of this county or this country for centuries. We have hunted across these fields beyond these windows for generations. Generations, Lord Powerscourt. The Gresham stirrup cup, the hunt has always said, is the best in the county, if not in the country.'

She stopped briefly. This woman's spirit would never be broken, thought Powerscourt. They could tie her to the stake for her beliefs. She wouldn't make a sound. Greshams don't cry.

'Edward is the latest in the line. The long line, Lord Powerscourt.'

Something softened in her voice as she talked of her son. Suddenly Powerscourt could see them, Edward and his mother, rowing round the lake in the summer, the sun caressing the golden curls of the pretty boy, the power of a mother's love caressing his heart. Then the softness went away.

'I expect you want to ask me about his marriage, Lord Powerscourt. I will spare you the trouble of framing what might be an embarrassing question. I expect you have heard the gossip, what they are saying down there in London.'

She made London sound like Sodom, thought Powerscourt, keeping still and silent in his chair, his eyes flickering outside to the frozen landscape.

'I never met the girl. I did not attend the wedding. I did not attend the funeral, dare I say it, a happier event for me. I believe she was called Louisa. Such a common name. Shopgirls are called Louisa, I believe. So are grocers' daughters. The marriage was simply impossible. Greshams don't marry shopgirls. They don't marry Catholics. They never have.'

But they did. They had, thought Powerscourt, wondering how he could steer the conversation in the direction he wanted.

'Did Edward ever bring Prince Eddy here? To Thorpe Hall?'

'Prince Eddy? That one who has just died? Yes, he did. He came on a number of occasions. Very feeble young man, I thought. Bad blood, thin blood. Something wrong there. Fancy being carried off by something so mundane as influenza at his age. It just proved there was something wrong with his breeding.'

'Did Prince Eddy know Louisa at all?' Powerscourt tossed it in lightly, like a hat into a ring.

'My dear Lord Powerscourt, do you expect me to know the answer to that question? I have told you. I did not attend the wedding. I did not attend the funeral. I was hardly likely to pop over to that place where they lived for grocer's tea.'

'Forgive me for asking, but do you know anything of the circumstances of her death?'

'I do not. I did not ask. I did not inquire. I did not regard it as any of my business. I was merely glad that Edward was rid of her.'

Powerscourt wondered if a mother's love was strong enough to send Lady Blanche over to the little house, bought by the grocer father, and push a daughter-in-law she had never seen down the steps to her death. He didn't think so. Nearly, but not quite. But he felt she was not telling him all she knew. But then, she never would, even if he waited until the frosts had thawed and the lake could welcome rowing boats once more.

'And where is Edward now, Lady Gresham?'

'Edward? Oh, he went away after his time at Sandringham. He came back looking quite pale, terribly pale. I expect it was the weather up there in Norfolk. Some people say he was still upset about the death of that girl.'

She couldn't say Louisa, thought Powerscourt. Not again. Once, or was it twice, was all she could manage. Greshams, some Greshams at any rate, don't say Louisa.

'And where did he go? When he went away?'

'He said he was going to Italy, Lord Powerscourt. He only left last week. Edward said he had to make a journey to Rome. I never asked him what he meant by that. Maybe it had something to do with that ghastly religion. Do you know Italy at all, Lord Powerscourt?'

She made Italy sound like a next-door neighbour, the nearest county family perhaps.

'I do, Lady Gresham. I know it quite well. Did he say if he was going straight to Rome?' He's gone straight to Rome already, thought Powerscourt, like Newman and Manning and all those other converts to Catholicism, hundreds, if not thousands of them in his lifetime. But he felt it wiser not to mention that.

'He did say something about that. I think he said he was going to Venice first.'

There were two fires burning in the long long room. All the time he sat there Powerscourt had felt cold. The room was cold. Maybe it would never be warm again.

'I took him to Venice for his first visit when he was sixteen years old, Lord Powerscourt. Just the two of us.'

Powerscourt could see the two of them, not in a rowing boat, but in a gondola edging its way down the crowded waters of the Grand Canal.

'Edward adored Venice. He always said it was the whole business of being there that made it so attractive. He loved walking round some of the poorer quarters, you know, Lord Powerscourt, rotting palazzos falling into the street, washing hanging out above the windows.'

'I know exactly what you mean, Lady Gresham. I do indeed. How well you put it.'

She smiled a condescending smile. Powerscourt had a great

urge for train timetables. Trains across Europe. The fastest way to get to Venice before Lord Edward Gresham, one-time equerry to the late Duke of Clarence and Avondale, moved off on his journey to Rome. Maybe he could telegraph to Rosebery's butler from the railway station.

At least Lady Blanche didn't offer me any fruit cake, Powerscourt said to himself as he left, the rich mixtures of Shapston coming back. In fact she didn't offer me anything at all. Maybe she found the whole business pretty distasteful.

He saw her watching from the windows of her long long room as his carriage skidded across her frozen park towards the station, an old woman, icy with pride, watching her last visitor depart from the Gresham home at Thorpe Hall. She was alone again in that huge cold house with its baroque ceilings, alone with memories of her long-departed husband and her wayward son, memories of the Greshams of old haunting her from the walls of her salon, greeting her from their cold marble tombs in the family vault when she went to worship. Maybe she's not all that lonely, he reflected. Maybe she lives through today by living in the past.

Greshams don't cry. Not then. Not now.

Anyway, he thought, you couldn't see Lady Blanche Gresham making a fruit cake. She'd have to send out to the shop for one.

To the grocer's shop.

'Seven o'clock train to Dover, my lord. Connects with the boat to Calais. Quickest route, my lord.'

A note from William Leith, Rosebery's butler, waited for Powerscourt back in St James's Square in reply to his telegram. He hasn't wasted much time, Powerscourt thought. Then he reflected that for a man with Leith's resources, shelves and shelves of timetables, this was probably child's play. Calcutta might prove a challenge, or the twin cities of Minneapolis and St Paul.

'Express to Paris. Arrives at 4.30. Gare du Nord, my lord. Would suggest Parisian taxi to Gare de Lyons. Night train to Milan, my lord. Departs at 7.30. Breakfast in the station. Very fine rolls in the Milan station buffet for breakfast, my lord.

Connections to Venice every hour on the hour from 8 o'clock. Could reach Venice by lunchtime or early afternoon, my lord. Have taken the liberty of making you reservations on all these conveyances. Except the taxi, My Lord. Prior booking difficult if not impossible. Rooms reserved at the Danieli. Central location. Recommended by My Lordship.'

How on earth, wondered Powerscourt, did the man know about the rolls in the buffet? Maybe his customers reported back, to add to the encyclopedias of railway knowledge in his little eyrie half-way down Rosebery's basement stairs.

As the train rolled southwards from Paris the following evening, past the ten crus of Beaujolais and alongside the waters of the Rhone, Powerscourt was counting his dead.

Prince Eddy, in that charnel house of a room in Sandringham. Lancaster, suicide in the woods. Forever Faithful. Semper Fidelis. Simon John Robinson of Dorchester on Thames, place of death unknown. Lord forgive them for they know not what they do. The two gentlemen from the homosexual club in Chiswick. Lady Louisa Gresham, interred in some Catholic chapel in the Midlands, unmourned and unloved by her mother-in-law.

Six of them now. Six corpses. What was the thread that held them together? Was there indeed one single thread? Was the answer in Venice or in London? Or neither?

As his train turned eastwards and began its long ascent into the Alps, Powerscourt fell asleep. He did not dream. Clarence hath murdered dreams, he thought to himself, as the roar of the great steam engine met the deep silence of the mountains.

Santa Lucia railway station is one third of the way down Venice's Grand Canal. Santa Lucia, thought Powerscourt happily. They've even named a railway station after Lady Lucy. How nice of them. I think she's got a church just round the corner too, maybe a palazzo. But he wasn't sure about the palazzo.

An aged gondolier, wiry moustache and that red beret they always seemed to wear, secured Powerscourt's passage to his hotel. As they pushed off from the bank, the gondolier took a deep breath and filled his lungs with the dank Venetian air.

'Please,' said Powerscourt, holding up his hand just in time. 'Please, *per favore*, no singing. *Niente opera*,' he went on desperately. '*Silenzio. Per favore. Niente aria*. No singing.'

The gondolier looked dumbstruck. 'No arias? Not one, signor? Not even a little one? Drinking song from *Traviata* perhaps?'

'No arias.' said Powerscourt firmly. 'Not one. Not even that damned drinking song.'

The gondolier gave one of those special shrugs reserved for foreigners and resolved to add yet more lira to his bill. Powerscourt felt he had had a narrow escape. Singing Italians, usually out of tune in his view, on the way down the most romantic street in the world were an abomination not to be borne.

Palazzos drifted by on either side. When he was a boy Powerscourt had a map with all the great ones marked, their dates of construction, the famous and the infamous who had lived there. When he was nine or ten, he could remember most of them. The names, he thought, such poetry in the names.

Palazzo Vendramin Calergi, one of the most beautiful Renaissance buildings in Italy. Palazzo Giovanelli where they had bribed their way into the aristocracy with 100,000 golden ducats. Ca' Rezzonico, home of yet another Venetian Pope. Palazzo Falier, home to the traitor who tried to become king and lost his head for his pains, cut off on the top of his own staircase. The vengeful aristocrats, Powerscourt remembered, had given him one hour's notice of his execution. Palazzos built for the great families with their names in the Golden Book.

Families with Doges. Families with Procurators of St Mark's. Families with Popes. Families with Admirals. Families who traded in spices. Families who traded in silks. Families who traded with Shylock.

The waters of the canal were choppy now, boats being unloaded, the gondoliers picking their way skilfully through the traffic. They were passing the Rialto Bridge, once the financial heart of Venice, the City of London on the water where two banks went bankrupt when they heard of the great voyages of Columbus back in the 1490s, Venice's monopoly of trade with the East supposedly broken. Venice took three hundred years to die.

The gondolier was humming now, humming quite loudly as

if in revenge. Powerscourt thought it was the drinking song from *Traviata*, the noise blending in with the wider noises of the city, boatmen shouting at each other, porters warning the public to beware, other, better treated gondoliers bellowing away into the Basin of St Mark. The great bulk of the church of Santa Maria della Salute loomed up, a giant in Baroque, built to commemorate the salvation of the city from the plague. One million piles were sunk into the soggy ground to build it, one third of the population wiped out before they started. Even syphilis, Powerscourt thought bitterly, even syphilis hadn't managed that yet.

The porters at the Danieli must have been warned of his arrival.

'This way, milord. Your coat, milord, your hat, milord. Cup of tea, milord?'

The interiors were all gold leaf and dark red velvet, huge chandeliers of Murano glass hanging everywhere. Ornate rococo paintings, imitation Tiepolo, filled the walls with nymphs and satyrs from some imaginary Venetian past.

The place was full of Americans, their nasal twang echoing round the great reception room that looked out across the water to San Giorgio and the Lido. Americans rushing around on the Grand Tour, thought Powerscourt, who rather liked Americans. Buffalo come to meet Byron. Boston embraces Botticelli. Grand Rapids hails Giorgione. Tampa salutes Titian.

'Five days in Venice, five whole days,' one bulky matron was telling her compatriots indignantly. 'I can't believe it takes five whole days to look at Venice. The place isn't a quarter the size of Philadelphia! Then we're down for seven days in Rome! Seven days! I mean, after you've seen the Pope and his pictures, what is there left to do?'

A solemn little man with a small moustache, very correct in a frock coat, greeted Powerscourt. 'Lord Powerscourt? Welcome to the Danieli. My name is Antonio Pannone. I am the manager here.'

He led Powerscourt to a quiet table by the window and removed the reserved notice.

'Lord Rosebery telegraphed to say you were coming. He is an old friend, Lord Rosebery. Any friend of Lord Rosebery must be a friend of the Hotel Danieli, no? It is so.'

The little man looked round. Tea appeared as if by magic. He poured two cups, his eyes watching steadily as the crowds passed by his windows.

'Lord Powerscourt, Lord Rosebery said you were probably looking for somebody, no?'

Powerscourt told him about his quest for Lord Edward Gresham. 'He is a young man, in his late twenties, with fair hair and brown eyes. Lord Edward Gresham always dresses well. His friends used to tease him about his clothes.'

'Here in Venice,' said Antonio Pannone sadly, 'everybody likes to dress well. It is the fashion. Do you have a picture or a photograph of him by any chance?'

Powerscourt did. Johnny Fitzgerald had pressed it into his hand minutes before his train left London two days before.

'For God's sake, Francis.' Fitzgerald was panting after his long run up the platform, searching for his friend. 'Why do you have to travel in a compartment right at the front of the bloody train? I nearly missed you. Now then. If you're going looking for somebody, then it sometimes helps to have a picture of them so everybody else can see what the bugger looks like. I thought even you would have realised that by now.'

Powerscourt hadn't. In his haste, he had quite forgotten. Lord Johnny pressed a copy of the *Illustrated London News* into his hand.

'Page twenty-four.' he said firmly. 'Or maybe page twenty-five. There he is, on the steps of a house party somewhere in the country, looking very handsome too.'

'How on earth did you get this, Johnny?'

There was a lot of activity up at the front of the train. Whistles were blown, flags waved. Almost imperceptibly, the seven o'clock express to Dover and Paris began to move.

'It's my aunt, Francis. Christ, I'm going to have to do some more running to keep up with you. I'm not running all the way to bloody Venice, Francis. She collects all these magazines, my auntie. She's got rooms full of them. She says they'll be valuable in the years to come. She's quite mad. She's potty . . .'

Lord Johnny ran out of platform. The train gathered speed. Powerscourt just heard a parting message, shouted through the smoke.

'Don't go falling into any of those bloody canals now, Francis. And don't talk to any strange women, courtesans or whatever they're called. Bloody place is full of them.'

Powerscourt handed over his *Illustrated London News*, opened at page twenty-five. It was indeed a formal photograph of the guests at a country house weekend. The hosts and the older people were seated uncomfortably in front of a set of steps. The young women, clutching their parasols against the sun, were lined up behind them. Draped around the steps and the flower-pots were a group of young men, boaters tilted. Most elegant of them all, lying languidly on the topmost step, one elbow on the ground, the other hand checking the precise angle of his exquis-ite hat, was Lord Edward Gresham. He was staring insolently at the lens, as if it was disturbing his afternoon.

'This one here. The one lying down. That's Lord Edward Gresham.'

'Thank you. Thank you, Lord Powerscourt. He looks the bit of the dandy. It is so?' Pannone peered intently at the picture, checking perhaps, to see if there were any regular clients of the Hotel Danieli in the frame. 'Now, Lord Powerscourt. May I borrow this picture? Or I could get one of the local people to make a copy? Whichever you prefer. I have a plan. Have you looked for people in Venice before, Lord Powerscourt? It is more difficult than you think. Sometimes we have done this before. For the authorities, you understand.'

More Americans were pouring their way into the great recep-tion room. They were complaining about the prices, prices of Murano glass to take home, prices in the hotel, prices for hiring gondoliers, operatic or not. Don't they realise, thought Powers-court, people have been complaining about the prices in Venice for centuries, the price of salt, the price of silks. But they kept coming back.

'Mr Pannone, sorry. I drifted off in my mind, like one of your gondolas. Of course you may keep the magazine. Now, tell me about your plan.'

'My plan depends on the waiters, Lord Powerscourt. Every-body has to eat, it is so? So, they go to the hotels and the restaurants. Waiters serve them. Waiters have eyes and ears, none better. Now then, in a moment, I take the picture to

Florian's in Piazza San Marco. Many of the tourists go there a lot. My friend, the top waiter in Florian's, he and I circulate your young man round all the hotels and the restaurants. For a day or two this Lord Edward will be the most famous man in the city! All the waiters looking for him!'

Waiters, thought Powerscourt. How very neat. The waiters of Venice would be pressed into service on his behalf. His very own secret service. Waiters as spies, his spies, their eyes flickering across faces as they served the Spaghetti al Vongole or the Fegato al Veneziano, spies with the claret or the Chianti or the grappa. Such a secret service might have existed centuries before in the days of the Council of Ten or the Council of Three, running Venice's domestic intelligence services from their shadowy headquarters in the Doges' Palace, the victims dumped unceremoniously out to sea, or found in the misty Venetian mornings, buried heads down in the pavement by the waterfront.

Take care what you are ordering in Venice. Mind what you say. There are informers everywhere.

'That sounds excellent, Mr Pannone. May I say how grateful I am for your assistance? I do not know how long Lord Gresham intends to stay here. He may have already left.'

'Everybody stay in Venice longer than they intended,' said Pannone loyally, 'except for these Americans.' He looked regretfully at the throng of transatlantic visitors crowding round his bar. 'Always they are in the hurry. Always they want to be somewhere else. It is as if they have some strange disease, the not able to sit still disease. Do you understand Americans, Lord Powerscourt?'

'I think I find them as confusing as you do, Mr Pannone. But tell me, how long do you think it will take to find Lord Gresham?'

Pannone rubbed his hands together thoughtfully. 'Two days at most, I should say. At most. The man has to eat. This system has always found people in that time before. Is he dangerous, Lord Powerscourt?'

Powerscourt didn't think it would help if he said that he was suspected of murdering the heir presumptive to the English throne.

'No, I don't think he is dangerous. I just need to speak to him.

212

I shall be at Florian's, or in here, every day at lunchtime, and from five o'clock in the afternoon. I shall be waiting for him. We could have some of your excellent tea together. Or dinner.'

'Good, Lord Powerscourt. Very good. Inside two days, I promise you. Now, let me show you to your room. It is the one Lord Rosebery stays in when he comes.'

As they climbed to the first floor, Powerscourt wondered just what he was going to say to Gresham when he found him. If he found him. He had a terrible suspicion that he had already gone further south on his journey to Rome.

'Did you kill Prince Eddy? Why did you want so much blood? How did you get into his room?'

20

What had the mother said about Rome? Powerscourt dodged his way round a mountain of crates heading from a waterfront boat towards the Danieli. He was walking, the following morning, round Venice in an anti-clockwise direction, hoping against hope that he might catch a glimpse of Lord Edward Gresham on the way. 'Edward said he had to make a journey to Rome. I never asked him what he meant by that. Maybe something to do with that ghastly religion.' The old lady had sat as stiff as a ramrod in that cold room, fingering her pearls as she spoke.

Maybe something to do with that ghastly religion. You didn't have to go to Rome if you were a good Catholic, did you? It wasn't like Mecca or wherever it was where the Muslims went on their pilgrimages. What was so special about Rome? Had he promised Louisa that he would take her there? Was this a journey of expiation, Edward going where Louisa wanted to take him? In Memoriam?

Powerscourt had now reached the forbidding gates of the Arsenal, half-way along the city seafront. A quartet of melancholy lions stood on guard outside, a fifth perched arrogantly up a gate. They stole those lions too, the Venetians, Powerscourt remembered, just like they stole the ones on top of the Basilica of St Mark's in the Piazza San Marco, just like they stole the body of their patron saint St Mark from some tomb in Alexandria. Pirates, all of them, the inside of St Mark's a pirate's cave full of booty plundered from Constantinople and the trade routes of the Venetian ships. They were built in here, those ships, thought Powerscourt, as he turned left and walked along the side of the great red walls that guarded the Arsenal's secrets. They could turn out a warship a day at the height of their power, he recalled, a mass production line running from keel to a full set of sails inside these walls in twenty-four hours.

Up here were the poorer quarters of the city, where the Venetians lived in hovels rather than palazzos, the streets paved with rubbish and hungry cats forever on the prowl. Lady Gresham had mentioned something about that too. Powerscourt's memory clicked into action as he crossed a small canal by a delicate wrought-iron bridge. 'He loved walking round some of the poorer quarters, you know, Lord Powerscourt, rotting palazzos falling into the street, washing hanging out above the windows.' There's plenty of washing round here, thought Powerscourt, as a sheet escaped from its moorings and fell on to the narrow street a couple of feet behind him.

Bells were tolling right across the city, distant bells, nearby bells, sad bells, old bells, new bells, all calling the Venetians to Sunday Mass. Mass, Powerscourt thought. Did Mass have something to do with it? Before he could pursue the idea, he realized that he was lost. The baffling topography of Venice had struck again. You could never keep your sense of direction in the place, he remembered, where you thought the waterfront must be turning into some landlocked campo of the interior, St Mark's itself appearing when you thought you had finally reached the railway station. Mass. The Venetians were turning out for morning service. Some of them were carrying flowers. Old ladies were carrying flowers, grandmothers bent nearly double with the weight of them. Where did the flowers come from, Powerscourt wondered? Perhaps they stole them too, like they stole the lions, early morning pirate flotillas despatched on missions of theft to the mainland.

Then he knew. The old ladies were taking the flowers to the cemetery, not to Mass. Perhaps they'd been to Mass already, an early morning special for the bereaved. If he followed the old ladies he would come out at the landing stage where the boats sailed for Venice's Island of The Dead, San Michele in Isola, a cemetery ringed with water, its entire surface covered with graves and tombs and ornate Italian statuary. Just the kind of place Queen Victoria would like to visit for her holidays, Powerscourt thought, surrounded on all sides by the dead.

He followed patiently behind a convoy of Venetian grand-mothers, twisting their way slowly through a maze of passages and dark streets towards the waterfront at Fondamente Nuove. 'We have erred and strayed from thy ways like lost sheep.' Powerscourt remembered the high clear voice of his parson in his little church at Rokesley. 'We have followed too much the devices and desires of our own hearts ... Spare thou them, oh God, which confess their faults.' You had to confess your sins before you could partake of the sacrament.

They had reached the waterfront. A couple of boats stood ready to take the bereaved on their short journey to San Michele.

Confession. Lord Edward Gresham's confession. That was it. If you hadn't confessed your sins you were not meant to share in the body and blood of Christ. If you were responsible for the body and blood of Prince Eddy then you had quite a lot of confessing to do. Maybe he's looking for somewhere to say his confession. Maybe the journey to Rome ends in the confessional box.

The old ladies set out, flowers still clutched tightly to their bosoms, the boat rocking gently from side to side. Behind them a dark funeral boat, manned by a crew dressed entirely in black, was making an even slower journey to the melancholy island. Business was going to be brisk on San Michele this morning.

He could hear singing now, a hymn drifting out from the rococo masterpiece of the Gesuiti. Jesuits, Powerscourt thought. Maybe Lord Gresham needs Jesuits for his confession, learning and casuistry combining to offer him some form of absolution.

He was lost again. Damn, he thought, looking at his watch. I am meant to be having lunch at Florian's in half an hour. Damn! Where is Florian's? Where has it gone? Where is St Mark's Square?

He plunged resolutely over a bridge. Then he stopped half-way across and looked around. There were campaniles soaring above the streets, but he couldn't tell which was which. He heard a voice behind him.

'You're not lost by any chance, are you? Most people look like that round here when they're lost.'

216

We have erred and strayed from thy ways like lost sheep, thought Powerscourt. A priest, clad in black, with a very smart biretta on his head, had come to rescue the straying.

'I'm afraid I am. I need to be at Florian's in half an hour,' Powerscourt confessed.

'At Florian's in St Mark's Square? I am going that way myself. Perhaps we could walk together.'

The priest was indeed English, he told Powerscourt, attached to Farm Street, the Jesuit church in London's Mayfair. Perhaps Powerscourt knew it? He did. Money, the priest said sadly, so much money there. He left Powerscourt to compute the sins that might be commensurate with that much wealth.

They discovered a common interest in pictures. The priest, whose name was Father Gilbey, was a devotee of Giovanni Bellinis. Had Powerscourt been to Murano to see the Bellinis there? Most tourists missed them.

Powerscourt promised he would make a pilgrimage there before he left Venice. They parted by the pigeons in the piazza, musicians already working their way through the drinking song from *Traviata*.

'I hope you find what you are looking for, Lord Powerscourt. I think you are looking for something. May God bless you.'

Powerscourt fled into Florian's with a terrible thought. Lord Edward Gresham had taken instruction before he joined the Roman Catholic Church. He wouldn't have taken it in the Midlands, Powerscourt felt sure. Had he taken it in Farm Street with Father Gilbey, in his biretta?

Had Gresham come to Italy with his very own father confessor in tow? And were the two of them now packing their bags for Lady Lucy's railway station and a further journey towards Rome while the Grand Inquisitor waited in the Hotel Danieli or ate plates of seafood in Florian's?

They didn't find Gresham that day.

They didn't find him the next.

Powerscourt roamed round the city, haunting the churches, patrolling the museums, walking endlessly along the seafront, up to the Rialto Bridge and back to the Piazza San Marco. He wrote to Lady Lucy. They knew him now, the waiters in Florian's and the pigeons in the square, the waiters shaking their heads sadly when he entered, the pigeons flying in formation for him to the sound of an aria from 'Aida'. Powerscourt thought about ordering some sheet music from London to widen the repertoire. Johnny Fitzgerald could get it here in a couple of days. He wrote again to Lady Lucy.

Mr Pannone, the manager of the Danieli, was worried. He could sense a growing anxiety in Powerscourt, a tenseness. He too, reflected Pannone, was catching the American disease, the not being able to sit still, as Powerscourt paced up and down the dark red corridors of the hotel, unable to sleep.

Signor Lippi, the top waiter at Florian's, came for a conference in Pannone's office, looking out from the first floor towards San Giorgio Maggiore across the lagoon. Signor Lippi was tall and thin, a glittering collection of silver rings on his fingers.

'I do not understand it, Lord Powerscourt,' said Pannone, gazing sadly out at his city. 'Every day we look for him. Every day we can tell you where you have been. Before you have even come back. We know. So where is this Lord Gresham?'

'Perhaps, as the Lord thinks, he has gone.' Signor Lippi was clutching a new set of his menus to his bosom.

He is risen, thought Powerscourt. On the third day he shall rise again and judge the quick and the dead.

'I do not think he has gone. I do not know why. And you, Lord Powerscourt, once you thought he had gone. Now you are not so sure. It is so?'

'It is so,' said Powerscourt sadly.

A waiter appeared and handed a collection of papers to Pannone.

'See, Lord Powerscourt. See, we have fresh reports. Every few hours we get these. Each time we check them out. Always we check them out. And they are nothing. Nothing.' Pannone turned over his pages, looking for hope. 'He is in Burano, it says here, walking by the sea. He is in the church of Santa Maria Formosa. He is at the Accademia, looking at the pictures. He is having lunch on the Lido. He is everywhere. And he is nowhere.

'Here is another one. He is on the island of San Giorgio,

218

walking with a priest by the little lighthouses. This but an hour ago.'

'A priest, did you say?' Powerscourt was leaning forward intently.

'Yes, a priest. But what of it? Venice, like Italy, is full of priests.'

Powerscourt told them about his meeting with Father Gilbey two days before and his cryptic words of farewell.

'You think he come here with the Lord Gresham? The father confessor?' Mr Pannone had left his seat and gone to his window, staring out at Palladio's church of San Giorgio Maggiore.

'I think it is possible. But look, gentlemen, look.' Powerscourt spoke slowly, slowing down the thoughts racing through his mind. 'Is it possible that you could stay in Venice and not stay at a hotel? Of course, you could stay in somebody's house or palazzo, but I don't think Gresham had any close friends in Venice.

'Suppose you were a priest. Could you not stay in a seminary, or in a monastery? And could you not, in exceptional circumstances, have a guest with you? So that you eat your meals in the monastery or wherever it is. Such a visitor would not visit the cafes or the hotels or the restaurants. He misses out on the waiters altogether. Your splendid intelligence system doesn't work. There wouldn't be any news at all.'

There was a brief silence. The three of them were now at the window, staring at the buildings on the island.

'There is a monastery on San Giorgio,' said Signor Lippi softly, 'a famous one. The buildings, the refectory and the library are also by Palladio. But they don't let people in to see them, not even Americans.'

Signor Pannone sounded more cheerful as he thought of places the Americans couldn't visit. 'All of this is true,' he said, 'it is true. So we must find out who is on the island. And who, perhaps, is their guest. How do we do that, Signor Lippi?'

The two men spoke rapidly in Italian, their gestures more pronounced. From time to time Powerscourt wondered if they were going to come to blows, so fierce did the exchanges seem.

'*Bene. Bene.* Now then, Lord Powerscourt, this is what we

propose.' It's like a waiter offering you the menu in France, Powerscourt thought. 'It may not be perfect, but we think it will work. Yes?' He glanced briefly at Signor Lippi, who nodded vigorously. 'We have just got the time. Now it is a quarter after seven, not too late to pay a call on the monastery before they start praying for the night or whatever they do.

'Our catering manager here at the Danieli,' he waved an expansive arm around the room and what was visible of Venice outside, as if that too was part of his hotel, 'he does a lot of business with the monks at San Giorgio. Not with the monks, pardon me, but with the housekeeper of these monks. She has worked there a long time. She know everything. She know everybody. She talk a great deal. Maybe because the monks are silent much of the day and do not talk to her. God knows, women need to talk.' He shook his head, weighed down perhaps by the speech and speeches of his own women. Powerscourt thought he must have daughters as well as a wife. 'I will talk to this man now. We send him to the island. He talks, perhaps he listens to this housekeeper woman. Then he comes back and tells us.

'And I have not told you the best part of the plan, Lord Powerscourt. We have to wait here till he come back, you and I. Sometimes she talk for hours, this housekeeper. I do not think we will like the waiting, you and I. So we send them with Venice's finest gondolier, the fastest man in the city. Signor Lippi here! Every year he wins the races for the gondolas. Every Sunday he practises up in Cannaregio. These races are like your Henley. You have rowing races at Henley, it is so?'

Powerscourt assured him that they did.

'Well, he is our man. Maybe he is not used to the rowing the gondola in his frock coat but he is happy to help. Come, we must go. There is not any time to lose.'

The two Italians rushed from the room.

'Don't forget the picture!' Powerscourt shouted after them. 'The picture of Lord Gresham!'

'My God, my God, we nearly forget the picture. We must not be in too big of the hurry, I think.'

Powerscourt stared out of the window. Beneath him the night

porters of the Danieli were on duty, great cloaks tightly fastened against the cold. To his right the lion of St Mark sat happily on top of its great pillar, still waiting to warn of invaders from the sea. To the right of San Giorgio, on the island of Giudecca, he could see lights on Palladio's other great church, the Redentore, built like Santa Maria Salute as a thanksgiving for salvation from the plague. Gondolas bobbed up and down on the waterfront. His pigeons still bustled about St Mark's Square, a lone orchestral group serenading the night air with Mascagni's *Cavalleria Rusticana*. Perhaps the sheet music had arrived earlier than expected.

There was a sudden burst of activity by the gondolas. Signor Lippi, in white shirt-sleeves now, his rings glistening from the lights on the waterfront, was preparing to leave with a small tubby figure in the back of the boat.

Powerscourt watched them go, the gondola moving swiftly across the waters of the lagoon, growing smaller and smaller as it reached the San Giorgio steps. Powerscourt thought he saw the tubby figure disappear through a door to the right of the jetty. But he wasn't sure.

Still he watched. Was this the end of his journey? A journey that began months before in Rosebery's tiny castle at Barnbougle with tales of unknown criminals blackmailing the Prince of Wales. He thought of the people he had met along the way, the impossible courtiers, the efficient Major Dawnay, Mr Simkins the naval historian up the steps in his archive, Lord George Scott, former captain of HMS *Bacchante*, spilling crumbs on his beard. He thought of the unhappiness, Princess Alexandra grieving for another son, Robinson, the red-faced man who told him to get out, his son buried in the Dorchester churchyard, Lady Blanche Gresham the proud old woman, alone with her ancestors in the great expanse of Thorpe Hall. He thought of Lord Johnny Fitzgerald, up his tree by the homosexual club in Chiswick. He thought of Lady Lucy.

He watched on. Nothing stirred by the steps. He thought he could see Signor Lippi waving his arms to keep warm. The waters were still. He thought of Lady Lucy, worried by the Round Pond in Kensington Gardens, happy and passionate as she told the story of *The Fighting Temeraire* in the National Gallery, radiant in her Anna Karenina coat at the bottom of St James's Square.

Still he watched, his eyes never leaving those shadowy steps by the façade of the church on its island. Maybe I shall bring Lady Lucy here to Venice one day, he thought. Maybe we could come for our honeymoon. We could stay here in the Danieli with Mr Pannone.

'What are you thinking of, Lord Powerscourt? Over there by the window?' Pannone had slipped quietly back into the room.

'I was thinking of getting married, Signor Pannone. But I have not yet asked the young lady. Perhaps I am too soon.'

'How charming, Lord Powerscourt. That would be a good change for you. This business with the Lord Gresham, it has been very difficult?'

Powerscourt watched on. What was he doing, deciding to marry Lady Lucy at a time like this? It wasn't the first time he had thought of it either. Was that a gondola, leaving San Giorgio, turning round to return to the hotel? No, it was only a shadow on the water.

Twenty minutes gone now. He checked his watch again.

'It has been difficult, Mr Pannone, yes. I shall be glad when it is over.'

Pannone was silent, as if he knew Powerscourt didn't want to talk. He produced a pair of binoculars and rejected them, saying you could see as well without.

A dark cloud passed over the young moon. The church was barely visible now, only the white tops of its lighthouses clear to the watchers by the window. How long could that woman talk for? Had the true nature of the mission been discovered? Was Pannone's man even now being interrogated by some of the monks? Had be been locked up in some dark cell beneath the waterline to await more skilled interrogation by the Jesuits in the morning?

Powerscourt thought he saw something move by the steps. He rubbed his eyes, and rubbed at the Danieli's windowpane, straining for a better view. It was nothing.

'Look! Look!' said Mr Pannone. 'I think they are coming now.'

The gondola was coming back by a different route. It swung

over towards the Customs House Point, zigzagging its way towards the shore.

'This will be the quickest way home, Lord Powerscourt. With the currents.'

He could see them now, Lippi rowing powerfully, white shirt gleaming in the night, the small tubby man not moving in the back.

'How much longer? How much longer?' Powerscourt was losing patience.

'Only a few minutes. This last passage is very quick. Wait here and I will bring you the news. My catering manager he does not speak English.'

Pannone departed to the waterfront. There was a hasty conference by the shore before the three of them vanished inside the hotel.

Powerscourt looked out again at the enigmatic façade of San Giorgio, no movement at all visible from the window. Down below a large party of Americans were heading off to a restaurant, celebrating their last night in the city.

Pannone came back into the room. He was carrying an open bottle and a couple of glasses.

'I think we must have a drink, Lord Powerscourt, after our long watch. To settle the stomach, we say. We were right. But we were also wrong. There is a priest staying in the monastery. And he does have a guest with him. And the priest is English. There the good news ends.'

Pannone poured out two glasses of Chianti and carried them to the window.

'There is no Father Gilbey. There is no Lord Gresham. The priest comes from Leeds, in Yorkshire, I think. Father Richards. He is very old, this Father Richards The guest is his brother, Leopold Richards.

'Leopold Richards has some terrible disease. He has come to Venice to die. The priest has come to administer the last rites. And then to bury him.'

21

Mist. Mist was everywhere in an invisible Venice at six o'clock in the morning. Powerscourt slipped out of a side door of his hotel to wonder at it and found he could hardly move.

The Lion of St Mark on its huge pillar, the gondolas, the gleaming domes of the Basilica of St Mark, had all vanished. Only the water was still there. You could hear it lapping monotonously against the quays. Venice has disappeared, thought Powerscourt. It's not surprising really. The whole place was too fantastic to be real in the first place. Venice, its astounding beauty, the delicate tracery on the Doges' Palace proclaiming its uniqueness down the centuries, Venice was only an illusion, a stage set. Now God has closed the production down and removed the scenery, plenty of angels waiting to take it into the wings.

Day had turned into night, a night of mist, a white night. Italian oaths could be heard near and far as the early morning traffic stumbled through the gloom. Far off, out to sea, distant sirens sounded notes of alarm and danger.

He reached out a hand and touched a reassuring pillar in the colonnade of the Doges' Palace. Maybe it was lifting now. A dark black shape seemed to bob rhythmically up and down fifteen feet in front of him, a gondola, hovering into sight. The pigeons, huddling in the corners of the buildings, wings folded, began trying experimental flights over St Mark's Square. As he turned on to the seafront, or what he thought was the seafront, the Bridge of Sighs loomed up, its sinister shape lording it over the waters of the invisible canal below.

Powerscourt wished his brain would clear, like the fog. He felt drained, emotionally exhausted by the events of the previous two days. Should he simply turn round and go home? How long could he wait here for a man who might never come? Should he be in the Piazza Signoria in Florence, or starting a long vigil in the colonnades of St Peter's in Rome?

The Danieli cat, sleek and prosperous, was beginning a leisurely patrol along the boats by the quays. God seemed to have changed his mind. The Venetian stage set was being restored to life, angels flying extra missions, blocks of marble and stone being put back in their positions.

But Powerscourt simply couldn't decide what to do. He was lost.

Salvation came at lunchtime. He had spent the morning drinking desultory cups of coffee in Florian's, brushing up his Latin on the inscriptions of the dead Doges in the church of San Giovanni e Paolo. There had been so many battles, he thought, hundreds and hundreds of miles from home, sea battles against the Turks, the Cypriots, the Greeks, the Turks again, admirals returning in triumph to Venice to be interred in black marble in this Venetian necropolis, their proud and haughty epitaphs giving them a kind of eternal life on the walls.

He wrote again to Lady Lucy. He said he hoped they could come to Venice together one day. He told her his abiding impression of the watery city, that it was a monument to the passing of a once great naval power. Maybe London will look like this when the Royal Navy's days are over, he wrote, gazing out at the pigeons in St Mark's Square, palazzos falling into the water, decay wrapped round the great monuments like a rotting glove.

'Lord Powerscourt! Lord Powerscourt!' Pannone found him in the entrance to his hotel. 'Quick! Quick! You must come to my office at once! I have news!'

The little man was beaming broadly, ushering Powerscourt into the room where they had waited for Signor Lippi's gondola the night before.

'I have seen him! The Gresham! He come! At last! At last!'

'Where did you see him, Mr Pannone? You saw him in person? In the flesh?'

'I tell you. This is the happy day. It is good, so? Now then, let me gather my thoughts.' He collected another sheaf of papers on his desk. 'This morning we get more reports. Oh, yes, the reports do not stop. They do not stop until I, Antonio Pannone, give the word. And we have this one, from half-past ten.'

He waved a piece of paper from his collection at Powerscourt who saw that it was covered by a spidery Italian handwriting, with a lot of exclamation marks. Maybe they write like they talk, he said to himself, emphasis and gestures flying all over the place.

'This report, he say that Gresham is in the city, staying at the Hotel Pellegrini near the railway station. Not a very good hotel, the Pellegrini, he should have come here to the Danieli. Much better, much more convenient.' He shook his head sadly at the ingratitude of lost clients. 'But this waiter at the Pellegrini, he is very clever, I think. He takes a look at the visitors' book. There it is. Lord Edward Gresham, of Warwickshire, staying for three nights.

'Lord Powerscourt, I have to tell you. I was excited, so excited. Maybe the young man unpacks, I think. Maybe he rests from his journey. So I go on a journey of my own! To the Pellegrini! And there he is! Just coming out of the front door, in a tweed suit and a big coat!'

A further batch of messages arrived, a young waiter backing deferentially from the doorway.

'Ah ha! Ah ha! See how well the system works, Lord Powerscourt. Now he is in the bookshop, buying guides to Venice and a book of religion! Now he is in Florian's! With Signor Lippi himself!'

Powerscourt smiled at the memory of Venice's fastest gondolier from the night before. How did they get the messages from one place to another, he wondered? Were junior waiters, as fleet on land as Signor Lippi by sea, sent hurrying across the city? Perhaps they used the pigeons. The birds might welcome a change from listening to all those bloody arias in St Mark's Square. Better not to ask.

'And he is just ordering lunch! Pasta, a bifsteak, some of Florian's excellent sauté potatoes. I can tell you this in confidence, Lord Powerscourt. The Florian sauté potatoes are better than ours. Impossible, but it is so. Come, what have we here? It is a message from Signor Lippi himself! I can keep him here for one or two hours if you wish. Please advise.'

'I think you need to think about what you want to do, my lord. On my way back from the Pellegrini I think to myself, we have got this business the wrong way round. We were not too late, as we thought, for the coming of the Lord Gresham. We were too early! Maybe he is the serious traveller. Maybe he comes here by Verona with the lovers and Vicenza with all that Palladio town hall. Maybe he goes to see the Giottos in the Cappella degli Scrovegni at Padua. Maybe.'

Powerscourt doubted very much if he would have gone to Verona. Romeo and Juliet were not likely to have much appeal to Lord Edward Gresham.

'Mr Pannone, this is wonderful! How can I thank you?'

Powerscourt found himself rising from his chair and embracing the little Italian. He drew the line at the kisses on either cheek.

'Now then. This is the difficult bit. Difficult for me, I think.' Powerscourt had walked to the window again. San Giorgio was now very clear, bright sunlight on the water. Just round the corner, not visible from his vantage point, Lord Edward Gresham should be on the bifsteak by now, accompanied by Florian's excellent sauté potatoes. Should he go and approach him? 'Mr Pannone, I think I need some more advice.'

'Lord Powerscourt, my dear Lord Powerscourt, I do not want to know your business. But I see how troubled you are in the mind. This interview, I think, it is very important for you. Tell me, does this young man want to see you as much as you want to see him?'

'I very much doubt it. I feel sure that he does not want to see me at all.'

'I thought so. So, you think, you do not want to go and meet him now. In Florian's.'

'I don't think so. There are too many people there.'

'And you do not want to invite him for dinner this evening. Not now, I mean. You fear that he may smell the rat and disappear.'

'Exactly. He may smell a rat and disappear.'

'I shall write a note to Signor Lippi and tell him so. So, Lord Powerscourt, you come all this way. We find the man. Now we must work out a way of bringing you together. We could seize him in Florian's and bring him here so he has to talk to you. But that would make him very hostile. Perhaps he does not speak at all.'

Pannone departed briefly to send his message to Signor Lippi. 'I shall be back in a moment. And the reports will continue. We have three days while he is in Venice unless he decides that the Pellegrini is so terrible that he has to leave before. So, we have three days to make the plan.'

Powerscourt was pacing restlessly up and down the room. Outside Venice gleamed in the winter sunlight, the visitors queuing up to visit the Doges' Palace or setting off on the boat trips across the blue water to the distant islands of Burano and Torcello. He had just one chance, Powerscourt felt. Just one. If that didn't work, then his chances of solving the mystery were almost gone. He might be able to make a very good guess as to who killed Prince Eddy, but it would only be a guess.

'Lord Powerscourt! We have the good luck today, I think! See, another report from Signor Lippi himself! They make the great fuss of this Lord Gresham in Florian's. They find the senior waiter, their best English speaker, to come and chat to him at the end. This senior waiter, he work in New York for a time. So he talks American. No matter. The senior waiter here at the Danieli, he work in London and Paris. Much better, I think.'

'Anyway, this senior waiter, he ask the Lord if he wish to reserve a table for dinner tonight. He does! He comes back at 7.30! Just two hundred yards from here!'

Powerscourt did not share in the little man's enthusiasm. He felt reluctance coming over him like a sleeping sickness.

'Do you not see, my lord? I think for some time that what we need is the private room. The dinner for two, the candles, the good wines, the fine food, everybody happy in the warmth of the fire. People are happy to talk then, I think. I hope that we can do it here at the Danieli. We have many fine private rooms for the gentlemen who come with the ladies who are not the wives.' Pannone shrugged dismissively. 'But they have rooms also at Florian's on the upper floors. So, you meet the Lord Gresham, as if by chance, in the piazza. You have the chat. What about the dinner together? Why, I have booked a table for one at Florian's. We make it two. What could be simpler? No?'

Powerscourt looked blank. He didn't want to commit himself. Not now. Not yet. Maybe not ever.

'Or, my lord, we also book the private room here. So you too can ask him to dinner with you. It is the good plan?'

Still Powerscourt looked reluctant. He smiled helplessly at Pannone. The little Italian smiled back.

'What you need, my lord, is the time for the thinking. I shall leave you for a little while. I make the arrangements in Florian's. I make the arrangements here. I have a little hotel business to attend to. I shall return, my lord. Good thinking.'

It's not that he is frightened, Pannone said to himself. But he has thought about this for so long that it has now come on him in a great rush. He's surprised. He's overwhelmed.

Powerscourt made up his mind. Two memories forced him into it. His own promise to the dead Lancaster that he would be Semper Fidelis to his memory. And the voice of Johnny Fitzgerald in his ear. Never give up, Francis, never give up. That's what you always said. Even at the bottom of that bloody great mountain in India.

All through the afternoon Pannone brought further reports of Lord Edward Gresham's progress around his city.

He was in San Marco itself, staring up at the ceilings. He's gone to the Frari. He's looking at Titian's *Assumption of the Virgin*. He's walking around the Zattere, the seafront between the district of Dorsodouro and the island of Giudecca. He's walking back to the Rialto Bridge.

'Good. Good,' said Pannone at half-past four. 'I think that means that he is going back to the hotel. Perhaps he takes the little rest before he come for the dinner down here. Now, Lord Powerscourt. You are sure you want to go ahead with the plan? Yes?'

'I am certain of it,' said Powerscourt. 'It is our best chance.'

'You are going to be like the gamblers in our casino here, I think. You put everything on the red.'

A golden sun was setting over the Grand Canal, bathing the dome of the Salute with colour. Behind it the rest of Venice glowed with the last of the light. In front, it turned once more into a black and white city, an etching before the coming of oils.

'Let us see if we can help you, Lord Powerscourt. Tonight we put some of our waiters on the streets for a little while. The watchers will be out in the open air. Service in some places will be a little slow tonight, I think. Come, come.' He drew Powerscourt to a map of Venice on the wall.

'Here we have the Piazza San Marco, this great empty space at the bottom of our map. On the south side, in the middle, we have Florian's. Round the corner, down here by the water is the Danieli. Up here to the north, way beyond the piazza, we have the Hotel Pellegrini. We hope that the Lord Gresham will come down from there. Now, Lord Powerscourt. Anybody who knows Venice and is coming from the Pellegrini to Florian's will walk past the Rialto and down the Mercerie here,' his finger traced the route of an imaginary Gresham, 'and come out here, at the top of the north end of the square. But the people are always losing themselves. So, he might come down the Calle Specchieri and end up even higher up the square. Or he could come down the Calle dei Fabbri here,' Pannone stabbed the map again, 'and finish almost opposite Florian's. Or he could go even further west and end up at the other corner of the square from the Mercerie.

'But, consider, Lord Powerscourt. Almost whichever way he come, he come out on the opposite side to Florian's. So he have to walk across the piazza. So we put our waiters at every entrance to the square on this north side. They send a signal to another waiter man in front of the Campanile here. He is wearing the hat of the gondolier so you know him, yes? The gondolier's hat, he send the signal to you. You, my lord, are at the side of St Mark's, by the door into the Doges' Palace. You can see all the square. It is unlikely that a man coming in from the north, through any of these entrances with the waiters, will see you. You get the sign, you walk into the piazza. There you meet the Lord Gresham. We all pray for you, yes? We hope we pray all night.'

The little man laughed.

Powerscourt was looking closely at his meagre wardrobe. He should have thought of something suitable before he left London, something mild and reassuring. Not that dark suit, he'd look like a policeman. Not that grey, even if it was well cut, he'd look like a policeman off duty. The brown suit, that was all there was left. That didn't look too threatening. A blue shirt. Anybody could wear a blue shirt. Now then, had he brought it with him? He had. Here was an Old Etonian tie, a currency still valid, even in Italy. Especially in St Mark's Square where you hoped to meet another former pupil. Maybe the headmaster would feel proud of these old boys' reunions happening all over the place.

Six thirty. Soon it would be time to go. He didn't have a plan. But he did have what he hoped would be the least threatening order of conversation. Your mother, Lady Blanche Gresham. I met her recently. She was looking well. Always good for a minute or two, people exchanging horror stories about their mothers. Religion. The road to Rome. I've often thought of it myself as a matter of fact. Louisa. My condolences to another who had lost a wife. God forgive me, Caroline.

Six forty. There was a knock at the door.

'He has not left the hotel yet, the Lord Gresham. He is still at the Pellegrini.' Pannone was looking nearly as anxious as Powerscourt. 'The waiters are taking up their positions. The night is clear. So they will be able to see everything. Sometimes it is so gloomy the Lord Gresham could walk past and you would never know he had been there. I have inspected the room at Florian's for the dinner. It is not as good as the one we have here, but it would do. You will try to persuade him to come here, Lord Powerscourt? I would feel that things were under the control then, you know?'

231

Powerscourt assured the hotel manager that every effort would be made to return to the Danieli.

Five to seven.

'Is it time to go yet, Mr Pannone? What do you think?'

'It is only two or three minutes to your position, Lord Powerscourt. But we don't want to be late. Not tonight, I think.'

Seven o'clock. The bells were very loud. Powerscourt jumped. Of course, he remembered. They're only a hundred feet away, those bells, on the far side of the Basilica of St Mark.

Behind him lay the Doges' Palace, the Piazzetta linking St Mark's Square with the waterfront, and the dark waters of the lagoon. To his left, the great square of San Marco was deserted now, save for a few visitors waiting for their evening meal. There was a cold breeze from the sea. Above, to his right, there was another lion, one of the studious lions, with the gospel between its paws. Pax Tibi Marce. Peace be with you, Mark. Amen to that, thought Powerscourt, shivering slightly with the wind and his nerves.

Ten past seven. Mr Pannone appeared suddenly without warning. He must have come along the front of the church where the light was poorest.

'Everything is ready. He do not leave the Hotel Pellegrini yet. Perhaps he is the fast walker. You see my man over there by the Campanile? With the gondolier's hat? The hat is the key, my lord. When he knows the Lord Gresham is just about to enter the piazza, Sandro over there, he wave the hat. To the right means he is coming down the Mercerie. To the centre, the Lord Gresham come down the Calle dei Fabbri in the middle. To the left, and he come out at the bottom of the square. Good?'

'Good. Very good,' said Powerscourt.

Idling over the little bridges, poised expectantly by shop fronts at the bottom of streets, reading the menus in the lighted windows of the restaurants, the waiters loitered for their prey. A wave to the end of the street, a lifted hat, sometimes a whistle, and the word would be passed on down those tortuous Venetian alleyways. Lord Edward Gresham is coming. He's coming this way.

Twenty past seven. St Mark's Square was virtually deserted. The pigeons had taken over, ruthless scavengers of the detritus of the day. It's a stage, thought Powerscourt. What had Napoleon called it, St Mark's Square? The finest drawing-room in Europe, that was it. But it was not a drawing-room tonight. Tonight it was the grandest stage in Venice, waiting for a two-man show. The actors are coming. The audience are waiting, peering through the windows in the grimy buildings, box seats available in Florian's and in Quadri's on the other side of the square, standing room only on top of the Basilica, up there with the four lions. Good view. Rather cold. Low prices.

Pannone had disappeared. Sandro the gondolier's hat was standing impassively under his bell tower. Only very close up could you see that his eyes were patrolling the far side of the square in regular arcs, like the beam of a lighthouse, only quicker. And that his eyes never stopped moving. They hardly blinked at all.

Seven thirty. Maybe he's not coming, thought Powerscourt. Maybe he's got cold feet. He's too tired. He smells a rat. He's going to eat at the Trattoria alla Madonna, or the Ai Gondolieri. He's going to eat at his hotel.

The management regrets. All those holding tickets for this performance will receive a refund in the foyer. Our sincere apologies, ladies and gentlemen, this performance is cancelled.

Mr Pannone waited at the desk in his office. He took a large pinch of snuff. He was a general waiting for reports from the battlefield. But there was no news. The reports had dried up. He walked to his window and looked out across the waters, his mind scurrying up and down the streets and the byways of San Marco. Where was the Lord Gresham? Was the Lord Powerscourt going to be all right? He looked tense, almost frail, waiting there under his lion. What had Rosebery said? His work is very difficult. Please look after him.

Twenty to eight. Powerscourt wondered if he ought to pray. After all, the church was only a few feet away, full of its pirate booty. He decided God wouldn't approve. A group of elderly nuns, bent into the wind, were crossing the centre of the square very slowly, as if the sins of the world were extra heavy this evening. The pigeons scattered as they passed. Their wrinkled hands moved slowly round the rosaries, late evening prayers in the heart of Venice.

The gondolier's hat! It was moving at last! Sandro's hat, under the Campanile, was pointing to the right. Gresham must be coming down the Mercerie after all. At last. Powerscourt found that his legs were shaking. Steady, he said to himself, steady. He walked out towards the middle of the Piazza San Marco to make his rendezvous with Lord Edward Gresham, sometime equerry to the murdered Prince Eddy, late Duke of Clarence and Avondale.

Behind him he heard running footsteps. Sandro, Sandro the hat was racing at full speed towards the Hotel Danieli. For Mr Pannone, the reports of the evening were beginning. Only fifteen minutes late.

22

The curtain has gone up, thought Powerscourt. The audience are settling down. The prompter is waiting in the wings. If he walked a fraction more to his right he should be in speaking range of Gresham in less than a minute. Grand view the audience must be having, the two principals right in the centre of the square. All the world's a stage, all the men and women merely players.

'Lord Gresham?' said Powerscourt, as if not sure that he recognized the figure in the long black coat.

The young man stared desperately round the square. Out of the corner of his eye he saw Sandro the hat, disappearing round the corner of the Doges' Palace.

'Lord Gresham! It is you! How very nice to see you. What a pleasant surprise.'

Was that a flicker of fear in Gresham's eyes? He looked round again as if thinking of running for it. The square was so big there was no place to hide.

Greshams don't cry. Greshams don't run away.

'Lord Powerscourt! My goodness me! Here in the middle of Venice. How nice to see you again.'

I'm not quite sure you mean that, Powerscourt said to himself, not sure at all. Uncle, he thought, I'm an uncle, I'm an old friend of the family. That's what the script says for now.

'Lord Gresham, you must be here on holiday, like me. Venice is always at its best in the winter.'

I'm on holiday, thought Powerscourt, I'm not here on business, definitely not business. And certainly I'm not investigating, I'm not looking for a killer, not here in St Mark's Square.

'But come, my dear Gresham, I was not looking forward to having dinner on my own. You can feel a bit lonely. Will you join me? I am staying in the Danieli just round the corner.'

'Lord Powerscourt, that is very kind. But I have booked a table at Florian's over there. I made it for one, but I'm sure they can manage two.'

'Are you sure? The Danieli is very pleasant, the food is good there . . .'

'Well, they were very nice to me in Florian's this lunchtime. I wouldn't want to let them down.'

They were inside Florian's in a couple of minutes, Gresham turning abruptly on his heel as they went in, staring, staring once more at the empty square.

So far so good, thought Powerscourt.

Another messenger was running round the corner to the seafront. Mr Pannone's report service was swinging into action.

'Lord Gresham.' Signor Lippi himself met them at the doorway, his silver rings looking extra bright this evening. The gondolier. 'At lunch you were one. Now you are two!' He laughed. 'Tonight we have the big family party in here. We were going to squeeze you in round at the back, if you were one. But now, you are two, why, we give you the little upstairs room. It will be more peaceful without the great noise of the family Morosini down here. And you can look out at the view over the piazza.'

The room was lined in a dark blue material flecked with gold. There were pictures of Venetian churches on the walls. The curtains were left open, the great square stretching away from them into the night. Perhaps they're letting more spectators in now, thought Powerscourt, these are the best seats in the house.

He looked carefully at the young man, now the candles shone on his face. This was not the Gresham he had met and talked to at Sandringham. The Venetian Gresham looked as if he might be falling apart. His collar was not properly adjusted. He hadn't shaved very carefully, a tuft of stubble on his neck. The eyes were wild.

'Have you been to Venice before, Lord Gresham?' said Powerscourt, man of the world.

'I have. I've only been once before. But I loved it so much I've always wanted to come back.'

That would have been with his mother, Powerscourt said to himself, when Gresham was sixteen years old.

'Have you been here a lot, Lord Powerscourt? Do you know the city well?'

'Are you two gentlemen ready to order?'

Gresham started as the waiter offered the menu.

'Please, do take more time if you wish.' There were echoes of Manhattan as the head waiter hovered round their little table. This must be the man who went to America, Powerscourt remembered, even if Mr Pannone thought it wasn't as good as London and Paris.

'Giovanni!' Lord Gresham smiled. 'How nice to see you again. This is Lord Powerscourt. Also from England.'

The waiter bowed. He took the orders.

Antipasto di Frutti di Mare, read Pannone in his office a few moments later, the seafood salad for the starter. His mind automatically translated all Italian menus into English. Then Brodo di Pesce, the soup of fish, Risi e Bisi, the risotto flavoured with the peas and bacon, two Faraona con la Peverada, the guinea fowl with the special sauce. The bottle of Chablis to start with. Then the Lord Powerscourt ordered the two bottles of Châteauneuf du Pape. That should be good with the guinea fowl. Pannone remembered his conversation with Signor Lippi earlier that afternoon.

'These English, they all drink far more than we do, I think. I have watched them. You must have watched them too, Signor Lippi. So I think we pour plenty of wine at the young man early on. Plenty of it. Maybe he talk more freely after that. Maybe he tell the Lord Powerscourt what he wish to know.'

'You were asking if I knew Venice well, Lord Gresham. I have been here a number of times. But I wouldn't say I know it well. I keep getting lost, even now. I don't think you can ever know Venice well. There are too many surprises.'

'I know what you mean,' said Gresham, inspecting a large lobster claw from the seafood salad. 'But I don't think you could ever get tired of it. Oh, thank you very much.'

Giovanni, the American waiter, was refilling Gresham's glass, for the second time. The Chablis went well with the fish.

'Have you been to all of these churches? The ones on the walls, I mean.' Powerscourt moved his religious pawn slowly up the board.

'I've been to Mass in San Marco. That was fantastic. And I went to the Frari this afternoon.' Gresham was looking closely at a mirror above Powerscourt's head.

'Forgive me,' said Powerscourt, dismembering a bright red spider crab, 'are you a believer? In the Catholic faith, I mean. I always think those services must mean so much more if you belong to that faith.'

'They do, they do,' said Gresham, polishing off the last of the prawns. 'And I am, I am a Catholic, I mean. I converted a couple of years ago. It means a lot to me.'

'I have often thought about it,' said Powerscourt. 'So many people make the journey to Rome these days. Is it difficult? The converting, that is.'

'The whole thing is quite difficult,' said the young man, with the air of a religious veteran. The plates were being cleared away. Fresh cutlery was being laid. The Chablis was nearly finished. 'But then, you wouldn't expect a proper religion to be easy, would you? I had terrible trouble with my mother. She couldn't see why I was doing it. She refused to come to the service where I was accepted into the faith. The priest said that she would understand in the end. I think the end may be a long time coming.'

Gresham laughed grimly. The last of the Chablis was poured into his glass. Risotto and fish soup replaced the skeletons of the seafood. Still he stared intently at the mirror.

'It was after my wife died. That was when I thought of converting to Catholicism.' Powerscourt was moving a knight, or was it a bishop, up the board. 'It was so terrible. I really wanted what they call the consolation of religion. I kept going to church services, different ones, all over the place. In so many of the Anglican ones I felt they were just speaking the words. Oh, the words are beautiful, very beautiful. But I didn't think they meant anything very much to the people saying them. How is that soup, by the way?'

Keep the proprieties going. Good manners to the end. We're British, aren't we? Old Etonians all?

'The soup is excellent. Your risotto looks very good too. But tell me, Lord Powerscourt, how long ago did your wife die?'

A flock of pigeons shot past the window, heading for calmer quarters. The wind had risen and was blowing the day's rubbish across the square.

'Caroline?' said Powerscourt, chasing his risotto's last few peas across his plate. 'Caroline died seven years, three months and five days ago.'

Silence fell across the table.

'She died in a shipping accident. She was drowned. Our little boy was with her. He was only two years old.'

Briefly Powerscourt hated himself. He hated himself for using these devices on the young man, unaware that the confidences were rehearsed, the intimacy merely a ploy. He looked out into the square, empty now. I wrote most of this script, he said to himself. He's making it up as he goes along.

'You can still remember the day after all these years,' said Gresham, leaning back in his chair as the table was cleared once more.

'Lord Gresham. Lord Powerscourt. Now we have the guinea fowl, and the vegetables, and the little salad. And we leave you for a while. Please, help yourselves to the red wine. It is far too good to waste.' Giovanni bowed deeply and closed the doors.

Another message sped round to the Danieli. First two courses gone. Serious talk. Not much laughter. Young man drinking too fast. Pannone added it to his pile and stared moodily out to sea.

'I can indeed remember the day,' Powerscourt carried on sadly. 'I don't think you ever forget it. I don't think you ever can.'

'My wife died too, Lord Powerscourt. Last year. It was 14th June. I shall always remember it.'

'I'm so sorry, so sorry,' said Powerscourt gently, refilling Gresham's glass with the red wine.

'Louisa and I were so happy.' Gresham chewed reflectively at his guinea fowl. 'She was a Catholic too. That's why I converted. She said her parents wouldn't approve of our getting married unless she was marrying another Catholic. She was so beautiful, Lord Powerscourt, so beautiful. I knew the minute I saw her that

I had to marry her. I knew we would be so happy together.'
Gresham drank absent-mindedly from his glass, eyes staring
inward now into some private memories of his own.

'How did you lose her? If you don't mind my asking?'
Powerscourt spoke in his softest voice. It could all go wrong
here, he thought. Terribly wrong.

'It's a long story. Do you mind if it's a long story?'
Powerscourt waved his arm at the room and the view outside.
Welcome to the confessional, he thought. May the Lord have
mercy on your sins.

'My dear Lord Gresham, the night is young. Time does not
matter much, here in Venice. They've had so much of it already.
Please go on.'

The young man refilled his glass.

'Shortly before we were married, Louisa and I met Prince
Eddy. I can't remember where. It doesn't matter now. It doesn't
matter at all. But, anyway, he used to come and see us a lot after
we were married. He'd just turn up out of the blue. Sometimes
he would stay. Sometimes he would stay for days. I think he too
was a little in love with Louisa. I mean, anybody would have
been in love with Louisa. She was so beautiful.'

Powerscourt poured himself a glass of Châteauneuf du Pape.
Did they use this wine in their services, those Popes from
Avignon all those years ago? The body and blood of Christ,
grown on the Pope's own vineyards. Drink this in remembrance
of me.

'Sometimes he would call when I was away with the regiment. You know, manoeuvres, training camps, that sort of thing.'
Gresham shivered slightly. He continued his demolition work
on the guinea fowl's leg, now staring intently at the wallpaper.
'He came to stay again last year when I was away. It took me
four months to find out what happened, what really happened,
I mean. You see there was only one other person in the house at
the time. When it happened. The maid. And she ran away. She
disappeared. She vanished right off the face of the earth as if she
had never existed. I looked for her everywhere. I looked for her
at her parents' house in the little village she came from in
Yorkshire. The funny thing is, she was called Louisa too. Louisa
Powell. From Yorkshire.'

He stopped and stared into the fire. The audience outside in the square were very still. They're mesmerised, thought Powerscourt. He said nothing.

'Then I bumped into her near the Tottenham Court Road one day. Quite by chance. She'd changed her name. That wasn't surprising. You wouldn't want to go on being called Louisa after that. She told me the story in one of those little tea rooms they have round there. Awful cakes. Terrible tea, I remember, terrible tea. I had to promise to give her fifty pounds. Christ, I'd have given her five hundred.'

Powerscourt leaned forward and refilled Gresham's glass in sympathy for the terrible tea. He spoke not a word.

'This is what happened. This is Louisa's story, Louisa Powell, Louisa from Yorkshire. Not my Louisa. Not the beautiful one. Not the girl I married. My Louisa.'

Powerscourt thought he might be going to cry. Greshams don't cry, he remembered. They didn't.

'Eddy had been making advances for days. I don't think he knew that Louisa was expecting a child. The house we lived in was built on a slope. At the back, opening out from the drawing-room, there was a great long flight of steps leading out into the garden. Louisa was very fond of gardens. She knew a lot about flowers and things like that. They had some sort of a row, Eddy and Louisa. The other Louisa heard shouting. My Louisa was saying No, very loudly, a number of times. The other Louisa came round to see if that would calm things down. Not in front of the servants, that sort of thing.

'She saw Eddy push my Louisa quite hard. Then he pushed her again. He pushed her down the steps. She thought she heard him shouting after her. My Louisa cracked her head open at the bottom. That was that. My Louisa was dead. The baby was dead. Eddy ran away. Louisa ran away. I've been running away too. Ever since. Ever since Eddy killed her. "There's no bottom, none, in his voluptuousness." *Macbeth*. Malcolm in Act Four. I played him at school. I've changed the words to suit him better.

> ". . . your wives, your daughters,
> Your matrons and your maids, could not fill up
> The cisterns of his lust."

Powerscourt thought you could add the sons and husbands to Prince Eddy's list. Droit de seigneur. Eddy had watched his father all those years. Take what you want. Come to bed with the Prince of Wales by Royal Command.

Except Eddy had men in his cistern as well.

He thought of the young Gresham on stage, like he was tonight in Venice's grandest auditorium. He thought of Lancaster reciting Byron's lines about the fallen at the age of twelve. Lancaster had fallen too. So many bodies.

The young man stared at Powerscourt. His eyes went wild again. He stared out of the window. Silence filled the square. Silence filled the little room with the dark blue walls, flecked with gold.

'I've been followed, you know, Lord Powerscourt. I've been followed ever since I arrived here in Venice. There's somebody behind that mirror above you, watching everything I do.'

Powerscourt was saved by the return of Giovanni the waiter.

'May I clear all this away? You have enjoyed the guinea fowl? Good. Now then, gentlemen, in a few moments, some fruit, a little tiramisu? We have a very good lemon tart this evening, a speciality of the cook. And then some coffee? A little grappa with the coffee?'

'That mirror, Lord Powerscourt.' The waiter was still closing the doors. 'The person watching us. I thought I saw a face in there earlier on during the fish course. Implacable eyes, it had – the face, I mean. Like it was Judgement Day.'

'They're out there too.' The young man rushed from the table and flung open the windows, frightening a group of pigeons into flight. 'There's more of them. They're all watching me. Don't tell me I'm imagining things, Lord Powerscourt. I've got a recess in my little room at the Hotel Pellegrini. There's somebody on the far side of that too, watching, listening. I shouted at them before I came out. I don't think it made any difference at all. They're still there.'

God in heaven, thought Powerscourt. The poor man's going crazy. He can't have been feeling very stable before he got here. Pannone's waiters are pushing him over the edge.

'Everybody sees things in Venice, Lord Gresham. I shouldn't worry about it. Come, let me walk you back to your hotel.'

Gresham was talking non-stop as they left, as if he couldn't control himself. He talked about the mirror, about the faces that followed him round the streets of Venice, about the gold fleck in the wallpaper, turning into snakes, hissing at him across the room. The cold night air seemed to calm him down as they left. The great square was deserted, the Campanile soaring into the night, the four lions on top of the Basilica of St Mark preparing for a night hunt across the rooftops of the city.

Out of the corner of his eye, Powerscourt saw two of the waiters vanishing up the Mercerie and the Calle dei Fabbri on the opposite side of St Mark's Square. Gresham shouted at the disappearing bodies.

'There they are! There they are! I told you!'

He ran at great speed across the stones, the racing footsteps echoing into the walls. Powerscourt found him a few minutes later, panting sadly by the door of a hotel. 'Bastards got away. Bastards. I'll get even with them. I will. I bloody well will.' The two men walked slowly up the narrow street. At the top there was a left turn, then a little bridge, then another long stretch of the Calle dei Fabbri. Three-quarters of the way up a face peered slowly out from an alleyway. When it saw the two people approaching, it disappeared.

Gresham was off again.

'Come back! Come back!' he shouted in despair, too late to reach the vanishing figure. He sprinted up the street, peering into the little roads that twisted off towards the Grand Canal.

'Lord Gresham, come, come. I think you need to rest. Here is the Hotel Pellegrini at last. Why don't you call on me in the morning, at eleven o'clock at the Danieli. Things will seem better in the morning. We could plan our day together.'

Powerscourt watched Gresham right into his hotel, the night manager solicitous, taking his coat and escorting him to his room.

As he walked back towards the seafront, he remembered that great brick building at Morpeth, set back from the town, filled with the isolation wards of the insane. The Northumberland County Lunatic Asylum, full of people with visions, snakes in the wallpaper, mirrors with eyes. It's full of Greshams, he reflected sadly, wandering round those long corridors, doctors with strait-jackets waiting to protect them from the demons in their heads.

It's a race, he said to himself.

A race between my ability to obtain Gresham's confession. If he has one. And Gresham's ability to go mad.

23

Very early the next morning Powerscourt took a trip out to sea in the Danieli gondola. 'I don't care where we go,' he said to the boatman, 'just bring me back here in half an hour. I need to think.'

The gondolier took him out towards the Lido, the great curve of the seafront, Riva degli Schiavoni, named after the Slav traders who had done business there years before, gradually shrinking into a pencil line on a map behind him.

Lord Gresham nearly told me something last night, he thought. At one stage we were just a second or two away. But that was in the evening when the messengers and the wine conspired to send him almost mad. Powerscourt didn't think there could be too many more of these heavy, confession-laden conversations. If he doesn't tell me something this morning, I shall just have to ask him a question.

Just one would do.

He finalized his plan of campaign as the gondolier brought him back to the landing stage with a last flourish of his oar. Powerscourt realized that the man had been singing solidly for the past fifteen minutes. He hadn't heard a thing.

He sent a cable by the hotel telegraph when he returned to the Danieli to William Burke, his brother-in-law in London, asking him to forward the message to Johnny Fitzgerald with all speed. The answer was needed by 10.30.

Various changes were made to Powerscourt's suite on the first floor. A large writing desk, adorned with many forms of pen and pencil, was installed in the centre of the room. Three paintings were removed from the walls. Three of Mr Pannone's finest mirrors replaced them, gold frames resting happily on the red walls. A reproduction Madonna and Child took over from the Canaletto *View over the Basin of St Mark*. A large silver crucifix now hung beside the window, directly in the eyeline of the person sitting at the writing desk. And above the bed an empty space was filled with a reproduction of Tintoretto's *Christ on the Cross*, suffering and despair dripping from the canvas.

I'm not sure I'd like to sleep in this room any more, thought Powerscourt grimly. But I need all the assistance I can find.

Mr Pannone hovered, offering hints on how best to achieve the desired effect. The crucifix had been his idea. He offered to organize a parade of priests, patrolling ceaselessly outside the window, ever visible from above. Powerscourt declined.

'So, Lord Powerscourt.' Mr Pannone checked the final arrangements. 'It is now half-past ten of the clock. He is due here at eleven. As ever, we know when he come, the Lord Gresham. You do not meet him in the entrance down the stairs. I take him up here to meet you.

'Five minute after he come, I bring you the message. You do not have the message yet, I think. Ah, you do have the message. But there is the blank space left. You wait for the answer from London, it is so?'

Powerscourt handed the hotel manager a piece of paper. He had written the message at eight o'clock that morning.

Lord Johnny Fitzgerald was late. Perhaps he couldn't find the answer. Perhaps he wasn't in London at all. Perhaps he was out when the message found him, though Powerscourt felt sure he would still be having his breakfast. He wasn't an early riser, Lord Johnny.

'He has left the Pellegrini now! The Lord Gresham! He comes!' Pannone looked rather nervous, flitting anxiously between the reception and the telegraph room. 'He is looking around a lot again. He's walking fast. He should be here in ten minutes.'

Powerscourt took a last glance around his room. A smaller stage this morning, maybe a more intimate piece of theatre to play across these boards.

'Now he is passing the Rialto!'

Powerscourt made a final adjustment to the pens on the

writing table. He checked that you could see the three mirrors from the chair by the coffee table near the window.

'He is just coming into St Mark's Square! Do you wish me to hold him up down below while we wait for the message? No?'

Powerscourt looked out of the window. It was a grey day, wind and rain whipping across the seafront, tourists hurrying indoors, the braver ones marching on towards their chosen place of pilgrimage, plenty of customers for the art galleries today.

'Lord Powerscourt!' Pannone rushed into the room. 'It is here!'

He handed over a telegraph form. Lord Johnny's not sparing the words this morning, thought Powerscourt. But I suppose William Burke is paying the bill.

'Is there no peace?' the message read. 'Just when I have a few days rest your message comes to wake me up. Am I never to be left alone? Name you want is General George Brooke. Not related to the Daisy. Beware the courtesans. Fitzgerald.'

There was just time to add three words to his earlier message. He could hear Gresham coming up the stairs. He slipped it to Pannone as he left.

'Lord Gresham! How nice to see you again!'

'Good morning, Lord Powerscourt.'

Gresham did not look much better this morning. The untidy tuft on his chin had gone. But his cravat was twisted. He was wearing the same shirt as the night before. The hair was unruly, the eyes rather wild.

'They're still following me about, Lord Powerscourt. In broad daylight.'

Gresham's eyes looked at the three mirrors, at the crucifix, at the Madonna and Child. They went back in terror towards the mirrors. Powerscourt wondered if he saw snakes, or eyes, or the faces of murdered Venetians peering out from those golden frames. Two Doges, he remembered, had been killed just round the corner from the hotel.

'Come, I have ordered coffee. We can make our plans.'

There was a knock at the door. Pannone entered, bearing a tray of coffee and a message for Powerscourt.

'This has just arrived for you, Lord Powerscourt. It was delivered by special messenger to the hotel. Thank you, my lord.' He bowed deeply to the crucifix and departed.

'Goodness me. Goodness me,' said Powerscourt, scanning the words he had written three hours before. 'The British Military Attaché to the Italian Government is in town. He is here with the Ambassador for some conference or other. He wonders if we would like to join him for lunch. Man by the name of Brooke, General George Brooke. Do you know the fellow, Gresham? This Brooke person?'

Gresham had turned pale, very pale. He stared at the mirrors as if General Brooke was hiding on the other side of the glass.

'I do. I do,' he said very quietly. 'He was my first commanding officer. For four years.' He fell silent. Powerscourt stared at the silver crucifix. 'I can't meet him. I just can't. I've got to get away.'

He looked round as if he thought of jumping straight out of the window. Tintoretto's crucified Christ bled slowly above the bedspread. The mirrors sent Gresham the cryptic messages inside his head. The Madonna and Child looked gravely down, the Virgin aware across the centuries that the child she held in her arms was destined to die on the cross.

'Lord Powerscourt, please help me. I've got to get away. I've got to get away from here.'

Powerscourt waited.

'Will you take a message to England for me? I don't think I shall ever go back.'

'I should be happy to take a message for you. Of course, my dear Gresham. Why don't you write it down? There seems to be lots of paper and things on the desk. I shall just go and sort out this lunch. This General Brooke will have to find some other guests to entertain him.'

Down in the entrance hall, a fresh party of Americans had arrived from Vienna. Pannone was efficient in his reception, bags despatched here, porters summoned, welcomes and good wishes exchanged with the transatlantic visitors. The Danieli cat, Powerscourt noticed, had fallen asleep, wrapped around a potted plant by the reception desk. Outside it was still raining, little streams of moisture running down the hotel's windowpanes in crooked lines.

I wonder if they have thought of it yet, Powerscourt said to himself, Father Gilbey and the Monsignors and the Cardinals.

Confession by letter. You don't need to speak inside those dark boxes, just leave your message, posted through the grille. You could come back later for the answer.

The Venetians, Powerscourt remembered, looking at a portrait of a sinister-looking Doge on Mr Pannone's wall, had a slightly different system. They believed in betrayal, not confession, through the post, betrayal through those little post boxes, *bocca di leone*, mouth of the lion. They were emptied every night. There were several of them in the Doges' Palace. You denounced your enemies, or your friends, or your husband, or your next-door neighbour. All you had to do was write the letter and put it in the lion's mouth. Or the lion's den. The secret police did the rest.

Fifteen minutes, thought Powerscourt. Surely he would have written his message by now. Pannone gave him a reassuring tap on the shoulder as he tiptoed back up the stairs to his room.

It was empty. Gresham had gone.

'Pannone! Pannone!'

The little man had never heard him shout before.

'He's gone! The bird has flown! Gresham has cleared off!'

'Don't worry, Lord Powerscourt. The waiters are watching. Very soon, we shall know where he has gone. But see, he has left you the message.'

The envelope was addressed to Lord Francis Powerscourt, The Danieli Hotel. The ink was still wet. Powerscourt took a paper knife and slit it open.

Dear Lord Powerscourt,

I would like you to take a message to my mother when you return to England. Please tell her I am well and that I shall write to her soon. I should have done it before. I think she gets worried when I am not there.

I am going to Florence. I cannot stay in Venice any more. I feel I am going out of my mind. Those mirrors don't leave you alone, not for a moment. Then I am going to Perugia. I may go to Arezzo on the way, then on to Rome. In Rome, or on the way to Rome, I shall make my confession.

Then I shall break some more commandments. I am going to shoot myself. You're not meant to commit suicide

249

in the Catholic Church. But they won't know about it until it is too late. I am going to join Louisa, my Louisa, on the other side. I hope they'll let me in.

'He is back in the Pellegrini now, the Lord Gresham. He is packing his bags. Maybe he go to the railway station. We have many waiters there.' Pannone rushed through his latest report.

One last thing, Lord Powerscourt. I am sure you know this already. I killed Prince Eddy. You know why. I climbed over the roof and into his room. I think Lancaster heard me battering that photograph of Princess May with the heel of my boot. He may have seen me climbing out of the window, I don't know.

I don't regret it. But I know I must make my penance after I have confessed my sins.

I wish you had met Louisa. So beautiful. And I wish I had met your Caroline, lying at the bottom of the sea. My Louisa. So beautiful, my Louisa . . .

I have no more time. Goodbye Lord Powerscourt. Goodbye.

Gresham.

Powerscourt read it again, his hand shaking slightly. He folded Gresham's last will and testament and put it in his pocket. This was what had brought him to Venice. For this he had planned and plotted for four days, waiters posted across the streets of the city, pictures rearranged on the walls, false messages concocted on an early morning gondola ride across the lagoon. He should have felt elated, pleased with himself. But there were no Hallelujahs sounding in his head, only a great sadness and the thought of another death, an Englishman found lying dead somewhere in Italy, another one dead before his time.

'Lord Powerscourt? You find what you want, I think. But it makes you sad. You have found what you came for?'

'I have found what I came for, Mr Pannone. I did not think I would like it very much when I found it. But I have found it. And I like it even less.

'But,' he went on, 'without your assistance I would never

250

have found it at all. And thank you for all the assistance you have so kindly provided since I came here. I shall always be in your debt.'

Pannone smiled. 'We have a new saying now, in the Danieli, Lord Powerscourt. Any friend of Lord Rosebery, he is the friend of the Danieli, we used to say. Now we say, any friend of Lord Rosebery or Lord Powerscourt, he is the friend of the Danieli!'

Powerscourt bowed in gratitude. I'm going to have to embrace him again, he thought. Maybe it's the two kisses on the cheeks this time.

'But tell me one thing, Lord Powerscourt, if I may ask the question. This lunch with the General, the General who never was. An Italian General I could have found for you, I am sure, maybe a French one. I am not sure about a German one. But I could not have provided the English General. What does it mean, that name that came from England? Why was it so important?'

'The reason that name was so important, my dear Pannone, was that it was the name of the General who used to be in command of Lord Gresham. I was sure he would not want to meet him. That was why I sent the message to London. To find out his name.'

'He was the Commandante of the Lord Gresham? So with that name, you were sure he would not stay here for the lunch. Even at the Danieli!'

'I was sure.'

They embraced. Powerscourt delivered his kisses to the two ample cheeks of the little hotel manager. It's over, he thought. It's nearly over.

'You must come back and see us again, Lord Powerscourt. Perhaps with the young lady you are going to marry? The honeymoons at the Danieli, they are the best in the world!'

Santa Lucia station. Lady Lucy's trains. Lady Lucy's trains were waiting to bring him back to London.

Back to Lady Lucy.

Back home.

Part Four

The Green Cape

24

Powerscourt was back in Suter's office in Marlborough House, the same room where the four men had met before in the autumn of the previous year when Suter handed over his memorandum about the misfortunes of his master the Prince of Wales. Sir William Suter was looking down at a great pile of documents on his desk, Sir Bartle Shepstone, Comptroller and Treasurer of the Household, his white beard clean and bright in the morning light, was inspecting the polish on his boots.

I've seen you very recently, thought Powerscourt. Only the other day I saw lots of you all over the walls of those Venetian churches, kindly saints with white beards, waiting for eternity beside some sad Madonna, mighty prophets with white beards, rallying their people to the justice of God's cause, apocalyptic old men, God with a white beard, dividing the population of their paintings into saints and sinners in some final judgement.

Powerscourt, slightly nervous, still tired from his Venetian odyssey, was clutching a new black notebook.

Rosebery was wearing the neutral face of the politician, mentally preparing his last report for Prime Minister Salisbury on the strange death of Prince Eddy. Powerscourt had told him the full story the night before in Berkeley Square.

'It's like some terrible *Revenger's Tragedy*,' had been Rosebery's verdict. 'Let us hope there are no more bodies. Are congratulations in order, Francis? You seem to have got to the bottom of it remarkably quickly in view of the difficulties.'

'Prayers for the dead would be more appropriate than congratulations. A whole lot of prayers. A whole lot of dead,' said Powerscourt, shivering slightly.

'Good morning, gentlemen,' purred Sir William Suter, urbane courtier. 'You said you wished to see us. You said in your cable from Venice that you had fresh news on the unhappy passing of the Duke of Clarence and Avondale. Were you in Venice on holiday, Lord Powerscourt? I believe the weather can be very inclement there at this time of year.'

'I wouldn't say it was a holiday, exactly,' said Powerscourt with a rueful smile. 'I went there as part of my investigations.'

Eight hundred miles away a young man with staring eyes was waiting for a church to open. The church was the Santa Maria del Carmine on the southern side of the Arno in Florence. A small sign, attached to the parish noticeboard, promised confession in English between the hours of nine and ten on Thursday mornings every week. Father Menotti SJ.

The young man was early. He was trying to remember what the Jesuits had told him about making a good confession. 'Hail Mary, full of grace, the Lord is with thee, Blessed art thou amongst women, Blessed is the fruit of thy womb Jesus . . .' He prayed while he waited.

Underneath Masaccio's fresco of the expulsion of Adam and Eve from the Garden of Eden, two figures fleeing in shock and terror from their crime, the beginning of sin, the original sin, Lord Edward Gresham was preparing to confess his murder.

Powerscourt had asked Rosebery the night before how much he should tell Suter and Shepstone. Everything? A sanitized version of the truth? Just the name of the killer?

'For God's sake, Francis, they've never been helpful to you. The roots of this affair go back such a long way. They're used to hiding the truth. They never say yes, they never say no, as I said to you at the beginning. Just for once I think they should hear the truth. The whole truth and nothing but the truth.'

'I was originally approached about the affairs of the Prince of Wales and his family in the latter half of 1891,' Powerscourt began. 'At that time there were suspicions that the Prince of Wales was being blackmailed and there were fears, justified fears as it turned out, for the life of the Duke of Clarence and Avondale. I propose to refer to him as Prince Eddy from now on in this narrative of events.

'Shortly after I arrived on the scene the blackmail question seemed to go away. There were a lot of complicated manoeuvres in the affairs of the Prince of Wales and Daisy Brooke and an intemperate letter intercepted by Lady Beresford.'

Cisterns of lust, he thought to himself. He couldn't get the phrase out of his mind.

'These matters could easily have given rise to blackmail, but I was not entirely convinced of that. My inquiries revealed that there had been no blackmailers at large in what we call Society for at least twenty years. The cause of the blackmail must have lain elsewhere.'

Suter began taking notes. He would, said Powerscourt to himself. He'd be taking notes about the verdict of God on Judgement Day itself, preparing a memorandum for the Almighty's filing system.

'We then come to the murder itself.' Powerscourt looked down at his book once more. 'On the night of January 8th, or the morning of January 9th, Prince Eddy was murdered in the manner we all know.' Better spare them something.

The confessional was very dark, dark brown wood surrounding the penitent. There was a strange smell, floor polish perhaps. Or fear.

Gresham knelt at the feet of his confessor, Father Menotti, invisible on the other side of the little booth.

'Bless me, father, for I have sinned.'

He bowed his head, his eyes closed, as his confessor blest him. Gresham made the Sign of the Cross with the slow deliberate movements of the recent convert. A school choir was rehearsing in a distant part of the church, youthful voices singing the Kyrie. *Kyrie eleison, Christe eleison, Kyrie eleison.* Lord have mercy, Christ have mercy, Lord have mercy.

'I confess to Almighty God, to Blessed Mary ever Virgin, to

all the angels and saints, and to you, my spiritual Father, that I have sinned.'

'The Prince of Wales decided,' Powerscourt continued, 'for reasons which will become all too apparent, that he wished to hush the matter up, to conceal the truth. The convenient fiction was adopted that Prince Eddy had died of influenza.'

'Influenza, yes, influenza.' Sir Bartle Shepstone nodded wisely, as if he were an old friend of the disease.

'The result of this was that the death was not officially announced to the world until January 15th. In the meantime Lord Henry Lancaster, one of six young men, equerries to Prince Eddy, who were staying in the house, was found dead in Sandringham Woods, shot through the head. At first sight it looked like a second murder. But the medical evidence was convincing. Lord Lancaster killed himself. He left me a note.'

Suter looked up from his papers. Shepstone sat upright in his chair. Powerscourt had not told them about the note before.

'It wasn't a very satisfactory note. I mean it didn't clear anything up. If anything, it made things worse. This is what it said.'

He took the note from his pocket. ' "By the time you read this, I shall be dead. I am sorry for all the trouble I am causing to my family and friends and to yourself. I am sure you will come to understand that I had no choice. I could do no other. Semper Fidelis." ' Powerscourt folded Lancaster's note carefully and returned it to his pocket.

'I was greatly puzzled by the Semper Fidelis. Faithful to whom? To his country? To his friends? To Prince Eddy? To his regiment? At first I was confused. Things became clearer later on.

'So this was the position, as it presented itself to me when the business of the cover-up was over.'

Lord Edward Gresham was shaking in his confessional. The church cleaners were going about their daily duty with mops and buckets. The youthful choir had progressed from the Kyrie to a Sanctus. They kept making the same mistake. The opening notes echoed round the building again and again as the music master tried to correct the error of their ways.

'Father, I was at confession at Farm Street in Mayfair at the very beginning of this year. By the grace of God I received absolution, performed my penance, and went to Holy Communion. Father, I have sinned most grievously since then. I have murdered a man. I have broken the Sixth Commandment. May the Lord have mercy upon me.'

'What were the circumstances in which you broke the Sixth Commandment, my son?' Father Menotti's voice came from far away. The other side of the confessional box seemed to Gresham to be a world he had lost, one he might never re-enter.

'We could rule out the possibility of any outsiders having committed the crime. There were reports of Russians and Irish in the neighbourhood. Both were traced. Both were completely innocent. There were, it seemed to me, three possibilities.'

Powerscourt was delivering his verdict in the cold neutral tones of a judge summing up a complicated case. Sir Bartle Shepstone was stroking his beard.

'The first was a disgruntled army or naval officer who had served with Prince Eddy and thought the country would be better off without him. I can assure you that there are many such officers who despised his morals and his way of life and thought him unfit to be King.'

'This is outrageous, outrageous!' spluttered Shepstone.

'He was a fine upstanding young man!'

'No, he wasn't,' said Rosebery. 'He was a disgrace. I have met many senior officers with the views of which Lord Powerscourt speaks. Pray be quiet.'

'The second possibility was that it was one of the equerries. One of six, or rather five, after the death of Lancaster. I decided to find out everything I could about their lives, and about whether any of them might have good cause to murder Prince Eddy.

'The third possibility was that the blackmail was connected in some way with the murder. I discovered that the Prince of Wales had been outspending his income by £15–20,000 a year for over ten years, since 1879 in fact. That was the year in which the two young Princes left their training ship HMS *Britannia*, and were sent round the world on a two-year cruise on HMS *Bacchante*. One of the naval officers concerned believed that the main purpose of the voyage was to keep Prince Eddy out of England.

'There was a great scandal that year on board HMS *Britannia*. Five young men contracted syphilis, after sexual contact with Prince Eddy. He was believed to have contracted the disease from some prostitutes in Portsmouth.'

Cisterns of lust, thought Powerscourt. Cisterns full of it. Five of them on board the *Britannia*. Wouldn't one of the boys have done? Two, at the most? Suter carried on with his notes. Rosebery was looking carefully at Powerscourt, his features carved from stone.

'Since that time the Prince of Wales has been paying regularly to all those families. You could call it medical assistance, help with treating the terrible disease. You could call it compensation for those young lives destroyed. You could call it naval pensions. Somebody did. Or you could call it blackmail, if you like. I suspect that one, or both of you gentlemen, knew all about this matter. But you did not see fit to tell me.'

Powerscourt looked up at the two servants of the Prince of Wales. They did not reply.

'I was on the way to establishing whether or not any relatives of the victims could have committed the crime, a father or a brother. Revenge is a regular motive for murder. Two of the brothers were, in fact, in Norfolk at the time. But neither of them could have committed the murder. I was beginning to work my way through the rest of the families when a piece of news reached me about one of the equerries.'

'Father, my sin concerns my wife. I met her two years ago near Birmingham in the middle of England. She was called Louisa. She was very beautiful.' Lord Edward Gresham paused in his confession. Loving somebody wasn't a sin, was it?

'Continue, my son. Continue with your confession.' Father Menotti's voice was soft, but firm.

'We fell in love. She was of the Catholic faith. I was not. She wanted me to adopt the Catholic faith before she would marry me. I received instruction from the Jesuits in Farm Street in London and was received into the Church. We were married eighteen months ago.'

A grunt, or was it a cough, came from the other side of the grille. Perhaps Father Menotti was clearing his throat. Perhaps he was rejoicing in the salvation of a Protestant heretic, in a land all too full of Protestant heretics.

'Father, the man I killed was Prince Eddy, the son of the Prince of Wales, grandson of Queen Victoria herself. After we were married he came frequently to my house. He often came when I was away on army business. I am an officer in the British Army. Prince Eddy wanted my wife to commit adultery with him. He pleaded with her to give in to him. Everybody else did.'

'Was he a regular fornicator with other men's wives?'

'He would have sexual relations with man or woman, Father. It didn't seem to matter.'

Powerscourt looked round his little audience. It's a soliloquy this time, he thought, somewhere towards the end of Act Five.

'Two years ago, one of the equerries fell in love with a beautiful girl in the Midlands, near Birmingham. The girl's father was very rich. But there was a problem. The family were Catholic. The equerry was not. To the horror of his mother he converted with the Jesuits in Farm Street, just up the road from here. They were married. The mother did not attend the wedding.'

What had Lady Lucy said to him, about Lady Blanche Gresham and the marriage?

'Not to a grocer's daughter', she said. 'Not to a Roman Catholic. Not in some pagan chapel, decked out with bleeding hearts and the false idolatry of Rome.'

'Prince Eddy was a regular visitor to their house after they were married, especially when the equerry was away. He made regular propositions to the equerry's wife. Equally regularly, she refused. He grew tired of these refusals. He was not used to them, from man or woman. One day he pushed her down a flight of steps and killed her. She was pregnant at the time.

'It took our equerry four months to find out the truth. The only other person in the house, the only person who knew what happened, a servant girl, ran away. Eventually, last summer, he found her. That will have been the time he was requesting to become an equerry to Prince Eddy, I fancy. It tallies with the note you sent me, Sir William, about the dates of service of the equerries at the time of the murder.'

The cleaning party had moved on in the church of Santa Maria del Carmine in Florence. The singers had moved on as well, to the Benedictus.

'One day she refused him again. He pushed her down a flight of steps. It killed her. It killed our child as Louisa was pregnant. So I waited for my chance and I killed him. Prince Eddy had killed my Louisa. She was so beautiful. I adored her. Prince Eddy had killed our child before it was even born. Father, I know I have sinned against God's Holy Law and Commandments. I know I have sinned against the Sixth Commandment. I do truly repent of these my sins and beg you for forgiveness.

'I accuse myself also of all the sins of my past life, especially of those against purity and chastity. For all these sins and for those I do not remember, I ask pardon of God with my whole heart, and penance and absolution of you, my spiritual Father.'

'On the night of 8 January or early morning of the 9th of this year, the equerry climbed over the roofs of Sandringham and murdered Prince Eddy. The equerry's name is Lord Edward Gresham.'

Sir William Suter turned pale. Shepstone turned red.

'Gresham? Gresham? Are you sure, Powerscourt? Dammit, I have known the family for years. I think I went to his christening in Thorpe Hall.'

'I am quite sure, thank you, Sir Bartle. I would not tell you if I wasn't.'

'Dammit, Suter, this is unbelievable. Do you believe it?'

'How can you be so sure, Lord Powerscourt?'

'I told you I was sure of it. Gresham told me himself in Venice three days ago. Do you want any more confirmation than that?'

'Dear God,' said Suter, laying down his pen. 'What a terrible business. A terrible business.' He stopped and looked down at his notes again. 'Could I ask you to clear two little points up for us, Lord Francis?'

The Private Secretary, the bureaucrat, must ensure that all the facts are included in the report to his master.

'I have been haunted, ever since you told us, by Lancaster's Semper Fidelis. What does it mean?'

'I think he saw Gresham in the room. Maybe he heard him crushing the picture of Princess May into small pieces. Maybe he saw him climbing out of the window. He knew who the murderer was. He was being faithful to his friend. He wasn't going to betray him. So he is faithful to him for ever. Forever Faithful. Semper fidelis.'

'You have sinned, my son. You have sinned most grievously against God's Holy Law and his Commandments.' Father Menotti paused.

Lord Edward Gresham was still on his knees, tears on his face, terror in his heart. Father Menotti's voice was very close now. This is my last judgement, Gresham thought, here in the middle of Florence. Father Menotti has turned into Savonarola. This is Judgement Day, on the Arno.

'*Agnus Dei, qui tollis peccata mundi, miserere nobis.* Lamb of God, who takest away the sins of the world, have mercy on us.' The youthful singers had moved on to the Agnus Dei, innocent voices soaring into the roof.

'The crime you have confessed is a most serious one. You are required to tell the authorities in your own country what you have done. Every day, from now until the end of your time on earth, you must say three Hail Marys for the mother of the young man you murdered. You must pray for the brothers and the sisters every day. You must pray for the soul of the bereaved every day. Each year on the anniversary of his death, you must say the Mass for the Bereaved. This you do in memory of him.'

'*Agnus Dei, qui tollis peccata mundi, miserere nobis.* Lamb of God, who takest away the sins of the world, have mercy on us.'

'Do you heartily repent of your manifold sins and wickedness?'

'I do.'

'Do you promise to repent most truly of your crimes that you may come at last into God's own gracious mercy and protection?'

'I do.'

'May Almighty God have mercy upon you, forgive you your sins, and bring you to life everlasting. Amen. *Ego absolvo te.* I absolve you. May the almighty and merciful Lord grant you pardon,' Father Menotti made an elaborate sign of the cross, 'absolution and remission of your sins.'

'*Agnus Dei, qui tollis peccata mundi, miserere nobis.*' Lamb of God, who takest away the sins of the world, have mercy on us.'

The words of the priest and the choir escorted Gresham out of the church and into the cold air of Florence. He had made his confession. The priest had forgiven him his sins. There was only one thing left he had to do.

'And the blackmail? The blackmail of the Prince of Wales last autumn?' Suter was still tidying up the loose ends, composing no doubt in his mind the final memorandum for his master.

'I am not certain about that', said Powerscourt. But I think what happened was this. One of the young men on the *Britannia*, name of Robinson, from Dorchester on Thames, died of his syphilis last summer. The payments from the Prince of Wales stopped. The family were hard up suddenly. So the father tried to restart the payments on his own. I saw both *The Times* and the *Illustrated London News* in the hall of his house. I can imagine him cutting them up with the scissors and paste. Then I think the other parents realised what was going on. The matter was cleared up. The payments started again. The blackmail notes ceased.'

'And where is Gresham now?' said Shepstone.

'He is in Italy still. He is going to Florence, maybe to Arezzo, then Perugia. His final destination is Rome. After he has confessed his sins he intends to shoot himself. That's what he told me. I believe him. I don't think he will be alive for Easter.'

'Lord Powerscourt, we are so grateful to you, so relieved that we know the truth of this sad and terrible affair.'

Sir William Suter seemed anxious to get rid of them, ushering them into the Marlborough House corridor. As they walked down the stairs, Powerscourt turned to Rosebery.

'Damn. I've forgotten my little black book. I don't want to leave it in there.'

He sped back the way they had come. As he opened the door, they looked surprised and embarrassed to see him. The efficient Major Dawnay had joined them. They were poring over a map of Italy, laid out on the table.

'My book. I forgot it. I'm so sorry. Good day to you, gentlemen.'

Rosebery was waiting for him outside Marlborough House.

'Well done, Francis, well done. That seems to have brought the affair to a close.'

'I hope you're right, Rosebery. I do hope you're right.'

25

Lord Francis Powerscourt was waiting for Lady Lucy Hamilton in a box at the Royal Albert Hall, waiting for a performance of Beethoven's Ninth Symphony.

That dreadful Prince Albert, he thought as he waited, there's his great gold statue just over the road, brooding over Kensington Gardens. There's his son, the Prince of Wales, whose life had not been improved by his father's tyrannical upbringing. There's his late grandson, murdered for his lust, the cisterns of his lust. Maybe they've met already on the other side. He didn't think Albert would have a lot in common with the late Prince Eddy, Duke of Clarence and Avondale.

'What good deeds did you perform in your time on earth, Grandson Eddy?'

'I gave a lot of people syphilis, Grandfather.'

Then she was opening the door, wearing that Anna Karenina coat again.

'Lady Lucy! How very very nice to see you!'

'How kind of you to invite me, Lord Francis. And a box too! I have always been very fond of Beethoven.'

They settled down, two of them, in a box large enough for eight.

'Lord Francis.' Lady Lucy was peering down into the auditorium one floor below them. 'The whole place is like one of those Roman amphitheatres like the one in Verona or Orange. Is there room for bread and circuses down there, do you think?'

Powerscourt wasn't sure about the bread. But there was plenty of room for circuses. He saw himself in the imperial box

266

at the Colosseum. He was Augustus, maybe Nero. Down beneath two gladiators were coming to the end of a brutal fight. Both were wounded, blood flowing fast into the hot Roman earth. One appeared to have vanquished the other, standing above his victim, sword poised, ready to strike. The Roman mob were baying for blood. Nero Powerscourt turned to his consort to ask what fate should befall the man below. His consort was touching his arm again.

'Look, Francis. The conductor.' Lady Lucy was oblivious to her role as Queen of the Games.

The conductor, Herr Dr Hirsch, from Vienna, was a very tall thin man, beginning to go bald. He was picking nervously at his shirt cuffs as he took up his position. He prepared his orchestra, a smile here, a wave of the baton there. The audience were still rustling in their seats, checking their programmes, chatting to their friends. Herr Hirsch brought Beethoven's Ninth whispering into action. Very softly, very gently. Then Beethoven summoned his audience with a fanfare of drums and brass. Pay attention in the back! Stop your chattering, good citizens of Berlin or Hamburg or London! I am taking you on a journey! I, Beethoven!

For two movements marches, dances, sometimes lyrical, sometimes martial, swept across the audience. The conductor used his baton in great stroking movements, never pausing to look down at the score in front of him. Already perspiration was forming a glistening sheen across his forehead.

But the third movement took them to a different world.

It started with what sounded like a hymn, a melancholy sound, a sound of ineffable sadness. Beethoven is lamenting the misery of this world, thought Powerscourt, sitting very still in his box. *Sunt lacrimae rerum.* That's what it is, Virgil's lines from the *Aeneid* translated into music by a fifty-year-old German genius. There are tears in the middle of everything, a sadness at the heart of the universe. Tears in the midst of all things.

Then it swept off into another mode.

Love flowed out into the Albert Hall.

Love floated through the roof and hovered over London.

Then love turned and went ever higher, spinning, sweeping, soaring, into a realm beyond the planets, beyond the Milky Way.

Shards of God's love floated back from the spheres and drifted down to earth like stardust.

The conductor was leaning forward now, his baton caressing the strings as if he was brushing at something ever so delicate, like a butterfly's wings. Down in the arena there was a terrible stillness as if the audience were preparing themselves for a journey to Beethoven's universe of love. Behind them in the box the six empty chairs waited. Angels are coming, thought Powerscourt, angels are coming down to listen to the music. They will sit here patiently, wings furled. Then they will float up and rise above the streets of Kensington to join the anthem of love in the constellations above.

Love suffers long and is kind: love beareth all things, believeth all things, hopeth all things, endureth all things. One of the angels is reading a lesson, thought Powerscourt, a lesson for Lady Lucy and me, here in our box at the Albert Hall. Love never faileth; but where there be prophecies they shall fail, where there be tongues they shall cease, where there be knowledge, it shall pass away. There abideth three things, faith, hope, love. And the greatest of these is love. The angel sat down again. The music soared on.

Love was now very far away, knocking at the gates of heaven, somewhere far far above the streets of London, sweeping majestically towards the infinite. Beethoven's love. God's love.

When the movement ended Powerscourt turned, very quietly, to look at Lady Lucy beside him. She was smiling gently, her eyes filled with tears. *Sunt lacrimae rerum.* As the fourth movement brought the Albert Hall back to earth, Powerscourt searched through his pockets. You couldn't speak. Not in here. Not now. Beethoven might get cross. God might send a thunderbolt. Did he have a pen? He must have a pen somewhere. He did. Was there anything to write on? No, only an old copy of a newspaper rolled up in his pocket. He picked it out. He found an empty space inside an advertisement for Colman's Mustard. He composed his message.

'Lucy. I love you. Will you marry me? Francis.'

He tapped her lightly on the shoulder and passed her the crumpled paper, pointing shyly to his proposal.

Lady Lucy smiled at him. The tears had gone. She made

writing gestures at him. What on earth was she doing, making those signs with her hand? Then he realised. Lady Lucy didn't have a pen. He gave her his. This is what life is going to be like from now on, he thought. Sharing things, sharing pens, sharing programmes at the Albert Hall, sharing love.

The paper came back. The reply was hidden inside another advertisement, this one for Bird's Eye Custard. Powerscourt thought he would have preferred the mustard. He'd always hated custard.

'Francis. Of course I will marry you. Love. Lucy.'

She took the newspaper from him and placed it carefully in her bag. You couldn't trust men to remember to keep things like that, she thought. Not even Francis. Well, maybe Francis.

Beethoven was now on the final movement of his symphony. The chorus were on their feet. Schiller's 'Ode to Joy' bellowed out across the auditorium. The waltzes and the marches from earlier on returned to take another bow.

> 'May he who has had the fortune
> To gain a true friend
> And he who has won a noble wife
> Join in our jubilation!'

Lady Lucy sent out a small hand to hold Powerscourt's. It was all right in the dark. Nobody could see. Suddenly she didn't care who saw. She wanted to shout, to sing out her own hymn of love and happiness found with Beethoven and with Schiller. And with Francis. Her own Ode to Joy.

> 'Be embraced, Millions
> Take this kiss for all the world!
> Brothers, surely a loving Father
> Dwells above the canopy of stars.
> Do you sink before him, Millions?
> World, do you sense your Creator?
> Seek him then beyond the stars!
> He must dwell beyond the stars.'

*

'Francis.' Lady Lucy Hamilton and Lord Francis Powerscourt were returning to Markham Square in a cab, rattling along the Cromwell Road. 'I don't need to call you Lord Francis any more, do I? Not now, I mean. And you don't have to call me Lady Lucy either.' She was nestling against his shoulder. It was very cold outside.

'Well, I always think of you as Lady Lucy. In my mind, I mean.'

'Oh, I shan't mind at all if you want to go on calling me Lady Lucy. It shows proper respect, don't you think?'

Powerscourt laughed. 'What are you going to tell Robert?'

'Ah, Robert. Robert,' said Lady Lucy, snuggling ever closer into Powerscourt's shoulder. 'Do you know, he asked me the other day if I was going to marry you. Just like that. I think one of the boys' mothers at the school has just remarried. That must have put it into his head.'

She remembered the conversation, Robert glad to be diverted from Latin nouns, second declension homework, she herself struggling with the latest Henry James.

'Are you going to marry Lord Powerscourt, Mama?'

Lady Lucy composed herself. What a strange thing for Robert to say. Why, she'd only been thinking about it herself a few minutes ago. It was hard to get into, this Henry James.

'Well, darling . . .' She wondered what to tell him. I'd better tell him the truth, she thought, best to start early. 'I would if he asked me. But he hasn't asked me yet.'

'Is he going to ask you?'

'I expect so. I expect he'll get round to it one day. Probably.'

'And then you'll say yes?'

'Yes,' his mother laughed. 'Yes, I'll say yes.'

Somehow Robert knew that Lord Powerscourt would ask the question. After all, his mother was so pretty. All the boys at school said so.

'What will you think about that, Robert? If we do get married.'

'Well, he's not very good at knots and things like that for my boat,' said Robert, practically.

'I expect he's thinking about other things. He usually is.'

Lady Lucy told Robert that Powerscourt was an investigator, that he solved mysteries, sometimes murders. Sometimes he did secret work for the Government, like when he went to Venice. The little boy's eyes grew bigger and bigger.

'Was he doing secret work when he went to Venice? Was he thinking about the mystery when we were at the Round Pond? Wow! Wow!' There was a pause while this intelligence sank in. 'Mama?'

'Yes, my darling?'

'Can I tell the boys at school? If you decide to get married. About what he does. Lord Francis, I mean. The Investigator.'

'Just a little, darling. Just a little.'

The cab was on the final stretch now, progress slow along the King's Road in Chelsea. There was a full moon, occasionally visible above the roofs of Sloane Square.

'So, you see, Francis, I don't think there will be any trouble from Robert.'

'I see. Will I have to turn up in disguise sometimes? To give a good impression to Robert, I mean. False beard? Dressed as a washerwoman?'

The cab had drawn up at 25 Markham Square.

'Francis, won't you come in for a while? Would you like a cup of tea?'

'That would be delightful, Lady Lucy,' said Powerscourt, paying off the driver. 'Quite delightful.'

It was late when he let himself into his sister's house in St James's Square. Lady Rosalind was still up.

'Francis,' she said, pretending to rearrange the cushions on one of her settees. 'You're back very late. How was the Beethoven? How is Lady Lucy? Any news?'

Powerscourt knew as surely as if she had written it on the windows that she suspected he might have proposed to Lady Lucy. She'd been dropping hints for days.

'The concert was excellent. Lady Lucy is very well.'

'Anything to report? Anything new?'

'No, I don't think so.'

'No news then?' said Lady Rosalind sadly. But she was looking at her brother very closely indeed as if he was hiding something.

Powerscourt smiled an enormous smile. I can't help looking happy, dammit, he said to himself. But I'm not going to satisfy her curiosity at a quarter to one in the morning. 'I think I shall go to bed now, Rosalind.' He kissed his sister on the cheek.

'Pembridge! Pembridge! Are you asleep?'

Lady Rosalind shook her husband vigorously. He gave the impression of being asleep, but it was best to make sure.

'Pembridge! Listen to me!'

Pembridge struggled back to life. 'For God's sake, woman. Look at the time.'

'That's precisely what I mean. The time. Francis has just come in. Just this minute. At a quarter to one in the morning. That concert will have finished by 10.30 at the latest. And he's grinning from ear to ear. I think he may have done it.'

'Done what?' said the sleeping Pembridge.

'Proposed to her, you fool! To Lady Lucy!'

'Did you ask him?' said Pembridge sensibly.

'I did. Of course I did,' replied his wife testily. 'He said there was no news to report. He said that twice. But he was smiling all the time. I do wonder, though. I just wonder.'

Early the following morning Lady Lucy Hamilton was lying in bed in Markham Square, wondering where she should be married to Lord Francis Powerscourt. Should they go to her family home in Scotland, a chieftain's castle full of the relics of war and long cold corridors? Should they go to Francis' place in Northamptonshire? Or should they have the service in London, in St James's Piccadilly or St George's Hanover Square? She wasn't quite sure what you should wear for a second wedding. Whatever it was, she was sure she hadn't got it. She began thinking seriously about a new outfit, and, most definitely, a new hat.

Lord Francis Powerscourt was lying in bed in St James's Square, wondering where he should be married to Lady Lucy

Hamilton. Could they have it in Rokesley, he wondered, in his own little church, the service conducted by his own vicar with the beautiful voice, with the local choir singing out of tune? Maybe Lady Lucy would want to be married in Scotland where her people came from. No doubt, he sighed, his sisters would have their own views.

There was a great noise coming up the stairs. Someone was pounding up them very fast.

'Francis! For God's sake! It's still in bed you are! Will you look at the time, man. Look at the time.'

'Lord Johnny Fitzgerald, good morning. You're in my bedroom at a quarter to eight in the morning. Has there been a revolution or something? Is the nation in danger?'

'Get dressed, Francis. And then you can read this.'

Fitzgerald was clutching a copy of *The Times*.

'I can read the paper before I get out of bed, if I have to. I do believe I may have done it before. Which section of *The Times* do you wish to draw to my attention? Births, Marriages and Deaths? The financial pages? The football scores?'

'I don't understand how people can be flippant before they have even got out of bed, Francis, I really don't. Look, it's here. Page four, small piece down near the bottom.'

Unrest in Ireland. Train Derailed near Crewe. No, not those. Presidential Election News from Washington. No. This must be it.

Mysterious Death in Perugia
From our correspondent
The body of a man was found early this morning in one of Italy's most distinguished pieces of sculpture. His throat had been cut from ear to ear. The major arteries in the rest of his person had also been cut. There were marks on the hands and feet, said to be similar to those of Christ crucified.

The corpse was discovered in the Fontana Maggiore in the centre of Perugia. The Fontana was designed by Nicola and Giovanni Pisano in 1275 to be the symbol of medieval Perugia. Artistic experts believe it to be one of the finest examples of thirteenth-century sculpture in Europe.

'Is there any breakfast in this house, Francis? Any hope of breakfast? Why don't I go downstairs and get something to eat. You can catch me up, if you can manage to get yourself out of bed.'

The body was discovered by a group of nuns on their way to an early morning service in the Cathedral. They described the fountain as running with blood. They also reported that the water was still red when they left the Cathedral, even though the body had been removed.

Powerscourt could see Lord Edward Gresham, his eyes staring into mirrors with messages, running up and down the alleys of Venice, describing the great love affair of his life. My Louisa. So beautiful. Had he gone to join her like this, his throat cut by some unknown assassin, comforted by nuns at the last? He read on:

Superstitious elements believe that the blood was a sign from the Almighty. Groups of the faithful have gathered to pray beside the fountain.

The Italian authorities have not been able to identify the body. They believe that the dead man, described as being in his late twenties or early thirties, was not of Italian extraction.

Powerscourt read it again. He felt very cold. Then he read it a third time, fixing the report in his memory. He went downstairs.

'Powerscourt, good morning to you. Wife believes you've got engaged to that nice Lady Lucy.' Lord Pembridge greeted him through a mouthful of buttered toast.

'What's that?' said Powerscourt, pacing round and round the fountain by the side of Perugia's cathedral.

'Engaged. You. To Lady Lucy. That's what the wife says.' Lord Pembridge launched into a plate of kippers.

'Oh, yes. That's quite right. I have.' Powerscourt admitted it before he knew what he was saying. He was still in Perugia, thinking of train timetables and another long journey across Europe. He found himself submerged by congratulations. Fitzgerald embraced him. Pembridge shook his hand. His sister materialised and kissed him warmly on both cheeks.

'You old devil!' said Fitzgerald.

'Congratulations. I hope you'll be very happy,' said Pembridge.

'Better late than never,' said his sister.

It's like receiving a whole batch of simultaneous telegrams, thought Powerscourt. He wondered how he could stop the flow.

'Please! Please!' He banged a fork very loudly on the table. A piece of toast fell out of its rack and rolled to the floor. Reproving crumbs lay at Powerscourt's feet. 'Please! I know it's very important, getting engaged and all that sort of thing. But Johnny has just brought me some terrible news.

'You see, I thought my last investigation was over. But now I don't think it is. I think there is another chapter waiting for me, as terrible as the first. I've got to go back to Italy, I think. I've got to go back today.'

Suddenly he looked forlorn like a child whose toys had been taken away.

'I need to confer with my best man here.' He managed a sad smile at Fitzgerald. His sister noticed that his eyes were far away, as if he had already left them. Pembridge had always thought his brother-in-law a bit eccentric, a good man of course, but a bit odd every now and again. Now was definitely one of those now and agains. He went back to his kippers.

'Do I get to make a speech, Francis? Do I get to tell lots of stories about you? Do I get to kiss the bride?'

'You do, Johnny, you do. But we must make a plan first. Why don't we go into the drawing-room and pay homage to Rosalind's curtains? It'll be quieter in there.'

Powerscourt looked out at the early morning bustle of St James's Square. It was a cold grey day. The delivery boys had thick mufflers round their necks.

Lord Johnny had brought a plateful of toast with him. 'Do you think that's him, Francis? The body in the fountain? Is it Lord Edward Gresham?' He crossed himself as he spoke.

Powerscourt thought for a long time before he replied. 'I think it might be. I think it probably is. But that's only a hunch. Consider, though, consider what we know. We know that

Gresham was going to Perugia on his way to Rome. So he could have been there. Now you have to ask yourself who might want to kill him in such strange circumstances. Even in Italy, famed for its murders and assassinations, they don't go round cutting strangers' throats and leaving them to bleed to death in some bloody fountain.'

'It's no ordinary fountain, Francis. I looked it up in a book before I came here. It's one of the most famous fountains in Italy, like it says in the paper.'

'Forget the fountain for now. If we don't think it was an Italian who killed the man in Perugia, then who was it? Supposing that Gresham is the corpse. Consider who knows he was the murderer. Gresham, I mean. The murderer of Prince Eddy. You, me, Rosebery. Nobody else knows. Nobody at all.'

He looked out into the square again. It was raining now, great puddles forming on the tops of the coal carts. 'Nobody at all. Except, that is, except Suter and Shepstone.'

He spoke the names very quietly. He fiddled with the edges of the curtains. He looked at Fitzgerald, crunching his way through the last of his toast.

'You don't think those two gentlemen have been taking a quick holiday to Umbria, Francis, do you?'

'No, I don't. But they know people who might. They could have sent people. Last Tuesday I told Suter and Shepstone the identity of the murderer. This is Friday, ten days on. They were looking at a map of Italy back there in Marlborough House when I went back for my book. They weren't expecting to see me.'

'Christ, Francis, Christ Almighty. You know what we're saying, don't you?'

'I do, Johnny. I do. I've been thinking it ever since I read that story in *The Times*.' Powerscourt thought of the efficient Major Dawnay, of Shepstone's special detachments, of the very effective means employed to disguise the death of Lancaster. Certainly they could have done it. But did they?

'Johnny, until we know whether it is Gresham or not, we're wasting our breath. I must go to Perugia and see if I can identify the body. I must make one or two calls here before I go.'

'Francis, don't you think I should go to Perugia? I know what

276

Gresham looks like. I haven't just become engaged to be married. You don't have to do everything yourself. And they say that some of the local wine round there is worth a tasting.'

'That's very noble of you, Johnny, very noble. But I feel I owe it to Gresham after our conversations in Venice. I wouldn't be happy with anybody else going. Even you.'

'You don't think I should come with you? Maybe this whole thing is getting dangerous now. We don't want you ending up head down in some Italian fountain. I wouldn't get to make my speech at the wedding then. I've been thinking of one or two good stories already.'

Powerscourt laughed. 'I'm sure I'll be all right on my own. But I would like to know that you're in London. I could send you a cable through William's office if I have to.'

'That's fine, Francis, if you're sure. Now then, I wonder if there's any of that breakfast left. Those kippers looked rather good to me.'

Powerscourt wrote to William Leith, Rosebery's butler and train expert, asking him for an immediate route to Perugia, leaving today, probably in the early afternoon.

He wrote to the Commissioner of the Metropolitan Police, requesting an immediate interview, later that morning if possible. He apologized for being so importunate. It was vital he see the Commissioner today.

Two cabs carried his notes away. A third took him to Markham Square. He hoped that Lady Lucy would be at home.

Her elderly maid answered the door. Yes, Madam was at home. Perhaps Lord Powerscourt would like to wait in the drawing-room. Madam would be down presently.

'Francis. Francis.'

Her fiancé was pacing up and down the room.

'You look terrible. You haven't changed your mind, have you?'

'Of course I haven't, Lady Lucy. Of course I haven't.' He held her very tight. 'It's just that I have to go away again. Now. Today, I think. I know it's awful when we've just got engaged and everything, but I don't have any choice.'

'I thought you said your last case had finished.' She wasn't angry. She just wanted to know.

'I thought it had. I was sure it had. But it hasn't. That's why I have to go back to Italy.'

'Francis, poor Francis. But why do you look so worried, so sad?'

'I am worried, Lady Lucy. I am sad. I think there is another dead person waiting for me in Perugia. I left him in Venice about a week ago. Now I think he's dead. There have been too many dead bodies in this business already. And I was thinking about the wedding only this morning.'

'So was I. How nice that we were both thinking about it together. Have you made any decisions?'

'Well, I think we both have to decide where it should be after I get back. But I have found my best man. He's very excited about kissing the bride.'

'That must be Johnny Fitzgerald,' said Lady Lucy. 'I shan't mind being kissed by him. Not that it won't be much nicer being kissed by you, Francis.'

'I can't stop,' said Powerscourt rather desperately. 'I have to catch a train.'

'Poor Francis.' She held him by the lapels on his jacket and kissed him on the lips. 'I shall be here when you get back. But you will take care, won't you? You will keep yourself safe, won't you? Sometimes I think your work must be very dangerous.'

Powerscourt remembered as he left that Lady Lucy was used to seeing her men go off to war. The first husband must have gone away a lot. But then one day, he never came back. He was dead.

Leith's message was as brief as ever. He read it on his way to the Commissioner's office.

'3 o'clock from Victoria, my lord. Dover Calais. Express connection to Paris. Suggest station hotel above Gare de Lyons for the night. 7 a.m. express to Milan. Arrive Milan 4 p.m. 4.30 connection to Florence. Arrive Florence 9.30 p.m. Reservation at Hotel Rivoli, close to station. Former Franciscan convent, my lord. Train to Perugia, 8 a.m. Arrives 12.15, my lord. Mountainous terrain. Reservation at Hotel Posta, Corso Vannucci.'

'Lord Powerscourt. My dear Lord Powerscourt.' The Commissioner of the Metropolitan Police was looking old and tired and rather frail. Maybe it's been a bad week for crime in London too, reflected Powerscourt. The four large maps on his wall were still there, great blobs of criminal red marking out the East End.

'Sir John, I shall be brief. And let me say before I begin how much I value the assistance you have already provided. It has made my life much easier.'

'I wish we could have been more helpful.' Sir John shrugged. 'All our information was in the negative. As far as we know, there are no blackmailers operating in Society at present. Then there were five people checked for their whereabouts on a certain night in January this year.' He looked closely at Powerscourt as though he suspected the true reason for the requests. 'All of them have been lawfully accounted for. How can we help on this occasion?'

'Two things, Sir John. Forgive me if the first sounds fanciful. How easy is it to hire a professional killer in this country? How long would it take? And would they, the professional killers, be willing to commit murder outside this country? And, following on from that, how easy would it be to hire a killer abroad? In Italy, in particular. And finally, do you by any chance have a contact in the police force in the Italian city of Perugia? Somebody you could recommend me to in pursuit of my inquiries.'

'The last part is the easiest.' The Commissioner rose from his desk and selected a thick file from his shelves. 'You'd be surprised how often we have contact with other police forces. Runaway children, stolen jewels, thieves believed to have fled their country of origin. We keep records of all the policemen we have to deal with. And I am sure they keep records of our own officers.

'Padua, Palermo, Parma, Pavia, Perugia. Here we are. Perugia. The man you want is called Ferrante, Captain Domenico Ferrante. He speaks very good English. I shall cable him that you are coming and that we request him to assist you in your inquiries.

'You ask about hiring killers like you would hire a cab. It is very easy, far too easy. But I don't think British assassins would happily operate outside these shores. Maybe Captain Ferrante could help you with the Italian end of your business. And I presume you would like us to listen at the doorways and find out if any of these killers have been approached in the last few weeks? Weeks or months, would you say?'

'Weeks,' said Powerscourt firmly. 'Definitely weeks. In the last ten days to be precise.'

26

Mountainous terrain, my lord. Leith's phrase came back to Powerscourt as his express toiled its way through the tunnels towards Perugia. Down there on his right he saw a great expanse of water, Lake Trasimene with its three islands and the olive slopes above. Hannibal, over a thousand miles from home, his elephants trampling across the Apennines, had waited there for the Roman army in the mist and fog of an early morning. Fifteen thousand Roman soldiers were slaughtered between the hills and the lake, the carnage going on for hours. The little river flowing into Lake Trasimene was named the Sanguinetto in memory of the blood it carried two thousand years before.

A very young Italian policeman greeted Powerscourt at Perugia station. He drew himself up to his full height and gave his best salute. His jacket was at least two sizes too big for him, only the tips of his fingers visible at the bottom of the sleeves. The trousers, freshly pressed, drooped over his shoes. His mother thinks he's not finished growing yet, Powerscourt suspected. No point in wasting good money on a uniform that'll only last a year. Even a policeman's uniform.

'Lord Powerscourt? Welcome to Perugia, sir. I am to send your bags to the hotel. I take you to Capitano Ferrante, sir.'

The Capitano was in a little cafe, drinking coffee and staring moodily at a long report on his table. More coffee, strong and black, arrived as Powerscourt sat down.

'Lord Powerscourt, how very nice to meet you. I have the long message from the Commissioner about your visit. How is the Commissioner?'

'He is well. He looked tired the last time I saw him in London.'

'Everywhere the policemen are tired, I think. There is too much crime, there are too many of the criminals. Not enough time to catch them all.'

Captain Ferrante was a well-built man in his early forties. His hair was greying at the temples. He looked cheerful, in spite of the prevalence of crime.

'This Commissioner and I, we work together, three or four years ago. The English milord, a very stupid young man, he steal a painting from one of the churches in the city. Maybe he think he hang it on the walls of his palazzo back in England. I have to go and bring the painting back to Perugia. The Commissioner, he is very helpful. He is fond of paintings, I think, the Commissioner. Yes?'

'He is. He is.' Powerscourt remembered the reports of gruesome watercolours of the Thames, painted in his spare time.

'We bring back the painting. The Commissioner says that if it was painted to hang on the walls of San Pietro in Perugia, that is where it belongs, that is where it must live. But come, Lord Powerscourt. I believe you think you may be able to identify the body in the fountain? Bodies without names, they are so difficult. Our procedures for the dead people, they are very proper, very respectful, but they all assume that we know who they are.

'We have our coffee here, because the body is in that building over there.' Ferrante pointed to a large imposing building across the street. 'That is the hospital. The morgue is at the far corner of the hospital. That is where the body is. The nuns, you know, the nuns who found him by the fountain, they insisted on washing the body, cleaning it up, all that sort of thing. The Mother Superior, she insists.'

The Deposition of Lord Edward Gresham, thought Powerscourt, a companion piece to all those earlier depositions, weeping women removing a limp body from a bloodied cross under threatening clouds, the air thick with meaning.

'Come,' said Ferrante. 'We can have some more coffee when we come back. Then I will take you to the fountain.'

They made their way across the street and into the hospital. Sick patients were being wheeled along the corridors for their operations. Legs in plaster, arms in plaster made their first experimental journeys out of the surgeries and tottered on to the main thoroughfare. Doctors checked their notes as they went from ward to ward.

'It is down these stairs. Down quite a lot of stairs.'

Their boots echoed back up the stairwell. The walls were an antiseptic pale green, adorned at regular intervals with paintings of the Virgin. Two men, dressed in black, undertakers of Perugia, passed them going the other way, their faces locked in the piety of their profession.

'I must find the attendant. He has the key.' Ferrante disappeared through a side door.

There was no natural light at all down here, just the flickering of the lamps. Powerscourt wondered if he had come to the end of his journey, watched over by a beatific Madonna, fifty feet underground.

'This way, please.' The huge door creaked slightly. Ferrante and the attendant made the sign of the cross.

The room was very cold. There were no windows. The walls were white. A couple of lamps threw long shadows of the living against the walls of the dead. The morgue was about fifteen feet square with tiers of bunks reaching up towards the ceiling. But they weren't really bunks, Powerscourt noticed. They were shelves. On each shelf lay a corpse.

'*Questo. Si, questo. Per favore,*' Ferrante whispered to the attendant. This one. This one please.

The attendant pulled the second shelf on his right out from the wall. The body in its box came out slowly, as if it didn't want to be recognized.

It was the cravat he noticed first, the same cravat he had worn that last morning in Venice. A silk cravat. A bloodstained silk cravat marked the presence of Lord Edward Gresham. His face was calm, in spite of the great cut running across the throat. The nuns had cleaned him up well, Powerscourt thought, prayers washing the blood away from Gresham's wounded face. He saw the marks on the hands, the knife forced in and twisted round with great force. He noticed the thick dried blood all the way down his jacket. Maybe they weren't allowed to clean that up until the body had a name. Something in Gresham's face

283

reminded Powerscourt of those earlier Greshams, hanging on the wall of the Gresham family home, maybe even something of his mother. Aristocrats embrace their ancestors, even in death. Especially in death.

Ferrante coughed very quietly. 'Lord Powerscourt, do you know this man?'

'I do.'

'You are certain? You must swear that you are certain. We have to fill in the forms. For the authorities, you understand.'

'I am certain,' said Powerscourt, and whispered a last farewell to Gresham as the body slid back into the wall. Lord, now lettest thou thy servant depart in peace, according to thy word.

'When did you last see him?'

'I saw him in Venice about ten days ago.'

'Come,' said Ferrante, 'we can do the paperwork in the office. Not in here, I think.' Powerscourt could see why Italian policemen were always busy. Ferrante was filling in forms as fast as his pen could write.

'Name?'

'Lord Edward Gresham.'

'Address?'

'Thorpe Hall, Warwickshire, England.'

'Occupation?'

'Army officer.'

'Married or single?'

'Had been married. His wife was dead. No children.'

'Call that single. Religion?'

'Catholic.'

'Next of kin?'

'Mother. Lady Blanche Gresham, Thorpe Hall. Same address.'

'Reason for visit to Perugia?'

'Tourist.'

'Address to which body should be conveyed for interment?'

'Thorpe Hall again.' The family vault, watched over by his weeping mother. Surely even a Gresham would cry when her son came home in a coffin.

'Thank you so much, Lord Powerscourt. Now, while I finish off the forms, perhaps you would like to have a look at these.' He took a small bag from the desk and shook the contents out on to the table.

'This is what we find in the pockets and so on. Nothing has been touched, except by the blood.'

There was a train ticket to Rome, first class, valid for travel some five days before. Gresham must have been on his last day in Perugia when they killed him, the last stop before Rome. There was an assortment of small coins and a receipt for a bill from Florian's in Venice. My God, thought Powerscourt, that was with me, and the waiters, Sandro the gondolier's hat waving across St Mark's Square, the mirror on the wall. There was a letter, written by Gresham to himself. My Penance, it said at the top, from Father Menotti SJ. There followed a list of prayers, Acts of Contrition, arcane references to the intricacies of the faith that Powerscourt didn't understand.

But wait, he said to himself. If Gresham has his penance to perform, then he must have been to confession here in Perugia maybe, or in Florence.

'Captain Ferrante.'

'Yes, Lord Powerscourt.' The Captain was half-way down a very long form indeed. He carried on writing.

'I need to ask you a question about the Catholic faith.'

'I am not the priest, you understand.' Ferrante was refilling his pen with official blue ink. 'But my brother is. And my wife, I am afraid, she is very devout.'

'Lord Edward Gresham had converted to Catholicism. Early this year he killed somebody. It was revenge. The somebody had killed Gresham's wife. Gresham was on a journey to Rome. Somewhere en route he was going to say his confession. This piece of paper makes me think he had already done so.'

'There is no Father Menotti in Perugia, Lord Powerscourt. We have checked. I believe there is one in Florence. I have written to him but so far he does not reply. The mails are very slow sometimes. Most of the time.' Ferrante shook his head sadly at the inadequacies of the postal service.

'If he had said his confession, would he be able to go to

heaven? You see, he was very keen on going to heaven to meet his dead wife. Louisa, she was called. He was sure she was in heaven.'

'I think it is like this,' said Ferrante, continuing to write furiously. Powerscourt saw that he was now signing his name to a number of documents, a great flourish on the F of Ferrante. 'If he makes the confession, and the priest absolves him, and he performs the Sacrament of Penance, then the state of sanctifying grace is restored to his soul. He will be in the State of Grace. God will receive him into heaven. He can meet the Louisa again, perhaps.'

Powerscourt felt relieved. He didn't like to think of Gresham missing Louisa, somewhere between heaven and hell.

'So it is the story of the doomed lovers?' Ferrante bundled his papers into a folder. 'Like Romeo and Juliet in Verona, or Heloise and Abelard. This time we have Eduoarde e Louisa. Maybe we should write the opera, you and I, Lord Powerscourt. Italians would love it. *Eduoarde e Louisa.* The final act could be here in Perugia by the fountain, a huge chorus singing away as the body of Eduoarde is discovered. There is blood everywhere. The lights go down over the cathedral. The ghost of the dead Louisa, she come to sing to her lover's corpse. Maybe there is the duet. Eduoarde and Louisa on top of the Collegio del Cambio in the piazza. Two ghosts, but what a great aria. That would make the audience look up. Maybe they would cheer. Maybe they would cry.

'Sorry, Lord Powerscourt. I get carried away. I am very fond of the opera. Mrs Ferrante, she say I spend too much money going to the performances. Now it is time for some more coffee. These forms,' he waved triumphantly at the folder, 'these forms are finished. Thank God.'

They were now in some quiet room at the back of the cafe. More black coffee had appeared and a plate of pastries.

'Lord Powerscourt.' Captain Ferrante was devouring a small lemon cake. Powerscourt saw that there were a large number of these cakes on the table. Perhaps they were Ferrante's favourites. 'I think we should speak freely. Nobody can hear us in here. Nobody will disturb us. We can decide what to put in our reports later on. Yes?'

'Of course.'

'I think, when you came here, that you expected to find that the body was that of Lord Gresham. Is that right? The Commissioner sent me a summary of what it said in *The Times* about Perugia the day you went to see him.'

Powerscourt hadn't mentioned the report in *The Times* to Sir John. He was quite sure of that. He had mentioned Perugia, of course. Maybe it wasn't that difficult to combine the two.

'Yes, I was expecting to find that Gresham was the dead man.'

'May I ask you, Lord Powerscourt, why you thought it was Gresham? You read this report in your newspaper, you drop all the other things you are doing, and you come to Perugia as fast as you can. Why?'

Powerscourt could see why the Commissioner held Ferrante in such high regard.

'We are speaking confidentially for the moment, Captain?'

'We are. I give you my word.'

'It was the way he was killed. Those wounds.'

'And why did those wounds make you so sure? Forgive me, I have a report to write about this murder. It may have been an Englishman, not a native of Perugia who died, but I am still charged with the task of finding the murderer. As you may be too, Lord Powerscourt, but a different murderer perhaps. For you, I sense, this is an end. For me, it may be only the beginning. I can always write in the middle of the report that he was killed by an unknown person or persons. That I have done before, God help me. But I come back to the wounds.' Captain Ferrante advanced towards another of the little lemon cakes. 'What was it about the wounds?'

'In the earlier murder,' said Powerscourt, 'the one I spoke of, the victim's throat was cut, the arteries were slit, everything was done to make sure there was as much blood as possible. It was terrible. Your Perugia murder was a copy of the one in England, a direct copy, wound for wound, cut for cut. Once I read the report in *The Times* with the details of the death, I felt sure it was Gresham. Here, I suspect, the fountain washed away some of the blood. With the other one, there was no water, only the sheets and the carpets. The blood was lying in puddles on the floor.'

'I do not think I want to know very much about your earlier murder, Lord Powerscourt. I am forgetting that.' Ferrante took another cake as an aid to amnesia. 'Do you think, forgive me, that the killer was the same person in both our murders, that these wounds are some terrible trademark?'

'I am absolutely certain,' said Powerscourt, deciding that he too had better try one of these little pastries before they all disappeared, 'that the killer is not the same person. There are two different killers.'

'Perhaps they should sing an aria together in our opera of *Eduoarde and Louisa. The Murderers' Duet.* They could be sharpening their knives on the steps of the Duomo, pricking their fingers so they can splatter blood all over their nice white shirts.'

'I think we may become rich from this opera,' said Powerscourt diplomatically. 'But let me ask you a question. Suppose you were English. Suppose you wanted to murder Lord Gresham. You know he is going to be in Perugia. Could you hire a gang of killers here, to do your murder for you?'

'I think you could, if you were in Palermo. Or if you were in Naples. Maybe even in Rome.' Ferrante was thinking carefully about what he was saying. 'In Perugia, no. I think not. Of course we have murderers. But these are the citizens murdering each other for love or betrayal or passion or whatever they do these things for. In Perugia we do our own killing. We don't ask outsiders to come and do it for us. And anyway, who in Perugia would want to kill the Lord Gresham? Nobody even knows who he is. We couldn't find out who he was until you came.'

'So your experience tells you that somebody outside the city must have come to find him. And then to kill him.'

'Exactly so, Lord Powerscourt. And there is something else.'

Ferrante walked to the front of their alcove to check there was nobody listening. He came back with more coffee.

'We have found a weapon. It may be the one used to carve the Lord Gresham's throat. It is long and very sharp. We found it in the corner of the piazza about one hundred yards from the fountain. There is something special about this knife. I tell you what it is in a moment.

'My men, they go round all the butchers' shops, all the cafes, all the restaurants, all the hotels, all the big private houses where a cook might use such a knife. Ordinary people like the Mrs Ferrante, I tell you, she would not have such a thing. There is no need. My men, they ask these cooks and butchers if anybody has lost a knife. Or if they recognize the one we find by the fountain. They do not. This knife, it is a stranger in Perugia, a foreigner.

'And in the very small letters, along the blade, it says Made in Sheffield. Now, we do not know if this is the murder weapon. But it may be. And it may have come all the way from England. I know the Sheffield steel is famous, but here in Perugia, nobody buys the knives made in England. They buy the knives made in Italy, or in Germany, or in France. Not the knives from Sheffield.'

Ferrante paused. He smiled at Powerscourt. 'Let me try to sum up for you, Lord Powerscourt, where you stand. Then you have to do it for me. They make us play this game in the police college. Sometimes it is very good.

'You come to find out if it is Gresham in the fountain. In your heart you think it is, even before you see him. So, you find him. In your heart also, I think you know who killed him. Not necessarily the name of the person. Maybe someone tells some- body else to do it for them. Maybe the killer is obeying orders. I think you know that this killer, the killer of Gresham, may have gone back where he came from, probably to England. True?'

'Very good,' said Powerscourt. 'Now let me try.' Ferrante was eating the last of the lemon cakes very very slowly, one tiny mouthful at a time. Powerscourt hoped Mrs Ferrante made some of them for him at home. 'You have a body in the morgue. You did not know who it was. Now you do. You also know, I think, that the murderer will not strike again here in Perugia. The reason he came was simply to murder Gresham. He has done that. Now he has probably gone back where he came from. He may have left his murder weapon behind him. You could close your case, Captain Ferrante. Your report could say Lord Gresham was murdered by an English killer, sent here for the purpose. By the person or persons unknown. Your case is closed.'

'I think you are right, Lord Powerscourt. I can close my case. But I wonder where the murderer may strike again. Take care, my lord. These are very dangerous people with the sharp knives.

But, come. We must go and see the fountain before it gets dark.
And we must think some more about our opera. Maybe we
become like those English people, Sullivan and Gilbert? Powerscourt and Ferrante.'

Captain Ferrante hummed a little tune to himself.

'The beginning, I think I have the beginning. It is in an old
English castle at sunset. There is the Lord Gresham, sitting on
his battlements, sick with love for his Louisa. He looks out to
the great lake in his grounds. She is coming to him in a boat. He
cannot see her yet. Listen. He begins to sing . . .'

27

'Don't look back. Don't look round. Not yet anyway.'

Captain Ferrante was leading the way along the Via del Priori that joined the hospital and the morgue in the university district to Perugia's main square. 'I think we are being followed. I have thought it for some time.'

He looked across at Powerscourt. Powerscourt seemed more interested in a couple of very old Italian ladies, bent almost double, their bags of vegetables trailing along the road, streams of Italian pouring towards the pavements.

'Can you tell if they are Italian or English?'

'I cannot. They are a quick sight in a doorway here, a drawing back into the shadows there. The brown coat, I think. Sometimes the hat, sometimes not. Have you been followed before, Lord Powerscourt?'

'I have, Captain Ferrante. But that was many years ago in India.'

Delhi, was it, or Calcutta? Delhi, he thought. And it was so difficult, he remembered, because there were so many people, so many faces that looked at you automatically if you were a white man. But only two of them were following you with knives, following the Englishman, one of the rulers. He remembered the urge to run, to get away from his pursuers as fast as possible, to sprint across the Maidan and disappear into some Government building and the safety of its files. A white man's building, a ruler's building. In there you would be safe. And then the knowledge that to run was to make yourself even more conspicuous, more visible still.

'Well, we must think what to do about it. Or who it might be. Do you have any idea who it might be, Lord Powerscourt? Come, we shall talk of it later in your hotel. See, here is the Piazza IV Novembre. And here is the fountain where they find the body.'

On their left stood the Cathedral of San Lorenzo, the outside still unfinished after four hundred and fifty years. To their right the handsome Palazzo dei Priori with fine windows and Gothic sculptures, chains and bars of gates serving as memorials of ancient victories over Perugia's enemies. Stretching away towards the Piazza Vittorio Emanuele, the Corso Vannucci, named after Pietro Vannucci, Perugia's most famous painter, Perugino. A great statue of King Vittorio Emanuele Due himself stood in the piazza. Powerscourt wondered if anybody had counted the numbers of statues of this Vittorio Emanuele all across his newly united country. He was always on his horse. He was in every major town and city in Italy, looking down on his people. Sculptors must have built their own memorials to him, so much business had he brought.

The fountain rose in three graceful tiers, a pair of twenty-four-sided pools topped by a bronze basin.

'The people come to look at this fountain from all over the world,' said Ferrante sadly. 'Always, I think, they tell of the sculptures round the side, the delicate workmanship of the craftsmen, the little statues that show the heroes of Perugia's history. They forget what it meant to the people of the city. They come here to get the fresh water. They come to do the washing in the little pools. I am sure all that was much more important to the people six hundred years ago than the sculptures. Fresh water on top of this hill, they must have thought it came from God.

'But look.' Ferrante drew Powerscourt right to the edge of the fountain. Two nuns were praying on the opposite side, their heads bowed. 'They dump the body in the upper tier here. The doctors think the Lord Gresham was dead before they take out the knives. Then I think they cut his throat and the other parts. The blood flows over the top of this marble rim and down into the lower pool. I think they block up the passage of the water out of the fountain over there. So the fountain fills with the blood of the Gresham.

'That is what the nuns see, on their way to the cathedral behind us. They see the marks on his hands and in his side. And because the water cannot find the way out, there is still a great deal of blood in here when the nuns come out from their service, even though the body has been taken away. Blood mixed with water is flowing over the rim of the Fontana Maggiore, down on to the street.'

A small group of pilgrims joined the nuns, kneeling on the hard stone of the square. The water flowed on, clear again now, dancing its way down into the fountain, the sound of its passage drowned out by the prayers and passing crowds.

'Why do you think he was left here, Captain Ferrante? Did they mean to do it? Or were they surprised?'

'I think they mean to make all these wounds. But I do not think they wanted to leave him here. I think they come into the piazza by one of these narrow streets. They mean to come out by another one, perhaps the one we walked down just now. Then they hear the noise. Maybe they hear the nuns coming. Do they sing, on their way to the church, those nuns? The killers panic. They make the quick cuts to the body. They run away. The good sisters find the corpse, the marks, the blood. They think it is a sign from God. When they come out from their praying, the body has gone. My men, they take him away. What do the nuns think? He has risen perhaps, risen from the dead. Here in Perugia, we have a second Resurrection at four o'clock in the morning. They are still praying now. They have never stopped. Always now there is a nun by the side of the fountain.'

Captain Ferrante made the sign of the cross, thinking perhaps of his brother the priest, the pious wife reminding him of his duties.

'Let me buy you a glass of beer, Captain Ferrante. My hotel is just down here. Please, I insist.'

The two men set off down the Corso Vannucci. Stone griffins, symbols of Perugia, watched their passage. Living eyes, human eyes, spies' eyes marked their short journey. University students were everywhere now, walking arm in arm up the street, sitting in the cafes, talking about their lectures, planning revolutions, falling in love. The sun was setting far away across the Umbrian hills in a pink sky, criss-crossed with black.

'Accidents. Always it is the accidents that make our life difficult.' Ferrante was sipping slowly at his beer in a quiet corner of the hotel. Powerscourt saw that he could watch the entrance without being seen from the street. There were no lemon cakes here, only a few olives.

'I think, Lord Powerscourt, I think of what was meant to happen, probably meant to happen. The assassins kill the Lord Gresham. They mean to leave the body somewhere. Nobody knows who he is. After a time he becomes another unknown dead person, buried with the other unknowns in the graves with no name over in the camposanto. But no. There is the accident. They are surprised, the killers. They panic. They dump the body. The nuns find it. They make the great fuss about the sign from God. It appears in your *Times*. You come to Perugia. Now we know who he is. But maybe they wait for you too, the killers. Somehow they know you are going to come. Maybe killers read *The Times* like everybody else in England. They think the Lord Powerscourt too, he will come to Perugia.

'I tell you one thing, my friend. They will not kill you here. They will not kill you in Italy. They will have to kill Domenico Ferrante first!'

Powerscourt laughed and clasped him on the shoulder. This is getting to be a habit, he thought, embracing Italians, Pannone and Ferrante both. Two in less than a month.

'Captain Ferrante! I am most grateful to you. I am sure that the answer to my problem lies in London, not in Perugia. Tomorrow I must go home.'

'How do we get you home, though, my friend? That is the question. I do not think you should go back the way you came.' Captain Ferrante was lighting a large cigar. Great clouds of smoke billowed round their little sofa, as though they were at the front of a train. 'I did not like the look of that man who came in just now,' he said, creating yet more clouds of smoke. 'If we are hard to see, so much the better. Tonight, Lord Powerscourt, I keep the watch on this hotel. Very discreetly, you understand.

Maybe we can catch one of these watchers and get the truth out of him. Maybe.

'Tomorrow morning I shall come for you very early. We go to Assisi. I put you on the mail train for Rome. You go with the parcels and the letters, you understand. There are no passengers. From Rome there is the train that goes to Paris, I think. Two of my men will come with you. Just in case.'

Ferrante remembered the words of his friend the Commissioner of the Metropolitan Police. He may be in more danger than he realises. Please send him back safely, however difficult it may be.

'My friend. My friend.' Ferrante ordered two more beers and another foul cigar.

'I remember the case we had here in Italy two years ago, I think. In the end three people were killed. The first was the victim the killer intended to murder all along. But he make the mistakes along the way. Two other people know that he is the murderer. He cannot bear that other people know his secret. They could betray him. They know too much. So he kill them too. Is that how it is with you, Lord Powerscourt?'

Powerscourt thought of Suter and Shepstone in that drawing-room in Marlborough House, poring over their map of Italy, Dawnay waiting for his orders beside them. Probably they had killed Gresham. He knew they had killed Gresham. But he, Powerscourt, knew about the blackmail, he knew about the thirteen years of payments to the boys from HMS *Britannia*, he knew about the young man dead from syphilis. He knew the reason behind the useless voyage round the world with Lord George Scott and the parson person on HMS *Bacchante*. He knew about Prince Eddy and that secret homosexual club in Chiswick. He knew who killed Prince Eddy. He knew who killed Prince Eddy's killer.

He knew too much.

If you were Suter and Shepstone, you wouldn't want all that knowledge wandering round London or Perugia. You wouldn't even want it wandering round Northamptonshire. You'd want it killed off for good.

Lord Francis Powerscourt. RIP.

He turned back to Captain Ferrante. 'I think that is how it is with me. At the beginning of this case, my friend, I think all I have to do is to find a murderer. So, I find him. Then I have to find who killed the murderer. I think I have found them too. Now I have to find a way of stopping them before they kill me. Because I am the man who knows too much.'

That night Powerscourt had a dream. It was night-time in the Cathedral Square. An opera was in progress. The sides of the cathedral and the Palazzo dei Priori were lined with singers. Trumpeters stood sentry on the roof. Flaming torches threw long shadows across the audience in the square below. A girl was singing an aria, leaning on the edge of the fountain, her hand trailing in the water. A man was rushing at great speed through the square. The man, Powerscourt, paused briefly to sing a last duet with the girl. A mob was following him. Three soldiers in splendid uniforms held the mob back. Powerscourt could see that Captain Ferrante, in medieval costume, was leading the defence. Ferrante fell. The mob surged on towards the man by the fountain. The man turned, running desperately down one of the narrow streets, his feet slipping on the slope.

The woman by the fountain sang him a last goodbye.

Powerscourt raced off down the street. The music came to a great crescendo. Two gunshots rang out into the night, filling the silence left by the last chords.

He woke up.

William Leith wouldn't approve of mail trains as a means of transport, Powerscourt said to himself the following morning. It was hard to see the elegant figure of Lord Rosebery crouching in the dark, surrounded by black sacks of Italian post. Dawn came in slivers through the slits of the carriages, the countryside slowly lit up in stripes outside. There was no glass. The wind whistled in and rushed around the sacks and the three people surrounding them, Powerscourt and his police escort, two very serious men with thin moustaches and long black gloves.

'They will come with you to Paris,' Ferrante had said, pressing a small heavy package into Powerscourt's pocket as they left. 'The gun. It is loaded. Just in case, my friend. Just in case.'

They embraced again, in the cold of Assisi station, guards patrolling the length of the train, smoke rising from the front.

In Rome the escort changed into uniform, splendid hats giving extra authority to the dark blue of their jackets and the shiny black of their trousers. Only one of them spoke English. Powerscourt and he had strange conversations on the journey, about the man's family, about his grandfather who had marched with Garibaldi and his grandmother who had never forgiven him for leaving home for such a long time. All these marches, she said, they're a waste of time, if you ask me. It'll be just the same if there is a king as it was before, everything costing too much in the shops. Powerscourt told him about Lady Lucy and the fact they were going to get married. He got very excited about that, Giulio, translating rapidly for his friend outside in the corridor, endlessly watching the doors, his hand clutching something heavy in his pocket. Giulio wanted to know if he would ask Queen Victoria to his wedding. Somehow Powerscourt didn't think so. He didn't think he'd be inviting any members of the Royal Family.

If he lived long enough to get married.

Always they watched, north from Rome through the mountains, into the plains of Lombardy. They watched as they crossed the Alps in the dark. They watched as the train made its way north along the banks of the Rhone in the sunlight. They watched as they drew near to Paris, eyes never resting, every stranger who passed by their compartment inspected like smugglers' luggage at the customs point.

They came with him to Calais, even though their orders said to leave him in Paris. 'You cannot imagine the Capitano Ferrante when he is cross,' Giulio had said. 'It is very frightful. He say, see you safe to England. So, Lord Powerscourt, we see you safe to England.'

They watched across the flat expanses of northern France, the church steeples the only relief from the monotony of the plains. They watched him on to the boat. They inspected all the other passengers. They watched as the boat drew out, waving vigorously to Powerscourt as he stood on the deck.

'*Arrivederci! Ciao!*' they shouted from the shore. They watched until the boat had gone almost out of sight, ears straining for pistol shots or screams. They watched until there was nothing left to see, except the dark grey waters of the English Channel.

Lady Rosalind herself opened the front door of her house in St James's Square.

'Francis, Francis, you are back. At last. Thank God you are safe. Come and sit down.'

'Why should I not be safe, Rosalind?' said Powerscourt, relieved that the curtains in the drawing-room were still intact.

'Francis, it's Lord Johnny, Lord Johnny Fitzgerald. He's been shot.'

'Christ,' said Powerscourt. Christ in heaven. Great waves of anger rushed through him. 'When was he shot? Is he all right? Is he dead?'

'No, he's not dead. But it's a miracle he's still alive. He's going to pull through. I went to see him yesterday in Rokesley.'

'He's in Rokesley?'

'Yes, he went there two days ago. He said he was tired of waiting for you to come back to London. He said you must have wandered off to look at some bloody frescoes or something. He wanted to go and look at the birds.' Rosalind spoke very softly now. 'He'd gone out for a walk towards Fotheringhay. He said he'd seen a pair of kestrels. He heard shooting. He thought it was just an ordinary shooting party. He turned suddenly because he thought he saw one of these birds off to one side. Somebody fired. The bullet went into his chest on the right-hand side. If he hadn't turned it would have gone right through his heart.'

The bastards, thought Powerscourt. The bastards.

'A farmer found him and brought him back to the house. The doctors say he can't be moved. I'm afraid there was a great deal of blood all over your hall and up into your bed. They said it would be the best place for him. He's very weak. He's lost a lot of blood. But he'll get better.

'The point is this, Francis.' Rosalind looked at him as if he had come back from another world. 'He was wearing your big green cape. On his walk. The one you always wear when you are in Rokesley. Lord Johnny told me before he passed out again. He didn't think they meant to kill him. They meant to kill you.'

'I must go to him, Rosalind. I must go at once.'

Powerscourt went to the window and pulled the precious curtain back a fraction. He peered outside into the square. He waited until his eyes got used to the dark.

'Rosalind, can you see anyone out there? Anyone who might be watching the house?'

Together they stared into the wet London night. There was nothing suspicious. A policeman patrolled round the gardens in the middle. A couple of cabs delivered their passengers. A stray dog barked for its lost people.

What was that, down in the corner? Was that a coat, ducking into the shadows?

Powerscourt waited. The shadows refused to give up their secrets. You couldn't tell. He sat down and wrote some letters. To William McKenzie, requesting his immediate presence at Rokesley. To Lady Lucy, telling her about Fitzgerald's injury. To Rosebery, asking for an urgent meeting. To William Burke, saying that he wished to ask his advice at the earliest possible opportunity.

Outlines of a plan were forming in Powerscourt's mind, a plan that might keep him alive, alive to marry Lady Lucy and to welcome the flowers of spring, a plan that required the presence of William Burke, financier, man of business, director of Finch's & Co. in the final scene of the last act.

28

Powerscourt took a cab from Oundle station to his house. Normally he would have walked. Not tonight, he thought, as they rattled past the dormitories and playing fields of Oundle School, not tonight.

He thought of Johnny Fitzgerald lying on the road a couple of miles away, his life saved by a passing kestrel. He thought of him being bumped along the road back to the house, probably unconscious. I'm like one of those animals in the pictures now, he thought, the Powerscourt at Bay, waiting for a sudden explosion, the rattle of a pistol in the dark.

Rokesley Hall is under siege, the enemy disguised as shooting parties, scouring the countryside by daylight, looking for big green capes along the road. Strangers with rifles are lurking in the forest, able to pick a man out at five hundred yards distance. Wait for the knock at the door, opening into the perfect target for a gunman firing across the fields.

Men went from my house to fight at Agincourt and Crécy, he reminded himself. Perhaps we can summon their ghosts to stand sentry on the roof, deadly arrows waiting to defend their master, crossbows to the rescue.

Fitzgerald was asleep when he reached home, a troubled sleep, turning over and over in Powerscourt's bed.

'He keeps asking for you,' said Mrs Warry, his housekeeper, who kept watch over the invalid. 'He wants to know when you'll be here.'

'Well, I'm here now, Mrs Warry. You go and rest. What did the doctor say?'

'The doctor came this evening, my lord. And he'll be back again in the morning. He says he'll be fine but that he has to rest. He gives him some medicine each time he calls. He says Lord Fitzgerald mustn't have anything alcoholic to drink. Not for a while anyway.'

'I shouldn't think that went down too well, Mrs Warry. Not well at all.'

Mrs Warry laughed. 'Only this evening he was asking for a drop of brandy. Just a drop, he said. For the pain.'

'If he's asking for brandy, then he's definitely getting better. He's on the mend.'

Powerscourt rose early the following morning. He went to the desk in his little sitting-room looking out over the garden and the churchyard. Early snowdrops were peeping through the grass. Soon, he remembered, the lawns all around the house would be ablaze with daffodils, blowing and bending in the wind. It was his favourite time of year.

He began composing a letter to his sisters in case the assassins found him. He thought of Johnny Fitzgerald, sleeping the sleep of the drugged and wounded upstairs, his shoulder still stained with blood. He thought of Lady Lucy, giving Robert his breakfast no doubt, making sure the homework had been completed. He thought of the message of the dead Lord Lancaster. In time I am sure you will come to understand that I could do no other. Semper Fidelis.

Powerscourt took out his pen and composed the last memorandum on the Strange Death of Prince Eddy. He set out the facts from beginning to end: the blackmail attempt on the Prince of Wales, the fears for the life of Prince Eddy, the terrible murder, the suicide in Sandringham Woods, the quest for motive which led him back to the *Britannia* and the voyage of the *Bacchante* all those years before. He set out the facts about Gresham: the death of his wife, Louisa, so beautiful; Gresham's discovery of the true circumstances of Louisa's death; Gresham's expedition across the roofs of Sandringham to kill Prince Eddy.

He set out his own pursuit of Gresham across the streets and canals of Venice, the confession in that red room with the three

301

mirrors, looking out over the waters of the Basin of St Mark's, his own disclosure of the true nature of Prince Eddy's death to Suter and Shepstone in Marlborough House. He set out the facts concerning the murder of Gresham in Perugia, the knife made in Sheffield, the corpse dumped in a fountain. He set out the facts concerning the attempted murder of Johnny Fitzgerald. Or himself.

He made two copies. A panting William McKenzie came to see him.

'I ran most of the way from the station at Oundle,' the tracker from Scotland explained. 'I thought things must be pretty serious from what you said in your message.'

Powerscourt had put Most Urgent three times at the end of the cable.

'Somebody tried to kill Johnny Fitzgerald three days ago. He was walking over towards Rockingham. He's going to get better. He's in my bed upstairs. He was wearing my cape at the time. He thinks they were trying to kill me.'

McKenzie peered closely out of the window as if a gunman might be lurking in the long grass or hiding in the trees.

'I see, my lord. I see. I presume you would like me to keep an eye on things for you. I shall begin straight away. I would be advising Your Lordship not to leave the house just now. Not until I have taken a look around, you understand.'

McKenzie disappeared out of the window and vanished round the side of the house.

Another visitor arrived in style in a cab at the front door. William Burke had left his counting house and his investments to pay a call at Rokesley Hall.

'William! How very kind of you to come all this way.'

'I felt I had no choice,' said the financier. 'Your life is in danger. God knows what may happen next. How can I help?'

Burke took off his coat and gloves and sat down beside the fire. His wife's portrait, painted by Whistler many years before, looked down on him from the walls. She was flanked by her two sisters, looking rather younger than when he had left them.

'You've got them all here,' he said, nodding to the pictures in their heavy gold frames, 'all three of them.'

'I can keep an eye on them here,' said Powerscourt cheerfully.

'It's the only place in England where I can be sure my sisters will do what I tell them.'

'Must have its advantages, that. Maybe I'd better get another one done of Mary and hang it in my study at home. I could keep an eye on her there.'

'Now then, William. I think you'd better read this. I wrote it this morning.'

Powerscourt stood by the window and looked over at his church. William Burke, spectacles fastened on his face, read through his memorandum. The organist was practising. Strains of Bach or Byrd carried across the headstones.

'My God, Francis. This is terrible. Terrible. What do you want me to do?'

'I want you to come with me to Marlborough House to see Suter and Shepstone. I need a witness. Rosebery is abroad and the Prime Minister is unwell.'

'What are you going to tell them? Suter is the Private Secretary to the Prince of Wales, isn't he? What's Shepstone's official title?'

'Treasurer and Comptroller of the Household, William. Whatever that means.'

Powerscourt turned back from his window. A posse of rooks were flying in formation from the tall trees by the bell tower to scavenge in the fields beyond.

'The thing to remember is that they do their master's bidding. They do what the Prince of Wales tells them. I do not believe they would have killed Lord Gresham, or tried to kill me, if they did not think they were carrying out his wishes. I have to convince the Prince of Wales, through these two officials of his, that it is time to stop.'

'How are you going to do that, Francis?'

Powerscourt told him. A slow smile spread across Burke's face.

'Would he do that? Rosebery, I mean?'

'I'm sure he would. Absolutely sure. The whole thing started with blackmail. It's going to end with a different sort of blackmail.'

'Pressure, Francis, pressure. That's what we say in the City about these kind of transactions. Pressure is a much nicer word than blackmail. Come to think of it, I can bring a little bit of pressure of my own to the meeting. And the Prince of Wales won't like it at all. There are all sorts of pressures in this wicked world, Francis. But money pressure is one of the most powerful of them all.'

Burke looked at his watch. He had left the cab waiting at the front door.

'I must return to London, Francis. Do you have a date for this meeting?'

'I have said that we propose to call at eleven o'clock in two days' time. On Thursday. I shall see you on the steps outside.'

'Goodbye, Francis. Take great care of yourself.' His cab was turning to ride up the hill to Oundle. A small figure, it might have been McKenzie, was standing behind a clump of trees two hundred yards from Rokesley Hall, staring out at the bare landscape. He had a gun in his hand.

'Your sister sends you a message from London, Francis. Stay indoors, she says. At all times. Very dangerous place, Northamptonshire.'

'And where have you been?' Lord Johnny Fitzgerald was propped up on a mountain of pillows in Powerscourt's bed. The doctor had called. The dressings had been changed. Powerscourt thought he looked a little better. 'Really, Francis, I don't think you're the man I'd ask to come to see me on my deathbed. You'd never get here in time.'

'I would if I thought I'd hear your deathbed repentance. That would be quite something.'

'I've got nothing to be ashamed of,' said Fitzgerald, heaving himself up on his bolster, 'well, not very much. The point is, Francis, as I'm sure they told you, it's you who should be lying here in bed, not me. I'm sure they thought I was you, if you see what I mean.'

'Greater love hath no man than this, that he lay down his life for his friend,' said Powerscourt happily. 'Seriously though, I am most grateful to you, Johnny. But come, the doctors say I must not talk to you for long. How soon will you be able to walk again, do you think?'

'Here I am. Look at me. Nearly dead, for God's sake. And all you can ask is when I can walk again. Do you want to get rid of me, Francis?'

'No, I do not. Certainly not. But I was thinking of something I want you to do for me. And you would have to be able to walk.'

'They say I will be up and about in four or five days' time, definitely in a week. Where do I have to walk to, for God's sake?'

'I can't tell you yet. I'll tell you in a couple of days' time when you're stronger. I brought you this, by the way. It might help the recovery.' Powerscourt drew out a small hip flask from his pocket and laid it on the bed.

'Is there anything in it? You wouldn't be bringing me one of those things just to torment me, would you? It's not full of bloody water or anything like that?'

'Medicinal brandy, Johnny. Purely medicinal. The doctor thought this little flask should last you three or four days.'

'Three or four days? Will you look at the size of it? Three or four hours more likely. But I tell you this, Francis. You keep up regular refills of our little friend here, and I'll be walking about in three days' time. Just three.'

Suter and Shepstone were at their usual positions in the office at Marlborough House. William McKenzie had brought Powerscourt to the meeting by a devious and roundabout route, travelling south by a different line, changing trains as they went. They had left McKenzie in the doorway of Berry Bros and Rudd, an occasional glance at the bottles in the window, a more regular scanning of Pall Mall. A policeman seemed to have joined him on his watch, pacing regularly up and down between the entrance to St James's Palace and Marlborough House.

'Lord Powerscourt. Mr Burke. Good morning to you both. You requested this meeting, I believe, Lord Powerscourt. Do you have something further to report? Some further intelligence you wish to impart?'

'I do.' Powerscourt told them about his trip to Perugia, the mutilated body of Gresham in his fountain, the attempt on the life of Lord Fitzgerald. 'There is only one explanation that is consistent with the facts, Sir William. Only one.'

'And what is that, pray?' Shepstone was shifting nervously in his chair.

'Only four people knew that Lord Gresham was the murderer of Prince Eddy.· Me, Lord Rosebery, Lord Fitzgerald, the Prime Minister. And the household of the Prince of Wales.'

Powerscourt paused. It was very quiet in the room. Burke was shuffling a pile of papers in front of him. Shepstone was stroking his beard.

'None of the four went to Perugia to kill him. That leaves the Household of the Prince of Wales. Or people carrying out their orders. Orders to kill him, to kill him in exactly the same way as Prince Eddy, the same strokes of the knife, in the same places. Gresham could not be brought to trial in England of course. Once the Household decided on a cover-up, there had been no murder, there could be no inquiry, there could be no arrests, there could be no court case. There could be no judge putting on his black cap and ordering Gresham to be taken from this court to a place of execution where he would be hanged by the neck until he was dead. I believe the rope is kinder to the neck than the knife, gentlemen. Much kinder. But the Household could decide to take matters into their own hands. They could be their own judge and their own jury. Vengeance is mine, saith the Lord. I will repay.'

Shepstone and Suter started. They stared intently at Powerscourt. Could the man hear conversations when he wasn't even in the room? For he had, inadvertently, used exactly the same words as the Prince of Wales at Sandringham, discussing what to do once they knew the identity of Prince Eddy's killer. Vengeance is mine, saith the Lord. I will repay.

'Vengeance is mine,' Powerscourt went on, 'and it might embrace more than the murder of Lord Gresham. Vengeance could mean the elimination of all those who know the uncomfortable truth, uncomfortable for the Household of the Prince of Wales, that is. Vengeance could mean the elimination of those who know the full facts about the affair, the syphilis, the blackmail, the murders, the cover-up of the death of the heir presumptive. It might be much better if all those people were out of the way, all of them. Then nobody would ever know what happened in Sandringham. Or in Perugia. Or on board the HMS *Britannia* all those years before.'

Powerscourt thought of Captain Williams struggling along the beach at Amble, his career broken, his health ruined. It wasn't my fault, I tell you. It wasn't my fault. Was this a different form of vengeance, vengeance for all those ruined lives?

'An attempt was made the other day to kill Lord Fitzgerald. Maybe the killers mistook him for me. I cannot be sure. But I can tell you one thing for certain. If any further attempts are made on the life of Lord Fitzgerald or myself, or anybody else connected with this inquiry, the consequences will be severe. I suggest that you read this memorandum I have prepared. When you have both read it, you will return it to me, as you asked Lord Rosebery and me to do with an earlier memorandum of your own, Sir William.'

Powerscourt looked at the portrait of Alexandra above the fireplace. William Burke was writing more figures in his notebook.

'Interesting,' said Shepstone, and passed the document to Suter.

'Most interesting,' said the Private Secretary, handing the memorandum back to Powerscourt. 'And what is the point of this piece of paper, may I ask?'

'You may. You may indeed. If, as I said, anything should happen to Lord Fitzgerald, or myself, or anybody associated with us in this business, one copy of this memorandum will go to Queen Victoria. She has forgiven her son many things in the past. I doubt if she would forgive him this, murdering his own subjects. The second point is this. Lord Rosebery would call for, and be granted, an emergency debate in the House of Lords on the current state of the monarchy. As an opening statement, he would read this memorandum into the record.'

Powerscourt could imagine the sensation. Word would leak out, it always did, that some startling announcements were to be made in the Upper House. Peers, old and young, regular attenders and country backwoodsmen, peers curious, peers gossipy, peers sent by their wives to hear the news, peers in the Government, peers on the backbenches, peers would pack the House.

The great red benches would be in uproar by the time Rosebery sat down. There would be special editions of the papers. Suter and Shepstone had agreed to cover up the first murder for fear of scandal. Now they would get scandal on an unimaginable scale, a whirlwind, a typhoon of scandal from which the Prince of Wales might never recover.

Suter and Shepstone sat impassive in their chairs. Neither spoke. It was as if they were frozen, like Lot's wife, two courtiers turned into pillars of salt in Pall Mall.

'And that is not all.' Powerscourt continued in his role of the exterminating angel. 'Mr Burke.'

'I concur wholeheartedly with everything that my brother-in-law has said. His family are very anxious that he should remain alive. In one of my official positions, gentlemen' – Burke sounded as if he held hundreds of such positions. He probably does, thought Powerscourt, – 'I am a senior director of Messrs Finch's & Co., bankers to the Prince of Wales.'

For the first time in the meeting Sir Bartle Shepstone, Treasurer and Comptroller of that Household, looked pale. He stroked his beard anxiously. What was coming next?

'As of this morning,' Burke consulted an official document in his papers, 'the Prince of Wales owes Finch's & Co. the princely sum of £234,578 14s. 9d. That is without the computation of today's interest. Finch's would demand the immediate return of all monies owed. By the end of the month at the latest. Furthermore, they would request that the account be closed. And any attempts to obtain similar facilities with other banks would not be welcomed in the City of London. Our community of bankers is a small one, gentlemen. Word gets round. In the City, word gets round very fast indeed.

'But come, gentlemen.' Burke had applied his pressure. 'None of these things need happen. Lord Rosebery may never make his speech in the House of Lords. Finch's & Co. may never make such a request. You have the answer in your own hands. All you have to do is to issue the necessary instructions. All you have to do is to ensure that nothing further happens to Lord Powerscourt or any of his associates. It is quite simple.'

With that, Burke gathered his papers and strode from the room as if he had just left a rather disagreeable board meeting.

'We can see ourselves out, thank you,' had been Powerscourt's final words to the two courtiers. 'I've been here before. I don't expect to be coming back.'

Bells were ringing from the tower of Rokesley church. Happy bells. Joyous bells.

They could be heard in Oundle. They could be heard as far away as Fotheringhay where the noise shrank till the peals sounded like glasses tinkling on a tray.

Cheerful bells. Wedding bells. Bells for the wedding of Lord Francis Powerscourt and Lady Lucy Hamilton at two o'clock on a Saturday afternoon with the reception in Rokesley Hall.

Ten days had passed since the meeting in Marlborough House. Powerscourt had gone directly to Lady Lucy's house, McKenzie patrolling stealthily around the sedate purlieus of Markham Square.

'Francis! How nice to see you! How is Lord Johnny? Is he better?'

'He is fine. He is taking a little light refreshment now. Brandy to you and me. But I have serious things to speak of, Lady Lucy.'

'Serious things, Francis? What serious things?'

'I have to go away again, I'm afraid. The way things have turned out in this dreadful affair, I think it would be better if I were out of the country for a while until things settle down. People need a period of calm, I think.'

'Well, I shan't feel very calm if you're not here. I shan't feel calm at all. How long were you thinking of going away for?'

'I don't know. Six weeks? Two months? Something like that. Unless, unless . . .' Powerscourt left his unless hanging in the air. He was trying very hard to keep a straight face.

'Unless what, Francis? Tell me, my engaged one.'

'Well, I just thought . . .'

'Out with it, you old plotter. You're plotting something behind that sad face, I can tell. Out with it.'

'The thing is . . .'

Powerscourt, so upright and courageous in Marlborough House that morning, was feeling less brave in Chelsea that afternoon, particularly with those bright blue eyes boring into him. Perhaps he needed some of Fitzgerald's medicinal brandy.

'Well, if something happened, then it might all be different . . .'

'You're speaking in riddles now like a conjuring person. Robert saw one the other day at a fair. Rabbits out of hats, that sort of thing. Do you have a rabbit, Francis?'

Then she knew. She could never tell how she knew, but she did. 'Let me try a rabbit for you, Francis. I think what you were going to say might have gone something like this. Might have gone.'

She paused. She wasn't going to let him off lightly, not after all this delaying. 'Suppose we were married. Just suppose. It's only an idea, you understand. But suppose we were married in a church with bells and rings and vicars, all that sort of thing. Then we could go away together on our honeymoon. And you wouldn't have to leave me behind. You wouldn't have to leave me behind ever again. How about that?' Lady Lucy sat back in her chair and smiled a wicked smile.

Powerscourt laughed. 'You're right. That was what I was thinking of, exactly that. But then I thought it would be a bit sudden, getting married in ten days' time. There are arrangements and things.'

'Nonsense,' said Lady Lucy Hamilton, keen to be turned into Lady Lucy Powerscourt. 'I'd marry you tomorrow, Francis, if you wanted. So ten days' time is no problem at all.'

The Rokesley church clock said five to two. Powerscourt stood nervously at the altar, a pale Fitzgerald at his side. The pews behind them were filled with Hamiltons and Powerscourts, summoned at short notice. Powerscourt's three sisters and their husbands were all there, the little boys dressed in sailor suits. Powerscourt's only niece was bridesmaid to Lady Lucy. His sisters' children, William, Patrick and Alexander, had met Robert on the battlefield of Waterloo in the top of the Pembridge house in St James's Square a few days before.

'You could be Marshal Ney who led the last great charge of

the Imperial Guard, if you like,' William had offered generously. 'Or Napoleon.'

Somehow Robert had not been very keen on becoming Napoleon. He didn't like the thought of being sent away to that island in the middle of the ocean. Its name temporarily eluded him.

'I think I'll be one of the British generals defending the line, if that's all right,' he said, looking with amazement at all the uniforms spread out before him.

'You'll probably get killed,' said Patrick cheerfully. 'Most of them were.'

Robert felt that a British death would be better than defeat and a French exile.

The organ was playing Bach. The choir looked at the music in their stands. The vicar had the happy smile that vicars wear to weddings. Powerscourt hoped Lady Lucy wasn't going to be late.

'Francis. Francis. For God's sake.'

'What is it, Johnny?'

'You know I said I'd be fine for this wedding business. Well, I'm not. I'm feeling rather ill.'

There was a rustle at the back of the church. Lady Lucy, escorted by her brother and a trembling bridesmaid, was advancing up the aisle.

'Hold on to this pew very tight, Johnny. If that's no good, hold on me.'

Powerscourt saw himself suddenly supporting his bride on his left, trying desperately to keep his best man upright on his right.

Lady Lucy was passing the little boys in their sailor suits, penned in together under the stern eye of William Burke. She smiled at them, aunt-like. Well, nearly aunt-like. Robert was waiting in the bride's pew, looking very solemn in a new suit.

Fitzgerald was swaying slightly now.

'Hang on, Johnny. Hang on. The parson's got to do his bit now.'

'Wilt thou have this man to thy wedded husband, to live

together after God's ordinance in the holy estate of matrimony? Wilt thou obey him, and serve him, love honour and keep him, in sickness and in health?'

'I will,' said Lady Lucy, very firmly, smiling across at Powerscourt.

'I, Francis, take thee, Lucy, to my wedded wife, to have and to hold from this day forward . . .'

There was a sudden commotion three pews back. Two of Powerscourt's nephews were having a fight. William Burke was administering a terrible telling off. The way he frightens the Household of the Prince of Wales, thought Powerscourt, I'm surprised his children dare to breathe when he's around.

The organ played the Wedding March. A couple of local policemen, watching the proceedings benevolently from the roadway, saluted as they came out. A line of sailor-suited nephews, joined now by Robert, formed a miniature guard of honour. Johnny Fitzgerald limped slowly forward and gave Lady Lucy a huge kiss on the lips.

'I've been looking forward to that for ages,' he beamed.

'I hope you enjoyed it, Lord Johnny. It'll help you get better, I'm sure. Don't you have to make a speech now, or something like that?'

Fitzgerald's speech was short. He was looking very ill. He read telegrams from Rosebery – 'May all your mysteries be little ones' – from Signor Pannone in Venice – 'Everyone in the Danieli sends their congratulations, especially the waiters' – from Capitano Ferrante – 'Congratulations. Tonight I sing the aria for you both. The Marriage of Figaro perhaps. Or would you prefer Cosi Fan Tutti?'

The following afternoon Lord and Lady Powerscourt were leaning on the rails of their liner in the docks at Southampton. They were sailing to America for their honeymoon, to New York and Boston, to Charleston and Savannah. Powerscourt was excited about the architecture in Savannah, huge ante-bellum houses laid out in grids across the town.

'Have you seen our cabin, Francis? It's enormous. There are

312

great windows or whatever they call them looking out to sea, and all sorts of cupboards and things to put our luggage in. I've made it very cosy down there.'

Her husband patted her arm. A crowd had gathered beneath them, come to wave the great ship off.

In the telegraph room one of the officers of the Metropolitan Police was making his report to the Commissioner. 'Subjects safely aboard,' it said. 'No disturbances on the way. Will send further reports en route to New York. Handing over to the American authorities in the harbour. Johnstone.'

Ever since Powerscourt's return, he had been watched by the officers of the Commissioner of the Metropolitan Police, concerned for his safety. Ferrante had recommended it to his friend the Commissioner. 'You asked me to keep him safe,' his telegram read. 'I have. But he is not safe in England, I think. These people are very dangerous. Watch him if you can, Commissioner. Perugia grew very fond of Lord Francis.'

The great cables that held the ship to the shore had been cast off. An insistent hooter sounded above them. The dots left behind on the quay were still waving, waving at loved ones they might never see again, waving at friends departing, waving to the new world that would greet the boat at journey's end. England was growing smaller as they gathered speed. On the deck above, the band struck up the overture to Mascagni's *Cavalleria Rusticana*, the great hit in London the winter before.

'Lucy,' said her husband, putting his arm around her shoulder. 'I am so glad you are here.'

He wanted to say something to bind her to his last investigation, something that would join them both together in his mind. There had been too many deaths. He had almost lost count by the end. Prince Eddy, he didn't care about, one way or the other, he decided. Gresham has gone to meet Louisa. So beautiful, my Louisa. He must be happier now. He thought of Lord Lancaster, lying in the cold ground of Sandringham Woods, his life lost for wasted honour. He thought of Simon John Robinson at rest in the graveyard at Dorchester on Thames. Lord forgive them, for they know not what they do.

313

'Lucy. I give you a motto. May it see us across the Atlantic. May it see us across the future. I love you very much, Lucy. Forever Faithful. Semper Fidelis.'

'Oh, Francis, what a beautiful thought. Let me give it back to you. For our future. You and I. Francis and Lucy. Lucy and Francis. That sounds nice, doesn't it? Forever Faithful. Semper Fidelis.'